Paul Witcover

Elizabeth Hand

This edition of
EVERLAND AND OTHER STORIES
is limited to 100 numbered slipcased
hardcovers signed by Paul Witcover and Elizabeth Hand,
and 500 unjacketed hardcovers signed by Paul Witcover.

THIS IS COPY ___88___

In the quarter century since the publication of his first short story, "Red Shift," Paul Witcover has slowly but steadily produced an impressive body of short fiction alongside his critically acclaimed novels, *Waking Beauty, Tumbling After,* and *Dracula: Asylum.* Fusing elements of science fiction, fantasy, horror, and fairy tales, Witcover's work inhabits the borderlands of genre. *Everland* collects twelve of his best stories, seven previously published, including the Nebula Award finalist "Left of the Dial," and five appearing here for the first time, including the title story, which does not so much re-imagine as reinvent J.M. Barrie's classic tale of a boy who never grew up.

Ranging from present day New York to Central America, from Revolutionary France to a near-future United States convulsed by civil war, the twelve stories in *Everland* are both topical and timeless, showcasing Witcover's affinity for the strange that lurks within—or alongside—the familiar.

EVERLAND

PAUL WITCOVER

EVERLAND

And Other Stories

Introduction by Elizabeth Hand

PS Publishing 2009

PS Publishing Ltd / Grosvenor House /
1 New Road / Hornsea, HU18 1PG / England

e-mail: editor@pspublishing.co.uk • *Internet:* http://www.pspublishing.co.uk

CONTENTS

INTRODUCTION // vii

MAYALAND // 3

TWILIGHT OF THE DOGS // 15

RED SHIFT // 41

AFTER IVY // 67

LIGHTHOUSE SUMMER // 77

EVERLAND // 103

CHANGELING // 131

THE CATS OF THERMIDOR // 137

MOONLIGHT BECOMES MAGENTA // 155

THE SILVER GHOST // 173

WHERE BALLOONS GO // 199

LEFT OF THE DIAL // 219

v

INTRODUCTION

SOME LITERARY PUNDIT RECENTLY OBSERVED THAT, WITH writers, there's no such thing as genuine admiration of another's work; only envy. I will confess here to great admiration but perhaps greater envy of Paul Witcover, long before we ever met.

I'd been hearing about him for years. It was the late 1970s; I was living with a guy named Wayne, who regaled me often and at great length about his cousin, Paul, who was into the same stuff I was—we both wanted to be writers; we both were immersed in proto-punk like the Ramones and Velvet Underground and David Bowie; and we both loved science fiction, in particular the work of Samuel R. Delany, whose 1975 novel *Dhalgren* was a touchstone of that era. Aunt Marian, Paul's mom, confirmed everything Wayne said and more. Wayne and I saw her often, at movies and dinners at the Witcovers' home in the Virginia suburbs, where she'd comment on books Paul had read, bands he'd seen, the novel he was working on, the fabulous writers' workshop program that had just accepted him.

The upshot, of course, was that I was inclined to dislike, even loathe, Paul for some time before I laid eyes on him. This finally happened one summer evening in 1980, in a now-defunct Georgetown restaurant called Gepetto's, where Wayne, Marian, and I sat waiting for Paul to join us for dinner. I was steeling myself to be coolly polite to a shy, homely, bespectacled geek in a Ziggy Stardust t-shirt, carrying a copy of *Analog*. I literally did a double-take when a tall, drop-dead handsome guy in a black leather jacket walked in and sat at the table across from me. We started talking immediately, a long, intense, hilarious conversation about the Ramones and Velvet Underground and David Bowie and *Dhalgren*, Michael Moorcock and Hawkwind and the Clarion Writers' Workshop, which Paul would be leaving to attend the next morning. (It's worth remembering that in those pre-internet days, the odds against finding another Ramones fan, let alone one who could quote *Dhalgren's* opening sentence as well as that of *Ulysses*, were roughly a million to one.) Over almost three decades, it's a conversation that's never stopped.

His first published story, "Red Shift" (1984), was a masterfully assured take on the sort of dark carnival tale practiced by Ray Bradbury or Peter S. Beagle, but with the distinctly original gloss that would become a Witcover trademark. His work belongs to a form of American neo-transcendentalism that developed towards the end of the last century and has become wildly popular in this one: a homegrown magical realism steeped in pop culture and myth and sex, lyrically written and fearless in its refusal to remain locked inside the borders of genre.

Paul Witcover was one of the first people to stake his claim to this kind of literature, and he remains one of the best. The works in *Everland* (as well as his two novels, *Waking Beauty* and *Tumbling After*) mark the trajectory of an exceptional writer whose sensual, unsettling works encompass literary horror and postmodern fairy tales, science fiction and dark fantasy and the contemporary ghost story. All share a marvellously evocative sense of place: they're journeys as much as stories, exploring places the author has lived and loved—Central America and France; the suburbs of Washington, D.C.; Manhattan and the Delaware shore. From his first story to the more recent ones that make their debut in these pages, Paul has redefined and expanded the literature of the fantastic. As the narrator of "Red Shift" observes,

> *"Since that first vision the images haven't changed, but the readings always do. Jack and Jill, Medusa, the Grail, the Unicorn's horn: out of their constancy new patterns are constantly shuffled, and so, the more I used the Stone, the clearer it became that my first vision contained all others, even those as yet undreamed."*

It's a vision that, perhaps, reaches its culmination in the heartbreaking, elegiac "Left of the Dial," a finalist for the Nebula Award. It's a story I can never read without crying. It's also one of the best ghost stories I've read, period, and I suspect many readers who encounter it for the first time here will agree.

Over the years, Paul has never stopped journeying, never stopped exploring, never stopped writing—not just fiction, but book reviews and essays which, someday, may get their own volume. Knowing him has been one of the great joys of my life. Visiting the worlds created in *Everland* is another. It's one that can be shared by anyone who opens this beautiful, haunting collection by one of our very best writers of the fantastic.

Elizabeth Hand

For Cynthia

MAYALAND

THE BAR, CALLED THE POCO LOCO, WAS DARK AND FILLED WITH tourists, mostly gringos. It was the kind of bar where drifters washed up and stayed for months drinking and dancing in lazy eddies of movement and time. There was an incestuous feel to the place, a laconic desperation. A few hopeful glances swung toward Andrew as he entered, then seemed to lose interest. A mirror-ball revolved above the dance floor, where a drunken middle-aged Indian man in native dress was swaying alone to the New Wave beat. Andrew sat by himself in one corner, away from his countrymen and women.

The things that mattered to Andrew—the Indians and the land—seemed timeless, unalterable. There was a spirit investing every tree, lake, and volcano, a spirit, ancient but still green, that bided with the strength and patience of stone behind every Indian face just as the old temples persisted behind the mask of the jungle. Though crumbling and empty, defaced by tourists, the temples were still charged with life, as though they had been abandoned only yesterday by a people who had every intention of returning. The Guatemalans called their country the land of eternal spring, but it seemed to Andrew that whatever was essential to this country and its people, whatever had raised the temples and named the gods, was hibernating now through a long, cold season, a winter of white men who would one day melt away.

After a beer, Andrew looked up to see the Indian weaving over to his table. He was tall for his people, but his dark, handsome features were classically Mayan—thick lips, high cheekbones and forehead, and long, sloping nose. Andrew motioned for the man to sit down, glad to share his table

3

with a local; he'd been dreading the intrusion of some sixties reject who would gripe about the country then try to sell him bad dope.

The Indian introduced himself as Victor. His Spanish was slurred, difficult to understand. He said something about the music.

"I saw you on the floor," Andrew said. "You dance well."

Victor nodded energetically. "I like that man; what is his name?"

Andrew thought back to what had been playing. "David Bowie?"

"David Bowie. Duran Duran also. You buy me a beer, okay?"

"Sure." He walked up to the bar and ordered two beers.

"Watch out for that guy," the bartender advised. "He's in here all the time hustling drinks."

"He doesn't have to hustle me," Andrew replied.

When he returned to the table, Victor took his beer and guzzled greedily. Then he gave Andrew a bleary smile. "You think I am drunk, yes?" The smile vanished. "Okay, so look here, my friend." His brightly colored woolen shirt was belted below the waist, billowing it out into a sort of pocket at the belly, like a kangaroo's pouch. From it Victor took a handful of stones that he spread out on the table in front of Andrew. "Go on, pick one up."

They were light . . . in fact, not stones at all, but large seeds of some sort, carved into faces.

"Avocado pits," said Victor with pride. "I carve them myself. So I drink too much beer, too much Quetzalteca; I am an artist!"

The detail of the work was breathtaking, seemingly beyond the power of Victor's shaky hands. Andrew was reminded of Mayan relics he had seen at Tikal and Bonampak. And, in fact, he recognized among the carvings the monstrous faces of Mayan deities: Chac, the rain god, with his great hooked nose like an elephant's trunk uplifted to spray water; the blank, saucer eyes and slack, buck-toothed mouth of the sun god, Kinich Ahau; and the skull-masked Ah Puch. There were also human faces, of both Indians and gringos, yet even they seemed terrible, with expressions twisted to inhuman extremes of emotion as if they had absorbed the attributes of gods only to find their bodies too frail to contain them.

"They're fantastic. Are they for sale?" Andrew asked.

Victor opened and shut his mouth, groping for words as though he had been insulted. He seemed both angry and hurt. "What do you take me for," he asked at last, "one of those peasants who haunt the old places to sell their worthless imitation relics to stupid gringos? Look in front of you. These are not lies, made to look old. I did not come up to you and say, 'See what I have plowed up in my cornfield!'" He made to sweep the pits back into his shirt, but in his fury missed and scattered them to the floor.

Andrew bent down with him to gather up the carvings. When they had finished, Victor seemed calmer. He was a proud man, but then he had every right to be. Andrew had not meant to offend him. He apologized.

Victor smiled warmly. "I, too, am sorry. Again this night I have drunk too much. So for you, my friend, I will carve something special. Let us drink to friendship!"

Andrew bought two more beers.

"Why do you sit alone tonight," Victor asked. "Where is your girl-friend?"

Andrew shrugged. "Too many tourists. If I'd wanted to see this kind of place, I would have gone to Atlantic City."

But Victor was interested in one thing only. "That is bad. Even I, who am married, have a girlfriend."

Andrew laughed.

"My wife is across the lake in San Lucas; my girlfriend lives in Sololá. Between the two of them, I will soon be a dead man."

"What's it like in San Lucas?" Panajachel was proving too touristy for Andrew's tastes. In such places he always felt ashamed of his country and angry at himself.

"Ah! There it is beautiful and quiet, not like here. We fish and farm the land at the foot of the volcanoes just as we have always done. There I do my carving. The women are like flowers, and the children are always singing. The soldiers have taken men from all the villages around here: San Pedro, San Pablo, San Jorge. But never from San Lucas. We are good workers."

"How is it possible to get there from here?"

Victor clapped him on the shoulder. "Tomorrow you will come with me, stay at my house."

Andrew didn't think he would ever grow used to the spontaneous generosity of the Indians; at least he hoped not. He accepted with pleasure.

"Where do you sleep tonight?" Victor asked.

Andrew said the name of his hotel.

"Tell them to wake you at sunrise. The first ferry to Santiago Atitlán leaves at six. We must be on it if we mean to catch the ferry from Santiago to San Lucas. There is but one each week; should we miss it, we must walk sixteen kilometers."

"Where should I meet you?"

"The ferry leaves from the Hotel del Lago Azul. Walk down to the beach and turn left; you'll see the dock."

"I'll be there."

The next morning, Andrew woke with a hangover and had to hurry to catch the ferry, arriving just as it was pulling out. Victor was suffering too; they greeted each other and sat side by side in silence as the noisy boat labored across the lake.

This was Andrew's first trip onto Lake Atitlán. Soon he no longer noticed his hangover. The water was a deep, still blue over which the ferry passed as though gliding across glass. The air was clear and crisp. He could see across the lake, to where the thickly forested cones of three volcanoes humped one behind the other like vast green pyramids. Faint smears of smoke drifted from the sides, and bits of orange sparked now and again; Victor explained that the farmers, who could not grow enough to support themselves on their own land, set these fires at night and then took possession of the resulting fields. There they would grow food crops for a season or two before the landowners decided the patch could more profitably support coffee and either hired or simply evicted them. The results of this process could be seen to the right, where a fourth, smaller volcano stood, its sides an orderly patchwork of plowed fields.

As they drew closer to the opposite shore, Andrew could make out splendid homes tucked like castles amid unspoiled tracts of pine: the estates of the landowners and vacation homes of top army officers, according to Victor. Then the ferry rounded a bend and Andrew saw the village of Santiago Atitlán.

Dugouts from the village dotted the water to either side of them; the fishermen paused in the lowering of their nets and waved to the passing ferry. Andrew waved back. Up ahead, two rickety docks splintered out over the lake. A crowd of Indians in their bright costumes stood on one, waiting to load up for the trip back to Panajachel; it seemed as though the dock must collapse beneath their weight. More dugouts were drawn up to the shore around the docks, interspersed with heaps of seaweed left to steam in the sun. Behind the docks the grass grew thick as the ground sloped sharply up to a narrow cobblestone street lined with modest shops, restaurants, and houses. Farther up rose the blue and green dome of the church, topped with a red cross.

No sooner had he stepped from the boat than Andrew was surrounded by a flock of small girls who thrust bouquets of woven bracelets up into his face, chirping for him to buy. Victor waved them away. They dropped back, following at a discreet distance as Victor led Andrew to the San Lucas ferry. It turned out they had half an hour to wait. Victor stretched out on the grass to nap, but Andrew felt like exploring the town.

Away from Victor, the girls beset him again. He tried to be firm, but in the end their dirty faces, full of the intense youth and beauty that passed over Indian girls like a shadow whose substance they would never know, persuaded him to buy a bracelet from each. Anyway, they made good gifts; generally, he bought them from one group of girls only to give them away to another.

As he walked up toward the market, Andrew saw that the influx of tourists that had overrun Panajachel was spilling over into Santiago. This was perhaps inevitable, but still it saddened him to see how many stalls were hung with goods no Indian would buy.

The market itself preserved much of its traditional flavor, however: here, Indians still traded with Indians. The atmosphere was boisterous but jolly, like a festival. The stalls burgeoned with plantains and vegetables, clay pots and clothes of synthetic fibers. The crowd was in constant motion; it was impossible to stand still without receiving a poke in the back. Nonetheless, groups of women held their own around certain stalls, gossiping as their dirty, barefoot children chased each other and tussled underfoot. Now and again a rooster loudly asserted its importance. Andrew bought some bananas for breakfast.

On the way back to the ferry, he heard a sudden roaring on the road behind him and leaped aside. A truck sped by, filled with soldiers who stood uncomfortably squeezed together, rifles poking skyward. The oldest among them looked younger than Andrew. To a man, their faces were blank, without individuality or intelligence. The Indians quieted and kept their eyes to the ground until the truck had passed.

Back on the ferry, he and Victor were the only passengers. As they ate the bananas, Andrew asked about what he had seen. Victor pointed toward the land they were passing, the same thickly forested slopes Andrew had noticed earlier.

"The army says there is danger through here from guerrillas."

"But isn't that the way to San Lucas?"

Victor nodded. "Don't worry. There are no guerrillas."

"How do you know?"

"Villagers die there. Some gringos, too, a while back." He fixed Andrew with his gaze. "But never has a soldier died there."

Andrew shook his head. "I don't understand what's happening here. The guerrillas. The soldiers. You people in the middle. So much death wherever I go in this beautiful country."

"We do not speak of these things," Victor said.

"It is a stain on the memory of the Maya," Andrew said with feeling. "I wish there was something I could do."

Victor did not reply. He was carving an avocado pit.

Half an hour later, the ferry docked at San Lucas. The contrast with Santiago Atitlán was considerable. Here the docks were empty, the streets deserted save for strutting chickens and wasted, scavenging dogs. There was no one to cry for Andrew to buy their wares. The houses were smaller and in poor repair. But Victor was all smiles as he hopped down from the boat.

"What did I tell you, my friend? Here the air is clear!"

To Andrew, it smelled of cows and pigs.

Now a few people were making their way down to the dock; the weekly ferry brought mail, as well as hard-to-find goods ordered from Panajachel.

Victor knew them all; he sang out his greetings, and they answered in kind. Like Victor, they had pronounced Mayan features, more so than the Indians Andrew had seen in Santiago. Victor introduced him around, then they set off for his home.

It was a good way, somewhat outside of the village proper. All the way, Victor was talking, telling him who lived where, pointing out the local bar, the school, the place where, fifteen years ago, he had fought and killed his chief rival for the hand of the woman who became his wife. They passed fields where women and children bent beneath the hot son over dusty furrows, porches where men relaxed in the shade sipping Quetzalteca and spitting into the street. Victor called out to them all with pleasure; whatever they thought of him in Panajachel, Victor was obviously highly respected in his own village.

They stopped at a rickety wooden fence. Behind the gate the ground was torn and muddy; a line of thin planks led up to the house, a dubious-looking amalgamation of dried clay bricks, tree limbs, and rusty sheet metal topped with thatch. Behind the house, Andrew could make out a leaning shack of rotten boards: the outhouse. And behind that, a chicken coop set round with wire than seemed in better condition than the house.

Victor opened the gate and ushered Andrew through, kicking meanwhile at a weasely piglet that had insinuated itself between his feet. It scampered off, squealing mournfully.

The door to the house was wide open, as a consequence of which several hens were bobbing peremptorily toward Andrew as he entered. Startled, they careened about like cackling buzzsaws, causing him to step back into Victor.

"They scare you, eh?" laughed Victor, pushing past him into the room. "Sit down, my friend." He kicked a small stool to Andrew, who perched atop it, his knees pressing his chin.

Andrew was relieved to see that the inside of the house did not mirror the outside. Here the dirt floor was packed tight and neatly swept. In the center of the room sat a fat cookstove with a blackened pot on top. A hammock was slung in one corner; a washbasin and cooking implements hung from nails along the walls. There was a long table upon which rested an oil lamp and a small transistor radio with its innards spilling out. A sheathed machete leaned against the door. In another corner nestled a shrine to the Virgin Mary, draped with crepe paper and fronted by rows of festively colored candles burning down to puddles of wax. The space behind Victor was cut off by a curtain. Excusing himself, he ducked behind it only to reappear seconds later with his arms about the waist of a shrunken, smiling woman and two sleepy-eyed children, a boy and a girl. "My wife and my youngest, Juan and Concepción," he introduced, laughing as the two children, neither of whom looked older than ten, pressed back into their mother's skirts, eyeing Andrew with something like awe.

Andrew smiled and winked at them, provoking squeals of delight. Remembering the bracelets he had bought that morning, he reached into his pockets and held out two closed fists. "Go ahead," he said to the girl. "Pick one."

Timidly, Concepción inclined her head toward his left hand. When he opened it, she beamed with pleasure and took the bracelet. Emboldened by her example, Juan pried open the other fist and snatched the bracelet there.

"Thank our guest," Victor directed.

His son and daughter looked at each other, then ran out of the house without a word.

"Thank you," said Victor's wife, smiling and nodding.

Andrew waited for her to be introduced, but Victor merely guided her back behind the curtain. Then he took Andrew by the arm. "Come. There is a place I will show you."

Andrew was tired, but he did not feel he could refuse. "Where are we going?"

"To an old place up in the mountains. Don't worry, it will be safe; no one knows of it but me. I show it to you because I think you will understand."

Victor filled two jugs with water. He gave Andrew a candle and kept one for himself. Then they set out.

They climbed for hours up the side of a volcano that Victor called Atitlán; he did not know whether the lake had been named for the volcano or the other way around. It was hard going, their only companions the birds and lizards that fled before them into the thick forest. Victor led him down into a ravine cut by a waterfall. Obscured by dense foliage there, an opening winked large enough for a man to crawl through. Victor lit his candle and entered on hands and knees. Andrew followed.

"We must be noisy to frighten off the snakes," Victor said.

Andrew had to force himself to continue. The air grew cooler and drier the deeper they went. After a time—he could not have said how long—the passage widened. Soon they could stand.

Andrew gasped. Around and above him, illuminated by candlelight, the cavern vaulted out of rock and shadowy echoes of rock. Somewhere far away, water dripped.

It was a Mayan site. Untouched by time or archeologists. The walls were covered with painted glyphs and figures. Andrew brought his candle close. A red figure in a snake headdress held a man's head in one outstretched hand; before him knelt his victim, chalky blue, blood spouting from the neck to form a lush green cornstalk. Close by, a woman passed a thick, thorny rope through her tongue, catching the blood in a bowl at her feet. In the center of the cavern was an altar, a round, green stone ringed by carved skulls and inlaid with turquoise and shell. Behind it was a throne in the shape of a jaguar devouring a human heart. Stelae stood around the altar, some marked with dates in the Mayan bar-and-dot system that Andrew could recognize but not read, others blank-faced. The terrible faces of gods and goddesses leaned out from the walls as though the rest of their bodies would soon follow. There were four of the rain god, Chac, each facing a different direction and colored white, black, yellow, and red.

Andrew turned to Victor, who was silently watching him. "What is . . . was . . . this place?"

"This is where I come to carve," he said. He placed his candle on the altar. Andrew did likewise. They sat facing each other. Andrew reached for the water, but Victor stopped him. He gave him the second jug, which Andrew had thought contained water. "This is *balche*. It is an old drink made from honey. Here we should drink what they drank."

Andrew nodded. The *balche* was thick and heady. He felt as though he was taking part in some ancient ceremony.

"I found this place as a child," Victor said. "At first it frightened me, but I could not keep away. I heard the builders of this place call out. Though my mind understood nothing, my bones shook with the old language. I listened and learned much. I came here and carved, thinking about what I had learned, and more became clear to me."

"What is this place?" Andrew repeated.

"Listen." Victor had taken out his knife, was carving an avocado pit.

There was only the distant drip, drip of water.

Andrew sipped the *balche*. His head was spinning. The candlelight flickered over the walls, making the scenes painted there come alive. It was not water dripping, but blood. It poured down the walls in red streams. Andrew screwed his eyes shut, but the vision persisted. And then he heard Victor's voice echo through the cavern of his skull.

"You cannot escape the blood, my friend. That is why I brought you here. To understand from these things that what happens in my country today is not a stain on the memory of the Maya, as you put it, but that same memory, a living force still for all it may be forgotten by some. This place, this country, this people—everything is soaked in blood, as much today as centuries ago."

Andrew found that he had lost all feeling in his body. He felt as though he were floating in darkness, borne up by the steady voice. He could not speak.

"We are the true guerrillas. The others merely do our work. Army or rebels, the gods are served."

Andrew opened his eyes as though waking from a deep sleep. They were no longer alone in the cavern. All the Indians from San Lucas stood around. Some held torches, others swung censers from which an acrid, sooty smoke leaked, stinging his eyes and making them water. The smell of *balche* was strong. He looked down at his body: he had been stripped naked and painted a chalky blue. He still could not feel his limbs; he was being supported by two old men who wore masks of Chac. One of the men was painted yellow, the other red. Two more Chacs stood before him, black and white.

Then he saw Victor. He was dressed like one of the figures on the wall. He took something from his belt and held it up for Andrew to see. It was an avocado pit carved with his likeness, only twisted by pain. "This is your god face," he said. "In this way you will be honored among us, my friend." He paused, then added, "You asked what you could do."

Then the four Chacs grabbed hold of him by his arms and legs and bent him back over the green altar. He could not move, or scream, or feel; out of the corner of one eye he saw the thin, braceleted wrists of Juan and Concepción. He heard Victor speak in a language he could not understand. His heart was leaping against his chest like a wild thing that had caught the scent of freedom.

TWILIGHT OF THE DOGS

WE WERE WATCHING THE NETCAST OF THE FIGHTING IN Hampton Roads, looking for Dad or anybody else we knew, when the bombs started falling. Until that instant, I'd been certain the war would pass us by. Nothing interesting ever happens in Urbanna. But Reverend Samuels always said the Jacks would come sooner or later, and now it looked like he was right. He generally was.

At the first explosions, Amber and Cyndi began to scream in terror and what sounded like every car alarm in the neighborhood went off at once. I felt myself freeze up. This wasn't how I'd imagined myself acting in a combat situation. Two days ago I'd sworn up and down to Dad that I would fight like a veteran if given half a chance. Now I willed myself to spring into action, but it was no use. My body was no longer mine to command. I could only sit there on the couch, aghast and helpless.

Then Mom's steady voice filled me with a shame that took the place of courage. "Come on, Jon. You know the drill!"

She was already hustling the twins out of the room, making, I knew, for the church. That's where everybody was supposed to gather in the event of an attack. Even before the miracle of a week ago, when elements of the army and national guard went over to the side of the Hampton militia and took control of Langley Air Force Base, Reverend Samuels had been insisting that we plan for the worst. The miracle of Langley had only increased his sense of urgency.

"You think it's finished because of what happened at Langley?" he'd thundered from the pulpit to the crowd that had gathered to give thanks. "It's not over by a long shot. It's just beginning. You think because we're

15

godly folk here in Urbanna, wickedness won't seek us out? I tell you, it will come for that very reason! And when it does, there will be only one protection. One salvation." He flung his arms out to either side. "Behold, the wicked are overthrown, and are not, but the house of the righteous shall stand."

It was my job to get Gran to church. Gran was Dad's mom. She sat on the sofa now, eyes glued to the neTV as if she didn't hear the bombs bursting or feel the house shaking, as if those chaotic images of war broadcast by cambots miles away in Hampton were more real than the war that had suddenly shown up on our doorstep.

"Come on, Gran. We've got to go."

She looked up at me, her clouded blue eyes like glass bubbles that could shatter at a word, and pursed her lips in annoyance. "Quiet, you, Mark," she said.

It wasn't the first time she'd mixed me up with Dad. I didn't bother correcting her. I just reminded her that Reverend Samuels was waiting.

"The reverend?" Gran had a crush on Reverend Samuels. There was no other word for it. Whenever she was around him, she batted her eyes, giggled, blushed, the whole nine yards. It was embarrassing, watching my seventy-six-year-old grandmother behave like a thirteen-year-old girl. But it did come in handy sometimes.

"That's right." I eased her to her feet. Her body had the heft of porcelain. The bombs seemed to be drawing nearer. My legs were trembling with the need to run. I had to shout to make myself heard. "He's waiting for us at the church."

"Fetch my yellow scarf." Flakes of dandruff fell over the shoulders of her blue dress as Gran smoothed her hair. "The reverend says it sets off my eyes right nice."

"There's no time." Gripping her arm, I impelled her forward, trying to herd her out of the room. "You look fine."

She stopped. "Where are you taking me, Mark?"

I grimaced. Gran would pick today of all days to act up. Her biggest fear was of being put into a nursing home like Grandad. And like him, dying there. On bad days, when the Alzheimer's was at its worst, the slightest departure from routine left her confused and suspicious, fastening on vaguely imagined conspiracies to explain her sense of shadows gathering and closing in around her.

"Where are you taking me?" she repeated more fearfully now.

"I told you, to church!"

It must've come out harsher than I'd intended, because Gran started to cry. She stood there, limp as a dishrag, tears running down her face. I tugged at her arm, but I couldn't budge her. It was amazing how someone so frail could fix herself so stubbornly to one spot. The house was shuddering and groaning, and the sky was full of screaming. I felt like joining in. I realized I was going to have to throw Gran over my shoulder and carry her to church. She'd probably fight me every step of the way, but what else could I do? Leave her? I thought for a moment about hitting her: a tap on the chin, enough to knock her out, and when she woke up she wouldn't remember anything. But what if she didn't wake up? Besides, I'd remember. I'd know. And God would know.

"Take it easy, Gran," I said soothingly and reached for her again. Then I thought of the HK91. *The armed man fears nothing, is equal to anything.* How many times had Dad told me that? He was gone now, fighting against the godless government, but I'd sworn on the Bible to protect the family in his absence. Once the bombs stopped falling, the Jacks would come. I was going to need that rifle. I should have thought of it sooner; Dad sure as heck would've. "I'll be right back, Gran."

She ignored me, fleeing back to the sofa and the comfort of the neTV. The wall screen was still showing live feeds from Hampton. The city had been bombed by both sides and was little more than smoking ruins now, but Jacks and militiamen were fighting it out in what remained of the streets, as were the cambots of church and state, tiny arachnoid shapes recapitulating in miniature the warfare they recorded, edited, and broadcast via the network of themselves. Packs of dogs scavenged among the dead, moving purposefully through the debris as if they, too, shared a link.

After Dad and most of Urbanna's able-bodied men, along with plenty of kids my own age and even younger, had gone to the relief of Hampton, I'd moved his guns to the foyer closet, placing them high on the top shelf where the twins couldn't reach. Now I wrenched open the door and stood on tip-toe to grope for the HK91. As my fingers closed around the familiar shape of the assault rifle, something huge crashed down behind me with a roar like a freight train derailing into a pit of glass, and I felt myself lifted as if by the scruff of the neck and thrown forward.

The next thing I knew, I was lying half-buried in down coats and chunks of plaster. I had a feeling I was forgetting something important, but I couldn't stay focused long enough to figure out what. My head was throbbing so violently that I thought I was going to puke. When I touched it, pain like I'd never imagined shot through my brain. Then the sickness came rushing up and out of me.

Afterward, I began to wriggle my way back, inch by slow inch, more to escape the reek of my own vomit than anything else. I kept having to stop, coughing and gasping as my stomach heaved, but soon there was nothing left to come out. Moments or hours later, I glimpsed the stock of the HK91 protruding from a pile of coats, and only then did I wake up to where I was. The hardness of the weapon in my hand filled me with fresh and unexpected strength, like grace.

Then I remembered Gran, and that thought filled me with strength as well, a strength that rose from within me like the sickness had, and which felt almost like a kind of sickness itself. I backed the rest of the way out of the closet and stood on shaky legs, supporting myself against the wall with my free hand. My fingers were red with blood, and I wondered vaguely whose it could be.

"Gran!" I called, or tried to; no sound emerged from my lips. There was no sound anywhere. The explosions, the sirens . . . all gone. Vanished. Just a hissing noise like sand blowing over sand. I smelled burning things.

I pushed away from the wall and staggered through an obstacle course of debris—upended, smashed furniture, pictures and photographs hurled from their perches on walls and tables, the contents of shelves and cabinets dumped unceremoniously into the snowfall of plaster and broken glass blanketing the floor. It was as if a giant had lifted the house, shaken it like a snow-globe, then set it down again.

I reached the family room . . . what was left of it. The neTV was gone, along with the wall in which it had been set, leaving an opening that looked out into the front yard and the street beyond. I saw no sign of Gran or, for that matter, the couch on which she'd been sitting. This time, when I shouted her name, I heard the faint rasp of my voice, felt it in my bones like distant thunder, and I realized the world was not as silent as it seemed. The bomb that had wrecked the house had left me temporarily deaf. At least, I hoped it was only temporary.

I began to search the room, looking for Gran, but there was nothing. Had she been blown out of the house by the explosion? Or perhaps just wandered off, dazed and confused? Perhaps she had walked to the church and was waiting there now, along with Mom and the twins. I imagined how glad they'd be to see me, how they'd laugh and cry when I stepped through the door, the answer to their prayers. How Amber and Cyndi would come running to hug me. How Gran would be flirting with Reverend Samuels as usual. All of them safe.

Then I took a deep breath and wiped wetness from my eyes. Who was I kidding? Gran wasn't at church. And I'd better stop telling myself fairy tales if I wanted to get there. Urbanna had been attacked; that much was plain. I glanced at my watch: it was nearly seven. I tried to remember what time it had been when the bombs had started to fall. An hour ago? Two hours? I wasn't sure. But I must have been lying there in the closet for a long time, dead to the world. Had the Jacks come while I was unconscious? Were they here now?

I had to assume they were. Disgusted at my slowness to comprehend the obvious, I clicked off the safety of the HK91 and made my way to the opening in the wall, keeping low and availing myself of every shred of cover. I didn't know who might be out there, watching. There could be snipers waiting for a clear shot. With my hearing gone, there would be no warning crack, just the sudden impact of a bullet, like effect preceding cause.

Hugging what remained of the wall, I advanced to where it ended entirely. I crouched there for a moment, fighting down my fear. Then I peeked out. The cars and homes of our neighbors lay smashed and smoldering. Small fires were burning themselves out as though they'd burned for hours already. There were bodies sprawled in the street and across the singed and cratered lawns. I counted three in our yard alone. Two wore the uniform of the Jacks; the other was a militiaman. I couldn't make out the man's face, or even his unit, but his hair was blond, like my dad's. But Dad was miles away, in Hampton.

Meanwhile, some other part of my mind was fitting the pieces together. Following the bombing, the Jacks must have entered the town, only to be attacked by militiamen in turn. A battle had ensued . . . one I'd as good as slept through, to my shame. Now I saw no trace of life or movement. It appeared that both sides had withdrawn, leaving their dead behind.

Just as I'd been left behind. First by Dad, then Mom and the twins. Even Gran was gone. Perhaps I was as dead as the men outside, only I didn't know it. If I retraced my steps, would I find my body sprawled on the closet floor? No. I was alive, not some walking ghost. I might be deaf, but I wasn't blind. The important thing was to get to the church. It occurred to me that the Jacks, in their wickedness, might have violated the sanctity of God's house. It wouldn't be the first time. They were known for such atrocities, and worse ones. Of course, they denied everything, but we, the faithful, knew the truth. We'd heard the testimony of survivors, seen the footage netcast by CCP cambots from all across the country.

I stepped over the wall and outside, muttering a prayer. The sun was a pale smudge behind gray clouds and drifting smoke. A hot breeze was blowing. I didn't think I'd ever heard a noise quite as loud as this silence. It made me want to scream, fire a burst from the HK, anything to shatter it. Instead, I hurried toward the body of the militiaman, passing the two dead Jacks on the way. One of them was a woman—a Jill. I knew that women fought alongside men in the federal army, but it disturbed me to see. It must be a hard thing for a Christian man to have to kill a woman, even if she is the enemy. But God doesn't ask the easy things, as I'd often heard Reverend Samuels say and was coming to understand for myself.

The militiaman lay as if asleep, curled into a fetal position and turned away from me. His hair was blond and bloody. I couldn't see any indication of the man's unit, but the shoulder patch on his camouflage fatigues bore the insignia of the Church of Christ, Patriot: the white cross with the black silhouettes of two rifles stacked on either side and leaning together beneath the bar, propping it up. I took a breath and steeled myself. I had a terrible premonition that I was looking at the corpse of my father. Dropping to one knee, I turned the body face up. Or tried to. It was stiff, heavy, as if rooted to the ground. I braced myself and heaved.

I fell back onto my butt as the body abruptly rolled over. The dead man's eyes were gone. Blood-rimmed sockets gaped in a face that looked nothing like my dad's. It didn't even seem human. The crows had been at it. And not only crows. The nose and one cheek had been torn away, revealing bone-white teeth and a bloated, purplish tongue. The body remained curled around its death, like a spider. I scrambled to my feet and backed away.

A movement out of the corner of my eye was the only warning I got before a dark blur bowled me over. My hand came up instinctively, and I felt something sharp tear at my wrist. My screams were swallowed in the hissing silence as I struggled to throw off my attacker. The absence of sound made what was happening seem like a dream or a movie, a violent dance without music. Somehow I got my feet up and kicked free. Only then, as it prepared to spring at me again, did I realize that my attacker was a dog. I swung up the HK91 and fired off a burst.

The spray of bullets cut the dog nearly in two. I turned away, feeling my gorge rise, and saw another dark blur vanish around the side of the house. I tried to stand but fell twice before I was able to do so. My wrist was bleeding freely, the skin torn. I felt no pain, just a tingling sensation that climbed my arm in pulses synchronized to the throbbing of my head, the beating of my heart. It rose, then fell, then rose again a little higher than before, creeping up in a numbing tide. I don't know why I didn't turn and run back into the house. I wasn't thinking too clearly. I took a lurching step, as if stumbling downhill, then another, moving like a zombie as I crossed the yard in pursuit of the other dog.

Turning the corner, I came upon a sight that froze my blood. A pack of dogs was tearing at something on the ground. I saw a flash of blue amid the seething mass of fur and limbs. Then I was firing into the thick of it. A few dogs fell. The rest ran off.

I ran to Gran. Had I shot her as well? Once again, I hadn't thought things through. Some fighter I was turning out to be. "Gran! Gran!"

She couldn't hear my voice any better than I could. She was in far worse shape than the militiaman; if not for the dress, I didn't think I would have recognized her at all, so thoroughly had the dogs mauled her. I forced myself to kneel beside the torn and bloody body and look for some sign of life. A breath. A pulse. There was none. The Earthly vessel was shattered; Gran was with Jesus now.

I stood on shaky legs and checked the dogs I'd shot. One of them was still alive. It looked like a mutt, part beagle. It wasn't moving, but its mouth hung open, its long tongue lolling out, red with blood—whether its own or Gran's, I didn't know or want to know. It was watching me intently with brown, intelligent eyes. I raised the gun . . . but then a prickling along the back of my neck made me turn around.

The dogs had returned. There seemed to be more of them than before. The pack stood perhaps twenty yards away in the next yard, watching me, their bodies tensed and ready. I recognized neighborhood dogs among them, dogs I'd seen a thousand times being walked or running free in the park. But there were also dogs I'd never seen before, dogs of all breeds and sizes, as if they'd come from miles around. There didn't seem to be a leader; at least, no dog stood out from the rest. I fired a burst over their heads. They didn't flinch. They stood firm, like soldiers prepared to accept certain losses rather than retreat an inch. Cold fear uncoiled down the length of my spine.

I bolted. I didn't have to look over my shoulder to know that the pack was coming after me. I pounded up the walkway and onto the front porch of our house. Then I was inside, slamming the door behind me. A second later, the dogs smashed against the door so forcefully that I was afraid it would splinter. But it held.

I wasn't safe yet. The dogs would find the collapsed wall of the family room and get in that way. I wouldn't even be able to hear them; for all I knew, they were already inside. Gasping for breath, I ran to the basement door at the end of the hall. Only as I reached it did it register that I wasn't holding the HK91. I must've dropped it outside. I hesitated. Was there time to search the closet for another gun? But even as I glanced back, a dog shot out of the family room, paws scrabbling almost comically as it saw me and sought to alter its headlong trajectory. I didn't waste any more time, just wrenched open the door and flung myself through.

The musty odor of the basement filled my nostrils. I stood in darkness on the top step and groped for the light switch. It didn't work; the power must have been knocked out in the attack. But Dad kept a flashlight hanging on the wall for emergencies. I found it and played its beam over the stairs that descended steeply to the cement floor where I'd knelt and prayed three days ago. Dad had called me down after supper. As I descended the stairs, I'd been hoping that he'd changed his mind and was going to let me come along to Hampton after all. But when I reached the bottom, he'd pulled out the family Bible and made me kneel and put my hand to the vow-smoothed leather and swear that I wouldn't come after the militia . . . that I'd stay behind to protect Gran, Mom, and the twins. I repeated the oath he demanded of me though the duty it imposed seemed neither fair nor necessary. And it had seemed even less so the next morning when I watched history pass down Main Street in a festive parade. I'd watched and waved as the column departed, a false smile stuck to my face while inside I was burning with rage and humiliation at the sight of so many kids my own age and younger among the men. The injustice of it had made my heart seethe with bitterness against my father. Years from now, I'd thought, when people spoke of how the righteous had risen up to take back their country, I would have nothing to tell. But Dad had been right to make me stay. I would have a story of my own now. I was smack dab in the middle of it.

I tried to think clearly and logically of what was happening and what I should do. WWDD—what would Dad do? Well, he wouldn't have dropped his gun, for starters. I leaned back against the door. I felt it shuddering in its frame as the dogs hurled themselves against it; I was glad I couldn't hear whatever noises they were making. My heart was thudding. My head was pounding, and the tingling from the bite in my wrist had spread all the way up my arm, though the bleeding had stopped. I could barely move the fingers of that hand, or feel them. My watch was gone, torn away in the dog's attack. Could it have been rabid? Even if it had been, the sickness wouldn't be on me yet.

What had turned the dogs so vicious? Had the noise and bloodshed of war snapped something civilized in them, returning them to a wilder, more savage existence? Did the same thing happen to men? Perhaps that was war's secret allure . . . the knowledge I'd seen in the eyes of my dad and the other veterans as they'd driven off, a look that had called to me with a promise of revelation and transformation, like the look in Reverend Samuels's eyes on the day of my baptism, when he'd plunged me down into the warm water of the pool and held me there. I'd opened my eyes and watched my former self and all its sins go streaming away in the bubbles rising up all around me until the burning in my lungs had grown too great to bear and I'd begun to fight against the strong hands that held me down—which, as if they'd been waiting for just that signal, pulled me gasping into the sweet air of a new life. It struck me now that this was a second baptism, sanctified by blood and a silence similar to that which I'd experienced in the baptismal pool. When I surfaced now, how would I be changed?

Reverend Samuels had been right; wickedness had come to Urbanna. That the dogs were possessed by demons, I had no doubt. I'd always known that this fight was for the future of the country, but what if even more was at stake? What if the final struggle was being played out here and now? Were these the last days of conflict and conflagration leading to the Rapture? Or, and the thought staggered me like a punch, sent my shoulders sliding down the trembling plane of the door until I was sprawled on the top step like one of my sisters' rag dolls on a shelf, had the Rapture already come and gone while I lay unconscious, the godly lifted bodily up to Heaven, leaving the Earth to sinners? I'd always thought of myself as among the elect, the saved. Had that certainty been sinful, an excess of pride? If so, I repented it now. But I knew that repentance, however sincere, wasn't enough. I could still be saved, but I had to earn salvation by being strong in my faith and actions. That was the way of the Christian Patriot, of the righteous men like my dad who had left their families behind and gone to Hampton in the service of something bigger than themselves. I realized that it didn't matter what had happened, whether the Rapture had taken place or was still to come. I'd sworn to protect my family; that I would do to the best of my ability, or die trying. But I couldn't do it from here. One way or another, I had to get to the church. If, when I got there, it was empty, I'd know and rejoice for the sake of Mom and the twins and all the others so blessedly ascended. And if it were not empty, I would be needed more than ever.

But first I had to get past the dogs.

Yet I felt so tired, so drained. I couldn't even get to my feet. I felt the dogs scratching away on the other side of the door as if determined to claw their way through. I imagined their claws working inside me as well, scratching furiously at some inner barrier that would break sooner, and with more terrible results, than the door at my back. I sensed something in me akin to the dogs, a fierce and ravening potential desperate to be born. I didn't know what it was or where it had come from. I only knew that it would crack me open like an eggshell. I clutched my knees to my chest and shivered. Gazing down the narrow beam of the flashlight as though peering into the shaft of a tunnel, I prayed with all my heart, asking for strength and guidance. I'd never felt so afraid. So alone.

The glittery drift of dust particles in the flashlight's beam reminded me of driving home through snowfalls after a day of deer hunting, Dad sitting quietly behind the wheel and me quiet beside him, weary to the bone and half-hypnotized by the beautiful chaos of white flakes shining in the head-lights, tempting me with the promise of a deeper, hidden order, a pattern that would make sense of everything if only I had faith enough to surrender to it. Now I did surrender, letting myself sink into the bottomless swirl of dust, though it was exhaustion rather than faith that moved me.

I felt as if my soul had slipped from my body into a river of light in which countless other souls hung suspended, carried by fateful currents to whatever destination their lives had merited. My fear had left me; I felt only wonder. The dust motes were like windows I could peer into as they tumbled past. There I glimpsed entire lives; not in the way of earthly seeing, for the brightness around me was blinding, but with a new kind of sight that bypassed my eyes. Here there was no time, no sequential ordering of images. The totality of each thing, each person, was present simultane-ously, the whole contained in every part, conception to death, like a hologram existing in dimensions I'd lacked the senses to perceive until now. I wasn't seeing men, women, children . . . or, rather, that was the least of what I saw. They were strangers, like the bodies outside; yet I knew them. And knew that I was equally exposed to their gazes. I felt no shame or modesty. On the contrary, I'd never felt such acceptance and love. It came pouring into me from all directions. It was absolute, unqualified, like no human emotion I'd ever known or imagined. I realized then that I and all the other souls here were parts of a totality far bigger than ourselves, a construct so vast and multifaceted that only God could possibly perceive it. Yet—and it was this which truly awed me—that totality was present in me, in each of us, though as far beyond the grasp of even my current, height-ened comprehension as that comprehension had been beyond the grasp of my former senses. I was part of a hierarchy in which every place, however humble, was equally essential and valued in the eyes of God, just as all militiamen were of equal value in the eyes of the officers above them, whose orders were for that reason carried out without question or hesitation, an obedience founded not on fear, as with the Jacks—little more than slaves, really—who served the federal government, but, rather, on faith. *Lord*, I thought, so overwhelmed by this vision of a heavenly militia that I could only abase myself before it, *I am not worthy* . . .

None are worthy unless made so by the Redeemer's grace.

It was Gran's voice! Suddenly I felt the warmth of her love infusing me, though there was no visible sign of her presence. But I didn't need to see her; I knew she was here. And somehow it didn't seem at all surprising or unusual that she should be speaking to me, though I hadn't forgotten for a moment that she was dead. *I-I'm sorry, Gran. I failed you.* I didn't know if I was speaking the words aloud or only thinking them.

Don't be sorry. Rejoice as I do.

It's my fault you died . . .

This is not death, but life everlasting. I am born again in the communion of saints.

My heart leapt. *And me? Is there a place for me in that communion?*

For you and for all mankind.

Then it's true. These are the Last Days.

No, she answered. *The First. But it is not to speak of this that I am come. We have need of you, Grandson.*

We?

All of us here, freed from the prisons of our bodies. We can see—oh, so much! But we cannot act directly.

What, Gran? What have you seen?

You must go to the church, Jon. Your mother and sisters and all those sheltering there are in mortal peril.

What's happened? Is it the Jacks? Have they—?

Hush. There is no time. You must hurry, or it will be too late.

But the dogs . . .

Have faith, Jon. I will be with you in spirit. If you show no fear and trust in me, the dogs will not harm you.

I—I'm afraid, Gran.

Does death still frighten you so much? After all you've seen, all I've told you?

I was ashamed, but couldn't lie to her. *Yes.*

A time will come when you will throw open the door to Death and invite him in gladly. But that time is not yet.

It seemed impossible that such a time could ever come. But surely if I opened the basement door now, the death waiting on the other side wouldn't wait for an invitation. It would charge right in, all snapping teeth and rending claws. *I can't do it, Gran. My faith isn't that strong.*

Then your mother and sisters will perish. And not just in the flesh. The communion of saints will be denied them. Their voices will be forever absent from the heavenly choir. Will you let that happen when it lies in your power to prevent it?

But how? What power do I have?

When the time comes, you will know. God will provide.

I wish Dad was here.

He is.

It took me a moment to grasp her meaning. *No!*

Your father fell in Hampton. He fought bravely and died well. He has joined the communion. Will you deny him the joy of a reunion with his wife and daughters?

So many impossible things had happened, but this struck me as the most impossible of all. How could it be? Dad dead. Gone from the world, and me left behind . . . again. *I want to talk to him*, I demanded, as though this were a telephone conversation. *Like I'm talking to you.*

You can't, Jon. He hasn't adjusted to his new state among us. The transition is . . . confusing.

I felt a weight that hadn't been with me before, as if Dad had borne it until now. A chain of fathers and sons forged across the generations. Now that heavy chain was mine to carry forward, mine to pass on . . .

Jon? Are you listening?

Is it over? I asked then. *Have we lost?*

There was laughter in her reply. *How can we lose? With each death we grow stronger.*

I'll need a weapon.

Faith must be your weapon. And your shield.

But—

Enough!

I jumped at the sharpness of her tone. It was as if whatever stood at the far end of the chain of fathers and sons—the very first father of all, perhaps—had yanked the chain taut, bringing me abruptly to heel.

There is no more time for talk. You must act, Jon. Now, this very instant!

Even as she spoke, I felt myself expelled from the light of her presence. The sensation of weightless suspension gave way to the hardness of the stairs on which I sprawled, the door at my back. My muscles were stiff, protesting the awkward position. I felt a fierce thirst. Had I fallen asleep? Had it all been a dream? My face was wet with tears. The weight of Dad's loss was still with me. I knew it always would be.

I got to my feet with a groan—an audible groan. I could hear again! And that wasn't all. My head no longer pained me, and though the numbness in my arm remained, I found that I could move it, and the blood-smeared fingers of my hand, easily. Gran had healed me . . . or God had, working through her spirit. Just as she'd been healed, for no trace of the Alzheimer's had been evident in her words or in the luminous intelligence I'd perceived behind them. What more proof did I need? Yet I didn't open the door. Pressing my ear to the wood, I listened intently but heard nothing. Only the muffled, mindless, yet somehow mournful wailing of car alarms. Perhaps the dogs had gone. If only I could see what was behind the door!

Gran?

But I knew she wouldn't answer. Blessed are they that do not see, and yet believe. I thought again of Dad's sacrifice, of Mom and the twins and our neighbors all huddled together in the church, praying for deliverance. In some way I didn't understand, I was that deliverance. Or could be, if I had faith and courage enough. And hadn't I sworn already to protect them? I reached a trembling hand to the door, turned the knob, and pushed it open.

The dogs were waiting, as I'd known they would be. They filled the hallway. But they didn't charge. They didn't make a move or a sound. They sat or stood, watching expectantly, anxiously, tails lowered, brown and yellow eyes shining in the beam of my flashlight with the unnatural intelligence of the devils residing there.

Steeling myself, I took a step forward, gripping the flashlight tightly in my hand, like a club. The nearest dogs drew away, opening a path between them. Another step, and more dogs retreated, whining as they went. It was like Gran had promised; her spirit was pushing them aside, protecting me. Armored in her grace, which came from God, I advanced with increased confidence into the midst of them. When I reached the closet, I paused, thinking to procure a better weapon than the flashlight, but no sooner did I turn than the dogs drew close to bar my way, warning me back with growls and bared teeth and bristling fur. The other dogs had closed ranks behind me, cutting off my retreat. I had nowhere to go but forward. To the church.

Outside, the sun had set, and the night seemed darker than any I had ever known, with a thick haze of smoke drifting through the air, obscuring the stars and moon, and my flashlight the only source of illumination apart from guttering fires. Everything was the same, but changed: the wreckage of houses and cars, the bodies of the dead, all rendered at once less real and more terrible in the flashlight beam. The stench of burned wood and rubber and other things I didn't want to think about curled in my nostrils. I saw my HK91 in the driveway where I'd dropped it, but I didn't bother trying to retrieve it. The dogs herded me past. Now that I could hear again, the clamor of the car alarms was making me wish for silence.

I walked to the end of the street and turned up Main. It was hard to believe the militia had driven down this street just days ago, the whole town lining the sidewalks to cheer the parade of pick-ups and SUVs. It had been a regular Fourth of July: horns honking, people shouting and waving upside-down American flags, guns being shot off into the air. Now Main Street was cratered from the impact of shells and bombs, strewn with smashed cars and broken glass. I passed more bodies, but the dogs wouldn't let me stop to examine them. I thought of Dad, lying dead somewhere in Hampton, and of my friends who had gone with him to fight. How many of them lay sprawled in the graceless contortions of death; how many of their martyred souls had joined the communion of saints? All, surely all. But then why didn't I feel happier for them? Why wasn't I rejoicing? The noise of the alarms reminded me of Amber and Cyndi, how they'd screamed in terror when the bombs had started falling. How would I tell them that they no longer had a father? And Mom . . . She was a widow now, thinking she still had a husband.

I began to run. The dogs paced me to either side, barking and yapping in excitement, or perhaps frustration. Every so often one would dart in to snap at my legs, but my faith held firm, and I was not bitten. When I reached the steps of the church, the pack dropped back, and I knew then that I was safe. What was in them could not come close to such a holy place.

I ran up the steps, looking for some sign of life within the church, but the windows were dark. The door was locked tight. Was I too late? I pounded at it, shouting for admittance. "Open up! It's me, Jon Jensen!"

The door cracked open suddenly, and a strobe of light flashed into my eyes. Someone grabbed me and pulled me inside. I heard the door slam shut. I cried out and swung the flashlight blindly, more out of instinct than anything else, but the blow never landed. My wrist was seized in a grip of steel, and what must have been a forearm caught me under the chin and pinned me back against the door. The flashlight dropped from my fingers as the voice of Reverend Samuels rasped in my ear. "Don't fight me, Jon! You're safe now. Safe. Do you understand?"

I managed a nod, and the pressure on my windpipe slackened. I gasped for air and would have fallen, but Reverend Samuels bore me up. My vision was beginning to clear when, with the click of a switch, the lights came on, blinding me a second time. The church had its own generator; even if electricity were out in the rest of Urbanna, there would be power here. I let myself be guided through a soup of blotchy shapes and colors.

"Here, sit down," came Reverend Samuels's voice again.

I sank gratefully into a chair. A hand fell onto my shoulder, squeezed. "Drink this."

A plastic bottle was thrust into my hand. I raised it to my lips and tasted cool cider. I drank greedily.

"Where's your grandmother, Jon?"

I shook my head, unable to speak. The round, red, sweaty face of Reverend Samuels swam into focus. He was squatting in front of me in his baptismal robes of brilliant, arterial crimson—for there could be neither birth nor rebirth, whether of an individual or a nation, without the shedding of blood, as Jesus and Jefferson had said. One of the altar pieces, an M-16, dangled from a strap at his shoulder. His eyes looked big as blue marbles behind his glasses. They stared into my soul, judging me.

"Everyone made it but you two." Reverend Samuels dug his fingers into my shoulder. "You were supposed to bring her."

"I—I couldn't!" I blurted out. "I—"

He interrupted: "Is she still alive?"

Tears came welling up at the question. I wiped my eyes fiercely, ashamed. "She's gone, Reverend Samuels."

"I'm truly sorry, Jon." With a sigh, Reverend Samuels released me and stood, holding the M-16 steady against his side. "I know how much you loved her. But you mustn't blame yourself. It was her time. God called her home."

"I know," I said.

"Then dry your tears. The arms of Jesus will comfort and avenge."

The windows of the vestibule were covered with thick blankets to keep the light from shining out. The double doors leading to the sanctuary were closed. Behind them I heard, for the first time, faint strains of organ music. "Is everybody okay, Reverend Samuels? My mom and the twins?"

"They're fine, Jon. Everyone's fine here."

The surge of relief was so strong that I was sobbing before I knew it. I'd arrived in time! Mom and the twins were all right. I could still save them. Save everyone. But from what? Gran had said only that my task would be revealed to me, and that God would provide the means to accomplish it. I had to have faith. "Take . . . take me to them."

Reverend Samuels gently pushed me back as I tried to stand. "I will. But calm yourself first. Seeing you like this will only upset them."

I nodded, struggling to master my tears.

"What's it like out there, Jon?" Reverend Samuels asked meanwhile, lowering his voice to a raspy whisper. "The neTV is down. The phones are dead; even cells aren't working. And there's nothing but white noise on the radio. We're cut off. I know there was a battle; we heard the fighting. But then nothing, only the howling of dogs."

"They're devils, Reverend Samuels."

"You saw atrocities, then?" he said almost eagerly. "The Jacks—"

"Not the Jacks," I interrupted. "The dogs."

He blinked in surprise.

"They're possessed."

"Possessed?"

I told him how the pack had ravaged the bodies of the dead and tried to kill me. He listened expressionlessly, but I could tell that he didn't believe me, not even when I showed him my wounded wrist.

"That's a nasty bite," he said.

"I'm telling the truth, Reverend Samuels. I swear it!"

"You've been through a lot, Jon. One thing for sure, God was looking out for you today."

I nodded. "I'm here for a reason."

"We all are, son."

"No, something's going to happen, and I have to stop it."

"What do you mean? What's going to happen?"

"I don't know! But Gran said—"

"Jon, whatever your grandmother may have told you before she died, you have to remember that she was sick. Her mind was gone."

"No . . . " I didn't know how to explain it to him. But he already thought I was crazy, so what did I have to lose? "She's with the angels now, Reverend Samuels. She spoke to me. Said everybody here was in some kind of danger and that it was up to me to save them."

Reverend Samuels blinked owlishly behind his thick glasses. "This is God's house, Jon. No danger can touch us here. And we don't need any saving. We're already saved, in Jesus. And so are you."

"You don't understand. She guided me. Kept the dogs away. I—" My insides twisted painfully, and I felt sure that the danger, whatever it was, was at hand. There was no more time to talk. I lurched to my feet . . . or tried to. My legs wouldn't support me. I couldn't even feel them. I hit the floor hard, the plastic bottle that Reverend Samuels had given me bouncing from my hand and rolling away. What was happening to me? I tried to get up, but my arms were useless. "Gran," I moaned. "Gran, help me . . . "

"Don't be afraid." Reverend Samuels's face loomed over me, round and red and dripping with sweat, his glasses shining like moons. "I've got you."

The next thing I knew, I was blinking up into bright lights. The organ music had grown louder. "Reverend Samuels?" I called weakly.

There was no answer. The organ played on. It was a familiar tune, but I couldn't concentrate enough to recognize it. A red-hot knife was slowly sawing its way through my guts. I turned onto my side and heaved. What came up was black and foul-smelling. The sight of it was so wrong that I couldn't keep myself from whimpering.

Where was Reverend Samuels? Why had he abandoned me? And Gran, too. Where was the comfort of her voice? They had all abandoned me.

At least I could move again. Gritting my teeth against the pain, I forced myself to sit up. I was in the sanctuary, upon the rostrum. The pews of the church were filled with people, all the citizens of Urbanna who had remained behind: women, children, old men. There were perhaps a hundred. I could almost believe they were sleeping, lulled by the sweet sounds of the recorded music. Crawling to the lectern, I pulled myself slowly to my feet. I saw Mom right away, in a pew toward the back. Amber and Cyndi sat slumped on either side, sheltered in her arms. I cried out, but their heads did not rise. No one stirred. No one woke. I thought of how I'd wanted to spare them the news I carried, thinking to shield them from death, when all the while, death had already claimed them. Now they were beyond me and my news.

A fit of coughing seized me, and I clung to the lectern as bile and blood spattered from my lips onto the pages of the hymnal that lay open there. I read my own death on the white pages. The cider had been poisoned. And I had not been the only one to drink. Why hadn't I realized sooner? Because I'd known about this; we all had. It was the worst of worst-case scenarios, a sin permissible in order to protect the weak and innocent from the depredations of the Jacks. With communications down, and fighting in the streets outside, Reverend Samuels and the rest must have given up hope, lost faith in the militia. Or fallen back on a higher, purer faith. Yet God was not pleased. He had sent me here to stop the sacrifice. I remembered Gran's warning: *Your mother and sisters will perish. And not just in the flesh. The communion of saints will be denied them. Their voices will be forever absent from the heavenly choir.*

Only, I'd come too late. I groaned, imagining the scene, how the reverend had stood where I was standing now, leading the congregation in hymns as bottles of cider were passed from hand to hand along the pews, mothers helping children to drink, then drinking themselves and passing it on, the voices slowly growing softer and fewer as time went on, until only one strong voice remained. And then that, too, falling silent. But not in death. No, Reverend Samuels wasn't dead.

At that moment, I felt such anger and hatred for him that my whole body shook with it. I had no illusions about my survival, but I prayed for the strength and time to make him pay for what he'd done. He was carrying one of the altar pieces, but the other remained, also an M-16. It was behind me, leaning against the big wooden cross that stood in front of a pristine white curtain at the back of the altar. I took a step toward it, but without the lectern's support, I fell. As I lay there, trembling with rage and frustration, the poison carving me up inside, I seemed to hear my father's voice. *The armed man fears nothing, is equal to everything.* At that, new strength flooded my limbs, and I crawled to the altar and took down the M-16. It was, of course, loaded. I clicked off the safety.

And not a second too soon. From behind the curtain, I heard the sound of Reverend Samuels's voice raised in song. It was faint at first, but growing louder, and I realized that he was climbing up from the basement, returning to the sanctuary.

> *Let us with undissembled love,*
> *Like children in one band,*
> *March to our Father's house above,*
> *And to the promised land.*

It was the hymn, "Ye Pilgrims, That Are Wand'ring Home." The words seemed twisted by circumstance into something sinister. Or maybe I had never understood them correctly until now.

> *My little flock, I bid adieu,*
> *Our parting is to-day;*
> *O may we all to Christ prove true,*
> *And try to watch and pray.*

I positioned myself behind the altar and waited. If I'd been here, as planned, would I too have drunk willingly of the poison, accepted it like a communion cup, sure of my place in heaven?

There is one thing that wounds my heart,
And grieves my soul full sore;
To think we must in body part,
Perhaps to meet no more.

The curtain rustled, then parted. But instead of Reverend Samuels, a Jack stepped through. Surprised, I hesitated, and in that moment of hesitation he strode past my hiding place without a glance, raised his gun, and began to fire short bursts, raking the pews. At that, I reacted at last, aiming my rifle and firing a single shot. It struck the Jack in the side; he spun and went down, the rifle flying from his hands.

I dragged myself over to the fallen soldier, who lay face up in a spreading pool of blood. It was Reverend Samuels. His face was gray, his lips bloody. His glasses were gone; his blue eyes had a brittle shine, as if they were turning to glass themselves. They blinked, then seemed to focus on me, widening with something like wonder.

"Why?" I croaked. Meaning, why everything? The poison, the uniform, the fighting, the dogs. This last, senseless desecration. All of it.

But his eyes had hardened, their transformation done. There would be no more answers from Reverend Samuels. Unless he himself was the answer, the final answer to every question.

A furtive sound drew my attention, and I glanced over my shoulder in time to see a handful of cambots scuttle across the ceiling and behind the curtain like daddy longlegs. They had recorded everything. Perhaps transmissions were down, or being blocked, in our area, but the cambots were capable of traveling for miles. One of them at least, and the truth it carried, would get through. In days or weeks, footage would appear on neTV, and the world would see me shoot Reverend Samuels.

Except no one would know it was Reverend Samuels. They would see a militiaman shoot a Jack. A Jack who had just massacred a church full of innocent people. The atrocity would further discredit the government and bring fresh sympathy to the Christian Patriot cause. Reverend Samuels hadn't panicked, after all. He'd wanted this. Arranged it. Convinced Mom and the others that there was no other choice but poison. Then, when its work was done, he'd started his. I pictured him moving along the pews, carefully arranging the bodies, preparing them for the cambots, for his grand entrance in the role of the evil, murderous Jack. Only, I'd interrupted the performance. Like some returning prodigal, I'd been welcomed back into the fold, even given a place of honor upon the rostrum. A brave young militiaman, cut down attempting to protect the innocent. A martyr. But I'd played a different role. Avenger. That was what people would see. And I knew it would be a powerful message, more so than the original, even if it wasn't true, or not the truth that it would be taken for. But there was nothing I could do about that now. I slumped back against the lectern. I could no longer feel my legs, and instead of a hot knife twisting in my guts, a heavy ball of ice seemed to have settled there. It was too late for me. Too late for everything.

Gran? Why don't you answer?

But she had forsaken me. If I hadn't dreamed her up in the first place.

I don't know how long I sat there, drifting in and out of consciousness, before the sound of a dull, muffled boom roused me. The floor trembled. The lights gave an ominous flicker and then went out. I felt as though I had never known darkness until that moment. It was like being buried alive. Assuming I was still alive. I couldn't feel my body, and it began to seem to me that I was floating free in that oceanic dark, a lone thought in a fading mind. It was a solitude so stark, stripped of every consolation, every hope, that I found myself longing not for light but a deeper darkness, a final extinguishment of the spark that was me. I wondered if the noise I had heard was the resumption of bombing, and I prayed for one to strike the church, reached out with all the desperation of my yearning to pull oblivion down from the sky. How different this was from the vision I'd experienced on the basement stairs of a vast communion of souls, a heavenly militia! I could no more join in that communion now than I could make myself rise and walk, or return the dead to life.

I heard no more explosions. But after a time impossible to measure, colors began to bloom in the dark: pale, pulsing blues and oranges and pinks, as though the sun were rising inside the church. I watched in awe, enraptured by a beauty so simple yet inexplicable that it could only be a miracle. I rejoiced then in my heart and chided my lack of faith, sure that the intensifying colors presaged an angelic visitation, that Gran was about to speak to me again, or to appear before me wrapped in the glorious raiment of heaven. She was so close now that I could almost see her shape, rosy as the dawn. A veil as thin as gossamer was all that separated us. And then it parted, pierced by a wing whose feathers were bright as flames.

But no angel stepped through. Instead, in the garish light, I saw that the curtain behind the altar was on fire. So that was what Reverend Samuels had been up to in the basement! That was the sound I'd heard: an incendiary. He had planned well; there would be no evidence to disprove the testimony of the cambots. I laughed at the joke that had been played on me, that I'd played on myself. Then laughter gave way to another fit of coughing.

The curtain burned quickly, falling away in sections that draped across the beam of the wooden cross, setting it ablaze in turn. I watched as the fire spread, numb in mind and body. I wondered if the poison would complete its task before the flames reached me, or, if not, whether it would insulate me from the pain. I tried to build my courage by telling myself that any suffering would be brief, and that soon I would be following Mom and Dad and the twins. They were waiting for me, and Gran with them, Grandpa too, and all the rest, all the martyrs and saints, the Christian Patriots, the virtuous dead. Waiting to welcome me into the godly communion that was the reward of a steadfast faith.

Yet had my faith really been steadfast and true? Even as the flames curled up the walls to lick at the high ceiling and the sanctuary began to fill with smoke, so that I coughed out as much of the tainted air as I breathed in, I knew the shameful answer. I had given in to doubt and despair. I had been quick to dismiss my vision as no more than a foolish dream, ignoring the warnings Gran had given me. In any case, I'd told myself, I was too late; the poison had done its work by the time I'd arrived, and there was no one left to save. But it seemed to me now that Gran had been referring to souls, not bodies. She'd said that I was saved already, but not so Mom and the twins and all the others gathered here. Perhaps the manner of their deaths was blocking their souls from entering the heavenly kingdom: as suicides, they were not welcome. That seemed unfair; if anyone should be barred, it was Reverend Samuels, surely. But that judgment was God's to make, not mine. If Gran was right, and I had the power to redeem their souls, how could I give up without at least trying to exercise it? Why else, though I'd drunk the poisoned cider the same as everyone else, had I alone been spared a quick death? I was still alive for a reason. There was something I had to do.

But what? I prayed for an answer.

And then I remembered something else Gran had told me. *A time will come when you will throw open the door to Death and invite him in gladly. But that time is not yet.*

And now? Had it come now?

I knew at once that it had. This was another test of faith, just like earlier in the basement. And that test, I understood with a sudden clarity that seemed more than merely rational, had been a rehearsal for this one. In a sense, they were the same. I had opened the door to death, but death had not touched me. The dog pack had parted to let me through, and I had walked among them unmolested, like Moses across the floor of the Red Sea. Now the dogs were waiting outside the church. Waiting for me to open the door and admit them.

And then? Would they enter despite the flames and fall upon the bodies here, as they had those outside? Whatever happened, I didn't think I would escape as I had before. But there was no escape for me anyway. I could either lie here and let poison and fire dispute for the honor of finishing me off, or I could attempt what had been asked of me, even though I didn't understand its purpose, how letting a pack of devils into the church could be the salvation of anyone. But wasn't that the whole point of faith, that it went beyond human understanding? God doesn't ask the easy things.

The flames had engulfed the cross and the altar. The smoke was thickening, and it was growing more difficult to breathe, though I'd managed to pitch myself over onto my side, closer to the floor, where the air was fresher. Walking was beyond me, my legs numb and useless, but though I couldn't feel my arms either, I found that I could use them to drag myself forward. At the edge of the rostrum, I pulled myself over the lip and fell the short distance to the floor. I lay there a moment, then began elbow-crawling up the center aisle. It was slow going, with the hiss and crackle of the fire loud in my ears and growing louder. When I glanced to the left or right, I saw the feet of kids in sneakers and sandals dangling above the floor, and the feet of grown-ups resting upon it, and in the shifting light of the flames their legs seemed to jiggle and dance in place like the legs of frantic marionettes. I saw the wet shine of vomit and urine and blood, and it was plain, too, as it hadn't been from the rostrum, that some of the congregation had lost control of their bowels. After a while I stopped looking and kept my eyes glued to the floor in front of me, measuring the winking inches of my progress. I didn't even look up when I passed the pew where Mom and the twins were sitting. I was afraid that if I did, I wouldn't be able to go on.

Reverend Samuels, in his hurry, had left the sanctuary doors open when he'd carried me in. The vestibule beyond was sunk in shadows only fitfully disturbed as yet by the flames behind me. Though my arms felt heavy as lead weights, I didn't dare rest. I knew that my time was running out.

I had no memory of crossing the darkened space. All at once, it seemed, I had reached the front door. The golden knob glittered above me. I reached for it, but I might as well have been reaching for the moon. My hand fell back, defeated, and as it did, a wordless howl broke loose from somewhere deep in my chest: a raw, primal cry of fear and pain and failure, of loneliness and anger, anguish and loss. It was a howl of accusation, of imprecation, of prayer.

Answer came from the other side of the door.

Not one voice, or a dozen, but what seemed a hundred voices, a thousand, howling out in response. Strangely, it wasn't terror that flashed through me then like lightning, but hope. A bright and wild energy came crackling through my veins—from where, I didn't know—and all the hairs on my body stood up at once, lifted by some invisible force that pulled my arm up too. A will greater than my own surged through me, not to be denied. Nor did I attempt to deny it. I watched as though in a dream, a spectator within my own body, as my fingers, with a dexterity and strength they had lacked seconds earlier, closed around the knob and turned it. At that, as if the action had opened a sluice in me, I felt the motivating force depart my body in a rush, returning to its source. I fell back, emptied, and the door swung inward.

The dogs poured through. One small, snarling tributary split off to engulf me. I tried to raise my arms to fend them off, but weak as I was, I could do nothing. Teeth tore into me, and I cried out. But soon enough I was beyond all pain, all terror.

I did not dwindle; I did not die. I felt myself disperse into the dogs that consumed me, into all the dogs, and I was not alone there, for everyone they had tasted was present in that host, Gran and Dad, Mom and the twins, even Reverend Samuels, Jacks and militiamen too, all reconciled now, part of a vast and lively communion. I added my voice to the choir, joining the unending hymn. Then we spilled out of the burning church and into the night, hungry to spread the good news.

RED SHIFT

MR. MARLEY'S WAGON SEEMS PERPETUALLY FADED EVEN THOUGH Tiny touches it up once a year, sometimes twice. Upon each side is a sign that reads "Marley's Astounding Traveling Acrobatic Wonder Circus and Animal Menagerie" in exuberant blue, green, red, and gold brush-strokes. Mr. Marley's paternal grandfather founded the Wonder Circus sometime around 1912. One day Mr. Marley's father took over, and in the fullness of time passed it on to his son, the present Mr. Marley. There is a Marley IV now, my own age, but I doubt there will be a circus for him to inherit; like Marley IV himself, the Wonder Circus is the last of a once-proud breed.

The rest of the wagon is crammed with scenes tracing the history of the Wonder Circus like a third-rate Sistine Chapel. The scenes crowd together like nostalgic ghosts mourning the living with tears of turpentine; oh yes, the Wonder Circus is dying, a decrepit elephant staggering toward some august graveyard. (Just try and explain this to Marley IV, however, with his funny ringmaster dreams!)

May I direct your attention to this plank, jigsawed with age like a dried-up riverbed, which preserves the slithering, slippery charms of Slytha the Snake Goddess, who shed her last skin (so Tiny informs me) in 1952? And there, in the top corner, one stumbles thirstily from the parched ex-river, through desert, and into an oasis where billowing tents pitched in the fore-ground of distant pyramids suggest an advertisement for Camel cigarettes; veiled beauties gather water in clay jugs which they balance adroitly on cranium while camels of the mammalian variety doze beneath lush palms. (Our last camel died when I was two.)

41

In fact, these days the Animal Menagerie proclaimed so boldly with a golden flourish is reduced to a scrawny crew of cantankerous apes (lower left-hand corner, beside the elephant, now deceased), Precious and Lad's Lady, two aging show horses who double as beasts of burden (appearing for a limited time only, thanks to a busted engine, hitched to the front of Mr. Marley's wagon), and Vladimir Karamazov, the dancing, juggling, and wrestling bear (seen ambling head-over-shoulder from the oasis like a beast cast from Eden).

From this auspicious exterior, dusted with a few dimming stars among shrunken dwarfs and nova afterglows, I can envision the interior with a sorcerous acumen which would make even Madame Sosostris, famous clairvoyant, somewhat envious. (Well, not totally sorcerous; I was born there, after all, and I don't suppose things have changed that much in fifteen years.)

I see a cluttered space, half office, half home. I see an untidy desk with stacks of bills and a safe without the funds to pay them. I see, in another pile on the desk, letters from anxious creditors and notices of canceled bookings. All of this I remember from the frenzied hours immediately following my birth and Mother's death (frenzied, that is, for everyone save myself and, presumably, Mother; I passed the time in observation and meditation).

But I see something else on the desktop as well, a smaller stack of correspondence pushed to one side, its existence perhaps forgotten, certainly postponed. These letters represent the long arm of the law, of fabled reach and as many fingers as there are misguided Samaritans in the world. Surely (they ask) a more supportive environment could be provided for that unfortunate girl than a flea-bitten itinerant circus; a better parent than an alcoholic ex-strongman; friends of her own age and, frankly, species. A minor headache amidst brain tumors to Mr. Marley, but not to me. I like the Wonder Circus and don't want anyone to take me away from Tiny. Here in our wagon, a boozy Tiny playing watchdog, I shiver at the thought and move on.

To the man seated behind the desk, also nursing a bottle. His ringmaster's suit of red and gold is a faded sunset, his hair prematurely gray, his forehead, well, I could count the furrows but I'm not supposed to be that smart. In bed behind him, Marley IV cavorts in dreamland, cracking that leather whip at pretty showgirls' behinds, center ring, spotlight please, on the new, improved Wonder Circus.

Well, Not bad. Of course, if I'd been in the Wonder Walk, my hand on the Star Stone and around me the tarot of Medusa's petrified head, Jack and Jill the two-headed fetus, the genuine Holy Grail, and the horn of the last Unicorn, the reading would have been much, much more exciting: escape velocity from present to future achieved every time.

Which puts me in mind of Tiny's trips in the opposite direction. Births and deaths are as ephemeral as the shadows of clouds to Tiny, so even though his heavy drinking started after I was born, I don't think I caused it as people say.

At the age of fifty-five, his fantastic strength undiminished, Tiny's mind, never a pristine chapel, began to lose itself behind a lifetime of scrawled graffiti. Madame Sosostris used to tell me stories of how, by the end, Tiny would cower in the center of the ring and whimper like a trapped animal as the crowd hooted and Mr. Marley screamed directions to simple strongman tricks he'd forgotten from the night before. Soon Mr. Marley retired Tiny, although he gave him a job as a handyman so he could stay with the Wonder Circus.

Tiny began to drink: not to punish himself, not to remember, not to forget. He drank and he drinks to catalogue in dreams that endless list of days that never were and might have been.

Then he is happy, but the necessity of dreaming is a weakness Tiny carries like an old injury from the one weight he could not lift.

At each performance, Tiny was a backstage fixture. Propped in the wings and reeking of cheap booze, he would preside over the decay of the Wonder Circus in a drunken fugue, his eyes wide open but tuned to another channel.

One night Tiny was in his usual position as two of the clowns gamboled into the big top leading Vladimir Karamazov through the sawdust by two long leashes. (Vladimir Karamazov is something of a fixture himself. A twenty-year veteran of the Wonder Circus with untold years of European service behind him, for a bear he's ancient.)

He trundled along as though on wobbly wheels, some kid's neglected toy, bent into a patchy black-furred ball that rarely uncurled anymore. I sometimes imagine him as he must have been in his prime: erect, six feet tall and four feet wide, all muscle, ladies and gentlemen, that black fur bristling as if electricity rather than blood was rushing underneath it. At such moments he must have transcended his identity and become something beautiful and terrible, a savage god, although really it was just another trick to impress the crowd, even simpler than the juggling and mincing dance steps, to tell the truth.

Curled in upon himself in those threadbare years of his life, Vladimir Karamazov must have, like Tiny, reinvented past performances, again bringing the crowd to its feet by batting a record-breaking eight oranges from paw to paw while balancing on one leg or gyrating madly in an authentic kazatska.

Each night he was dragged into the spotlight by clowns, and he would allow them to break for a while the spell of bearish memories he was hibernating in as though through a hard winter and bat pathetically at two oranges, reduced now to mere comic relief but still a crowd pleaser, still a money-maker, valuable until death and, who knows, perhaps beyond, stuffed and mounted like some fearsome museum relic along the Wonder Walk.

But that night Vladimir Karamazov curled so tightly into his past that he must have turned himself inside out, because no sooner did he reach the center of the ring than he reared back and with two mighty tugs wrenched the hapless clowns off their feet and tumbled them headfirst into the sawdust. His huge head snaking from side to side, his breath rasping in deep growls, his eyes orange marbles, Vladimir Karamazov lurched toward the closest seats like Boris Karloff on the late show.

The audience screeched their good-humored terror, although some parents, I'm sure, felt the Wonder Circus had gone a bit too far with this particular act. But who wanted to be remembered for years as the first to bolt for the exits?

At that first cry from a hundred throats, Tiny, in the midst of lubricating his own throat with some Old Forester's, seemed to slide deeper into his dreams. Setting the bottle on the ground without spilling a drop, he glided forward like a sleepwalker, utterly quiet, his face serene.

Vladimir Karamazov pricked his ragged ears at the soundless footsteps and turned. Like two wrestlers they circled, each gauging the other, respectful and cautious, as Mr. Marley tore at his hair and yelled for the clowns to call the police, the fire department, the National Guard, before Vladimir Karamazov mauled Tiny and the Wonder Circus out of existence.

And then, as if at some prearranged signal, they rushed together, colliding with a thud that shook the big top. Back and forth through the sawdust they raged, first Tiny, then Vladimir Karamazov in control. Like a boxer, Tiny hammered away at Vladimir Karamazov's belly and snout. Recalling old acrobatic skills, Vladimir Karamazov whipped his clawless paws through deadly pirouettes and danced his kazatska with swift kicks to Tiny's shins.

Finally they wrapped their huge arms about each other and fell to the sawdust, where they flapped around like fish out of water. In five minutes it was over. Nonchalantly, Tiny stood up and offered his hand to Vladimir Karamazov. The two wrestlers sauntered from the ring on two and four legs, respectively, to where Tiny had left the bottle of Old Forester's. Breathing heavily, he grabbed the bottle, upended it and guzzled half, then held it steady as Vladimir Karamazov tossed off the rest. Then, two old troupers, they exited to the wings. The applause was deafening and lasted for fifteen minutes. Mr. Marley clapped loudest of all.

So Tiny got his job back, but the funny thing is that in order to wrestle he has to be drunk, so he drinks just as much as ever. And, like a friend under the bad influence of an old war buddy, Vladimir Karamazov joins him on his binges. They sigh and belch together, exhaling dreams like smoke through a spotlight.

I've forgotten the name of the town we pulled into this afternoon. Buildings change, and people, but something beneath all that seems to remain as constant from town to town as the peeling, silver-coated Civil War markers spiked along the back roads or the well-meaning welfare representatives who pester Mr. Marley to give me up to the affections of the State. It's enough to start creepy thoughts, like we're some Dutchman circus doomed to wander in circles and play always to the same town, a town that sprouts new buildings and bodies at each intersection . . . .

Herndon, that's it. Of course, the good people of Herndon don't see themselves as I see them; in their eyes they are far superior to, say, the people of Oakton, upstate. I understand that I do them a disservice, but they get revenge: I don't believe they ever notice how the Wonder Circus dwindles each year, how the shows get shorter and old acts vanish, never to be replaced. Or if they notice anything, it is the rise in ticket prices from one year to the next.

This afternoon a tribe of footballers from the local high school arrived bearing girls and six-packs to help us set up.

Not that it's a big job anymore, with just four wagons left from the glory days when Marley's Astounding Traveling Acrobatic Wonder Circus and Animal Menagerie boasted fully eleven wagons, and plenty of horses to pull them too. But it's still more than Tiny can handle, especially with the enthusiastic assistance of Mr. Marley, Marley IV, Madame Sosostris, and the rest of the group. I'd like to help Tiny, but even such meager activity as planting stakes for the tents is well beyond my supposed capacity for purposeful thought and action.

I was resting in the shade of the famed Animal Menagerie as the two carloads of local heroes made their timely, dusty entrance. After parking on the fringes of this field we have appropriated, they clustered, joking among themselves, fully aware of the nascent Wander Circus but in no hurry to acknowledge it.

Then one of them, big-boned and sandy-haired, a fullback glory boy, sashayed up to Tiny and offered him a beer in that eternal gesture of respect and equality between the strong. Tiny—dear Tiny, named not for his size or his heart but his intellect, a fitting dad for yours truly—wanted to accept but was unsure of Mr. Marley's reaction. So he grinned instead and pawed the sweat from his brow as Mr. Marley himself walked up.

As usual, quite inadvertently, Tiny managed to stumble into the center of attention; at the edge of the field, the kids nudged each other with tanned elbows and chuckled as Tiny's grinning face swung from side to side like a well-used saloon door.

Hearing their laughter, Tiny turned, but the laughter roosting on his own lips died there as he noticed, for the first time, the retinue of nymphets. Tiny's grin melted in a nuclear blush; he swung clumsily at a tent peg with his sledgehammer, provoking additional mirth.

I wondered if Tiny was punishing his body for failing to follow the lazy currents of emotion that, in his mind, pass for thought. Or was his outburst meant to express frustration at the kids' taunts? The tent peg that he drove into the hard dirt was only the most convenient member of that frighteningly large class of objects and things which he must view as "not-Tiny," like the kids themselves.

But Tiny cannot stay upset for long, whether at himself or others; in moments the offensive scrawl on his memory's slate is lost, scribbled over, impossible to locate again. Soon he was grinning as though nothing had happened, back to square one.

And by then, with a solemn yet hearty shake of hands, agreement had been formalized between Mr. Marley and the fullback. Out came the free passes Mr. Marley carries for just such occasions. Around went the beers (even to Tiny, who nodded appreciation yet still seemed wary of drinking). From one of the cars, an old, old black Buick streaked with red flourishes about the fenders, a tape-deck began to spit rock and roll of the holy, hollow variety so popular in the South and Midwest. Down came the sun; up, like dreary and dutiful ladies, rose the tents, up into the cool evening, canvas cracked smartly by the wind.

As the men worked, the girls grew bored, and soon began to cast curious eyes around the rest of the grounds. From the Animal Menagerie, I fielded a few glances; in the dusk I must have seemed like one of them, only more so, a teenage trapeze-artiste or horse trainer, gypsy girl (on Mother's side) of the sawdust. But as they hesitantly stepped forward, Marley IV swooped to intercept, graciously offering the full tour, which they were pleased to accept. Throughout, Marley IV radiated superior disdain, as though possessed, by the rigors of the circus life, of some great Secret which, for an unspoken price, he could be persuaded to share, although inside I knew he was terrified by their nearness. As they approached I heard:

"It must be great to live in a circus."

"It's okay. Hey, you wanna see the monkeys?"

"Monkeys!" Long pause. "You mean like little, cute monkeys, or gorillas?"

"Oh, you'll see," bwana Marley IV replied.

By which time he had brought the girls close enough to see plainly that

I was not one of them, could never be. As they walked past, the girls fell into an awkward silence, as though out of respect for the dead.

Marley IV, meanwhile, chattered on. "That's just Judith; don't mind her. Come on in here, up these steps."

Inside the wagon, Vladimir Karamazov barked gruffly; the girls squealed with delighted fear.

"We keep these tranquilizer rifles in case he escapes," drawled Marley IV, thinking, I knew, of other game.

Twilight is kind to me. Cloaked by shadows I can move with greater freedom than in the daytime, yet I'm not totally shrouded in darkness. When people see me in twilight, a blur among other blurs, they rush to supply what's missing, and I become, for a time, one of them. Conversely, I sometimes enjoy pretending that each hazy shape I see delineates a being like myself in every way.

So, as they labored, the footballers looked more and more in my direction the darker it got, their imaginations working best when supplied with least. One in particular, the fullback who had offered the beer to Tiny and bargained with Mr. Marley, would prop himself against his sledgehammer, sip at his warm beer, and stare thoughtfully toward where my inky outline seemed to dissipate into the night sky, seep into the ground, and melt into the Animal Menagerie all at once.

I returned his stare, seeing a patch of dark just more solid than the night, imagining all sorts of asinine romances. I thought of what a blessing blindness might be, for one. Or a world of utter, polar darkness, where fire had never blossomed, sparing us forever its petals and its thorns.

Finally, the work completed, or as nearly completed as the day would see it, the fullback started over. As he approached, I played the Eternity Game: first he was halfway to me, then closer by half, then half of that again, and so on, so that I could label my reactions as he neared and rank them however I chose, by order of occurrence, by strength of feeling, by length of same, et cetera. For example: fear first and foremost, delicious and precognitive; guilty excitement because I dreaded that he would stop, turn around before reaching me; anger that I could say nothing to him, and humor at the whole ridiculous misunderstanding about to take place—which, I also realized, I was doing nothing to avert even though it certainly lay within my power to spare the both of us an embarrassing confrontation. But I wanted to hear his voice, to know that he saw me truly, as I am, despite the night.

But he stopped well away from me, respectful of whatever barrier I may have imposed around my solitude. He could see more of me, I knew; yet, seated on the ground as I was, my knees drawn up to my chin and a hooded jacket bunched around my shoulders, I remained ill-defined.

"Hey. Howzit goin'?" he asked, hands in jeans pockets, elbows splayed at a jaunty angle.

I, of course, could not reply; but I moved a bit, stretched my legs, to let him know I had heard.

"You live here?" Taking my motion for invitation, he walked a few steps closer and squatted on his haunches. "Say, I'll bet you've been all over the place, huh? What's your name?"

He nodded his head after a time, as though my silence had confirmed some guess of his. "You know, that kid took everyone else for a look-around. How about you doing me?"

I had been watching Tiny and Mr. Marley creep up on the fullback for a while, but he'd been too absorbed in questions to hear their approach. Now a flashlight beamed into my face and a huge paw of a hand clapped itself onto the fullback's shoulder. He yelled mightily, whether at the sight of my face or the sudden pressure of Tiny's hand I don't know—both must certainly have been unexpected—and fell back onto the grass. He was up in a flash, battle-honed reflexes on twenty-four-hour alert, but Tiny kept that shoulder in a vise.

"This is Judith," Mr. Marley said. "Tiny's daughter. We're very solicitous of Judith because of her condition."

"Yessir," rasped the Fullback. His eyes were bulging, his skin pale, as if he'd been caught masturbating by the Coach before the Big Game.

"She has hydrocephalus. Do you know what that is?"

Good old Mr. Marley, ever the ringmaster.

"Nosir."

"Well, it's a condition characterized by an abnormal increase in the amount of fluid in the cranium, causing enlargement of the head, wasting away of the brain, and loss of mental powers."

Whew! You've got to admire a man with a tongue that oily; for Mr. Marley it was either salesman, sportscaster, or ringmaster.

"Yessir." The fullback swallowed, taking it better than I'd expected. "I'm real sorry."

Mr. Marley nodded. "We all are, son." Tiny dropped his hand and just stood there. He looked pretty sorry all right. "It was dark; you couldn't really see. No harm done."

Together, they strolled back to the others.

"But that's terrible," I heard the fullback complain as they walked out of sight. "She looks so healthy too. I mean except for her head; the rest of her body."

I like to imagine that people ascribe my silence to shyness at first, that they see me in a romantic light, like the heroine of some terribly out-of-fashion novel. Then, when they discover I'm mute, their admiration balloons with sympathy. Only then do they notice my swollen head, bloated and sagging with sudden depressions like a month's-old pumpkin, not a Jack but a Judith-o-Lantern, symbol of some private Halloween.

At this point I generally imagine how, practically gagging on charitable impulses, they adopt me and finance the operation to correct my hydrocephalus; or, alternatively, the brilliant young surgeon, out to the Wonder Circus on some boyish whim he barely understands, vows to love and care for this proud but tragic figure of a girl.

Of course, the first thing they really notice is my head, and I'm rarely spoken to after that, so most folks never learn the muteness addendum. People point or pointedly do not point; children giggle, mistaking me for a clown, and are shushed by red-faced mothers who seem angry with me for some reason; rowdy teenagers engage in good clean malice or wander off confused and thirsty into the sunset like my fullback, never to return.

I try not to be bitter, and mostly succeed, because I remind myself that, although dumb, I am no idiot. I can read and write circles around most fifteen-year-olds if Marley IV is any indication: self-taught too. People see me and make faulty assumptions that I know better than to correct.

Having grown up in a circus, I've learned enough about freaks to recognize myself, enough about hydrocephalus to know that my brain should be too soggy to spark, floating in my head like Jack and Jill in their formalde-

hyde universe. I also figure that the circus is the best place for a freak like
me to hide. Here, as long as I behave the way people expect, I am rewarded
by their pity or disgust or indifference; out there I would be an object for
study, psychological (at least) dissection, and I'd hate that! I like people, and
even though I sometimes frighten them and make them uncomfortable, I
don't think they dislike me; I think that when they see me, they see themselves or their children gone bad. We circle each other warily, blind animals
afraid of touch, and we touch. Then maybe we lose a little of our fear,
because at least there's something genuine formed when we collide: a brief
bond between strangers reassuring us both that we exist.

Which is why the welfare agents frighten me with their good intentions.
State care means visits to the doctor, operations, all sorts of risks I do not
care to take with my fragile and precious consciousness, which, after all, I
figure I possess only by a fluke anyway. Frighten people too much, and
science overpowers the best intentions. Instead of pity, they learn to kill.

When I think like this, which is often, I wind up at the Wonder Walk.
Let my fullback comfort himself with friends and drink. I have my own
methods.

It is always gloomy inside the Wonder Walk. Partitions jut sharply from
walls and other partitions to form angular passages that direct and misdirect
patrons as in an Egyptian tomb where the false passages and dead ends are
meant to ensure that only the wise and worthy reach the center. Stepping
inside is like entering an optical illusion, a singularity. The farther in you
go, the bigger it seems to get, until, by the time the center is gained, it
seems inconceivable that you have not left the wagon through some mazy,
other-dimensional corridor. (Of course, I know the secret. At the entrance
are arrows, provided by Mr. Marley, to point the way. I go in the opposite
direction and come to the center after turning three corners; I've never
believed it necessary to purchase illumination with the scrip of suffering.)

The Wonder Walk was deserted. I ran to the center, then paused and
shut my eyes tight, feeling out for the Star Stone with my hand, letting it
fill my thoughts with sight.

At this point in the real show, spotlights flare on each exhibit in turn,
accompanied by the thunder of Mr. Marley's pre-recorded pitch.

The first thing the patrons see is a large glass jar. It flashes, tossing back the blue-red lights, but if the audience members peer closely, they can make out one form . . . no, two . . . or is it only one? It is Jack and Jill, the two-headed fetus, shrunken, wrinkled, and as peaceful as a drowned, mutant Buddha.

"Tragedy of Science or triumph of black magic? Dead or sleeping? And, if asleep, what dreams etch such shrewd smiles on their wizened faces? Perhaps, ladies and gentlemen, it is best not to question but to accept; perhaps we have spied for too long already, and our own faces, one by one, are slipping, as though onto a movie screen, into the endless, ageless dream they share . . . ."

Suddenly Jack and Jill vanish, and before the audience can *ooh* so much as a single *ahh,* a violet spotlight sparks onto a glass dome. Within the dome, a fluted horn, spiraling more gracefully than a gazelle's, of a color so white as to appear fluorescent in the violet light.

"Ladies and gentlemen. How often has science scoffed at the myths of the ancients only to discover their essential truth? Surely, deep within the collective unconscious we all share, each of us recognizes this horn of the purest ivory, this symbol of purity and truth from an age more pure and true than our own."

Again darkness, before the more skeptical audience members can step forward to discover if the horn is ceramic. Then a single, cold blade of white light; struck with the light, a rainbow blazes from jewels crafted into the sides of a golden goblet rimmed with silver.

"It was the glory and the ruin of the greatest knights of the Round Table: Lancelot and Galahad; the triumph of Sir Perceval. In a sense, the sad epitaph of King Arthur and the Age of Chivalry. The last goblet to touch the lips of our Savior, ladies and gentlemen."

The light dims; the image of the Grail lingers as though the jewels are flickering embers. Then a green light leaps.

"The most terrible visage in all history, ladies and gentlemen. In the golden age of the poet Homer, it was said that anyone who met her gaze was transformed to solid stone. For centuries she tyrannized the world, until the hero Perseus turned her power back upon itself with a mirrored shield. It is said that if ever another mirror holds her image, the stone will soften, the asps nesting in her brain will writhe anew, and Medusa will live again. Is there an adventurous young lady with a compact, perhaps, who wishes to test this prophecy?"

But the light is gone before anyone can react. Now all the colors of the spotlights are thrown onto a coal black stone the size of my fist, where they dance from the tips of embedded crystals. "All the objects you have seen here tonight, ladies and gentlemen, have come from the past. Now we give you the future. A stone tumbled from a star, a Star Stone, bathed in countless radiations unknown to science over the billion years or more it took to reach our planet. Did it arrive by accident, or was the Star Stone sent to us by beings as far above us as we are above the amoeba? Perhaps, even as we speak, it is waiting, waiting for the signal that will instruct it to release all its energy and transform us into gods . . . or destroy us."

Melodramatic, but it sells papers.

As usual, when the power surged into me I was also drawn into the Stone, as though a vacuum had been created between us, an invitation offered to let go of my body and escape into the Stone itself, to become a new crystal blazing upon its surface with unimaginable energies. I won't deny I've been tempted at times to test the depths of the Stone's abyss, especially at first.

At first I was inside Mother, the predecessor of Madame Sosostris, a (self-proclaimed) full-blooded gypsy who called herself Orlando. There, in the fluids of Mother's womb, I floated and understood many things. I knew of the hydrocephalus that even then was wasting my brain; without fully comprehending the idea of speech, I understood that power was to be forever denied me. There was no part of my body or Mother's that I did not know, down to the thin uterine wall which would burst as she birthed me, me nearly drowning as she hemorrhaged to death in Mr. Marley's wagon, the Wonder Circus fifty miles from the nearest town. These were not happy truths.

But they came to me magically. Perhaps all children of gypsies are natural fortunetellers, or perhaps it was the Stone, although I had not yet come to associate the gentle tug I felt behind my consciousness with the Star Stone: indeed, hadn't conceived of its existence at all. It was only later, "outside," that I realized others were different from me, and later still before I realized just how different . . . .

Behind my still-sealed eyelids, I saw:

A golden chalice, rimmed with silver, filled with wine. And in the wine I saw:

A fetus with two heads, one male, one female, floating, dreaming. And in those dreams I saw:

A white mare with a single ivory horn, shivering in labor. And from that mare was birthed:

A woman with a woman's full body and a misshapen head that crawled with snakes.

The snakes struck the mare. The mare turned to stone. From her ivory horn, blood dripped to the earth, filling it like a chalice.

It seems straightforward now, but then it was my first deal of the tarot packed into the Wonder Walk. Even so, I read the meaning right: Mother's death, my sickness, all as I've mentioned already.

Since that first vision the images haven't changed, but the readings always do. Jack and Jill, Medusa, the Grail, the Unicorn's horn: out of their constancy new patterns are constantly shuffled, and so, the more I used the Stone, the clearer it became that my first vision contained all others, even those as yet undreamed.

Still, I was not prepared for what I saw tonight. I ran out into the crisp night air, which seemed to shimmer with stars and the chatter of insects. I stood there, looking up at those stars, and tried to force the vision from my mind (I still can't bring myself to write it down). For the first time in my life I felt small and insignificant, as though I had lost control of my destiny or just pierced the illusion of ever having had control. Thank God Tiny is here now, asleep beside his empty bottle, or I'd be too shaken to write at all.

As the shock ebbed, I knew I had to be with someone. It was late, but Madame Sosostris would be up.

As I approached her wagon, I heard the music of Pink Floyd and smelled marijuana. Madame Sosostris was nowhere in sight though, so I sat on her wagon steps to wait.

After a moment, her head poked from the doorway above me. "Judith, you gave me a fright! Thought you were a hick cop or something. Be right down."

In her early fifties, Madame Sosostris is one of the youngest Wonder

Circus regulars. She's a mystery, having shown up looking for work in the fortune-telling line just a week after Mother's death. Aside from Tiny, she's my only friend, the only one who accepts me without censure or embarrassment.

Chuckling to herself, Madame Sosostris picked her way carefully down the stairs. "A beautiful night. I thought the clouds would stick around, but you never know, you just never know, do you? Ah, give me a moment," she said, bustling away from the wagon, "and I'll be all set up. Then you'll see something." I followed to a spot some yards away.

There was a lounge chair. Beside it, on a tripod, her telescope was mounted. A small table stood within easy reach; on it lay a notebook, an ashtray containing two joints, and the cassette recorder playing Pink Floyd.

Madame Sosostris settled into the lounge chair, then leaned forward to adjust the telescope, fussing with an assortment of eyepieces. "I don't need cards or stars to divine where you've come from; just like your mother, people tell me. I never much cared for the Walk, though. Maybe it's too much competition in the bizarre." She laughed and looked up from the telescope, beckoning me closer.

"I can only give you a quick peek tonight, Judith, because I have some very important observations to make in about a half hour. Do you know, I think I've discovered another comet!"

I enjoy stargazing with Madame Sosostris. A respected amateur astronomer (she really has discovered a comet: Westland's Comet; I looked it up), Madame Sosostris seems to take no notice of my condition and explains things to me as though she really believes I can understand.

I stood on tiptoes to squint into the eyepiece as Madame Sosostris lit up a joint. Another reason I enjoy stargazing is that it reminds me of the Star Stone. I feel that same pull when I put my eye to the lens that I feel when I touch the Stone. It's as though I'm tugged out of myself, tumbled down a narrow tube of mirrors, and bounced into the midst of the stars. In fact, the first time I looked into a telescope I was scared to death; because it was so similar to the Stone, I was certain I'd be trapped out there forever. Now that I know I can come back, it relaxes me and makes it easier to resist the Stone's pull.

But after tonight's vision, instead of reinforcing my sense of will, it made me feel more helpless than ever. As I looked, Madame Sosostris began to lecture, a habit she falls into when high.

"See that group of stars? Don't look much like dogs, do they? But that's what people call them: the Hunting Dogs. If you look real hard, maybe you can see a blur of light, like someone squashed a firefly on the eyepiece. See it? That's another galaxy, like the Milky Way where we live. It's called M-51. I wonder why some galaxies have names like Milky Way and Andromeda and others are stuck with labels like M-51. Doesn't seem fair, does it? Of course, if there're people living out there, I don't suppose they call their own galaxy M-51." She chuckled, then came the whistle of breath as she drew on the joint.

"You know, Judith, they do kind of look like dogs, though, don't they? I mean, there's one with its mouth open, like it's barking at something. What do you suppose they're hunting? Ah well, we'll never know. All those stars are moving away from us at different relative speeds. In a thousand years, the Hunting Dogs will be gone; some new constellation'll take their place. Kind of sad in a way. M-51 is moving away too. Fourteen million and some odd light-years away already and hightailing it off at about three hundred twenty miles per second. Everything's getting more and more distant, and all we can chase them with are telescopes." She sighed. "That's why I like comets, I guess. They're friendly. They travel around like hoboes, but sooner or later they come back. You can depend on comets. Of course, they end up by smacking into the sun!"

I drew back from the telescope at this terrible knowledge so casually imparted by Madame Sosostris. Everything was breaking up, flying apart. One day only isolated stars would exist in all of space, nothing between them but their own faint flickerings; ultimately, even their own light outstripped, the reasons for their flight forgotten, they will race on and on, drunk on the fumes of an old combustion.

I almost returned to the Stone then and surrendered to its pull, but I decided to say goodbye to Tiny first. And when I saw him in the wagon, sleeping his exhausted sleep, the bottle of Virginia Gentleman half full beside him and Vladimir Karamazov's smell in the air, I changed my mind. Because, after all, what does it matter if stars abandon each other so long as people stay true?

But trite sentiments are no substitute for sleeping pills. I was awake all night wrestling with the vision despite Tiny's reassuring snores, and by the time he opened his bloodshot eyes this morning, stumbled to his feet and lurched out of the wagon to find breakfast with a slurred admonition to "Get some sleep," I had decided that I'd seen what amounted to a hitherto unmatchable portent even though its meaning was still unclear.

As the morning passed, I lay in bed trying to decide if I wanted to search out that meaning. One thing you learn in a lifetime of fortune-telling is that fate has a way of playing itself out like a game of solitaire whether you're aware of the process or not, and that generally it's better, all things considered, to at least have an idea of what to expect so that you don't blunder through life laying red nines on red tens or vice versa. On the other hand, I remember very well what happened to Mother the first time I had this vision, and if there is anything remotely similar looming in my future, I don't want to know about it. Some cards are best left unread.

Finally I decided to try and forget the entire episode. I got up, shrugged on a dress (backward, for appearance's sake), and wandered out into the early afternoon to watch the last of the Wonder Circus get slapped together.

Wouldn't you know, the first person I saw was the state welfare rep. It was just blind luck that I managed to spot her first and could duck into an empty tent before she saw me (even so, I sensed her head swivel suddenly; these types have built-in radar for the afflicted). I peeked out after a moment to watch her stalk off on spindly crane's legs, her sharp-nosed face jerking to follow each sound or movement.

If I hadn't been so preoccupied with the vision, I would have remembered that today would bring the customary visit from the local agent and remained in bed feigning sleep for another few hours. Too late for that, I could at least take refuge in the Wonder Walk, closed to the public until six p.m. But after a half-dozen steps, I stopped and considered that I really didn't want to go back just yet, did I? Not if the same vision were to repeat itself, which seemed likely. In the past, obscure visions had worked themselves out by hammering resolutely away at me until suddenly light dawned. Well, I didn't want light to dawn, so no Wonder Walk. Equally strong, however, was my desire to avoid the woman who even now was probably bringing the full brunt of her considerable moral artillery to bear against Mr. Marley in an effort to win his cooperation in persuading Tiny to give me up. Since I couldn't use the Stone to eavesdrop, I decided to spy on them the old-fashioned way, that course of action having the advantage of eliminating all chances of being captured by the woman, since she'd always be in range of my sight or hearing.

Or so I thought. Ear pressed to the side of Mr. Marley's wagon, I hadn't heard more than a muffled word or two when someone's hand clamped onto my arm.

I jumped, would have yelled if possible, and struggled briefly before deciding to bluff my way through on the strength of my supposed handicap. I turned, expecting to find I don't know who, certainly not Marley IV.

He relaxed his grip slightly; in his other hand he idly twitched a riding crop that he had taken to carrying in emulation of Mr. Marley's ringmasterly style. "Dad's looking for you," he announced with a grin. "Some lady wants to meet you." He commenced dragging me to the front of the wagon.

Then I really fought: scratched, bit, twisted, kicked, and spit.

You'd think I'd've maybe inherited some of that fabled Tiny strength? Not so. But I annoyed him enough so that he stopped to twist my wrist behind my back and lever my arm up to my shoulder blades.

"She's gonna lock you in a hospital forever," he hissed through hair into my ear. The crop stung the backs of my knees, and Marley IV shoved me ahead of him, jerking me roughly up when I staggered. Then we stopped again, suddenly, and through his hand encircling my wrist I felt Marley IV shudder.

"Just what do you think you're doing to her, young man?"

I recognized the voice; it was Madame Sosostris!

Marley IV dropped my hand. I backed against the wagon.

"She just tripped," he said, "you know Judith, and I helped her up. Anyway, my father wants to see her."

Madame Sosostris lowered her head as though preparing to charge, and Marley IV stepped back, bumping against me. "Don't you lie to me, John Marley," she said. "Your father might own this circus, but I can break you over my knee any time I feel like it!"

"My dad'll fire you!" Marley IV whispered; then, bravado notwithstanding, fled.

I rubbed at my sore wrist. Madame Sosostris put a gentle arm around my shoulders. "There, Judith, don't be afraid. He won't hurt you anymore. Come back to my wagon, and you can watch me tell fortunes and read horoscopes."

I had to smile at that; my skills in the fortune-telling line are far superior to her own, but I didn't want to hurt her feelings, so I came.

Inside, Madame Sosostris's wagon is like a maze. Thick, faded tapestries hang from the ceiling, dividing and subdividing the space into a kitchen, bedroom, and parlor. Whenever Madame Sosostris brings me to listen to her spin fortunes, she hides me behind one of the curtains so that I can see and hear everything while at the same time being invisible to the customer. I don't understand why she treats me almost as though she suspects my interest in her fortune-telling attempts (which I view with the bemused indulgence of a master toward a gifted novice), but I am grateful.

Behind the curtains I am spirited off to a gypsy wagon; much of Madame Sosostris's paraphernalia was used originally by Mother. The tapestries leak years of smoky incense and have absorbed as well, I like to imagine, whispers of fanciful and tragic divinations long come to pass. Sometimes Madame Sosostris's voice, muffled through layers of trembling cloth, sounds like how I remember and/or imagine Mother's, and it's as though she's speaking to me from behind a veil as deep and black as the insides of the Star Stone.

Madame Sosostris puttered about her parlor as I watched from a chair, arranging her tarot deck and astronomical charts and sliding her handy *Skeleton Plots of One Hundred Great Novels* into the open-faced back of her reading table. Rummaging through her cassettes, after much indecision she inserted something by Brian Eno into the tape deck. As the music crept from speakers hidden behind the tapestries, Madame Sosostris opened another cassette, removed a joint, and lit up—to "open the channels of communication," as she put it. Then, after lighting two sticks of cinnamon incense, she shooed me behind a tapestry, opened the door to the wagon, turned her shingle around, and sat back in her rocker to wait for business.

Moments later, the welfare rep herself walked in. She stood still, hands on her narrow hips and elbows pressed against her sides as her eyes flicked across the space. I placed another tapestry between us.

Madame Sosostris reached out one finger to solemnly tap the top card of the tarot deck. "Yes, I'm the fortune teller, if you're wondering. Have a seat."

The welfare rep's neck turned; her body remained motionless. "I'm here for the girl, Judith Lessing. Young Marley told me he saw her come in here."

"Well, she did, but that was some time ago. What do you want to see her for?"

"I don't see how that could be any of your concern." She began to circle the room stiffly, slowly.

"This is my wagon," Madame Sosostris said.

The welfare rep grasped the edge of a tapestry in her small fist and tugged it back an inch. "Then you can tell me if there is room back here for a small girl to hide."

Madame Sosostris stood. "So you're from the welfare department. I should think you'd have better things to do than harass Judith and her father."

"I was given this case, and I don't intend to fail like so many others have." The welfare rep released the curtain and moved to the other side of the room, keeping the table between Madame Sosostris and herself. "I've already talked to Mr. Marley; I gather it's useless to speak to the father. I understand the girl's a hopeless case as well, but I'd like to see her anyway to get a better idea of what to put in my report."

"Why don't you mention somewhere in your report how happy Judith is here at the circus? Or how it would break her father's heart if you took her away?"

The welfare rep paused. "That's an extremely selfish attitude. Just because you've grown attached to the child is no reason to deprive her of the care and comfort that could add precious years to her life. I know you think I'm cold and uncaring, but I only want what's best for the child."

"Sometimes it's wrong to preserve life," Madame Sosostris said.

"I hope no one makes that decision for you one day." The woman went to the door of the wagon. "Well, I've been searching through this circus for hours, and I think I can smell a conspiracy. No matter; I've enough for the report. When I show it to a judge, I'm sure he'll order an examination to determine whether Tiny is a competent parent. I think we both know what the results of that examination will be. Of course, you'll be able to visit Judith. Then I'm sure you'll agree that it was all for the best, even though it might seem a bit painful now."

"Get out of my tent," Madame Sosostris said. "It's your attitude that's selfish, but you're too narrow-minded to admit the possibility. Yes, I think you will succeed, if that makes you happy. Perhaps you'll even earn a promotion. Congratulations."

"I'm sorry you feel that way," said the welfare rep. She ducked her head and slipped out the door.

Madame Sosostris sat back in her rocker and quietly began to cry.

I crept out the back way and spent the rest of the afternoon wandering, oblivious to the stares and exclamations that everywhere accompany my presence and used to give me such welcome feelings of purpose and stability.

As the circus frantically geared up for the first show, and more and more townies pressed into the field to play the assorted games of chance before the main show began (at one point I thought I recognized my fullback at the shooting gallery, looked again but saw only faces as alike as apples in a basket), I began to build a decision from the day's disarray.

I wandered to the back of a tent where Marley IV was forking hay for Precious and Lad's Lady. "It's your fault I'm stuck with this shitty job," he declared. "That old witch ratted on me!" Then he came at me, brandishing his pitchfork, laughing as I stumbled away.

To the clowns' wagon, where, amid snickers and noxious cigar smoke, I was treated to a show of noxious postcards purchased from the proprietor of the local barbershop then ushered out by one of the more sober clowns.

To Mr. Marley's wagon, where a group of stout Girl Scout matrons were shrilly protesting the inclusion of Hermaphrodita in the magic show and Jack and Jill in the Wonder Walk.

To Madame Sosostris's wagon again, through the back to avoid the line out front, where, proceeding sequentially, Madame Sosostris had reached number forty-seven in *Skeleton Plots of One Hundred Great Novels: Lady*

Chatterley's Lover. A plain young woman with mousy hair wadded into a bun and glasses as thick as the bottoms of soft-drink bottles listened in rapture as distorted music from the Grateful Dead slid between fumes of strawberry incense.

To the Animal Menagerie, where, upon seeing me enter, the apes began to chatter and scold like old country gossips.

Then not to the Wonder Walk but instead to the cage in the back of the big top where Tiny and Vladimir Karamazov were huddled together in heaps of dirty straw, toasting each other with Stolichnaya Vodka and pissing all over themselves.

It was an hour to show time. Suspense was in the air; the best seats were filling up. No one noticed as I slipped into the cage and rousted Tiny. Vladimir Karamazov whined as I led out Tiny, who paused and with infinite generosity left his ursine friend the remainder of the bottle.

Back in our wagon, I had to get Tiny cleaned and sober enough for the act. Tiny compounded matters by passing out as soon as we got inside. I undressed him, bathed him (no easy task, shuttling buckets of water from the showers back to the wagon under the noses of people who, in less hectic circumstances, would have smelled a rat), and had him ready (somewhat less than more) after three hours. For his part, refreshed from his nap yet still swimming in the sweaty vat of his strongman fantasies, Tiny was anxious to wrestle.

I lagged behind as he tramped circuitously to the big top, where Mr. Marley was waiting, incensed; despite my efforts, the act was twenty minutes late and the crowd getting ugly.

Tiny swept his boss aside with a negligent shrug, spying his pal Vlad, fumbling with a few oranges in the ring, apparently unable to decide whether to juggle or eat them. The crowd roared, Vladimir Karamazov dropped the oranges and roared, Tiny roared, and they rushed together, happily reunited, and waltzed through the sawdust like old lovers as the crowd screamed for blood.

At that moment I knew I had to go back to the Wonder Walk and link with the Stone again. The show had another hour or two to run, depending on how much of a match Tiny and Vladimir Karamazov delivered, but for the time being the Wonder Walk would be deserted.

Once again I threaded the maze to the center and the Star Stone. Trembling, but resolved to act, I reached out to touch the Stone and was gone, no more myself but not swallowed up by the Stone either, a new creation tumbling in blackness that gradually became suffused with deep purples and oranges as I opened (or closed, depending on your point of view) my eyes.

There it was again, the vision I had seen first in Mother's womb, presaging her death and my crippled life, then for the second time a night ago, this time meaning what? As I watched the transformations repeat, Grail to Jack and Jill to Unicorn to Medusa and back again to Grail, I was struck by the remorseless cyclical nature of it all, offering no escape, as though people might choose destinies only from a list of roles—a pack of cards—forever fixed and incontestable.

But I had a way out. From the first, I had felt the Stone's invitation like the pull of a gently receding wave. Now, as my fear grew, the Stone sucked persuasively at my will, urging me to abandon my body for the solace to be found as another bright crystal studding its coal black form, existing only as others perceived me, no longer even observer but something more tentative still: the observed. In that moment, as in the zodiac wheeling endlessly through my head I replaced my mother with myself, I saw also that the vision of my calamitous birth could be read as escape as well as entrance. And I leaped; I did not hesitate for a second; I did not want to bring my own destroyer to life as Mother had.

But something held me back. Even as I strained to sever the threads binding me to my body I was pulled back and my hand torn from the Stone. In my mind, a door closed.

Someone was pummeling my body into the hard floor, groaning breath fetid with alcohol and vomit into my face as flesh tore between my thighs, and I cried out in my mind for the Stone, but my fingers could not reach it so balled into fists and hammered against the back above me. Then there was a spurt, a spasm, and it was suddenly clear what was happening to me as the body rolled off and lay face up and it was my fullback, breathing heavily, hands twitching at his sides.

At first I just lay there, unwilling to move, trying not to feel the blood seep from me. Then my fullback heaved; vomit frothed at his lips, and he began to cough. I got up and turned him over so at least he wouldn't choke to death, but immediately afterward I went to the case holding the last Unicorn's horn to smash it open, take the horn, and stab him to death.

I picked up the Stone to smash the glass and went spinning off into the vision again, no longer observing but actually a part of it now, and I realized that it was too late for escape, that it had always been too late. When the vision cleared, I left the wagon without looking back. How could I kill my fullback for playing his part? We all play our parts.

Madame Sosostris was righter than she knew, explaining to me about fleeing stars. We are no different. We flee one another because we must, colliding occasionally, in brief and brutal conflagrations then careening off in new directions toward new spectacles of destruction. Afterward, nothing remains to evidence our passage but the debris of our clashes strung into a single long ellipsis.

The rape only hours past, I write epilogues to things that have not yet transpired. I see the cancerous death of Mr. Marley, and Marley IV expiring in a fashion not unlike my fullback, strapped behind the wheel of a shimmying universe. I see my own death as predicted, not quick on the heels of my child's birth as it was with Mother, but years later from the hydrocephalus. I see your death as well, Madame Sosostris (for this is all written to you), but I won't reveal it, don't worry; all fortune-tellers should turn that final card themselves.

The law moves more slowly than the Wonder Circus, and by the time the court order for Tiny's examination reaches us, my son will be one month old, healthy and as familiar with the Stone as I am now. I will not stay to watch Tiny render the court order useless by stumbling during a wrestling match with V. Karamazov and breaking his own neck—which everyone takes for murder, carrying out swift sentence against Vladimir Karamazov on the morrow—so I cry for my father and his friend tonight.

I see myself delivering these pages secretly to you just before leaving the Wonder Circus to escape the vultures Tiny's death will bring, taking only my son and the Stone. They will look, but they will never find us.

I no longer have the consolation of ignorance to make life bearable, but some consolation seems necessary. As I leave the circus, and later too, when it is visible only as a memory dimmed and scratched by the hard years to come, I think I will pause long enough to look back, just as Vladimir Karamazov is pictured ambling from the oasis on the side of Mr. Marley's wagon.

AFTER IVY

THE BULLDOZERS KEPT STONE AWAKE. HE WAS USED TO THE white noise of the surf, and without it he felt stranded, left high and dry where sleep could not reach. He listened as the baseboard heaters came on through the house. The clicks and pings reminded him of faucets dripping.

She slept through it all. Her long, big-boned body was turned away from him, curled upon itself. The light of moon and stars through the sun- and salt-glazed window painted her a stranger. Stone felt with a pang how far she was gone from him, asleep. How alone he was with the bulldozers and dripping water.

Storms had raged without waking her while he, afraid for his boat, which had shared her name, paced the creaking house and gulped bourbon until his head swam. Stone knew better than to wake her now just for the sake of company. She needed her sleep; each morning he watched her struggle up from its depths when the alarm sounded at six, coming to the surface as if carrying the sun on her shoulders, already exhausted by the effort.

After she had left for school, where she taught the sixth grade, Stone would rise and begin again the tired routine of reading the help-wanted ads in *The Wave*. He did this with meticulous attention over eggs and coffee, circling likely prospects with a red felt-tip pen bought especially for the task before going out to watch the bulldozers carve up the beach. Afternoons he drove into Ocean City to drink with Lamar, who, like him, had lost boat and business when Ivy struck in the ebbing of September. Insurance barely covered their drinks.

He could use a drink right now, he thought; something to help him sleep. As he rolled out of bed, she turned with a sigh and settled into the hollow of his leaving. Her fine dark hair had strayed across her cheek and nose. She lay under the blanket with one arm bent beneath her, the other stretched along her flank where shadows pooled. She was not beautiful, but the gulf between them made her seem exotic and desirable, a mermaid of sleep. How young she looked, this woman who was his wife. Her skin like pale ash.

In the shadowed kitchen Stone poured a shot of bourbon and gulped it down with a shudder of refined distaste. For all the pleasure it gave him, the smell turned his stomach like some noxious medicine he'd been given as a boy. He poured a larger glass and without turning on the lights began to pace the house in bare feet and bathrobe.

It was a small house, bright by day and always breezy, built long ago by his parents as a summer place but more than that to Stone from the first, much more: the only real home he knew, the only one they could not poison. If they had failed, it had not been for lack of trying, but because he had stayed through those summers with an assortment of aunts and uncles and their families while his parents, both of whom worked, came and went on alternate weekends, he rarely saw the two of them together from June until September.

After school he'd begun to come up in the fall, when the cold weather kept his parents away. He would take the boat out of sight of land, where the wind came sharp and steady and the sky was like blue ice above the churning dark waters of the Atlantic. Finally he would drop anchor to fish, not caring what he caught. That was freedom all the way to the horizon and even wider inside. Sometimes Lamar came and brought a bottle. Once he brought his sister: a teacher at the elementary school in Selbyville where Stone had gone in childhood summers to shoot baskets with his cousins.

She had only known his parents in their final years, husband and wife mired in hate and sinking fast like beasts in tar, snapping at whoever came close. Stone's father, a retired judge, rarely spoke except to wound; even his silences could wound, his eyes commenting with caustic irony on whatever passed before them in the courtroom of the world. His mother, while capable of equal venom if provoked, preferred a defense of self-pity and gin. They had killed each other right in front of him, as if in need of a witness, day by day over the long unhappy years of their marriage. When they died, months apart—his father of a massive stroke, his mother, he knew, a suicide, though her death had been ruled accidental, an absurd drunken fall from a ladder—the house and boat had come to him, there being no other children. They had not approved of her, of the marriage; of course, they had not approved of him either, for he had given up the law by then.

Upstairs Stone could feel the house tremble beneath his feet as the bulldozers rumbled up and down the beach. The vibrations came through the sand like electricity through a wire. On nights when the surf was up the dull, jarring *whump* of a wave would shiver the glass chimes on the porch and rattle the windows in their frames. And this two houses back from the beach. It really was amazing, like the footsteps of a giant.

Stone walked onto the deck and looked across the roofs of the neighboring houses—empty now until spring or later. A pale and hazy light hovered above the dunes. The rumble of the bulldozers was louder, interspersed with metallic clankings and the grind of shifting gears. A briny mist blew inland. The bourbon warmed him but would soon be gone. As a boy he had climbed the sheer slope of the roof to view from its peak the wide ocean across which shards of sun and tiny white sailboats skipped on their outward courses. If he could have flapped his arms and followed he would have done so.

Now Stone wondered again if he had been foolish to think that he could claim this house for his own and bring his bride to share it as though it had no history but what they would make together, out of themselves: sons and daughters. It seemed to him more and more that his parents had left some residue of their spiteful energies behind the walls to radiate slowly and invisibly outward with the pinging of the baseboard heaters like a second, barren, inheritance.

After three years of trying there were no children, and the doctors could not say why. Relax, was their considered and expensive advice. Stone could not talk to her about it, in fact could not talk to her about much of anything these days—and that, too, seemed a symptom of something dire, especially when, as now, he'd had a bit to drink and saw or seemed to see beneath the clouded surface of things.

Still, his alcoholic intuition could not predict the future, and this worried Stone because after Ivy there was not much left he could stand to lose. All month over drinks at the Green Turtle, Lamar had been trying to talk him into taking out a mortgage on the house in order to finance a new boat for the two of them. Stone could see the sense of it, but to Lamar's increasing disgust was unable to make up his mind. Nor had he discussed it with her, knowing that she would whole-heartedly endorse the idea of a partnership, sick as she was of his spiritless drifting. He was sick of it himself.

Back in the kitchen with sleep farther off than sunrise and the startling chill of a November night in his bones, Stone refilled his glass. A flick of the light switch revealed everything in place, the dinner dishes drying beside the sink, the refrigerator humming softly to itself, the clock above the stove keeping its unhurried time through the dead hours of the night. The sound of dripping water. The hush was heavy as stone but invisible, the air stuffy with sameness. Upon the beach, men were engaged despite the dark and cold in purposeful work against an encroaching sea.

In the bedroom Stone dressed, almost falling as he hurried into a pair of jeans. Too much to drink as usual, he thought, but so what the night was young and she still sleeping also as usual also so what. He wrestled a pungent wool sweater that had been his father's over his head then stood glass in hand and brought his breathing into harmony with hers which helped a little.

Just then she shifted onto her back with a languid motion as if lifted on a swell. One bare arm rose out of shadow dropping lightly to the pillow pale wrist up fingers curled over thumb in a loose and childlike fist from which she turned away, seeming to gaze right at him though he knew she was not awake. For all her restlessness she was a heavy sleeper. Occasionally tossed by some dream she would strike or kick him awake never waking herself; other times Stone slowly woke to find her moving against him with a blind and innocent desire he could not bring himself to shatter. Though aroused he would hold back to study the familiar loved features made strange and inscrutable by sleep, expressing emotions he could only guess at though he knew they had little if anything to do with him. Often as if at some internal signal she would open her eyes without hurry or surprise and pull him to her then without finishing what she'd started sink back where he could not follow, receding from him like a wave.

How was it that sleep could wash away the years of worry and disappointment and leave her looking younger than when they'd met, as though she were no man's wife and hardly yet a woman? Perhaps the virginity of girlhood had been itself a state of sleep to which she and all women returned each night to replenish some portion of what men took from them. Of what he took, lacking it himself, lacking even a name for it. In sleep she was free. Stone felt rebuked by her presence, her absence rather. He wished to wake her roughly, noisily, but was at once overwhelmed with shame, as if he were no better than his father. Her features seemed to radiate forgiveness; she would forgive him anything, he sensed. Was that what he could not forgive?

Sitting at the end of the walkway, Stone squinted into the glare of the klieg lights. He could hear nothing but the whine of the generator and the growls, clanks, snorts and roars of the bulldozers that moved through the haze below. The earth shook continuously; beneath his bare feet the trembling step was gritty and cold. The ocean smelled fresh and near.

From where he sat he could not see the gaping mouth of the iron pipe sunk beneath sand and water, only the furious torrent rushing past as if sprung from a breach in the ground. Following channels cut by the bulldozers, brown waters streamed seaward, leaving behind sloping mounds of sand around which shrieking gulls flocked to fight over every scrap edible or not dredged from the ocean floor. Stone raised the half-empty bottle he'd brought along for company and toasted with the quiet and only slightly mocking sincerity of his more than slightly drunken mood the lone bulldozer moving into the light its great toothed blade raised and glistening treads shedding sand and water as if freshly crawled from the sea.

It was a worthy cause but all things considered Stone would have rather had his boat back. More than a month since that night the winds at sixty and climbing fast they'd fled to the school with Lamar and his family and all the others who had no place to go a regular convention kind of fun though with flashlights and candles summer's last hurrah groups singing down endless bottles of beer on the wall and playing cards to keep the kids from crying others cooking over camp stoves between cots and sleeping bags laid out in tribal clusters across the slick gymnasium floor though some had wept and prayed as if the last judgment were at hand. Lamar had passed a bottle round till they were drunk and laughing *come on* she whispered later hot tongue to his ear and led him stumbling dizzy with lust down long hallways lined with watchful lockers to her dark haunted classroom he'd never seen her so eager so wanting *it's the wind* she said *the wind* he felt it too the force and nearness of those claws as he laid her back upon the desk papers flying their laughter drowned by the storm. The next day blue skies and no breeze to speak of, the power off but the house undamaged perhaps protected by the jealous spirits of his parents.

Others hadn't been so fortunate. As he and Lamar drove down the flooded streets of Ocean City, Stone had marveled less at the general havoc than at its capricious nature—homes shorn down the middle as if by a giant blade, one side utterly destroyed the other save for a missing wall as well preserved as a museum exhibit; cars parked upside down as though flipped by high-school pranksters; trees uprooted while, in front of city hall, flowers bloomed in cheeky defiance of storm and season. It was intensely surreal, landscape courtesy of Dali, the two of them unable to hold back nervous laughter all the way to the marina where seeing the collapsed roof the boats tossed like bathtub toys they'd known right away they hadn't been so lucky after all.

Stone had another swallow as the bulldozer clanked to the edge of the channel teetered there an instant then plunged into the stream. Gulls scattered wheeling their wings bright as mirrors spooked by the sudden splash and a thunderous bang that caused even Stone, expecting it, to jump. He drank again full of admiration for the dozer's operator, who righted his inelegant machine with a series of sharp grinding adjustments, not smoothly but with real style.

The man was of indeterminate age, dressed against the cold in a buffalo plaid jacket, open-fingered dark gloves and a baseball cap worn backwards. He gave no sign of having seen Stone or, indeed, anything else. Rather, his heavy-lidded eyes and the imperturbable smoothness of his expression made him appear to be more asleep than awake despite the cigarette glowing between his lips. Even the precise movements of his hands upon the knobs of shift and throttle as he simultaneously dipped the blade, spun the dozer on one track and began to push a mound of sand towards the opposite bank seemed reflexive, automatic, as if the man had surrendered to the will of the machine and the machine to the dreams of the man, the two fusing into a single entity, a centaur of blood and steel.

Stone ducked beneath the walkway guardrail to half-stumble, half-slide down the steep dune face. At the bottom he staggered senses reeling along the edge of the channel drunker than he'd thought. Missing the bottle he searched the sand then saw he'd left it at the top of the stairs. There was a quickening in his blood and in the crisp intoxicating air, a roar as of wind or water, as if this circle of fogbound light were the eye of all hurricanes past present future. Not far ahead the pipe jutted from the sand like some ship-wreck relic come to light water gushing hard and furious from its wide mouth.

He jogged to the pipe and put one hand to its cold wet rusty side, felt the force of the flow, the power of it. As if it were a shell he placed his ear to the metal and heard not the roar he expected but a hiss smoother than drifting sand hardly a sound at all something like the slow leak of steam from a radiator or the sigh of a sleeping woman.

Stone hoisted himself onto the pipe and climbed to his feet balancing only with the greatest difficulty as if perched on a swaying tightrope although the diameter of the pipe was nearly four feet, wide enough for a child or even a small adult to crawl into let alone walk upon with ease. Arms stretched to either side he slowly turned and as he did so spied far up the beach the headlights of two bulldozers bobbing like the lights of ships at sea then still turning saw the wide flat stretch of darkness edged in white that was in fact the sea and upon which tiny lights red and starwhite danced where the dredge was docked at the anchored platform pumping out the flood of sand whose swift passage underfoot tickled even through the metal like the dry rasp of a cat's tongue.

The explosion of sand and water from the end of the pipe sent up a fine and constant spray in which to his delight a rainbow shimmered like a ragged gypsy flag. Stone approached inch by inch along the slippery pipe.

Close enough to touch now the rainbow flared before his eyes like gaso-line spreading its gorgeous patina across a puddle. If only liquor mixed so prettily. With a shiver came the memory of a moonless September night, summer long since fled from the air though it would cling for a while yet to the water. Beneath the clamorous stars the sea quiet as a lake. It had been like floating or sinking into the sky like dancing to the music of the tides the gentle swells no higher than his chest rocking them in the same timeless rhythm their bodies knew so well it was in their blood after all the beating of their hearts a part of everything. He felt himself fall but did not know if he was drunk or dreaming.

The shock of cold wet cleared his head but though cushioned by the sand Stone was swept along by the force of the stream as if himself dredged from the ocean floor and pumped through the pipe, a curious merman spewed out in the company of other, smaller, oddities. Choking, unable to get his breath or his bearings, he wondered if he were going to drown, buried beneath heavy drifts of sand soon smoothed by the dozers so that by morning no trace of him would remain the dead weight of his body curled as if in sleep sinking deeper and deeper below the ground to achieve by imperceptible degrees the anonymous immortality of fossilization. Though the channel was not deep, the current was fast and strong, much stronger than it had seemed from the walkway. Amid flashes of light and dark he saw a cloud of gulls descend in a flurry a roar of wings. He threw up his hands to protect his eyes.

Stone felt himself rise effortlessly, as if he'd shed his body, grown lighter than air. Or perhaps the gulls were lifting him in their talons. Lamar, the boat, the insurance, the house, all of it fell away. The grasping shades of his parents fell away. He was flying into the eye of a whirling inexhaustible love.

Blinded by sand and light, Stone reached out then fell onto the sand where on hands and knees he retched up a gritty mix of bourbon and seawater. He felt like weeping though he was not sad, just empty as if something had swept through him.

The bulldozer plowed up another wave of sand, the operator grinning now, his cigarette an orange glow like sunrise in my body, she thought, waking, the dream a cooling ember in her mind, already half-forgotten.

She knew at once where he'd gone. With one hand resting upon her belly she wondered was it a sign. She was not superstitious but was late this month though he hadn't noticed; the rhythms of her body were more surprising to him than any storm. Late September seemed the best bet she decided after hurried calculations, maybe even that night on the desk, books and papers flying as if Ivy had clawed through the cinderblock walls of the school. Anyway that's what she would tell him for it seemed more romantic that way.

In the kitchen she put the kettle on and settled down to wait for her husband. *Ivy.* It was, she thought, lulled half to sleep by the soft clicks and pings of the baseboard heaters, such a pretty name.

LIGHTHOUSE SUMMER

ONE NIGHT WHEN I WAS TEN, A YEAR AFTER THE SEA TOOK MY
father, leaving us nothing to bury but what he had left behind on that
treacherous morning of clear blue skies—empty shoes, loose change, limp
clothes haunting closets, and the memory of a smile that clove my heart like
a beacon—my mother woke me with the news that she had decided to
marry Walter Hooper.

Framed by the weak light that spilled past my doorway from the hall, she
perched on the edge of my bed as if afraid the mattress might prove as
porous as quicksand. She breathed softly, waiting for me to reply to her
announcement. But I was determined to say nothing, wanting to punish
her for what seemed as much a betrayal of me as of my father.

"Mark . . . ?"

I turned away, unable to forgive a weakness I could not fathom. I felt a
touch on my shoulder, a shy pressure to which I returned a stony indifference, until it was withdrawn.

The weight of her lifted from the mattress, but my mother did not go. "I
want you to know I don't love him," she whispered. "No man can take your
father's place. But I have to do what's best for you, honey. I know your
daddy understands. Mr. Hooper is a fine man. Your daddy respected him.
He'll treat you right, as if you were his own. I promise."

I knew all about Mr. Hooper. He wasn't really an old man, but he
seemed like one to me then: his skin rough and wrinkled, his movements
slow and deliberate, even his words cautious. He smelled old. He'd been
after my mother ever since my father died, fishing for her with the same
dull persistence that he fished the waters off Cape Henlopen. He was a

gentle man, lonely, a widower with no children who, insisting I call him Walter, would sit me down from time to time and show me how to tie knots my Boy Scout manual had never heard of, his thick, blunt fingers, usually so clumsy, threading the rope with a thoughtless grace I envied desperately. At that moment I wished him dead.

I heard my mother sigh. Her lips brushed my cheek, hot and wet with tears that rolled down my face and neck as if I were the one who was crying. I wanted to brush them away, but didn't dare move until she had left the room, closing the door softly behind her. Then, to my utter surprise, a storm of tears burst from my eyes. I pressed my face into the pillow and wept as if there were an ocean inside me trying to get out.

Mr. Hooper just about lived at our house after that. He was there when I went to bed, was seated at the table when I got up for breakfast. He walked gingerly, padding in his white socks as if expecting the floor to buckle at every step. His dull gray eyes were clouded with an immense reserve. He never looked directly at me, seeming to think me too fragile to bear his glance without bruising.

I got the feeling that I was interrupting something whenever I came upon Mr. Hooper and my mother. The silence that arose then had a dangerous edge, punctuated by sudden attempts at speech that, as often as not, ended in a silence worse than that which had preceded it.

School was out for the summer, and as soon as I was excused from the breakfast table I would take off for the old lighthouse on Cape Henlopen, an hour's walk across the dunes and up the beach. My mother had forbidden me to play there, afraid that the listing wreck, abandoned for more than fifty years, would topple at the slightest breeze into the ever-advancing sea. But that dilapidated tower, romantic and mysterious as the ruins of a storybook castle, exercised an irresistible allure, as if its long-extinguished lamp were still ablaze in a nest of mirrors, beckoning to me with one long finger of light.

From the observatory, which I reached by means of a rickety spiral staircase, I would gaze past the shattered windows over the sparkling water—the keening of the wind loud in my ears, the tower swaying gently—until my eyes could no longer distinguish the thin line separating sea and sky. There I could be alone with my fantasies of pirates and spaceships or, unable to forget the reality awaiting me at home, plot elaborate schemes of escape and revenge, even more fantastic. It was there that I met, one day in late July about a week after my mother had accepted Mr. Hooper's proposal, the Captain.

There had been a furious storm the night before, huge thunderheads sailing in like immense gray battleships that opened fire with all their guns once the sun went down. For hours we had huddled in candlelight, the power gone, the house shaking like a frightened animal under the barrage of thunder and lightning as rain pelted the roof with such force it seemed the sky had been ripped asunder.

Coming over the dunes that morning, the storm's detritus all around me, I stopped short in astonishment at the thin trail of smoke rising from behind the lighthouse to smudge the blue sky. In an instant, the stark and comforting solitude of the place was ruined, my last consolation torn away. I was a little frightened, but I was also angry—curious, too—and so I approached from the sea side, intending to circle around and spy on whoever had usurped my refuge. Gulls challenged me with mocking squawks I hoped would not betray my presence, pacing me obliquely, their cruel yellow eyes watching me sideways with a hunger that made me think of dinosaurs. To my left, the surf rolled in, precise as clockwork, crashing with a dull wallop and hissing up the sand.

The lighthouse loomed white as bone against the sky, perched at the edge of a precipice and tilted at an angle that seemed impossible to sustain. The foundation showed through the sand, an irregular mass of cement and rusty iron rods upon which scattered clumps of bleached-out grass had somehow found purchase. Tides had scooped a yawning cavern that threatened to undermine the structure. That close, the bulk of the tower obscured the smoke, and for a moment it seemed again as ancient and innocent as my imagination had made it.

Then the wind shifted. I smelled bluefish frying.

I crept around the tower, sliding in the sand that rose steeply to landward. I wondered who could be cooking here. There was no sign of a boat or jeep, no sounds of a party. It was slow going, but finally I was close enough to hear the sizzle and pop of the fire. I stuck my head out for a peek.

Sitting on a cinderblock before a small fire kindled from the splintered remains of the keeper's house, a shack that had been crushed over the years by the shifting sands as if slowly squeezed in a giant's fist, was the strangest man I had ever seen. His back was to me, but even so I could tell he was an old man by the stoop of his bony shoulders, upon which a faded and tattered shirt hung loosely, flapping like a scarecrow's garment. His head was sunk in the hollow between his shoulder blades, as if the hat he wore, a navy blue cap of the type favored by weekend sailors, were made of iron. I could hear him muttering to himself in a low, gruff voice like a man clearing his throat as, with one finger, he gingerly poked the contents of a pan suspended above the fire on a grill propped between two cinderblocks. He looked for all the world like the sole survivor of a shipwreck, marooned in the shadow of the very lighthouse responsible for his fate. So great was my astonishment that I forgot to remain hidden and stepped out for a clearer look.

Without turning, as though he had been aware of my presence all along and, what's more, been expecting me, the old man called out in a clear and friendly voice: "Well, Mr. Sharp. So you've got here at last. Come and eat with me."

I looked around wildly for Mr. Sharp, expecting to see him emerge at any second from the lighthouse. But there was just the two of us. The old man turned to face me. I braced myself as he stood, ready to run.

Though his legs straightened, his back seemed to grow more bowed, so that he was scarcely taller than when he had been seated. I saw now that he was dressed in the remnants of a uniform trimmed with gold braid. His blue cap had a silver anchor blazoned above the ragged brim; gold laurels festooned the flukes. Long wisps of white hair emerged from under the cap.

"Mr. Sharp," he said after a moment, his voice gone hard and petulant. "Have you been drinking again? Don't you recognize your old captain? Come here at once!"

I took a step forward. "I'm not Mr. Sharp, sir," I called.

"What impudence!" The Captain stamped his foot, then shook his head sadly. With a shrug of his shoulders, he turned away and reseated himself upon the cinderblock. "Go hungry if you like, Mr. Sharp. I don't care."

The breeze blew another whiff of the bluefish my way. Cautiously, I walked over to the fire, dragging a cinderblock to a spot directly across from the Captain. With the fire between us, I felt safe enough.

The Captain looked up with a knowing smile and chuckled. "You never could resist bluefish, Mr. Sharp."

"Yes, sir," I agreed. His gaze seemed fixed on a spot behind and above me; white as sea foam, his eyes were occluded by cataracts like encrustations of salt. It was a wonder he could see at all. He struck me then as a sad but comical figure, a cross between Popeye and Mr. Magoo, a fitting keeper for the blinded lighthouse at his back.

The fish was delicious, fried with scallions of a sort I had never tasted. As we ate, the Captain continued to address me as Mr. Sharp. I assumed that he was an old man reliving his past, an escapee perhaps from a seamen's rest home or mental institution. I soon lost all fear of him, entering into his fantasy as if it were one of my own.

"More fish, Mr. Sharp?"

"Aye-aye, sir."

Mostly he talked of things I could not understand, of ships and storms, of far-off lands and the strange people who inhabited them.

"Remember the *Dorcas*, Mr. Sharp? Now there was a fine ship! The finest to ever sail the seven seas!"

"That she was, sir."

He never mentioned his name to me; he was, and always would be, simply the Captain. Listening to him speak, alert for any allusions to his recent history, I got the impression that he had been at the lighthouse for years, invisible until now. He had certainly made himself at home—when we finished eating, he took me inside. A hammock was strung in one corner, pots and pans hung from hooks in the walls, old books were stacked on a table in the center of the room, beside the spiral staircase leading up to the observatory. There were shelves lined with cans of soup and vegetables, a box stuffed with kindling and a sack filled with onions and potatoes. He had even hung rude curtains cut from burlap over the empty windows. I followed him up the stairs.

In the observatory, the Captain faced the open sea. The breeze feathered his white hair, and it was easy to imagine him on the bridge of the *Dorcas*, sailing bravely into unknown waters. He took a deep breath, then turned to me, seeming, as always, to be looking at someone creeping up behind my back. His sideways glance and hunched posture reminded me of the gulls that had paced me as I walked to the tower. He cocked his head at an even more unlikely angle, then pointed to his clouded eyes.

"Can't see worth a damn," he said matter-of-factly. "You can't sail with your nose, Mr. Sharp. Not even I can do that. So they retired me. Retired. And here I am, come to the very edge of land but still not afloat, no, even though this old lighthouse sways like a mast on gentle seas, even though the wind in my face makes me think I'm sailing. Well, there's no help for it. I'd hoped for something different once. Did you ever hear me speak the name of Willis?"

"No, sir," I answered.

He sighed, and seemed to grow older still. "Willis was a girl I knew long ago. Eyes the color of the sea. I don't mean blue, Mr. Sharp. No, not just blue but every color in the seven seas. The angry gray of sudden storms, the placid blue of calm waters ruffled by a fair breeze, the steaming, turgid yellow of tropical latitudes, the deep and murky green off the coast of Africa. We were to be married."

"Sir?"

"Are you married, Mr. Sharp? I can't recall."

"No, sir."

He nodded. "It's a luxury for young sailors but a comfort, I think, in our old age. Willis died before our wedding. Drowned at sea, like called to like. Though I didn't know it at the time, I was marrying her not for love but for her eyes, not for any present comfort but for my old age away from the sea, so that, in her eyes, something of the sea would be left to me." He sighed again. "Forgive me, Mr. Sharp. There's not much left for me now but memories and regrets. It was kind of you to come visit your old skipper. Will you be shipping out soon?"

"Not until September, sir," I said, thinking of school.

"Perhaps you will pay me another visit."

"I will, sir," I promised. With a tired salute, he turned back to the open window, his back bowed with the pressure of years and disappointments but his gaze steady for all that, sweeping the horizon as if in search of a distant, fabled shore.

In the days and weeks that followed, I visited the Captain as often as I could, bringing knickknacks from home I thought he might appreciate, old things of my father's I knew no one would miss: a rod and reel, an oil lamp, an oilskin slicker. I brought fresh water in soda bottles, used my allowance to buy him six-packs of Coca-Cola and fresh oranges. Although my mother suspected that I was disobeying her and playing at the lighthouse, she seemed unwilling to disturb the peace that reigned over our home, a peace as unstable as the lighthouse itself.

My mother and Mr. Hooper were to be married at the end of September, and even though they were planning a simple ceremony, performed by a Justice of the Peace, there was much that needed to be done. They had no patience with my sullen and resentful presence, and though they knew that they would have to deal with it before the wedding, they preferred to postpone the day of reckoning as long as possible. That suited me just fine.

Arriving at the lighthouse, I would call out: "Mr. Sharp reporting for duty, sir! Permission to come aboard."

The Captain would poke his head out the door or peer down from the observatory. "Granted, Mr. Sharp. What have you brought today?"

And I would present him with some candles, or some kitchen matches, or some milk. Best of all he liked citrus fruits, which he accepted with a wide smile: "Scurvy, you know. Can't be too careful."

We spent whole days wandering the beach like Robinson Crusoe and Friday. It was as if we truly were marooned on a deserted island, for though I constantly worried that someone would stumble across the Captain and take him away, return him to the home or institution from which he had escaped and in so doing rob me of my best and only friend, we never saw another soul, not even so much as a sail or plume of smoke on the horizon. If airplanes passed overhead, we did not notice them; our eyes were fixed on the sand, where we found the strangest things washed up: coconuts, shattered ceramic dishes that we painstakingly glued back together, bits of colored glass, smooth as opals, that were warm to the touch and glowed in the dark like fireflies.

Once we found a dead fish like nothing I had ever seen. It was the size of a small dog, its bloated body covered with dark quills, its mouth gaping widely to reveal row upon row of needle-sharp teeth. The Captain insisted that we bury it. "Poison," he said, and shivered as if at an unpleasant memory.

The Captain was the most marvelous fisherman I had ever seen. He made his own lures, which he never failed to spit on before casting. Thus primed, it took scarcely any time at all for a fish to strike. Suddenly the rod—my father's—would bend, the line taut and glistening in the sun as the Captain, laughing, his spine bent to an even greater degree than the rod he held, waded into the surf to claim his prize.

About the middle of September, the Captain began to prepare the lighthouse for winter even though we were in the midst of a heat wave that had stretched unbroken since the end of August—long, scorching, rainless days the likes of which no one could remember, nights dry and endless as deserts of black sand. Meanwhile thunderheads kept rolling in, turning the sky the color of the Captain's eyes. Behind that dense curtain, opaque as quartz, the best the sun could manage was a wan yellow light. After sunset, green flickerings ran through the sky like a fever. The petulant rumblings of thunder never ceased for an instant. People were irritable, glancing up nervously every few seconds even as they made jokes about the weather or placed bets on when the first drop of rain would fall. At home, my mother and Mr. Hooper seemed to feel the weather was a bad omen for their marriage. For the first time, they argued in front of me, and I began to have hopes that the wedding, now two weeks away, would be called off.

School had started weeks before, but I had yet to attend a single class. Carrying my books under one arm, I marched off to the bus every morning only to cut across the dunes once I was out of sight, running as though Mr. Hooper were after me. When I reached the lighthouse, breathless, the Captain would be hard at work installing shutters he had hammered together with nails I had brought from the hardware store or patching the roof above the observatory with shingles pulled from the wreckage of the keeper's house. Side by side we worked through the day, stopping only to eat a meal of fruit and whatever fish the Captain had caught that morning. Then, when it was time for school to let out, I would say goodbye and head back home.

Looking back, it seems amazing that I got away with this careless deception for as long as I did . . . though certainly no more amazing than the fact that, until the very end, no one discovered the Captain was living at the lighthouse. It was as if the lighthouse protected us, casting its blinding light into the eyes of anyone who chanced to look our way. But I suppose even then I knew it could not go on forever. And, sure enough, one Friday afternoon my mother was waiting for me in the kitchen with Mr. Hooper.

I let the screen door slam behind me, my usual greeting dying on my lips at the sight of their stern, disappointed faces. Though my heart quailed, I managed a weak, uncertain smile.

My mother and Mr. Hooper were seated at the kitchen table, a pitcher of iced tea between them. For a moment no one moved, the only sound a low growl of thunder that seemed to come from deep in the earth. Then, as if arriving at a sudden decision, my mother stood, the sound of her chair scraping across the floor as shrill as fingernails down a blackboard. I winced and took a half-step towards the door.

"How was school today?" My mother's voice was icy calm. Her hands smoothed the front of her dress.

How much did she know? I glanced at Mr. Hooper, hoping to find some clue there, but his wrinkled face wore a pained expression that told me nothing good. I shrugged. "Okay."

I had not thought my mother could move so fast. In an instant she had me by the arm. My books crashed to the floor. I squirmed to free myself, but she only squeezed tighter. "How dare you lie to me," she said.

I was on the verge of tears, more from the sound of her voice and the look in her eyes than the pain of her grip.

"Mr. Rowan called today. The principal. He said you haven't been to class once since school started. Not once! Do you have any idea how that makes me look? Do you?"

She shook me with each question. I did not know how to answer.

"No, you don't care about me. Only about yourself. You know this isn't an easy time, but do you try to help out? Do you make the slightest effort to be a help to me? You don't raise so much as your little finger! What's gotten into you, Mark? Answer me!"

I was afraid that if I opened my mouth I would start to cry. The best I could manage was, "I don't know."

"'I don't know.' And where have you been playing hooky every day? Do you know that? You damn well better! Down by the lighthouse?"

"No," I said.

"You're lying." And then my mother hit me for the first—and only—time in her life. It came out of nowhere, a slap that left the side of my face burning. I could hold back the tears no longer.

"Mary!" I heard Mr. Hooper's chair scrape back.

"Stay out of this, Walter," she warned. Then she addressed me, her hand raised as if about to deliver another slap. I saw that she was crying as much as I was. "For the last time, have you been playing hooky down by the lighthouse? I want the truth now."

All I could think of was protecting the Captain. "No," I sobbed.

The anger seemed to drain out of her all at once with my denial. Her hand dropped, and she turned me loose.

Suddenly Mr. Hooper was there, one arm around my mother's waist. "Your mother loves you, Mark," he said.

"She doesn't love you, Walter," I sneered. "She told me so."

He stiffened at that. Anger rekindled in my mother's face. "You ungrateful . . . Go to your room. Now!"

I ran past them, glad to escape. I slammed the door to my room and threw myself down on the bed, crying with shame and rage. I knew I had said something terrible, and though a part of me regretted it, another part gloated at the wound I had inflicted on them both. Faintly, from the kitchen, I heard Mr. Hooper and my mother shouting. I listened for a while, straining to make out the words, which grew more and more indistinguishable from the thunder, until I realized, with a start, that I had fallen asleep and woken in the middle of a storm.

There was a plate of cold rice and chicken on the night table beside my bed. A glass of tepid milk. Outside my window lightning flashed with manic intensity, illuminating a world of wind and water in which there was no up, down or sideways. The house shivered with each crash of thunder, and I thought fearfully of the Captain, riding out this tempest in the battered lighthouse. I pictured him in the observatory, his face hard into the wind, my father's oilskin slicker flapping about his crooked body like a tent come loose from its moorings. There he stood, immovable as a rock, gripping the window ledge as if sailing the lighthouse straight into the teeth of the storm.

When I woke the next morning, the sky outside my window was thick with clouds the color of ugly bruises. Thunder sounded muffled and peevish in the stuffy air. No breeze blew. It felt like a lull between battles. There was no calm, no peace, no sense of relief. Just a feeling of helplessness that swelled with each growl of thunder and flash of lightning until I could not bear to be alone another second.

Without bothering to change out of the clothes in which I had fallen asleep, I hurried into the kitchen, where, as usual, I expected to find my mother and Mr. Hooper. It was company I hungered for, not breakfast, and despite all that had happened I knew that the pressure of the impending storm would not seem so crushing and fearsome with them to share it.

But they were not in the kitchen. There was a note on the table from my mother. She and Mr. Hooper had gone out. They would be back by afternoon, when, as she put it, "we need to have a talk, the three of us." She told me to stay home, as the storm might break at any moment.

It was only then that I remembered the Captain. A terrible foreboding gripped my heart, and for an instant I pictured him lying broken and bloody among the stones of the tumbled tower, calling out in a weak voice for his faithful Mr. Sharp. Scarcely pausing to grab an apple and glance at the clock above the sink—it was almost ten—I rushed headlong out the door.

As I ran toward the lighthouse, the carnage of the storm lay everywhere around me. Trees had blown over. Parts of people's roofs had been carried away then deposited on the dunes as though the rest of the house were still attached, submerged beneath the sand. Here and there I encountered the mangled forms of gulls and, once, a huge black bird I did not recognize, whose leathery wings, even in their ruined state, stretched farther than I could stretch my arms. I stopped for a minute, marveling, then ran on.

Coming over the last dune, I saw the lighthouse standing upright as if by force of will alone. Its base all but destroyed, the tower slumped seaward with a curve reminiscent of the Captain's crooked posture. The slightest breeze, it seemed, would serve to send the whole structure crashing into the surf. It swayed perilously even as I watched. There wasn't a minute to lose. I ran up the beach, shouting for the Captain at the top of my lungs.

Then I saw the Captain himself hurrying down the beach to meet me. My father's oilskin slicker flapped around him like the wings of a huge, dark bird. Lost within its deep folds, he seemed hardly to touch the sand at all, as if a sudden wind had swept him up, blowing him along.

He came to a stop before me, one hand hugging the slicker to his body, the other holding his cap in place. Long strands of white hair whipped about his face, causing him to squint more than usual as he peered up at me with a sidelong glance that, as always, seemed directed somewhere behind and above me.

"She's come back to me, Mr. Sharp," he said excitedly. His clouded eyes shone with a diffuse yellow light, as if a flash of lightning had been trapped there, ricocheting back and forth with ever-waning intensity inside a cluster of crystals.

I took no notice of his words, speaking at almost the same time in a voice as excited as his own. "It's not safe here anymore, Captain. You've got to clear out, come home with me."

"She's sound as a rock," the Captain declared over a roar of thunder. "I'd as soon abandon a child."

"But the storm . . . "

"Bah! We've seen worse, eh Mr. Sharp? Remember that time rounding the Cape of Good Hope? Or in sixty-seven, the typhoon in the China Sea? Besides, I can't leave now. Didn't you hear? She's come back to me!"

For the first time, I registered what he was saying. "She?"

"Why, man, it's Willis I'm speaking of! Who else?"

It took a moment for me to place the name. Then my jaw dropped. "You mean . . . "

He nodded furiously, then seized my arm in a grip that put my mother's to shame, pulling me toward the lighthouse as he related what had happened.

"It was late last night. The height of the storm. I was in the observatory, looking out into that maelstrom for any sign of a ship in distress. I could see nothing, but I felt ships out there, whole crews bravely struggling for their lives as the world came to pieces around them, afraid and lonely but determined to live and, failing that, to die like men. What I wouldn't have given then for oil enough to light the old lamp! We know, you and I, how welcome is even the most feeble flicker of light from shore on a stormy night, when hope and despair alike have been washed overboard. It's a sight that steadies the shakiest heart like a slug of brandy and warms the coldest limbs like a roaring fire in a friendly hearth. But there was no oil, and the lamp itself was useless, the mirrors smashed and scattered. There was nothing I could do but watch with my useless eyes and . . . I won't say pray, but something very like a prayer was burning in my heart.

"The lighthouse was bending like a stalk of grass, but I had faith in her, Mr. Sharp. Sound as a rock she is! Besides, I wasn't about to give up my last command, abandon ship, not with so much depending on me. I felt that if I turned away for even a second, unseen ships would founder. And you know very well that nothing can make me leave the bridge in a storm.

"All at once, illuminated by a flash of lightning, I saw a body afloat in the surf. Pale white and gleaming like a fallen sliver of the moon, it was there for an instant then gone, swallowed up in the storm, the night. At first I thought it was just these old eyes playing another one of their damned tricks, lending substance to shadow, life to a drifting log. But then I saw it again, rolling in the trough between two waves, a body for sure but limp, lifeless, swept close to shore by some chance but already being pulled back out to sea.

"Without pausing to think of those ships depending on my vigilance, I ran from the observatory, nearly tumbling down the stairs in my haste. I burst out the door, into the thick of the storm. I knew at once that I hadn't a chance in hell of spotting the body again, much less retrieving it. The idea that it was still alive didn't even occur to me. Still, because it was a human being I had seen, for the sake of my conscience I didn't want to give up so easily. I made my way down to the edge of the beach. Long tendrils of sea foam snaked about my ankles, seeking to draw me in, until I didn't dare take another step.

"Just then, in a flicker of lightning, I saw her. Her shape rose from the frothy waters in one smooth motion, a wave swelling into flesh. Clothed only in foam, she hung limply on the crest, her body seeming to dance as the wave skimmed her over the water with a catboat's grace. She collapsed at my feet. I knelt beside her. Her eyelids fluttered. She gazed up at me, barely conscious. It was then that I recognized her."

By this time we had reached the lighthouse. The Captain paused in his narrative to usher me inside, then resumed after pulling the door shut behind him, pacing wildly back and forth as he spoke. I listened as before, understanding little of what he told me in his strangely stilted language but held spellbound by the passion in his voice. Every so often the lighthouse shifted with a groan the Captain ignored but which sent me edging closer to the door.

"I think I have told you once, Mr. Sharp, of Willis' eyes. How they contained all the moods of the seven seas, aye, and other seas besides. Every sea that ever existed or will exist, every sea dreamed of by man or fish. I had long ago forgotten her body, but her eyes . . . how could I forget them, with the sea itself continually before me? The body in my arms belonged to a stranger for all I knew or cared, but the moment I looked into her eyes I knew that, by some miracle, perhaps in answer to my prayer, Willis had come back to me. How didn't matter, or why, just the fact that she was there, in my arms again. I saw once more the oceans of my youth! Though my ruined eyes could not longer plumb the depths they once had, I floated on the surface of her eyes like a weary gull, content to rest there. I said her name, shouted it above the roar of the storm, but she recoiled as if repelled by my countenance. Had I changed so much that she no longer knew me? Well, even so, what did that matter now that she was mine again? I picked her up—she had lost consciousness again—and carried her into the lighthouse. Since then I haven't left her side for a moment, Mr. Sharp, until I saw you coming."

I looked around anxiously. "Where . . . ?"

The Captain pointed to the ceiling. "Have no fear, Mr. Sharp! You shall see her!"

There was nothing I wanted more. It seemed obvious that the Captain had rescued some poor, half-drowned woman, then assigned her a familiar identity just as he had done with me. The difficult part, I foresaw, would be to get her away from him, to get them both out of the lighthouse, which trembled beneath my feet, underscoring the urgency of action. I decided to humor him. "Don't you think, sir, that after all she's been through, Willis might be better off in a hospital?"

The Captain scuttled up to me as if I had disobeyed a direct order. I shrank back, afraid of him for the first time since that day three months earlier when he had addressed me from the fire. "She won't leave me again, I swear it! I won't share her with anyone! Not with doctors, not with you, Mr. Sharp!"

I spoke quickly, swallowing my fear, trying to salvage the situation. "I'm sorry, sir. I felt it was my duty as first mate to point out every option. Of course, I'll abide by your wishes."

That seemed to calm him. He nodded stiffly. "Quite right, Mr. Sharp. Quite right. It's only—well, you understand. You'll be an old man too one day . . . before you know it. Take my advice: find yourself a girl like Willis and hold on tight, as if she were the only thing between you and drowning!"

At that, he invited me up the stairs to see Willis for myself. As we climbed, I ventured to mention once more my fear that the lighthouse would buckle when the brewing storm finally broke. The Captain slapped the railing and replied, "No need to worry, Mr. Sharp. She's solid as a rock. I'd stake my life on it."

"And Willis'?" I asked.

He stopped, peering down at me suspiciously. It was strange to see the Captain from that twisted angle; I was used to looking down at him, and in the reversal of our usual positions I sensed that I had been fooling myself about the Captain's essential harmlessness.

"Mr. Sharp," he said in a clipped voice. "Your concern has already been noted. I forbid you to bring up the subject again. Is that understood?"

"Aye, sir," I said sadly, as if the end of summer had come not with the start of school but only now, with the Captain's harsh words. Dimly, I realized that this game I had been playing for months of *Treasure Island*

and *Robinson Crusoe* was no game, was in fact the realest thing I had ever done in my life. At that moment, I stopped thinking of myself as Mr. Sharp.

I don't remember what exactly I expected to find in the observatory. Probably I envisaged a poor, bedraggled girl wrapped in blankets, shivering with cold and fear, her eyes containing not oceans but simple tears. No doubt I pictured her hopeful look as I entered, my nod that would silently assure her that everything was going to be all right. If I had stopped playing one game, it was only to take up another; such is life for a ten-year-old . . . and not just a ten-year-old.

The staircase spiraled up through the observatory floor. The first thing I saw as my head emerged was a naked woman gazing out through an open shutter at the storm-tossed sea. Though her back was to us, her slumped shoulders and bowed head conveyed an impression of sadness and resignation. She wore her hair in a thick braid that coiled about her neck like a collar of dark leather. It flared into a hood around her head, accentuating her mournful aspect. A dull gray blanket lay about her ankles.

I blushed, but could not look away. Until then, my only knowledge of women's bodies had come from pictures passed hurriedly around the school bathroom or playground. Compared to those women, posed in positions that, though exciting, seemed somehow wrong, cold and manipulative and imbued with a cynicism that made me feel ashamed of my interest, Willis—for I had already begun to think of her by that name—was like a vision of purity, and my shame in viewing her came from another source entirely: I was ashamed not of myself, but for her, intruded upon in this way by the Captain and me.

The Captain motioned for me to come up, making no move to cover Willis. The room was lit by the oil lamp I had brought the Captain. A strange, mottled light, shot through with pale yellows and ugly greens, drifted through the open window whenever lightning flashed. The woman seemed unaware of—or disinterested in—our presence, gazing out the window as if yearning to throw herself back into the sea. Her wrists, I suddenly noticed, were bound by lengths of rope to the rusted iron railing that was set into the wall beneath the windows. She had room to turn or sit, but no more.

I turned angrily to the Captain, but before I could say a word he put a finger to his lips to shush me and motioned toward Willis with his head, inviting me to approach her. A peaceful look had spread over his features. He seemed to be asleep, enjoying a pleasant dream. I realized he was seeing something quite different from what I was, that he was, in fact, gazing back into the past, clothing the naked woman before him in the vestments of a bygone age just as he called her by the name of a girl long dead.

Time moved slowly in that room, as if the Captain's dream were reaching out to snare me in its thick folds. The rumble of thunder seemed strangely protracted, stretching into a continuous snarl. I couldn't speak, could barely summon the strength to cross the floor and, picking up the blanket, drape it gently around Willis' smooth white shoulders.

She jumped at my touch and whirled to face me, the blanket clutched to her throat, the rope taut at her wrists, her cowl of dark hair flaring around her head like a cobra's hood. Yet I believe I was far more startled than she. For though her body was that of a woman, her face was like nothing I had ever seen or imagined, and I knew with an instinct as swift and sure as any in my life before or since that I was in the presence of something utterly alien, unhuman.

Paralyzed with fear, I could only stare, struggling to make sense out of what I was seeing, to explain it all away. Not that she was ugly or monstrous—no, my fear stemmed rather from the overwhelming strangeness of her beauty, like a landscape too vast and exotic to be taken in by the eyes, by any of the senses alone or together, a beauty comprehensible only in bits and pieces, and even then but imperfectly.

Her white skin was lustrous as an opal, yet I knew, without daring to stroke it, that it would feel soft as a dolphin's belly beneath my hand. The plane of her face was absolutely flat. I saw no eyes, no nose, only lips that were wide and thin, colored a deep blue and stretching . . . I would say from ear to ear, but she had no ears, at least none that I could see. Instead, where her ears should have been, long, fleshy strips ran down her slender neck to culminate just above her shoulders. Dark red, almost purple in color, they fluttered like gills with each breath she took, flashing glimpses between their folds of a pink so bright that I thought at first I was gazing into a wound. I started to look away, unsettled by the sight, then froze, hypnotized by a glitter like sunlight skipping off water. Willis was opening her eyes.

The flesh above her mouth drew upward, revealing eyes as wide and round as portholes in a ship. For once, the Captain had seen correctly. I felt as if I were gazing through those windows at an ocean that stretched on forever, without shore or horizon. And then, abruptly, I found myself on the other side of her eyes, in the water itself, buoyed up gently just as the Captain had described. Whatever fear was in me vanished then. A sense of peace and well-being swelled my heart that is impossible to convey, like what a baby must experience while floating in the infinite sea of its mother's womb. I was surrounded not by water, but love. Above me, great birds circled lazily in the blue sky. One or two swept low, their wings grazing the water and sending up huge plumes of spray, as if hunting for fish. Yet I knew they posed no danger, that I was not in this strange world as much as it was in me.

Wonderful as it was to float there, I was not satisfied. I wanted to go deeper, to touch bottom if I could. The Captain's scabrous eyes kept him on the surface, but I had no such handicap. I was already jealous of Willis and did not want to share her with anyone. The thought that the Captain, in his own mind, was perhaps treading water beside me was unbearable. I would dive to depths he could not hope to reach.

My descent was effortless and seemed without end, a slow downward spiral past fish the likes of which I had never seen, some shaped so absurdly I had to laugh, others instilling a terror no shark could hope to match, still others gazing at me through eyes that brimmed with sad intelligence, like cows grown wise. I never needed to draw a breath. Soon the water turned dark as night. Fish drifted by like ghosts shedding a weak glow while far below I seemed to see thousands of shimmering lights, bright as a field of stars.

The feeling of love deepened in me, tinged with an urgency that I associated with thoughts of home and safety, of my mother waiting anxiously for my return and I as anxious to reach her. I realized dimly that Willis was attempting to communicate something to me that I was understanding only partly, if at all. But I knew one thing perfectly: if I could just reach those lights, everything would become clear.

But something was behind me, something large and terrifying. And fast . . . much faster than I. Soon it would overtake me. Panic welled up in me, Willis' on top of my own. I couldn't tell any longer whether she was in my body or I was in hers. Just then, without warning, it broke upon me like an undersea storm.

There was no time to react. Tumbled head over heels, I was pulled away from the lights, away from home. Everything was blackness. I (or, if you prefer, Willis—the distinction was meaningless at the time) felt as if I were being sucked into other oceans by the power of the storm, being drawn from one end of the seven seas to the other, across a distance so great I feared I would never be able to find my way home.

And then, in the midst of the darkness, I saw a single light. It shone bravely for an instant, cleaving the water to kindle a spark of hope in my breast, then winked out. But it was back again almost at once. I swam for it with all my strength, my heart beating to the rhythm of its bright pulse. But the storm was too fierce, the currents too strong. I was swept past the light. I saw it recede behind me, then all at once I burst into the air. A wave raised me high. For a second, I thought I glimpsed the stark, defiant outline of the lighthouse against the angry sky. Then I was flung down.

I stood where I had been standing minutes or was it hours earlier, as if the wave had tossed me right out of Willis' eyes. Tears were running down her face, and she was gazing at me with an imploring look that, despite her alien appearance, was as human as her tears. I was crying too. Beside me, the Captain stared into Willis' eyes with a dazed, enraptured look, rocked on peaceful swells. Baby noises came from his mouth. Then Willis turned away.

The Captain staggered. He would have fallen had I not grasped his arm. He leaned against me then shook free, mumbling curses like a drunken man dragged out of a doorway. But an instant later he was his old self again, squinting up at me suspiciously through his clouded eyes as he wiped his mouth on the ragged sleeve of his jacket. "It's time you were going, Mr. Sharp," he said.

Descending, my mind was awhirl with the images Willis had placed there. The emotions I had shared with her were so strong that I felt them as mine, though tailored to fit my own situation. I had to get home, had to see my mother. Nothing else mattered, not even Willis, bound to the observatory railing like Rapunzel in the stories my mother had read to me in the fairy tale days when my father was still alive.

As I left the lighthouse, the Captain called to me from the foot of the stairs. "You won't tell a soul, will you, Mr. Sharp?"

"No, sir," I said, already running.

"She's our secret!" he yelled behind me.

But even in the grips of this alien compulsion laid upon me like a magic spell, I knew that I could not share Willis with anyone, least of all the Captain. As I ran across the dunes under the lowering sky, passing once again the smashed carcass of the strange bird—a bird I now recognized—I was thinking of how I could steal her, hide her away from the Captain and everyone else, so that the oceans of her eyes would be mine alone to sail.

My mother and Mr. Hooper were still out when I arrived home. I paced the kitchen, unable to relax, eaten up by worry, by a longing so intense and desperate it seemed impossible to believe that the familiar sight of my mother could assuage it. Yet despite my preoccupation, a part of me realized that my suffering was but a shadow of what Willis was suffering in the observatory, looking out over the heaving ocean toward the home she had left behind, a home as close as the space between two heartbeats yet farther away than all the miles that ever were. I wondered if she had a family there. Perhaps she was married, with children of her own, children who missed their mother as badly as I missed mine . . . as badly as I missed my father.

I ran outside as soon as I heard the car drive up, barely waiting for my mother to step out before throwing myself into her arms. She flinched, then hugged me close. I breathed in the smell of her, never wanting to let go. Yet the longing imparted to me by Willis did not lessen one bit. If anything, it grew, until I felt her sadness, her loneliness, more keenly than ever.

Finally my mother pushed me gently away. She was looking at me with tenderness, yet also with concern, and she reached out one hand to smooth my hair while the other touched my arm. I was acutely aware of Mr.

Hooper, still in the car, watching with a bemused expression. It was all too much. I burst into tears.

"Whatever is the matter, Mark?" my mother asked, hugging me to her again.

I shook my head, unable to say a word. Even if I could have spoken, what would I have told her? And even if she had believed me, what could she have done? The Captain had been right to call Willis our secret. She was that and more: she was my responsibility as well. I understood that now. And so, though I hated to admit it, was the Captain.

All that day the skies rumbled ominously, yet the storm expected every second did not break. That evening, at dinner, Mr. Hooper mentioned that we might be evacuated further inland as a precaution. I listened in horror, as if to a death sentence passed on Willis and the Captain. Later, lying in bed, I could not sleep. Beneath the sounds of thunder, I heard Willis calling to me in her silent way. Strange images, invested with a nostalgic allure, danced in my mind like the notes of an irresistible song, and I pictured her facing away from the sea, her wide eyes open and shining inland, beaming her plea into the darkest reaches of my selfish and cowardly heart.

Finally, I could resist no longer. I climbed out of bed, got dressed, and slipped through my bedroom window. I crept past my mother's window, in which a light still burned, then began to sprint across the dunes.

The air felt supercharged, crackling around me with the pent-up energies of the storm. Just as I came in sight of the lighthouse, a tremendous crash of thunder seemed to split the sky; a flash of lightning turned the world inside out as hailstones the size of mothballs began to fall, their wicked sting goading me on.

When I burst into the lighthouse, the Captain was nowhere to be seen. The floor was pitching like the deck of a ship at sea. Held in place by a pool of hardened wax, a single candle guttered upon the Captain's table, bathing the room in a murky, undersea glow. Hailstones thudded against the closed shutters with a deafening clatter. A sudden crash sounded above my head. Stumbling to the stairs, I climbed as fast as I could.

Entering the observatory, I was just in time to see, in the soft orange light of the oil lamp, the Captain pick himself up and launch himself at Willis with a hoarse bellow. She lashed out with her fist, catching him on the side of the head. He dropped back a step, weaving like a boxer, then fell heavily to the floor. He lay there unmoving, but Willis did not seem to notice. Instead, she began tearing with her tiny sharp teeth at the ropes that bound her wrists. I hung back for a second, afraid the Captain would get up. When he did not, I went to his side and quickly slipped his scaling knife from his belt, where he always wore it. His lip was bloodied, and his left eye was swollen almost completely shut.

When I stood, Willis was facing me, her hands held out, wrists up, in a gesture of supplication. I hesitated, not wanting to lose her. She shook her arms impatiently. I stepped forward, raising the knife to cut her free.

It was then that I made the mistake of looking into Willis' eyes. They did not suck me in as they had before. Instead, she seemed to be regarding me from far away, from a distance I had crossed once but could not hope to cross again. A part of me was with her there, and I knew that I would never get it back no matter how long and hard I searched for it or how patiently I awaited its return. I saw, too, reflected in her eyes like the future in a crystal ball, the journey she was determined to take, putting herself once more at the mercy of the storm, hoping that it would carry her back across the seven seas but knowing just the same how slender her chances were. I did not want this knowledge, but it could not be refused. There was nothing I could say to make her stay, nothing I could do but help her go. I cut her loose.

Willis leaped to the window ledge and, kicking open the shutter, dove. The hail had turned to a heavy rain, and as I peered out a flash of lightning gave me a glimpse of her in the surf, a flicker of white in the dark and furious sea gone at once and forever. I was tempted to follow, dragged behind by an invisible thread.

And perhaps I would have jumped, following not just Willis but my father as well, had the Captain not grabbed me from behind. He yanked me away from the window, spun me around and threw me to the floor, plucking the knife from my hand. His wounded face contorted into a mask of rage, the Captain advanced upon me, brandishing the knife. "Mutiny, Mr. Sharp! Mutiny, you damned traitor! How dare you steal my Willis? I'll see you dead, do you hear? I'll cut you up and feed you to the sharks!"

The Captain was interrupted as the lighthouse sagged in a sickening lurch that sent him sprawling, arms spinning in an effort to save his balance. I stayed on the ground, crawling toward the stairs. "Come on, Captain! She's going over!"

He had fetched up against a wall. "That's a lie! She's solid as a rock and you know it!"

There was no reasoning with him. Following my example, the Captain dropped to his knees and began to crawl after me, pulling himself along the sloping floor by digging in with the point of his knife. "You'll not escape me, traitor!" he called. "I'll see you dead!"

The tower gave another lurch. I slid back towards the Captain, who, thanks to his knife, did not lose any ground.

"Now I've got you!" he cackled.

I scrambled away, barely keeping clear. One more lurch would deliver me into his grasp. The stairs seemed miles away. My strength was exhausted.

And then I heard my name shouted from below. "Here I am!" I yelled back. "Up here! Help!"

It was Mr. Hooper. My mother had sent him after me upon discovering my empty bed, sure that I had gone to the lighthouse. His wrinkled face popped into view not a moment too soon; the Captain was almost upon me.

Mr. Hooper pulled me out of danger. "Who are you?" he demanded of the Captain. "Don't you know this old lighthouse is about to collapse?"

"So it's you, Roberts!" the Captain cried, quick as ever to recognize a perfect stranger. "I'll get you yet!" He raised the knife to hurl at us, but lost his balance and tumbled against the far wall. The knife flew from his hand in a loopy arc, and smashed into the oil lamp. In a second there was a wall of fire between us.

The lighthouse shuddered again. Mr. Hooper started down the spiral staircase. I fought in his grasp: "No! We can't leave the Captain!"

"We'll be lucky to save ourselves," Mr. Hooper replied, tightening his grip.

"You don't understand . . . "

I slumped against him, exhausted. He carried me out of the lighthouse, into the stinging rain, then set me on my feet. He still held me by the hand, afraid I might try to dash back inside. But I had no stomach for that. The lighthouse was blazing like a torch. I watched anxiously for the Captain. Then Mr. Hooper said, as if to himself: "He's not coming out."

I knew he was right. I felt numb, drained. In a way it seemed fitting that the Captain perish with his last command. Yet I grieved for him just the same, despite his attempts to kill me. Like Willis, he would take a part of me with him.

Together under stormy skies, Mr. Hooper and I watched the lighthouse tremble, tilt, then topple in a slow arc. It hit the water with a roar, sending up a tower of spray and steam and sparks that faded gradually into the rainy night. Soon there was nothing to mark where the lighthouse had stood but an empty space, and even that, I knew, would be gone by morning. We turned around, still holding hands, and began the long walk home.

I'm an old man myself now, older than the Captain. I think of him often, and of his advice to me. Find a girl like Willis and hold on tight, he said. I spent my whole life searching and ended up here, on another beach, beside another ocean, as alone as when I started. That empty space where the lighthouse stood; it's been in my heart ever since.

The Captain's body was never recovered, and though I told my story a hundred times, described him again and again, he was never identified. Sometimes I think that he came from a place like Willis' home, only not so far away, not so different. For years, after every storm, I returned to Cape Henlopen, but nothing strange ever washed ashore. When the lighthouse fell, a gate clanged shut.

My mother and Mr. Hooper were married as planned. Though there were problems at first, he wove himself into our lives, and ours into his, with a grace as surprising to behold as his clumsy fingers at work on an intricate knot. When Mr. Hooper . . . Walter . . . died twenty-one years later at the age of seventy-three, not even his death could unravel that knot. My mother never remarried, and while I still lived in that part of the country I visited his grave twice a year—twice more than I visited the empty resting place of my other father, who, as the years went by, I came to remember less and less.

Each evening now I pause in my writing to watch the sun set over the Pacific. Bisected by the horizon, the sun glows like an orange ember, sending a russet beam across the water as if from a great lighthouse in the west. Sometimes I linger until the night opens up, clear and infinite as a saint's eye, rich in stars, and I think about the field of lights that Willis was trying so hard to reach and wonder if she made it home. And then I think perhaps there are other gates that lead across the seven seas, gates that are not blown wide by the gusting winds of storms but that swing open gently with a man's last breath. If that is so, if a light shines out in the dark time of my death, when hope and despair alike have been washed overboard, I will follow it over seven thousand seas.

Over seas without number.

EVERLAND

1. The Shadow

ONE NIGHT WENDY WOKE TO THE SOUND OF MUFFLED CRYING. Because her littlest brother, Michael, would sometimes wander into her room after a bad dream and ask her to tell him a story, Wendy wasn't too surprised, when she sat up, to see a boy huddled in the shadows at the foot of her bed. There was nothing that Wendy loved more than telling stories. She not only remembered every story she had ever heard or read, but she made up new ones all by herself.

"Michael, why are you crying?" she whispered.

Without raising his head, the boy pointed to the window behind him. The window was bolted shut although Wendy distinctly remembered having left it open. In fact, all the windows in the bedroom were shut. Her father would be furious. He was a firm believer in the healthful benefits of proper ventilation; even on the coldest winter nights he insisted on leaving the windows wide open.

Wendy was about to get out of bed when she noticed a filmy darkness flitting against the outside of the window with a sound like moths' wings. The boy cringed.

"It's only the wind, Michael," she said. "Don't be afraid."

"I'm not either!" The boy sprang to his feet, and Wendy saw that it wasn't Michael after all. Or her other little brother, John.

The strange boy, whoever he was, was dressed in a suit of green leaves and vines. He stood with his legs spread and his chest out and his hands on his hips. A long dagger hung at his belt. "I'm not afraid of anything!" he declared.

The boy looked so solemn, despite the tearmarks on his face, that Wendy clapped her hands and laughed.

He put a hand to his dagger. "Why are you laughing, girl?"

"Girl is what we call Nana, our dog," she told him. "My name's Wendy. What's yours?"

"Peter Pan."

Again, Wendy had to laugh. "That's a funny name!"

"It isn't!"

Suddenly it occurred to Wendy that her bedroom was on the second floor of the house. "I suppose you climbed up the old tree and swung in through the window, Peter. That's how I do it."

"Didn't either," Peter said. "I flew."

"Liar!"

Peter rose into the air until the top of his head brushed the ceiling like a balloon. He smirked down at her. "Now who's the liar?"

Wendy thought about what adventures she could have if only she could fly. "Show me how!"

"Take back what you said!"

"You weren't lying! It's wonderful! But how ever do you do it, Peter? Is it hard?"

"Anyone can fly. Even girls!" He drifted to the floor like a feather. "It's your shadow that weighs you down. It glues you to the ground. Get free of your shadow . . . and up you go!"

"Free of your shadow? How do you do that?"

"*I* know how. I'm the cleverest boy of all! And do you know what, Wendy? I haven't gotten older since I got rid of my shadow. Not by a day, not by a minute. I won't ever get old! The only problem . . . " He glanced toward the window with a shudder and dropped his voice to a whisper. "The beastly thing won't leave me alone. It's always coming after me, trying to reattach itself!"

"How awful," Wendy said.

"It doesn't make much noise, you see, and it blends in frightfully well with the dark and lurks about in shadows, waiting to pounce like a panther. It almost caught me tonight. Would have, if I hadn't ducked through your window."

"Now what will you do?"

"Don't know," Peter said glumly, looking as if he might start to cry again. "I can't get back to Neverland with that shadow hanging about. It's too quick even for me; I'd never get past it."

"Neverland?"

"It's where I live," he explained between sniffles. "With the lost boys. I'm the Captain."

"What about your parents?"

"There are no parents in Neverland. Never have been. Our parents didn't want us . . . and we don't want them."

"A place with no parents," Wendy said wonderingly. No drunken father, with fists as quick as his temper, to tell her how young ladies must behave, what they may and may not read or do or want to become. No timid mother to side with husband against children and sons against daughter. It sounded too good to be true.

"*I* have an idea," Wendy said.

"You do? Tell me!"

"First promise to take off my shadow so I can fly too."

Peter pulled out his dagger. "It's going to hurt."

"I won't cry."

It did hurt. Wendy didn't cry. When it was over, something very like her mother's sheerest black stockings lay rumpled upon the white sheets of Wendy's bed.

"Is it dead?" she asked.

Peter winked. "How do you feel, Wendy?"

"I feel . . . lighter than air." And somehow, just by thinking it, Wendy rose off the ground. She flew. She circled the room, turning cartwheels on the ceiling and somersaults over the bed.

But then Wendy saw something move out of the corner of her eye. Her shadow was flapping sluggishly on her bed like a flounder at the bottom of the sea.

"It's waking up," Peter said. "It'll be after you in a second."

Wendy felt sorry for her shadow, but she didn't want it any more, didn't want to be weighed down, unable to fly, growing older with each passing minute, turning into a grown up, a woman like her mother with children and a husband to care for and no time to read stories, much less make them up. She was eleven years old; she didn't have much time left. And there were so many stories to tell, stories she hadn't even thought of yet!

She remembered the locket her grandmother had given her at Christmas. It was silver, shaped like a heart. "Just look," Granny had said. "It opens up. You can put a picture in there someday, a picture of your sweetheart."

Wendy didn't have much use for sweethearts. But now she had a use for the locket. Quick as the thought came to her, Wendy folded up her shadow until it was as small as a postage stamp, and much, much thinner. She locked it inside the silver heart, just as if it *had* been a picture of her sweetheart, and tucked the locket under her nightgown.

"Now I can be eleven forever!" She flew into the air with a skip and jump and twirled there like a ballerina.

"That's fine for you," Peter sniffed. "But my shadow's wide awake. I can't fold it up like that."

"No, I don't suppose you can."

"But you said you'd help me."

Wendy wanted to help Peter. Not because she had to, but because she was happy. "Do you know the story of the mice who bell the cat?"

"What are stories?"

"Stories are, well, *stories.*" No one had ever asked her what a story was before. Wendy knew a lot of stories, and she certainly knew how to tell them, but as for what they *were*, that was something else again. It was something she'd have to think about. "I'll sew some bells onto your shadow. Then you'll always be able to hear it coming."

"Capital!" Peter cried. "Only how will we catch hold of it?"

"I'll open the window a crack. When your shadow flies through, slam the window shut as fast as you can. We'll trap it. Then I can sew on the bells."

"Shadows are very stupid as a rule," Peter said. "It's bound to work."

Wendy got a needle and thread and a small belled collar that she had been making for a neighbor's kitten. She went to one side of the window, Peter to the other. Outside, the shadow beat against the glass like a mindless thing.

"Ready, Peter?"

He nodded.

Wendy opened the window. The shadow darted in. It was fast. But Peter was faster. He slammed the window down.

The shadow's right hand fluttered under the pane, caught like a bird in a trap. On the other side of the window, the rest of the shadow pulled as if with all its might, its feet pressed flat against the glass. But it was no use. The bells jingled like a sleigh ride as Wendy carefully stitched the collar around the shadow's wrist.

"I hope I'm not hurting it," she said.

"Serve it right if you were. I say, Wendy, those story things of yours are the best!"

Wendy nipped through the thread and stepped back with a proud smile. "There. All done."

"Just listen to it jingle!" Peter howled. "I think I'll call it Jinglebell!"

Peter's laughter must have been a little too loud, for just then the voice of Wendy's father boomed, his voice slurred so that she knew he had been drinking, and his heavy tread shook the stairs.

Peter drew his dagger. "Don't be afraid, Wendy. I've killed lots of fathers!"

Wendy was often angry with her father. She often hated him for hitting her, for hitting her mother and her brothers. More than once she had wished him dead. But how much simpler, now that she had no shadow, just to fly away like a bird. "There'll be no killing, Peter!"

Peter looked disappointed. "But won't he give you a whipping, Wendy?"

"He'll have to catch me first." There were two other windows in Wendy's bedroom in addition to the one holding Peter's shadow. Wendy flung one of them open. The starry sky beckoned above the dirty gas lamps of London. "I'm coming with you to Neverland!"

"But I've never brought a girl back."

"I'll tell you lots of stories!"

Peter brightened. "That's different." He sprang out the window, thumbing his nose at his shadow.

Wendy followed with a whoop, her nightgown billowing behind her. "Which way, Peter?"

He pointed to a group of stars low in the east. "Second to the right and straight on till morning!"

"Last one there's a rotten egg!" Wendy cried.

Behind them, the door opened to an empty room, an open window, and a furious jingling of bells.

2.THE FLIGHT

Wendy and Peter flew for what must have been a very long time. They left London, and then England, far behind. They flew over an ocean, then over vast stretches of snow and ice, then out among the stars. But Wendy and Peter weren't worrying about time. To them, only a few minutes had gone by since they'd left... well, wherever it was they'd left. They weren't worrying about *that*, either. When you have no shadow, and stop growing up, time becomes a clock with a blank face and no hands.

Finally, though, as she and Peter played hide and seek in a comet's tail, Wendy began to wonder just what it was that she'd done before she started flying, and where it was that she'd done it. Life hadn't *always* been this wonderful. Once, a long, long time ago, things had been different.

But it was only with the greatest difficulty, as if remembering the foggiest wisp of a long ago dream, that Wendy succeeded in calling to mind the faces of her mother and father and her two little brothers. And even then she wasn't certain of their names or of who they were, no more than she could recall exactly where it was that she and Peter were going.

But Wendy *did* remember that the last one there, wherever "there" was, would be a rotten egg. Leaving Peter tangled in the comet's tail, she raced off as fast as she could in the direction of morning. And before long—or, anyway, it seemed very soon to Wendy—she caught sight of a green island sitting all alone in a sea that was the mild blue of seas on maps.

As she drew closer, her excitement mounted, as if she'd always known this place, as if she were coming home. The branches of the trees grew in such a thick tangle that all Wendy could see at first was a bristling mass of green—here a bright, shiny green like sunshine on spring grass, there a dark and threatening green like storm clouds frowning on a picnic. All together there were so many shades of green that she grew dizzy trying to tell them apart. If not for the many colorful flowers and birds—birds she mistook for flowers, flowers that turned into birds—Wendy might have gone blind with green.

At the very center of all that green stood a mountain, a volcano, itself covered in green, from which rose a thick and steady plume of smoke. I've never seen anything quite like this, Wendy thought. It seemed like a dream come true, a place out of one of her stories. And with that she remembered what the island was called.

"Neverland!" she crowed. "I win!"

3. THE ISLAND COME TRUE

Neverland from the air might have looked like an impenetrable jungle, but things were different on the ground. A network of paths criss-crossed the island from one end to the other. The paths were used by almost every creature that lived in Neverland: the lions, the wolves, the boars, the bears, the deer. And the lost boys, of whom Peter was Captain.

Some of the lost boys Peter had fetched back to Neverland himself, but most had simply woken one morning to find themselves on the island. Not one was younger than five or older than eleven. They still had their shadows and could not fly, so, unlike Peter, they grew up—only very, very slowly.

When hair began to sprout on a boy's face it meant that he was older than Peter, which, Peter being Captain and all, was against the rules. It was a sad day. Peter gave the offending boy a choice: battle or boat. A fair chance, he said. Anything less would be bad form. Some boys chose battle, thinking that they were better than Peter just because they had hair on their faces. Peter had to kill those boys. The others, the sensible ones, he cast out to sea in small boats stocked with a supply of food and water. They were never seen again.

There were other creatures in Neverland besides the wild animals and the lost boys. Creatures that kept off the paths and moved through the deepest, darkest heart of the jungle—a place the boys called the No-no-never-no—in a thrashing and crashing of foliage, uttering strange and fearsome cries. Even the lions cringed at those cries.

But not the lost boys. The lost boys loved to hunt the wild animals that dwelled along the paths. That was fine sport. They dressed themselves in the skins of bears and wolves and lions that they had slain. But most of all the lost boys loved to hunt the terrible creatures dwelling in the No-no-never-no. That was the finest sport of all, forbidden to the youngest boys. Not even the oldest boys would enter the No-no-never-no without Peter. Not that they were afraid: it was a question of respect, Peter being Captain and all.

So there they were, on the same morning that Wendy had her first view of Neverland, the lost boys, marching along the paths as they did every morning, daggers and spears and bows and arrows at the ready. It was hard to say how many there were; boys were constantly running ahead and scampering up from behind, climbing and tumbling out of trees, and chasing each other into—but not too far into—the jungle. It would have been very strange, with all the ruckus they were raising, if they had even *seen* a wild animal, much less killed one. And in fact they hadn't had any luck. They were in a nasty mood.

"I say, Bill," said one, a chubby little boy of six or seven wearing the fur of a bear, "I do hope that Peter comes back soon! It's never much fun without him!"

The boy addressed, whose lanky form betrayed the waning of boyhood and whose face was caked in a mask of dirt, smirked and gave the younger boy a shove. He was Peter's second-in-command. "Give a listen to Eric, mates! The little girl misses her mommy!"

Howling with laughter, the other boys surrounded Eric and began to chant: "Erica! Erica!"

Eric aimed a kick at the boy closest to him, who was both smaller and younger.

The laughter redoubled, now at the expense of Eric's victim, who looked in turn for someone on whom to safely vent his wrath.

And so the lost boys continued along the path, laughing and fighting among themselves.

Eric saw her first.

"It's Peter!" he cried, pointing up through the branches to where a figure in white could be seen flying through the air.

"Shh!" hissed Bill. "That's not Peter! It's a girl."

Hoots of derision.

"A *girl*? Never!"

"Girls don't fly!"

"This one does," Bill said.

"What should we do?"

"What would Peter do?"

"Peter shoots first and asks questions later," Eric said.

"Exactly so, Erica," said Bill. He notched an arrow to his bow and let fly. The arrow sped true. Wendy gave a cry and sank into the trees, the shaft protruding from her breast.

4. THE HOME UNDER THE GROUND

Wendy woke to a painful throbbing in her chest. She opened her eyes.

"She's alive!" someone cried. (It was Eric, but Wendy didn't know that.)

Wendy found herself looking into Peter's green eyes. Behind him was a crowd of fierce-looking boys. "What happened? Who are all these boys?"

"Welcome to Neverland, Wendy. These are the lost boys."

"Where are the lost girls?" she asked.

Peter smiled. "This is Wendy, boys."

The boys said nothing. Wendy didn't like the way they were looking at her. All at once she remembered an arrow sprouting from her chest. "Who shot me? Was it one of you?"

An ugly, dirty boy stepped up and gave a mocking bow. "Bill, at your service."

"A million-to-one shot," Peter said admiringly. "Look at this." He held up her locket. The arrow had pierced the little silver heart.

Wendy's hand flew to her chest; there was only a small wound, hardly more than a scratch. The locket had saved her life. "You might at least say you're sorry, Bill."

Bill smirked. "I'm sorry . . . Sorry I hit the locket and not you!"

The boys howled their appreciation of Bill's wit.

"You'll be even sorrier when I'm through with you!" Wendy cried. She flew at him, but something yanked her back. She tried again. The same result. There was a bracelet of steel around her ankle and a chain that led back to a thick, gnarled root. She tugged at the chain in disbelief, then looked at Peter. "Is this some kind of game? If it is, I don't want to play."

The boys laughed even harder at that.

Peter danced a jig in the air, holding up a tiny gold key for her to see. He placed the key on the thin silver chain beside her locket, broke the ends of the arrow off, then slipped the chain over his head and beneath his shirt of leaves. "I'm the cleverest boy of all!" he sang.

Wendy took notice of surroundings for the first time. She was in an underground room. The massive roots of a tree twisted and twined through the air to serve as walls and ceiling. She lay upon a pile of damp leaves and moss. Toadstools sprouted from the floor; some of the boys were using these as chairs. Light fell through small holes in the roof; every so often a worm or bug or spider fell down the same way. A fire blazed inside a hollow log that stood on its end like a stovepipe. The smoke made Wendy sneeze.

"What shall we do with her, boys?" Peter asked.

"Kill her!" cried what seemed like a sizeable majority.

Wendy grew a little frightened at that, but she vowed not to show it. She glared at the boys, daring them to do their worst.

"Not so fast!" Peter said. "This one knows stories."

The boys looked at each other in puzzlement. "Stories?"

Peter gave a condescending laugh. "Don't you know what stories are?"

Eric scratched his head. "I think I might have heard a story once, Peter. A long time ago. It was about a girl and a rabbit. A lady told me." (Actually Eric thought it had been his mother who'd told him the story, but it wasn't wise to mention mothers around Peter.)

Bill gave him a shove. "Shut up, Erica!"

"Do you know that one?" Peter asked Wendy.

"*Alice in Wonderland*," she said.

"That's about a girl. Tell us one with boys in it."

"I won't. You better let me go, Peter!"

"Never! Go on and tell. Maybe then I'll let you go. Or maybe I'll let the boys kill you."

"Dibs," Bill cried.

Wendy thought for a minute. She didn't think they could keep her down here forever. Sooner or later she'd get free. Then she'd remind Peter that he wasn't the only one who could fly, or play dirty either.

"Once upon a time, there was a boy named Jack," she began.

5. WENDY'S STORY

Each night, Peter and the lost boys gathered around Wendy and demanded a story before bedtime. They refused to hear the same story twice, nor would they listen to any story with a girl as hero. Witches and wicked stepmothers were the only roles open to girls in the home under the ground.

After a while, Wendy had exhausted the nine-hundred and ninety-nine tales of Scheherazade that featured boys as heroes, all the stories about boys in the Brothers Grimm, the Greek and Roman myths, and Aesop's fables, along with countless stories of her own devising. Wendy thought that years must have gone by in this way. Since time was a funny thing in Neverland to begin with, and even odder without a shadow, it might not really have been as long as all that.

On the other hand, perhaps it was even longer.

Finally she started telling stories that she'd left out the first time, stories about girls. She told Cinderella, only changing Cinderella to a boy, the glass slipper to a sword, the fairy godmother to a magic ring, and the prince to a giant. The lost boys never knew the difference. But Wendy began to think about stories in a new way. Why were boys always fighting things and saving girls? Why did the girls just lie there waiting for the boys to save them, like Snow White or Sleeping Beauty awakened by the prince's kiss? Even Scheherazade got married in the end, Wendy thought. She'd bet anything that boys had made up most of those stories. Wendy knew that no prince was coming to rescue *her*.

Wendy remembered her old life more clearly now, though everything about it seemed tiny and far away, as if seen through the wrong end of a telescope. Yet she never wished that she was back in London with her mother and brothers, under her father's roof. There had to be someplace else, she thought. A place as far away from Neverland as Neverland was from London. Everland, maybe. Once she got free, she'd find Everland. Or make it if she had to.

In a strange way, all the stories Wendy told came to be about herself, about how she had escaped from one kind of prison only to wind up in an even worse jail, and how she would escape from that jail too. They were all the same story.

Wendy's story.

Every day the lost boys acted out what Wendy had told them the night before. They split into two sides, one side playing the Merry Men, the other the soldiers of the Sheriff of Nottingham. They played cowboys and indians, boys and giants, elves and ogres, Gods and Titans, angels and devils, knights and dragons, sultans and genies. Great battles raged across Neverland, with many boys limping home in need of Wendy's nursing, which she was forced to provide, and a few boys not coming home at all. Practice for the No-no-never-no, Peter called it.

Sometimes tremors shook Neverland as if the volcano at its center was about to erupt. They went on for days and days. Then a strange solemnity descended over the home under the ground. No one laughed, no one fought, no one said a word. Even Wendy's stories were unwelcome.

Early on the morning of the day after the tremors stopped, before the sun came up, the younger boys were herded into a stockade that Peter had built to prevent them from following along. Then, heavily armed, the older boys filed into the jungle, into the No-no-never-no. When they returned in the evening, there were always a number missing, many more than were lost in the pretend wars that Peter called practice.

And yet, oddly, new boys were brought home from these trips into the No-no-never-no. Most were very young, no more than four or five. Wendy heard them whimpering as they were marched out of the jungle and into the stockade, where they were kept for some weeks and taught how to be lost boys. Wendy had the feeling that a lot of boys never made it out of that stockade.

When they weren't listening to stories or out hunting and fighting, Peter and the lost boys teased Wendy unmercifully. Peter kept threatening to open her silver locket and let her shadow out, so that she'd start to grow up again and lose the power to fly, even though the only flying she did these days was to hover a foot or so above the ground at the end of her chain while she dusted the ceiling; in addition to everything else, the lost boys made her keep house and cook. But Wendy teased Peter right back, and her fists taught the other boys the dangers of coming too close.

Then there was Bill. Bill was afraid of Peter, and kept in line when Peter was around. But every so often Peter's shadow, Jinglebell, made an appearance. The bells were so loud that they could be heard from miles away. Even so, Peter's face turned pale at the first faint jingle, and he would fly away from the home under the ground, sometimes for days, or what seemed like days. Then Bill would be in charge. And Bill was worse than Peter. Peter never did the nasty things to Wendy that Bill did when they were alone. Peter never touched her in bad places or made her touch him. Wendy hated Peter, but she wasn't afraid of him. Bill she hated *and* feared.

So it was the happiest—indeed, the only happy—day that Wendy experienced in the home under the ground when Bill was discovered to have . . . whiskers. It happened like this.

Peter had been gone for some time, and Bill was up to his old tricks. He had sent the lost boys out of the home under the ground and was wrestling with Wendy on the bed of moss, rubbing against her as he made strange growling sounds deep in his throat. The smell of his body and the stench of his breath made her want to throw up. Wendy fought at first, but Bill was stronger, and in the end there was nothing she could do except make everything into a kind of story in her head, a story that had a different ending than what was really happening, a story where she got free and took a knife and began, very slowly, to cut pieces of Bill away. She was just finishing with his face, when, out of nowhere, a deluge of cold water splashed over her.

Sputtering, Wendy opened her eyes to peals of laughter. Bill stood above her, soaked to the skin, his mouth open in shock.

Peter was back, with the lost boys gathered around him.

"What game is that, Bill?" he asked.

Bill tried to speak, but could only stammer.

"It looked an awful lot like you and Wendy were playing Mommy and Daddy, didn't it boys? We don't play that game, Bill."

Bill found his voice. "No, Peter. I was just punishing her is all. She was trying to get away!"

"Is that true, Wendy? Don't you like it here?"

"Someday I will get away!" she said. "Then you'll be sorry!"

Bill kicked her. "See what I mean, Peter?"

"I say, Bill," Peter said, as if changing the subject. "That's the first dunk you've had in ages, isn't it? Come to think of it, when the rest of us are hunting mermaids, you always stay on the beach. Now I see why. Some of the dirt's washed off, Bill. I can see your face."

Bill's hand darted to his chin.

"Bad form, Bill," said Peter with a cold smile. "Should have owned up to those whiskers from the first. Now what's it going to be? Battle or boat, a fair chance either way."

Bill scowled. "Fair? That's a laugh! I can't fly—I wouldn't have a chance in battle. I've seen you cut them down!"

"Boat then. Sorry to hear it. It would have been a good battle. But you're right: you'll have a better chance against the sea than you would against me. Boys, take him to the stockade."

"Aye, aye, Peter!"

And Bill had been hustled out, struggling and shouting curses.

Then Peter had turned to Wendy. "Why, Wendy. Is that a smile I see? I think you're getting to like it here after all!"

During the days, when the lost boys were out hunting and fighting, Peter left a boy behind to stand guard over Wendy as she cleaned up the home under the ground. Of all the boys who guarded her, Wendy's favorite was Eric. There was no honor in being left to guard a girl, and the task fell most often to Eric because he was held in such low repute by Peter and the other lost boys.

Eric reminded Wendy of Michael, her littlest brother, who was just about Eric's age. Like Michael, Eric liked to listen to Wendy's stories, even stories that had girls as heroes. He would whisper to her sometimes about his mother, whom he barely remembered.

"All I remember about my mother," he told her once, "is that she often said to my father, 'Oh, how I wish I had a checkbook of my own!' I don't know what a checkbook is, Wendy, but I always wondered why my father wouldn't give her one. *I* would have."

One day not long after Bill had been set adrift, Peter and the lost boys went hunting in the No-no-never-no. As usual, Eric was left behind to watch over Wendy, while the younger boys were put into the stockade to await Peter's return.

"What is it that happens in the No-no-never-no, Eric?" Wendy asked as she fixed up the beds with fresh moss. "What kind of creatures live there?"

A visible shudder passed through Eric, and his chubby face turned pale. "You mustn't talk about the No-no-never-no, Wendy. It's a bad place."

"Have you ever been there?"

"No." He squirmed on the toadstool where he sat. "Well, once. But I was little then, so I don't remember. Someday I'll go back. With the others. You're not a real lost boy until . . . " He broke off, fidgeting with his dagger.

"Until what?"

"You're just a girl, Wendy. You wouldn't understand."

"Wouldn't understand what?"

"Yes, wouldn't understand what, Erica?" croaked a voice from the shadows of the doorway.

6. WENDY BREAKS THROUGH

Eric held his dagger in a shaking hand and faced the doorway of the home under the ground. "Who's there?"

Something hideous shambled into the light. It was as big as a bear and just about as hairy. It wore a big black hat and a long blue and red coat and tall black boots. It was almost too big for the home under the ground and had to bend over like an ape in order to fit inside. Wendy knew there was a word for this creature, but she was too busy just then trying to pull free of her chain to remember what it was.

"What's the matter?" the creature said in its horrible gravelly voice. "Forgotten your old friend, Bill?"

"You're not Bill," Eric said. "Peter sent Bill away."

"I came back," it said, and big yellow teeth appeared in the thick tangle of black hair that Wendy suddenly remembered was called a *beard*. Her father had had a beard.

"You're a *man*," she said, remembering the word at last.

"What did you think I was, Wendy, a giant from one of your stories?" And he laughed; at least, she supposed it was a laugh, though it sounded more like splintering wood. "It's a pirate I am, my pretty. *Cap'n* Bill now."

Eric's mouth fell open. "It *is* Bill. But how . . . "

"I knew I'd find my way back," Bill said as if hardly able to believe it yet. "Thirty years sailing up and down the seven seas. *Thirty years.* Five ships, a dozen crews, and hardly a day's gone by here. No one grown older but poor old Cap'n Bill. But I said I'd come back and so I have. Come back to settle things with Peter Pan. So he's gone to the No-no-never-no, has he? He'll be wishing he stayed there before long!"

Eric jabbed the air with his dagger. "You'd better go, Bill. Peter'll fix you good if he catches you. It's not allowed to come back."

"Shut up, Erica!" Bill barely seemed to move, and Eric flew across the room. He crashed hard into the wall, sank to the floor and didn't get up. Then Bill faced Wendy. "Now it's your turn."

"I'm not afraid of you." She dug her fingernails into her palms to keep from trembling.

"You will be," he said. "Hasn't a day gone by over these last forty years that I haven't thought of you, Wendy. Waiting for me here, never growing up, perfect in every way. Pure as gold. We've got forty years to catch up on, right from where we left off. But first you're going to help Cap'n Bill settle things with Peter. I've got a ship at anchor off the coast with a crew of scurvy cutthroats such as would gladly send their own mothers to the bosom of Davy Jones for a chance at a girl like you. You'll help me, my pretty, or they'll get that chance."

But Wendy was thinking of a different kind of chance. "I want to settle things with Peter, too," she said. "Get me out of here, and I'll help you." She didn't even feel a twinge of guilt when she told this lie. She supposed she was past all that now.

Bill grinned. "It's true, you've got no end of reasons for hating him. More even than you know. Help me willingly, and things will go easier for you, my pretty. You can be Cap'n Bill's first mate, his own little nightingale. I'll clip your wings, and you'll sing pretty for me when the sun goes down."

Wendy could tell by the fall of light through the roof that the afternoon was waning. All she could think about was getting away from the home under the ground. She'd worry about getting away from Bill later. "They'll be back soon. We have to hurry!"

Bill took a key from a pocket in his coat. "This is a skeleton key. It opens any lock. I've had cause to use it many times in the course of my career, but never to unlock a greater treasure than you." He paused, then replaced the key. "But I'm being hasty. I could clip your wings right now and have a tumble before Peter gets back. You'd like that, wouldn't you? You've been missing me. I can tell."

Wendy drew back to the limit of her chain as Bill approached. "There's no time, Bill."

"That's all there is in Neverland, is time." He pulled a long, wickedly curved dagger from his greatcoat. "On my travels through heathen lands, I became acquainted with many a strange custom. There's places where women are burned alive when men die. Other places girls are killed as soon as they're born, before they take their first breath even. I've come to see that's all a waste. It's more girls we need, not less. I once visited a place where birds are kept in cages. Beautiful golden cages. And those birds sing like angels. Like bloody angels! You know why? Because they're *blinded*. A blind bird won't fly away, you see. Its wings are as good as clipped. It's got to fly with its song now. That's the only wings left to it. Wings of song. I saw that, and I said to myself, Cap'n Bill, that's for Wendy when you find her. You'll clip her wings in just that way, her tongue too, and then there'll be only one song left to her: the sweetest song a man can hear."

As Bill talked, Wendy was watching Eric out of the corner of her eye, hoping that Bill wouldn't see him as he dragged himself across the room. She saw by the way Eric moved that something was wrong with him, but somehow he managed not to make a sound. Even if he had, she thought that Bill was too worked up to notice.

At last, with an effort that made Wendy wince to watch, Eric pulled himself to his feet behind Bill, raised his dagger and brought it down hard into the man's back.

Bill screamed and dropped his dagger. He spun around and, with a hand squeezing Eric's throat, lifted the boy off the ground. Eric hung limply, his face turning blue. Bill reached over his shoulder and, groping, pulled the dagger from his own back. He rammed the blade into Eric's chest and threw him to the floor.

When he turned back to Wendy, Bill's black beard was stained a glistening crimson. He sank to his knees, his eyes searching the floor for his dropped dagger. At last he saw it.

It was in Wendy's hand.

That was the last thing he saw. His eyes went first. Then his tongue.

Bill had been right, Wendy thought as she worked her way down the rest of him in the dimming light. There was plenty of time after all.

7. The Pirate Ship

It was a moan that brought her to her senses. She didn't know where it had come from. Maybe from herself. When she looked down at what was left of Bill, Wendy didn't feel horror or fear, or satisfaction either. She felt only sadness. A sorrow so big it flowed out of her heart to fill up the whole world. She wasn't a girl anymore. She let the dagger fall from her hand. Then she heard the moan again. Someone was hurt. Eric. She crawled to where he lay.

Eric's eyes were open, but Wendy could tell right away that he didn't see her. He was seeing something, she thought, but not with his eyes. Not her. She took his hand. "Eric?"

Eric's hand tightened fractionally. He moaned again. Wendy thought that he was trying to say something. She leaned close. "What is it, Eric? I'm here."

His teeth had started to chatter. "C-cold, Mommy."

"I'm not . . . " Wendy began, then stopped. She thought of how Eric had always wanted to give his mother a checkbook of all things, and for some reason she began to cry. "Would you like to hear a story?"

The hand tightened again, more weakly now. She told a story she'd never told before, one that she made up as she went along, about a brave little boy who battled a giant in order to set his sister free. But the hand grew cold before she reached the part about how they all lived happily ever after.

Then Wendy heard noises outside, faint shouts and the rustling sounds of jungle foliage being tramped down and thrust aside. The lost boys were back.

Wendy knew there was no time to lose. She rummaged through the pockets of Bill's coat until she found the skeleton key. As she turned the key in the lock of her chains, she felt the rusty tumblers of her heart click open one by one. Then she was free. She grabbed Bill's bloody dagger and flew to the door, skimming inches above the ground. She nearly flew out, but she forced herself to take a peek first.

Peter and some lost boys were walking toward the home under the ground.

Wendy ducked back inside. There was no way to get out now without being seen, and she remembered very well what kind of target a flying girl made.

No matter what, she swore to herself, no one was going to chain her up again. Never.

When Peter entered the home under the ground, he stopped short at the sight that met his eyes. There was Eric, lying on his back, a dagger protruding from his chest. There was a creature of some kind, it was hard to say what, exactly, because there was so little of it left that was not sliced to ribbons, but he supposed it might have been a *man*, and not just a man, but, to judge by its clothes, a *pirate*; and where there were pirates, he thought, there were ships; and that made him wonder—because up until now no one had ever sailed to Neverland from outside—if this wasn't one of the lost boys grown up and come back for revenge, which is just what he would have done himself in their place. The idea of a war with pirates cheered him up a little. Things hadn't gone too well in the No-no-never-no. The lost boys were getting soft. Pirates might be just the thing to toughen them up. Then Peter realized that Wendy, too, was covered in blood and lying very still indeed on her bed of moss.

"Wendy?" he said. "Wendy! Wake up, Wendy!"

The boys with him looked at each other in surprise, for they had never heard Peter Pan sound so, well, *afraid*, except, of course, when his shadow, Jinglebell, drew near, and nobody blamed him for that. But this was different, they thought. Wasn't it? They didn't see any reason to be afraid of a dead girl. Didn't Peter always say that it was the live ones you had to watch out for?

Peter approached Wendy in stops and starts, the way the new boys moved when, roped together, they were marched back from the No-no-never-no and herded into the stockade to await their training. He fell to his knees beside her body and called her name once more, then reached a trembling hand towards her blood-streaked face.

The next thing anyone knew, a steel bracelet was snapped around Peter's wrist. He stared at his hand in disbelief as Wendy danced in the air.

"I'm the cleverest girl of all," she crowed.

Peter tugged at the chain, but it was fastened to the thick root as securely as ever. An odd smile cracked his face, as if he were happy to be outwitted. "I say, Wendy! Good form! But I've got my own key, you know. And how do you expect to get away? The lost boys will shoot you down whether I'm stuck here or not."

Wendy flew over Peter's head and came down behind him. She laid the curved edge of Bill's dagger against his throat. "I'm not going anywhere, Peter. One move from you or the lost boys and I'll carve you a new smile."

"Look, Wendy," he said. "Let's call it even. I chained you up, now you've chained me up. It was a game, that's all. You can go. Nobody will shoot you. I promise."

"I'm waiting," Wendy said.

"What for? If you kill me, the boys will kill you, and then who wins?"

"That's your problem, Peter. For you it's all a game. Winning and losing."

"What else is there?"

"You'll see," she said.

They waited. The crowd of lost boys grew until the home under the ground was packed, save for a clear space around Wendy and Peter and the bodies of Bill and Eric. Dusk ebbed into night. Someone lit the torches. No one said a word. The silence felt like the bottom of the sea.

Then they heard it. Faint and far away, a furious jingling of bells.

Wendy felt Peter's body grow tense; only the blade at his throat kept him from struggling.

"Wendy," he gasped. "Don't do it!"

"I want my locket back," she said.

"Take it! Take anything!"

She lifted the dagger from Peter's throat long enough to slip the locket over his head. "Tell the lost boys to clear out," she said, holding up the little silver heart and the golden key that dangled beside it.

"Wait for me outside boys. Go on!"

Grumbling, the boys left the home under the ground.

"Now what?" said Peter. The sound of the bells was growing louder.

Wendy stepped back, out of Peter's reach. "Now I go."

"But the key, Wendy!" Peter yanked desperately at the chain. "At least throw me the key! I cut your shadow off and taught you how to fly! I brought you to Neverland! Without me, you'd be old by now!"

"Say please, Peter."

"Please, Wendy! Please!"

She threw him the dagger.

He picked it up, a look of puzzlement on his face. "What's this?"

"It's your key."

"But this won't cut stee—" He broke off. His eyes widened. "You can't mean . . . "

"Jinglebell's almost here," she said.

Terror twisted Peter's features. The jingling of the bells had reached a clamorous pitch. Howling like an animal, Peter began to hack at his wrist with the dagger.

Wendy forced herself to watch. It sickened her, but she knew that it was important to see, to remember. She had never felt closer to Peter than now. He was part of her, a Siamese twin. In all the world, only the two of them were alike. Only they could fly. Only they would never grow up. Peter's pain gave her no pleasure, yet neither did she share it. It carved away at her, dull and relentless. She felt as if, bit by bit, without noticing it until now, she'd been cut to pieces just like she'd cut Bill, only *inside*. It had started with her shadow. Then, with each day she'd spent chained up, with each story she'd told, another piece of her had been cut away. She'd lost something when Eric died. With each scrap of flesh she'd subtracted from Bill's anatomy, she'd diminished herself even more. She had whittled herself almost down to nothing. Or, not to nothing, but into a new thing, a form not yet complete, that Peter was putting the finishing touches on now.

When he had cut himself free, Wendy thought, she, too, would be free. Free of him. Free of her old self. Then she'd know who or what she was. Who or what she had become. She waited to find out.

With a final shriek, Peter cut through. He turned to Wendy, the dagger raised, his green eyes empty of reason. He lunged for her.

A filmy darkness slipped between them. The dagger flew aside in an angry storm of bells. Peter howled again, and now Wendy covered her ears, for the agony in this cry dwarfed anything that had come before.

Peter and Jinglebell struggled on the floor. Then Peter suddenly grew still and pale as death. As Wendy watched, time sank its hooks into his body. She saw his skin sag in wrinkles and fat, saw a black beard bloom upon his chin, his limbs swell and burst the suit of greenery that he wore. A flow of flesh smothered his wound until only a bloodless stump remained, smooth and waxy as a candle with no wick. The collar of bells dropped to the floor of the home under the ground with a last jingle. He opened his eyes.

"Who . . . who am I?" he asked.

"You're the captain of a pirate ship," Wendy said, as if it were a story. "There was a mutiny. You were set ashore here with your loyal crew. Don't you remember?"

He sat up. And looked at his stump. "I remember . . . There was a fight. A betrayal."

"You have to go back. Take your ship. Leave this place."

He looked around, blinking. "What is this place? I almost think I know it."

"This is Never . . . I mean, *Ever*land," she said. "You knew it once, a long, long time ago. When you were a boy."

He nodded and got to his feet, stooping because of the low ceiling. "What happened to my clothes?"

Wendy pointed to the clothes she'd stripped from Bill. "Get dressed and I'll take you to your crew, Captain."

The clothes were a perfect fit. He picked up Bill's dagger and slipped it into his belt, took a torch from the wall and followed Wendy outside, into the night. Somehow, Wendy knew what she would find there. Sure enough, all the lost boys had grown up, just like Peter. None of them remembered who they were. But they remembered that Peter was Captain. They saluted at the sight of him.

"Good lads."

"Aye, aye, sir!"

"I believe we've got a ship to take back."

Under cover of darkness, Peter and his crew had no trouble taking the pirate ship from the men that Bill had left behind, who were too drunk and dispirited to put up a fight. Peter had bound Bill's curved dagger to his stump, and with every swing of his arm, men fell like wheat before a scythe. "No prisoners, lads!" he shouted. Even his crew feared him. They began to call him Hook.

Peter's eyes brightened when he heard. "Hook, is it?" He gave orders to raise anchor and set sail for the nearest port. "I'll have them make me a proper hook! A hook worthy of the name!"

8. EVERLAND

The ship got under way at dawn. Wendy watched until it was lost in the mists that rose from the sea each morning. Then she flew back to the stockade and opened the gates. Ten or so small boys came wandering out, rubbing their eyes in the light. They smiled when they saw Wendy, then burst into tears and threw their arms around her.

Wendy asked if they could take her back to where they'd come from. The oldest boy, who looked to be no more than five, and who said his name was Tristan, nodded solemnly and took her hand. The other boys gathered round, each of them touching her. They led Wendy into the jungle.

They walked for what seemed like hours. Soon the sun was well up in the sky, but even so a perpetual dawn or twilight lingered under the thick canopy of jungle foliage. The cries of birds and the sounds of unseen animals surrounded them on all sides. Wendy would have rather flown, but the boys would not release her.

Then one of them screamed.

Wendy looked.

There was a girl.

A dead girl. Her body prickled with arrows.

"Stay here," Wendy told the boys.

She went on. Now she saw the bodies of girls everywhere. Girls younger than her. Girls her own age. Wendy had to stop and sit down. She knew she'd found the lost girls. She remembered Eric saying that he wouldn't be a lost boy until he went back to the No-no-never-no and . . .

And what? she heard herself asking.

And this.

Wendy thought of flying after Peter. But what could she do, one girl against a ship of pirates? She knew that if she went after them, she'd never come back. After a while, she got up. She went deeper into the jungle. There were more bodies. Not only lost girls, but lost boys, too, boys she recognized from the home under the ground.

Then Wendy stepped into a clearing. She caught her breath. She was at the foot of the volcano. It rose up as if there was no end to it. It was covered so densely with foliage that it might almost have been a tree itself, the biggest tree that ever was.

Now she saw that there was an opening in the foliage at the very base of the volcano. She saw bare rock and, in the rock, a small crevice. When she drew near, an exhalation of hot air drove her back. There were bodies here, too, as if there'd been a last stand. No one was left alive. Wendy wondered if she was alive. Perhaps she was dead and didn't know it.

She remembered the locket around her neck. She took it out. Inside the silver heart, pierced by the stub of arrow, was her shadow. If she opened the locket, the shadow would emerge and reattach itself just as Peter's shadow had done. She hoped it wouldn't hurt as much. The fragment of arrow held the locket closed at first, but finally she was able to draw it out with her teeth. Wendy opened the locket.

It was empty.

Wendy sank to the ground with a moan. All the time she'd thought that bits and pieces of her were being cut away inside, it had been her *shadow* that was disappearing. Even when severed from her body, her shadow had still been connected somehow, invisibly. But now it was gone. She no longer had a shadow. She had never felt so alone. She began to cry.

"Why are you crying, girl?"

Wendy looked up, and there were the boys from the stockade. It was the boy called Tristan who had spoken. He repeated his question.

"Because I'm alone," she said.

"So are we," he said. "Can't we be alone together?"

Wendy drew the boys into her arms. "Yes, Tristan," she said. "I think maybe we can."

So they cleared away the bodies of the lost girls and the lost boys and buried them. Then they built a little house at the foot of the volcano out of branches and palm leaves and odds and ends that Wendy fetched back from the home under the ground. She was never going to live under the ground again, she told them. The boys said they didn't blame her. They started to call her mother, but Wendy put a stop to that: "There's no mothers in Everland. No fathers, either. Just brothers and sisters."

Every day, Wendy and her brothers went out into the jungle for food. There were fruits and vegetables of all kinds, and soon they had begun to grow their own food. There was no more hunting.

Every night, Wendy told them stories. Soon they were making up stories of their own. They took turns telling them.

One day, the tremors began again. They lasted a long time. Wendy and her bothers huddled in the little house, afraid. When the tremors ended, they went out to check for damage. Steam was pouring from the narrow crevice in the rock at the base of the volcano. As Wendy watched, a naked girl wriggled out. Then came a boy, then another girl, then two more girls and a boy, until three girls and two boys stood there, holding hands and blinking in the sunlight.

"I'm Corin," said one.

"I'm Callie."

"I'm Macey."

"I'm Emma."

"I'm Peter."

"I'm Wendy," she said. "Welcome to Everland."

A long time went by. Wendy's brothers and sisters grew up, though she never did. But she was never alone, because new brothers and sisters came to replace the ones that grew up. When they did grow up, Wendy didn't battle them or send them out to sea in a boat as Peter had done. One day, she'd flown to the top of the volcano and looked inside. Instead of fire and lava and smoke, what she saw was a window into the world she'd come from. It was a different place now, but she recognized it. Men and women were still fighting there. So whenever one of her brothers and sisters grew up, Wendy had them climb to the top of the volcano and jump through the window, into the world on the other side. They had children there, boys and girls who didn't wind up in Everland but who helped to build a new Everland bit by bit in the world on the other side. Every so often Wendy would fly up to the volcano and take a look at how they were doing. The world on the other side was changing, but very, very slowly. It was going to take a long time to build Everland there. But time was one thing there was plenty of in Everland, so Wendy wasn't worried about that.

There was only one thing that worried Wendy: the idea that Peter might return. She had never forgotten the dead girls and boys. She told all her brothers and sisters about what had happened and taught them how to defend themselves, how to fight. Boys and girls kept watch all day and night perched on the sides of the volcano, where they could see for miles.

One day, Wendy heard the cry she'd been dreading.

"Ship ahoy!"

She flew to see. It was a big ship with sails as white as clouds and a small black flag that flapped against them like a crow. She flew closer. The flag bore the skull and crossbones.

"Ahoy, Wendy!" cried a voice she recognized right away. Peter stood on deck, waving to her. At the end of his arm, a silver hook flashed in the sun. "It's Peter! Peter Hook! I remember everything! No hard feelings, eh, Wendy? Let's shake hands and make up!"

There was a flash of white. The air was rent by the most tremendous crash that Wendy had ever heard. Something big hurtled by. The pirates were firing cannon.

Wendy flew back to Everland as fast as she could. Her brothers and sisters were waiting. "It's Captain Hook," she told them. "He's come back."

"We're not afraid," said a small girl. "We'll fight for Everland!"

"For Wendy and Everland!" went up the cry.

And they did fight. Oh, how they fought!

The story of that fight would take a hundred pages to tell. A hundred

pages to tell how the pirates captured Wendy, and how she got free; how
Peter Hook plugged the crevice at the foot of the volcano with gunpowder,
and what happened when he blew it up; how the boys and girls of Everland
started a mutiny in Peter's crew; how Wendy and Peter fought to the death
on the lip of the volcano.

That would be a good story. And it's a story they never grow tired of
hearing in Everland.

But the important thing is this. When the fighting was over, and the
pirate ship had sailed away, the brothers and sisters of Everland buried their
dead and bandaged their wounds and went on living. And no matter how
many times the pirates came back—and pirates *always* come back—they
did just the same. They went on growing up and climbing to the top of the
volcano and jumping through the window into the world on the other side.

They are still doing it. If you look carefully, you can see them, and their
children, all around us. You may know them by a sparkle in the eye that
does not dim with age. They are in no hurry. They act as if they had all the
time in the world. They do their hard work the best way they can, with our
help or despite us. Perhaps it doesn't matter if we help or not. Perhaps
Everland is impossible in a world where children grow up so quickly and
forget so completely everything they once knew about being a child.

Perhaps.

But like the child I used to be, I will pretend in the face of all fact and
reason that it is not.

CHANGELING

BACK WHEN I LIVED WITH JUDY, THE APARTMENT ALWAYS
seemed too small. We were forever bumping into each other, getting
on each other's nerves. But once she was gone, it suddenly became full of
space. So much space, I felt lost in it all. I'd catch myself wandering from
room to room as though waking from a dream, look at my watch and see
that hours and not minutes had gone by. Yet though a whole month had
passed since Judy walked out, it seemed like just yesterday. I could still hear
the front door slam. I wondered if some obscure law of physics was at
work.

I started spending extra time at the institute. Late nights, weekends. I
even took up jogging. Jogging! But sooner or later, I always had to return to
the apartment and memories of Judy. Things weren't going too well.

That Sunday the parking lot of the institute was empty. The security guard,
watching a football game on a portable set, was surprised and put out to see
me. He eyed me with suspicion, plainly disapproving of my jogging suit
and sneakers, not at all the proper attire for whatever it was he imagined we
scientists did.

I had the whole place to myself. My footsteps rang in the empty corridors like the footsteps of a giant. Once in the cubicle I shared with Dr.
Sanford, I punched up last week's data and set to work.

This was the unavoidable drudgery of the search for new particles. They
were so rare, so maddeningly random, that only by amassing mountains of
data did we have a prayer of detecting them at all. And our method! Shoot

electrons at each other and watch the sparks fly. Like kids playing at marbles, as Judy used to say.

Even so, somewhere in each haystack of data a needle of proof might lurk to prick a probing eye. I wasn't hopeful, but it was easy to become lost and forgetful amid the simulated tracery of subatomic collisions generated upon the computer screen, brightly feathered trajectories suggesting an order invisible to the naked eye, like angels dancing on the head of a pin. There was a kind of comfort in that.

But not a lasting comfort. The tracks I followed did not lead away from Judy, but towards her. Her absence was everywhere; she was so much a part of my universe that she might have been an electron herself, a cloud of electrons spread wider than the Milky Way. Not once in all the years we'd known each other, not when we first met, or fell in love, or moved in together, had she seemed so beautiful, so desirable, so perfect to me as she did now, lover no longer, split up, moved out, gone beyond the reach of telescope and microscope. Gone.

I had her new number, but I'd promised not to call until I heard from her. She needed her space. I was determined to honor this open-ended promise in order to prove my worthiness and win her back. Of course at heart I was afraid to call, afraid to hear the tone of her voice as she recognized my timid hello. Afraid above all to hear the voice of my rival: for there must always be a rival. If there were no rival, it would be necessary to invent one.

But this particular rival was Judy's invention. Though I didn't know him by name or sight or smell, his existence was more than theoretical despite her denials. He was no particle indicated in the equations but not yet proved to be or not to be. That he was, I knew, and I knew, too, *what* he was: everything I was not, uninhibited Hyde to my too gentle Jekyll. I didn't hate him. On the contrary.

The urge to run came over me like it always did when I thought of Judy in the arms of her lover. The service tunnel to the institute's particle accelerator—the synchrotron—made a perfect track nearly five miles in circumference. Over the last month I'd gotten into the habit of doing a lap each weekend before leaving the lab.

I hurried down the hall to the small room that housed the target area, final destination of the accelerated particles. From there I entered the service tunnel along which, through shielded tubes attached to the ceiling, the particles were accelerated by the generation of electromagnetic fields to speeds approaching that of light.

I turned on the fluorescent lights and gazed for a moment at the tangled network of white pipes and dark cables. I was standing upon the metal grill-work of the technicians' walkway. Before me the tunnel curved gently out of sight. Behind, an identical view presented itself.

I took a deep breath, touched my toes to limber up, and began to jog. Though all portions of the tunnel were so alike I might almost have been running in place, I was able to gauge my progress by the appearance of a thin black line along the inside wall every tenth of a mile.

I imagined that the synchrotron was activated. My body tingled as if electrons streamed overhead, quickened towards the violent collisions out of which some unstable particle might be born to pass away in an eyeblink of decay. I felt like I was drawing nearer to Judy with each stride. Or, if not to her, then to my rival. How could I approach one without approaching the other?

The echoes of footsteps came from ahead of me and behind me, as if I, pursuing, were myself pursued. I stepped up my pace, hoping to overtake the footsteps in front while outdistancing those behind. But they matched me with mocking exactitude. I realized that the footsteps I was chasing and those chasing me belonged to the same person. But who that person was, my rival or myself, I could no longer say.

I was a quarter of the way through. I passed the halfway mark. Then three-quarters. Was that a stranger's back I glimpsed vanishing around the next curve? My side ached, my lungs wheezed, my legs were slabs of lead, but I spurred myself on with a final effort.

Just then I heard a dull wallop as if the air up ahead had hiccupped. But no alarm jangled; the fluorescents cast their edgy light without a flicker. The only sounds were my breathing and the slap of my sneakers on the grill-work. I rounded the curve and found myself back where I had started, outside the target area.

I reached for the door, only to yank my hand back. The handle was hot. "Hello!" I cried. "Anyone in there?"

From the other side of the door, I heard something like a moan. Removing my shirt, I wrapped it around my hand and, thus insulated, wrenched the door open.

A gust of hot air swept over me. I fell back, shielding my face with my muffled hand. Then I entered the room.

A naked body lay upon the floor. The body was so shrunken, the skin so shriveled, that it resembled a withered log more than a human being. The eyes were hard knots bulging beneath dry wood, the nose a branch snapped off, the limbs blunt stumps. Steam rose from the skin as if freshly pulled from a fire. The room and its equipment, as far as I could tell with a quick glance, were undisturbed.

I knelt beside the body. "Are you all right? Can you hear me?"

Once again I heard a weak but urgent moan, though I saw no sign of the mouth that made it. What must have been an arm rose in a gruff pantomime of pleading. The limb was like a rough-hewn club. A perverse fascination compelled me, despite my revulsion, to touch it.

Suddenly there was a hand where there had been no hand. It burst from the blunt end of the club in a flowering of flesh, strong pink fingers wriggling to intertwine with those of my own hand. I strove in terror to pull away, but could not. My limbs were petrified. My strength served only to raise the man—for I saw now that it was a man—higher, as though lifting him from a bed. At the sound of my shriek, the bark that was his face cracked in a sort of smile, and the knots that were his eyes ran with the sap of sight.

I felt myself shrinking as I watched the man grow. Before my eyes he took on the semblance of my very self, his skin soft and malleable as hot wax. Our hands were gloved in a single flesh; it was impossible to tell where I ended and he began.

All horror fled. How could I fear myself? No, it was not fear that I felt; I yearned to embrace the strange, familiar form, to feel its warmth, to taste its salt. But whose desire was this? What had overtaken me? I tried to put my questions into words, but no sooner did my voice begin to croak than it sputtered and fell away, stolen.

Our eyes locked. I shivered at what I saw there. Then his lips were on my lips. A powerful suction drew my tongue into his mouth. I felt my soul unspooling.

All that remained was a small green sapling. I took it with me when I left the institute and planted it in a pot on the balcony of the apartment. I whispered the old words to make it thrive, wondering what shape it would take. Later the phone rang. When I lifted the instrument from its cradle, I heard a voice like Judy's, only smaller.

THE CATS OF THERMIDOR

MY FRIENDS HAD INFORMED ME IN NO UNCERTAIN TERMS THAT anyone who was stupid enough to go to Paris that summer would deserve everything that he got. Didn't I read the papers? Didn't I watch TV? People were getting blown up every day over there in a rash of bombings that had the police baffled and the city terrified. To listen to them, it almost seemed that it might be safer to visit Beirut or El Salvador than a Parisian café, the preferred target of the terrorists.

I was traveling to Paris to gain access to certain documents in the Archives de France pertaining to that episode of the French Revolution known as the Reign of Terror. With them, I had reason to hope I would be able to make the original contribution to history that I had dreamed of for so long . . . and in the process shore up my shaky prospects for tenure at the university. It had taken more than a year to secure the necessary permission from the French government, and I wasn't about to let a few bombs stop me now.

I arrived at Roissy Airport on the evening of July 28th, the 10th of Thermidor by the old revolutionary calendar and, not coincidentally, the date of the execution of the dictator Maximilien Robespierre—the act which had rung down the curtain on the Reign of Terror in 1794. Months before, when making my plane reservations, it had given me a secret thrill to think that I would begin my intensive research into this bloody and fascinating period on the anniversary of its close; like most historians, when it comes to dates I am virtually superstitious.

I had already arranged through the university's housing exchange program to sublet an apartment for the length of my stay in Paris. I gave the address to a taxi driver in my untamed Midwestern French, then sat back to enjoy the ride. I must have dozed off, because for a time it seemed to me that the streets we drove through were those of revolutionary times, ablaze with lamps and crowded with carriages and people in a feverish mélange of misery and ostentation that threatened with each moment to explode into a riot, or worse. Everything was just as I had always imagined from reading the history books. But the screech of the brakes as we pulled to a stop outside 5 Rue Augereau woke me. Still half-asleep, I fumbled for the proper coins to pay the taxi, then hoisted my two suitcases and entered the building that was to be my home for the next month, all the time I had before the start of a new semester would end my research.

There was an ill-lit, narrow entranceway that extended back to angularly spiraling stairs of glossy dark wood. The apartment the university had procured for me was on the fifth floor. Squinting against the dark, I began to climb the staircase, which creaked ominously with each step I took. As I turned the corner to the fourth floor landing, I tripped over something in the shadows. A sudden, anguished scream nearly sent me tumbling back down the stairs, my suitcases right behind me. When I had regained my balance, I saw that a large black cat stood blocking my way. I didn't think I'd ever seen a cat so black, as if formed out of the darkness that pooled in the corners of the staircase. Its back was arched, its fur gone spiky. Its eyes burned into me like twin emerald fires and from its throat came an awful sound that made me fear, for a second, that it was about to throw itself upon me. Just then the door to my left opened, and the cat sprang inside. I had just time enough before the door slammed shut to smile weakly at the young woman there—but her eyes seemed no more forgiving than her cat's had been.

Continuing up the stairs, I noticed a sharp stinging in my right leg. When I finally got inside my apartment and turned on the light, I saw that the son of a bitch had clawed me right through my pants. Despite what seemed at first glance a lot of blood, the cut wasn't deep, and I managed to find some bandages and iodine in the bathroom

The wound tended to, I took stock of my new apartment.

According to the university, the place belonged to an artist who was vacationing in Tunisia. It was a small and tidy studio crowded with a bed, a desk, and a bookcase filled with old English and French paperbacks. There was a nook that served as kitchen—complete with stove, sink, and midget refrigerator—and a cranny for bathroom that boasted a toilet and shower. Two windows overlooked a small courtyard wrapped in the shadows of laundry hung out to dry in the sticky summer air. It was the refrigerator that claimed my immediate attention; tired as I was, I found that I was hungrier still. But the cupboard was bare; I would have to go out if I wanted to eat.

The street was empty and quiet between the skewed shapes of cars parked half on and half off the sidewalks. I picked a direction and started walking. The hot air was stirred by an occasional hot breeze. I rounded a corner, and there—burning high above the ornately frescoed fronts of the apartment buildings along the Avenue Rapp, like a ladder of pure light left leaning against the dull, yellow sky—was the Eiffel Tower. Farther up the avenue the tables and chairs of cafés spilled out onto the sidewalk like bright, inviting oases. People clustered there, eating and drinking and talking despite the lateness of the hour.

I took a seat at a table where someone had left a copy of that day's *Paris-Soir*. After ordering, I picked it up and read it while waiting for my meal. A story on the unsolved bombings caught my eye.

Five people had died in the latest attack, the twelfth in the series of bombings which, so far at least, had struck only in or close to cafés, a pattern the police felt was due primarily to the easy accessibility of such places. As with the eleven bombings that had preceded it, the choice of target in the latest attack seemed completely random and witnesses were unable to provide the slightest leads. The explosion itself had been powerful enough to destroy whatever evidence the terrorists may have left behind. Still, enough evidence had been gathered after previous bombings to convince the police that all the attacks were linked, probably the work of a previously unknown terrorist group despite the many calls and letters from known groups that never failed to claim responsibility in the aftermath of each attack. Though they had not yet solved the case, the police were confident, on the basis of information that was being withheld from the public for obvious reasons, that a breakthrough was imminent. The story closed with a quote from a police official urging people to remain calm but to exercise caution in visiting cafés. That advice sounded good to me, even if, as it appeared, my fellow customers had decided to ignore it. If these bombings struck only in and around cafés, then I would just make certain to stay away from them. I ate my meal quickly, paid the check, and hurried home.

Back in my apartment, the air was hot and stuffy. I went to the windows above the courtyard and flung them open, leaning out in hopes of a breeze. Then I jerked back, startled by the hiss of hot breath and the sight of emerald eyes blazing in the darkness. It was the same cat I had tripped over earlier, sitting patiently on my window ledge as if it had been waiting there for hours for me to poke my head outside. How it had climbed up so high I couldn't imagine. As soon as I pulled away, the cat jumped lightly to the floor, where it sat looking up at me with eyes glowing like green lanterns at the bottom of the sea, purring loudly and lashing its tail from side to side. It was a big cat.

I leaned down cautiously to pet it, remembering all too well the scratch on my leg, which was still stinging. But the cat was friendly now, pushing its head against my hand.

"Nice kitty," I said. "No hard feelings. I'd offer you some milk, but I haven't had a chance to go shopping."

The cat began to lick its paws as if to say that it had already eaten.

I had to laugh. "You want to stay for a while? I guess you can get down the same way you got up. Me, I'm turning in."

I had just taken off my shirt when there was a knock at the door. "Who is it?"

A woman's voice answered in French-accented English. "Your neighbor from downstairs. Have you seen my cat by any chance?"

I opened the door. "Come on in. He's here. You can introduce us."

I did my best not to stare; the woman was wearing a black silk dressing gown, loosely belted, the top open just enough to reveal the pale, moonish curve of one breast cupped in shadow. Her eyes were wide and almond-shaped, nearly as green as her cat's.

She hesitated in the doorway, seeing that I was half-dressed. "Excuse me; you were about to sleep . . ."

"That's all right. Please come in." I didn't want to let such a beautiful sight slip away so easily.

As she came in, the woman's eyes went straight to her cat, which, with almost the same motion, turned its eyes to her. I was to see it many times, this uncanny synchronization of movement between them, evidence of the deep bond they shared, but I never grew used to it. She held out her arms, and the cat leaped into them with a throaty meow. Then she turned back to me with a smile, absently stroking the cat, which rested in her arms as though cradled in the sturdy branches of a tree. "I hope he didn't get into any mischief."

"I think he wanted to apologize for scaring me before." I decided not to mention the scratch. "I'm just amazed he was able to climb up here."

She laughed. "He can climb just about anywhere he wants to. He's always getting into trouble."

"Sounds like a real terror."

"He can be."

We stood for a moment without speaking, looking at each other with timid smiles. I had the distinct feeling that she didn't want our encounter to be such a brief one any more than I did. "My name's Paul," I said. "You speak English very well."

She laughed, delighted. "I don't, really. I went to school in Chicago a long time ago. I'd like to go back some day. I've told Max all about it; he wants to go too."

I bristled at the name of a potential rival. "Max . . . ?"

"My cat. I'm Chantal."

"Enchanted to make your acquaintance, Chantal. You too, Max." I held out my hand jokingly to take Max's paw, but before I could touch it the cat flexed its claws and struck at me. The attack was so unexpected that I couldn't pull away in time. I watched in shocked surprise as blood began to well up from a gash in my palm, thick and dark.

"Oh, Max!" Chantal dropped the cat to the floor and took my hand in hers. "I'm so sorry . . . "

I didn't know what to say. I could have killed Max, but I didn't want Chantal to be angry with me. I decided to be a good sport, mumbling something about washing out the cut.

But Chantal did not release my hand. Instead, never taking her eyes from mine, she raised it almost reverently to her lips and, with her rough, wet tongue, licked away the blood. A hot tingling started at her touch that washed from my palm outwards, over my entire body, until my knees began to tremble. When she lowered my hand, I saw that her cheek was smeared with blood.

Without another word, I slipped my hands under Chantal's robe and pulled her down to the floor.

We kissed, teeth hitting teeth, the breath crushed from our bodies as we rolled over and over the hard floor. It was as if, since our passion had been kindled by blood, it could only find expression in bloodletting. Chantal was all over me, biting and scratching. I tasted the bitter stickiness of blood on my lips and felt its warmth dribble from my shoulders down my back. But my wounds only made me hungrier for more of these strange, excruciating pleasures. I felt as though I was continually dying and being reborn at her cruel, loving hands and mouth. I could deny her nothing. For the first time in my life, I was emptied of every desire but the will to surrender totally to another human being, and this I did gladly, opening myself to her invasion without guilt or shame or remorse. The pain lifted me right out of my skin until I couldn't hold back any longer. As I felt my control slipping, I spied Max's disembodied eyes glittering greenly in the shadows across the room like those of a demonic Cheshire cat.

It was only when the first pale light of dawn began to seep through the windows that we stopped. I led Chantal to my bed, and we lay down together as Max curled up by our feet. Though by all rights I should have been exhausted, I was too excited to sleep. All night Chantal and I had barely spoken, and now, clutching her to me with all the strength I had left, I wanted to tell her everything about myself, to reveal all my secret hopes and fears, and to hear all about hers, until nothing separated us.

I spoke of my reasons for coming to Paris, of the documents I suspected lay forgotten in the dusty vaults of the Archives and how they would bring me fame and fortune. I told her what it had been like growing up in a place called Lucas, Missouri, of my parents' dreams and how those dreams had ended in disappointment and divorce despite their best intentions, of my years in New York City as a student and, finally, a professor at the university, wrestling with the hard legacy of their dreams—my obligation to fulfill them.

Chantal listened, lazily scratching the bandage on my leg with one toe. "Is Max responsible for this, too?"

I admitted that he was, but said that I forgave him because he had brought us together.

"You're right; this was all his idea," she said.

"Do you always do what Max tells you?"

"Always, always."

I laughed. "And how does he tell you to earn a living, for example?"

"Right now I design jewelry. Pet jewelry."

"Are you serious?"

"Pet jewelry is going to be the next big thing, Paul. For example, cat collars. All too often these collars are merely restraints, shackles used to make pets into prisoners. My collars are designed with cats in mind—fashion statements of feline personality."

"I see. And you sell them in pet shops?"

Chantal shook her head. "The idea was too revolutionary for them. But I don't need their help. Max is always bringing stray cats home. I feed them, slip on a collar with my name and phone number attached, and send them back into the streets. It's free advertising."

"And people call you?"

"Well, not many. Not yet. But business will pick up once the idea catches on. You'll see. Every day there are more of my cats in the city."

It sounded like a crazy idea to me, but I knew that Parisians were supposed to be more than a little eccentric when it came to their pets. Maybe Chantal was a marketing genius. We talked a little while longer, but at last jet lag caught up with me, and I fell asleep.

I dreamed I was wandering the deserted streets of Paris, picking my way past the abandoned shells of automobiles and the burned-out facades of buildings as the shadowy fingers of evening groped inch by inch across the city. It was as if whatever had taken place there had left no one behind to clean up the mess and start over again. The muggy air smothered all sound and movement save my own, and my steps were so light as to be themselves almost silent.

Yet I was not alone. It soon became clear that something was pacing me, out of sight and far more silent than I, herding me toward some destination as though by alterations in air pressure. I tried to break away from the unseen net that I felt tightening around me, but I could not. Wherever I turned, something was there, invisible but undeniable, forcing me to stay on course. I began to run, no longer aware of my surroundings, blindly trying to escape whatever it was that pursued me. At last I came to the Champs Elysees, stretching straight to the Arc de Triomphe.

I took a step, then stopped short, unable to breathe. My hand flew to my throat. There was a collar there. It dragged me back step by step, as though attached to an invisible leash. Finally the pressure slackened and I could breathe again. I turned around. On the tops of the buildings that lined both sides of the avenue as far as I could see sat hundreds and hundreds of cats, cats of every size and color, from mangy alley toms, their fur matted or coming out in patches, to pampered showroom breeds. The sound of their purring suddenly filled the air. At first, I was afraid, but then I realized that the noise was coming from my own throat.

When I awoke late that morning, Chantal had gone. There was a note pinned to the bathroom mirror inviting me down for dinner that night. I showered and dressed in a hurry, eager to begin my research at the Archives.

The Rue Augereau was much changed from the gloomy street of the night before. The cobblestones were puddled here and there from laundry hung on lines that stretched between the houses, and the smell of sunlight drying the clothes filled the hot air with a scent that bubbled to my head like champagne. I walked along, whistling, with a smile for everyone and Chantal's face constantly before my eyes. I even stopped for coffee and croissant at the café I had visited the night before. What bomb could touch me now? I was falling in love with Chantal, and the pleasure of surrendering to the emotion made me feel invulnerable, as though my life carried a secret charm.

The Archives were located in the Marais, the oldest section of Paris, in a group of colorless, decrepit buildings insulated from the bustling world outside by high, thick walls that seemed impenetrable even to time's patient infiltration. Like so many public buildings of Paris, those of the Archives had begun as private dwellings in the honeyed days preceding the Revolution. But not a shred of the laughter and light of those days remained. Walking across the dreary, cobblestoned courtyard, the echoes of my steps were muffled as if under the folds of a heavy blanket, and a slight chill in the damp air as I entered the main building made me wish that I had thought to bring a sweater.

The security was tighter than that which I had experienced upon entering the country, and it was some time, even with my letter of authorization signed by the director of the Archives, before I was admitted. I felt as though I was entering a prison, a modern Bastille. A frosty young woman led me briskly through a maze of dim corridors and down some stairs to the tiny room which, apparently, had already been prepared for me.

The room was lit by one ancient bulb that oozed its gray light unevenly over lopsided stacks of disintegrating boxes from which yellowing papers leaked like the stuffing of an ancient sofa. There was a dust-covered desk with a wobbly chair and a telephone that my guide told me was connected to the library in case I needed further assistance.

"We've supplied you with photocopies of all materials from the relevant period," she said, speaking in English despite the fact that I had addressed her only in French. "Should you desire to examine the originals, that can possibly be arranged at a later date. There is a bathroom down the hall to your right. Please do not leave this room for any other reason. I'll be back to collect you this afternoon at five o'clock precisely."

"But I didn't bring any lunch," I said in amazement.

"You can order something by telephone, and it will be delivered." And with that, she left.

I sat down at the desk, annoyed by the lack of common courtesy almost as much as the excessive security. The room gave me a constricted, abandoned feeling that I didn't enjoy much either and was cold into the bargain. I began to shiver a little. Tomorrow, I vowed, I would bring along a sweater and some food. I picked up the telephone and ordered a cup of hot coffee, then set to work with a vengeance, determined not to let physical discomfort affect my work adversely.

The more I read, the more it became clear to me that I was on the right track. Not only did I find one of the documents I was looking for almost at once, but indications kept cropping up that others might also exist, still more obscure. I could scarcely contain my excitement as I sat there, my coffee forgotten, reading the words set down so long ago by the most enlightened men of their times, men who had—most of them with the best of intentions—rung down a second dark age upon their country that had threatened, for a time, to plunge the rest of Europe into endless seas of blood and terror.

Here were the grisly accounts of cold-blooded murder and torture, the spontaneous and not-so-spontaneous massacres, the logical yet horrifying justifications used by lawyers become butchers to defend the regrettable necessities of their new profession. And every word in the faded photocopies came back to one man, the chief architect of the Reign of Terror and its most enthusiastic disciple: Maximilien Robespierre.

It was impossible to read that name, to pronounce it silently and feel its sharp edges scrape away at the inside of my skull, without a shiver of fear made worse by the claustrophobic chill of the reading room. Gradually, imperceptibly, it came to seem that his icy and vindictive spirit had cut its way free of his decayed body and filled the air around me like an evil cloud. I could almost sense his eyes glittering at my back, burning with revenge and envy and greed like a furnace run amuck, stoked on the souls of countless innocent victims. I found myself half-listening for the heavy tread of soldiers' boots and the sudden knock upon the door that would announce a fate from which there could be no appeal. More than once I had to leave the room, to step into the bathroom and splash my face with cold water before I could bring myself to continue, my reflection in the mirror haggard and drawn, like a stranger's. Yet, at the same time, I felt compelled to continue because of the amazing progress I was making.

When the knock at my door came at five, I gave a cry and nearly jumped out of my chair in fright. I grinned at the same frosty young woman who had led me down earlier, overjoyed to see even her unfriendly face. She looked at me as though all her worst prejudices against Americans had just been more than confirmed, but I no longer cared. I just wanted to get out of there, to see Chantal again.

But my heightened state of nervous awareness persisted even after I had left the Archives. The sidewalks were crowded with people heading home from work, jostling each other into streets jammed with noisy cars. It was only with difficulty that I was able to wade into that stream of packed humanity that surged all around me like one of the bloodthirsty Revolutionary mobs I had just been reading about. The sight of so many bobbing heads had obvious and unpleasant connotations.

I bought a paper in an effort to distract myself, but the headlines were once again concerned with bombings—another café had been blown up that morning. I found myself reflecting on the difference between the guillotine of yesterday and the bombs of today as instruments of terror. Behind the differing methods and justifications, wasn't the terror itself the same, not so much a result of the actions of evil or misguided men as the cause of those actions? I felt as though a dark and evil cloud had hung over Paris ever since the Reign of Terror, infecting first one, then another, would-be reformer. I seemed to sense that cloud now, settling over the City of Light cloaked in evening's sticky shadows.

It wasn't until I stood inside Chantal's apartment kissing her beside the door as Max twined his body in and out of the spaces between our legs that I was finally able to breathe easier.

"Good day?" she asked.

"A strange one. I'm glad to see you."

"Me too."

"And who's this?" A strange cat had wandered into the room to see what all the commotion was about.

"My latest salesman. Max picked him up today. I was just about to put the collar on. Want to see?"

"Sure," I said.

Chantal took me by the hand and led me into what she called her workroom, though I saw by the unmade bed along one wall that she also slept there. There was a large table cluttered with thin, dark collars of a material that resembled plastic, along with metal studs, tangled wires and chips of colored glass—to name only what I could make out in one quick glance.

Chantal picked up a collar that had been decorated with curls of wire and patterns of colored glass and handed it to me. "What do you think?"

"Heavier than it looks." I hefted the unexpected weight. "What is it? Plastic?"

She nodded. "Well?"

It reminded me of something the first cat in space might wear. "Very interesting . . . "

Chantal took back the collar. "It's okay if you don't like it. Cats do. Watch."

And, in fact, the cat seemed more than willing to have Chantal fasten the heavy collar around its neck. Max sat close by during the whole operation, purring loudly as if to explain to the other cat its responsibilities as a walking collar advertisement. When Chantal showed the cat out the door, Max followed right behind.

He came back as we were finishing dinner, alone, appearing suddenly in the open window behind Chantal's back like a materializing ghost. Though he made no sound, Chantal was aware of his presence almost before I was. Max leaped into the room and then onto her lap, from which privileged position he regarded me coolly, his head just above the edge of the table, his eyes gleaming in the light of the single candle we had been dining by.

As we sipped our wine, I began to talk, slowly at first, struggling to find the proper words to express myself without sounding too crazy, about the feelings that had come over me in the Archives.

Chantal listened, stroking Max all the while with the same regular, hypnotic motion. "I know what you mean," she said when I had finished. "It's because of all the bombings. The fear they cause infects everything. But you just have to forget about it. There's nothing any of us can do."

But it seemed more than that, and I said so.

"Don't think about it so much," Chantal insisted. "It's just your imagination running wild. You have to calm down, distract yourself."

"And how do I do that?"

Chantal's answer was to stand up, tumbling Max to the floor. She began to dance in the candlelight, stripping off her clothes as she went. Weird shadows splashed across her, sliding off as if they could find no purchase on the almost blinding whiteness of her body save where her black hair grew—

and there they crouched like cats ready to spring. I could only sit there, my heart hammering in my chest, my mouth gone suddenly dry, as she circled the table slowly, moving to a music that only she could hear. Finally she knelt before me and unzipped my pants. I was already hard, and when she took me into her mouth I felt a storm break loose inside me.

That night our lovemaking was like a dark and furious ritual, an angry appeasement of all that was cruel or violent in ourselves that left our bodies battered and exhausted but our gluttonous souls hungry for more. The sleep that came to me at last was a fitful one, and I began to dream, almost at once it seemed, with a vivid intensity such as I had rarely, if ever, known.

I was pushing my way through a thick, unruly crowd in pursuit of a woman I recognized immediately as Chantal. So intent was I upon overtaking her that it was some time before I realized where—and when—I was. But the throng of people that filled the wide plaza, the style of clothing that they wore and the shouts that came from their throats, and, finally, the guillotine I saw mounted upon a scaffold at the center of the crowd—surrounded by half a dozen heads impaled on pikes like grisly flagpoles and festooned in blue, white, and red bunting spattered with gore—left no doubt but that I was in the Paris of the Terror, at the Place de la Revolution, where all the executions took place.

It was the afternoon of a hot summer day; the sun beat down with an intensity that seemed to drive the crowd mad with the lust for blood. People were hanging out of windows, clinging to lampposts, balancing on the edges of roofs as though about to hurl themselves into the churning sea of humanity below. Dogs and cats were everywhere underfoot, chasing each other through the crowd and fighting over scraps of food. Carts filled with bound captives on their way to the guillotine—some in the tattered remnants of aristocratic dress, others plainly "of the people"—plowed through that sea at a snail's pace behind a prow of gendarme's pikes that flashed gaily in the sun. The men and women in the carts faced their deaths as differently as they had no doubt lived their lives. Some wept and shivered uncontrollably, others had their eyes shut tight, their faces turned up to the sky as if praying for a miracle or begging forgiveness, while others watched the crowd with tranquil curiosity or naked hatred or pure, sleepy-eyed boredom. Here and there a condemned prisoner was attempting to harangue the crowd, but it was impossible to hear a word over the frenzied cries of ten thousand raw voices calling the same name—Robespierre.

A shiver went through me when I heard that name, and I raised my voice to shout with the others: "Show us Robespierre! Show us the dictator!"

The gendarmes pointed their pikes to the cart that happened to be at my shoulder, and I looked up to see a man slumped on the straw, his eyes closed, his thin, sallow face pressed against the wooden slats. I knew at once that I was seeing Robespierre by the strip of bloody linen that held his mangled jaw together, the result of a bungled suicide attempt moments before his arrest for treason. Dirty beads of perspiration stuck to his high, pale forehead like sluggish flies. I thought he was surely dead. A woman sprang upon the cart and, clutching the sidebars in one fist while waving the other above her head, cried out: "Murderer of my family, your agony fills me with joy! Go down to Hell with the curses of all wives and mothers!"

To my horror, Robespierre's eyelids flickered open at the sound of her voice. The woman shrieked at the sight of his eyes and tumbled back into the crowd. I understood her reaction. All intelligence had fled those orbs, yet they still burned, in their depths, with a malicious green fire that flickered so stubbornly that I wondered if even death could put it out. I felt the envious dregs of his power tug at me as though seeking to flee the prison of his wasted body, and it was all I could do to force my eyes away before he dispossessed me from mine.

I spotted Chantal shoving her way to the front of the crowd clustered around the scaffold and pushed after her. A pretty flush came to her cheeks as the guillotine did its work, and her eyes shone with real passion. Every so often she would raise a delicate wrist to her face to wipe away the blood that showered down from above or, forgetting herself, lick it from her lips with the darting pink tip of her tongue.

Finally Robespierre himself was taken from the cart. Somehow he found the strength to climb the stairs supported by two gendarmes. When he reached the top, the executioner snatched away his sky-blue cloak and pitched it to the crowd, which trampled the hated garment underfoot. Then he was led to the guillotine, his eyes feverishly searching the crowd. But before getting on with his work, the executioner paused a moment. As if coming to a sudden decision, he ripped the bandage from Robespierre's face. Robbed of its only support, his lower jaw dropped to his breast in a spouting torrent of blood. There burst from him a piercing wail that froze every heart with horror, a sound better suited to a cat than a human being.

I woke with a start, the echo ringing in my ears, to a weight pressing on my chest and the seagreen eyes of Robespierre glowing inches from my own. I gave a howl of mortal terror and sprang out of bed, knocking the body from my chest.

The lights came on. Huddled at the foot of the bed, Max was peering up at me hatefully, ready either to run or strike. I looked quickly away. Chantal sat up, blinking in the glare. "What happened? Are you all right?"

I was shaking. I sat down heavily on the bed, causing Max to bound off. It was plain what had happened, but I still couldn't bring myself to look at Max; the memory of the nightmare was too strong, the resemblance of the eyes uncanny. "Just a bad dream. I'm okay now." But it was a long while, hugging Chantal to me in the darkness, before I fell back asleep.

The next morning, Max was nowhere to be found. Chantal was angry at me for having scared him away, but I was glad he had gone. As I walked to the Archives, though, I couldn't shake the feeling that he was stalking me from the shadows, just like in my dream. It was all I could do not to break into a headlong run. Then, once inside the tiny reading room, my apprehensions of the day before returned stronger than ever, making it impossible for me to work. Despite the chill, I was sweating, my heart pounding, my spine crawling with unreasoning revulsion. I had to get out, to get away. It didn't matter where.

I walked aimlessly, quickly becoming lost. The farther I wandered, the more anxious I became, as though the guillotine's blade hung suspended above my neck by a fraying thread. Afternoon came and went, and evening's shadows began to lengthen like black cats stretching after a long sleep in the sun.

It was then that I saw the cat that Chantal had collared the day before sauntering down a side street as though headed for some tom-cattish rendezvous. I followed it on impulse, rounding the corner just in time to see the cat enter a crowded café. Seconds later, I was knocked off my feet by a punch of hot air that came roaring out of the café's doors and windows like the fist of the devil himself. Bits of glass and wood and other things I did not want to examine too closely were raining down from the sky. I picked myself up and began to run toward the twisted wreckage of the café, where a hellish chorus of cries for help and inarticulate raw screams merged with the sounds of crackling fire and the distant howl of the first sirens.

And then, abruptly, I stopped. I knew. Chantal was the bomber; the collars her bombs; the cats her carriers. How . . . ? But how didn't matter; I had to know why. I had to hear the reasons from her own lips. Then I would know what to do.

I turned around and ran back the way I had come, fighting my way like a drunken man past the people who had already gathered to help or just to watch. I was looking for a Metro station, and as I ran through the streets I had the impression that the deepening dusk was swarming with cats, a black river rushing right over my head and sweeping me along with it.

Riding home, I did not notice the stares of the other passengers or answer any of their questions. I knew that I was wounded from the blast, but I couldn't feel a thing inside or out. When the train stopped at the Ecole Militaire station, I leapt out, fighting off the hands that tried to hold me back, that had wanted to help me. I didn't need their help.

I ran up the street, turning onto the Rue Augereau as a blast knocked the windows out of the fourth floor of number five. It did not seem to be as large an explosion as the one I had just witnessed, but it was large enough. I found Chantal in her workroom. Her head had been blown off her body. I picked it up, staring into her glassy brown eyes in horrified fascination.

The police found me in that position and promptly placed me under arrest. I spent the next two days in jail. Apparently, Chantal had been a suspect in the bombings for a long time, and the police had been very close to making an arrest before the accidental explosion had saved them the trouble of having to prove their case. But the explosion had also robbed them of a terrorist to put on trial, and they were determined that I should make good that loss. However, despite their attempts to incriminate me, it became obvious that, though I had been her lover, I had known nothing of her terrorist activities. Finally they were obliged to release me.

My apartment had been damaged in the explosion, but I had nowhere else to go. It didn't matter to me anyway. Without Chantal, even the prospect of continuing my research had no appeal. But when I got home, a familiar sight greeted me, one that I had given up all hope of ever seeing again: Max. He looked pleased to see me, and I was sure glad to see him. I picked him up and hugged him, searching for Chantal's image in his deep green eyes.

"You're coming back to New York with me, Max. What do you think of that?"

He purred loudly, arching his back to receive my caress, his eyes boring into mine. I felt myself drowning in murky green waters as, far away, the muffled report of a guillotine's blade sinking into the block seemed to echo down the centuries.

The one thing that had bothered me about Chantal's death was that her eyes, frozen in her severed head, had been brown, not green. I had said nothing about the discrepancy to the police, believing that she must have been wearing contact lenses to disguise her appearance. But that question was cleared up for me the next time I happened to glance into a mirror.

My eyes were nearly as green as Max's.

MOONLIGHT BECOMES MAGENTA

IN THOSE DAYS THE TOWN LAY HALFWAY BETWEEN THE mountains and the jungle, a bastard claimed by neither parent. The only trail in or out cut over the highest peaks by a route murderous in the dry season and buried underneath mud or snow the rest of the year. Visitors were scarce, more like fleeting hallucinations than people such as ourselves—fugitives, holy men, and prospectors who descended out of the clouds and vanished forever into the green cauldron of hopes and dreams behind us, drunk on desire.

My father was the first to leave town and cross the mountains in more than a century. He ran off at the age of eighteen, a burning curiosity lighting his eyes, and returned ten years later, his eyes reduced to ash, hero of a revolution that had swept the country but left the town untouched. With him he brought his wife, a young girl from a seaside town who became like a sleepwalker at her first whiff of the steamy jungle air.

A year later I was stretching my mother's belly. My father had already forgotten the revolution, as if he had never left town. But over the mountains there were those who had reason to remember what he had been and fear what he might become again. One day the coffee pickers looked up to see a score of exhausted soldiers stumbling down the slopes. They conducted the soldiers to our door, carrying on as though Simon Bolívar himself was at their head.

The commanding officer, not Bolívar but a snot-nosed lieutenant who never identified himself by name, accused my father of assembling and training a guerrilla army in the depths of the jungle for the purpose of overthrowing the Republic in a broken voice that assaulted the ears like a weapon. The troopers held their rifles pointed negligently, as if by a coincidence that surprised even themselves, at my mother and grandfather. My father saw that he could not resist.

"Those are lies," he whispered for my grandfather's sake.

"There are no lies," the young lieutenant brashly informed him. "Only guilty and not-guilty."

After the arrest and execution, which took place in the capital five hundred miles away, my grandfather stopped eating. It shamed him to go on living without a chance of avenging his son, prevented not only by his advanced age but by the blindness that had darkened all his days. He took to his bed and remained there for months, not even rising to answer the calls of nature—a baby again at the age of eighty-three. Doctor Nuñez, our mayor (who had received his medical training from antiquated textbooks), advised my mother to expect the worst. A casket was ordered and Padre Mendez—an old crow in crumpled black cassock—summoned to administer the last rites.

It was in these funereal circumstances that I was born, a month premature. Doctor Nuñez pronounced me healthy, and my mother rejoiced at my manhood, rousing herself just long enough to announce that God had taken pity on her trials by sending a son. She named me Pablo, after my father (though out of deference to his memory, I have always been called Pablito, right down to this day).

With my birth, my grandfather's appetite for life returned. He believed that the duty of avenging my father's death had settled upon my shoulders like a great cape at my first uncomprehending cry. It was big on me, though, and I needed his help to make sure I grew into it. Even before I could speak, when words were strange and wonderful sounds innocent of meaning, Grandfather was whispering the stern and implacable demands of revenge in my ear for bedtime stories. He raised me almost single-handedly—my mother was too deep in her murky widow's world to notice. I was to be his eyes and, when the time came, his hands.

Two years after my father's murder, the first in a series of details, each consisting of eleven men—ten soldiers and an officer—arrived to garrison the town. Although at first they took their duties seriously—drilling in the plaza each morning, marching up into the hills and making a start at pushing back the jungle where it was encroaching on the town—before long the muggy heat and monotonous way of life it spawned had wilted their enthusiasm. Once the first detail was relieved and able to spread the word, replacements began to arrive looking as though they'd been posted to the very ends of the earth. The duty came to be considered a black mark, a slap in the face. And after a while the army used it that way, sending soldiers not to police or even protect us but to punish them. Many deserted, disappearing into the jungle never to be seen again and heard of only in fantastic and improbable rumors that echoed the false charges against my father, rumors, related to us by the more civilized Indians with whom we sometimes traded, of a tribe of cannibals led by white men who were carving an empire out of the deepest part of the jungle.

When I was seven, a detail arrived that was still awaiting relief five years later. Rather than desert and take their chances in the mountains or the jungle or continue to live apart as though posted in some isolated monastery, after a few years the soldiers married local girls and started families. The sole exception was Captain Ramiro Benítez, the commanding officer, a thin and stern-faced man who contracted malaria within a month of his arrival and spoke in a voice that made people wince and cover their ears.

Though the captain had changed drastically in the seven years he had been away, the first time Grandfather heard him open his mouth he knew him to be the same man who had arrested my father. Suddenly Grandfather had a focus for the stories he told me, and as a result I grew up impatient to avenge my father on Captain Ramiro Benítez before malaria could beat me to it.

I badgered Grandfather constantly for a chance. But he always shook his head, smiling at my eagerness: "Ever since you were born a month early, nothing can happen fast enough to suit you! Revenge is a fruit that must be left to ripen. Besides, you're still too young."

The truth was that he was searching for some way to kill the captain that would satisfy all the demands of honor yet permit me to escape undetected—no small trick in a town the size of ours, where people knew you were pissing before your water had a chance to hit the ground.

As the years passed, I began to worry that Grandfather might die before such an opportunity presented itself. After all, he was the oldest person in town—as Doctor Nuñez never tired of reminding him. More and more often, impatient and frustrated to the point of forgetting his own advice to me, he exploded in rages as blind as he was. Red-faced and shaking, unable to speak a word, he struck me with his open hand as if I were somehow to blame. The thought that one of these fits might induce a fatal heart attack was enough to make me tremble helplessly. But once he calmed down, Grandfather only laughed at my fears.

"There are two things keeping me alive," he told me once. "You know one of them."

"And the other?" I demanded.

"The gypsies. How could I go before thanking them for saving my life?"

The most eagerly awaited of all our rare visitors were the gypsies, who seldom made the arduous journey across the mountains more than once each century. Though there were hundreds of stories, no one really knew much about them. Some said they were witches, agents of the devil cloaked in human guise, while others maintained they were more interested in filching purses than souls. Because I believed every story no matter how contradictory and outlandish, the gypsies loomed large and vague in my eyes, juggling all opposites at once. They were especially venerated in my family because Grandfather had been born on the final day of their last visit.

It had been a difficult birth. He was dying, dragging his mother into the grave with him. The local midwives could do nothing. Finally an old gypsy, drawn by my great-grandmother's screams, had pulled Grandfather from the womb. The story goes that upon seeing he was blind, the gypsy blew sharply into each tiny ear as if honing the acuity of his hearing to a point where it would surpass the vision of the most far-sighted. And in fact Grandfather still claimed to have heard the fusillade that cut my father down all those years ago.

When I was twelve, my grandfather ninety-five, the gypsies returned. It was early afternoon and the streets were empty even of dogs; forced inside by the heat, people sat lazily behind open windows hoping for an errant mountain breeze or lay abed or in hammocks in a state of stupefaction that bordered on catatonia.

I was awakened that afternoon by my grandfather. Tears were streaming down his cheeks that he made no effort to brush away. I'd never seen him cry before and imagined something terrible must have happened. I sat up. "Grandfather, what is it? What's wrong?"

"Wrong? These are tears of joy, Grandson. My prayers have been answered at last. Soon your father will be able to rest in peace, his honor avenged, and we can hold our heads up high again."

My heart surged. "How? When?"

"The gypsies are crossing the mountains. I hear them singing as they come, songs my heart remembers."

I strained my ears, hearing only the drone of jungle insects. But I never doubted Grandfather for an instant.

"They saved my life once," he continued, "and now they'll help me again. Go to them tonight, Pablito. Keep your eyes and ears open. Take note of everything."

I grabbed his hand, excited and afraid. "You've got to come with me, Grandfather!"

He shook his head. "It will be better if you come back and tell me what you've seen and heard. I'll know what's important."

A few hours later, the whole town knew about our visitors, and that night everyone turned out to watch the gypsy caravan parade singing through the street. It seemed as though the population had doubled in a flash. People were shouting and laughing, even more worked up than at Easter, when the street was paved with bright mosaics of flower petals and colored sand, a swirling carpet over which the holy relics of the church were carried by all the men in town. Now the men carried bottles of rum, their faces as splotchy in the pale radiance of the full moon as the face of the moon itself.

A great shout went up as the first wagons entered town, flanked by some gypsies on horseback. Everyone ran to greet them. It didn't seem possible that they could have brought so much across the mountains unless they truly were witches. They looked magical enough, with silver hoops dangling from the ears and noses of both men and women and bright scarves fluttering from all over their bodies. The sides of the wagons were painted like rainbows torn by arrows or feathers spilled in a war of jungle birds. Even their horses were like no animals we had ever seen—dark, spirited mounts with a dangerous and intelligent look that made me keep my distance until the surge of the crowd pulled me from my mother's side and pressed me up against a strong and sweaty flank.

The rider, an old, silver-haired gypsy who wore a long crimson robe that seemed to swallow light and exhale shadow, reached down to steady me. I clasped his hand, and when he pulled away a silver earring lay glittering in my palm. Without thinking, I quickly shut my fist and stuffed it into my pocket. When I looked up again, he was gone.

The gypsies drew their wagons into a loose circle about the plaza and unharnessed their horses to graze in a makeshift corral at the edge of the jungle. Flaps were raised, sideboards lowered, creating stages for the display of marvels. There were storytellers, mountebanks, and palmists; alchemists, astronomers, and astrologers. The smoky aroma of frying meat and vegetables filled the air as vendors invited passersby to sample food and hot spiced wine.

Soon I spotted the silver-haired gypsy again, his crimson cape like a fiery tongue in the torchlight. He had ten knives in the air at once, scrambling with hands, knees, and feet to keep them aloft. Just then, with all ten knives hanging at the apex of their orbits, the gypsy suddenly lowered his arms and walked to the edge of the stage through a rain of steel, as unconcerned as a man caught in a cloudburst. Shouts rose on all sides, then a solemn hush followed by wild applause. More than one woman had fainted. I rushed to the front of the crowd.

The gypsy bowed, a gracious smile frozen on his face. "Thank you, friends. I am Cesar."

I saw that he was wearing a silver earring like the one he had given me and reached inside my pocket to touch it. I tried to catch his eye, but his gaze passed over everyone without distinction, never lingering.

"Friends! You've seen me juggle! How old am I?"

Shouts came from all around:

"Sixty!"

"No, seventy!"

"Seventy-five, right, Grandpa?"

Cesar just laughed, as though he had long ago despaired of ever hearing the right answer. "I am two hundred years old."

"Come on, Grandpa, that's impossible," someone called. "Don't think we're easy marks just because we live over the mountains!"

"I agree it's impossible," Cesar said. "But it is the very nature of miracles to be impossible, is it not?"

With that, he had us.

"Friends, ladies and gentlemen, behind me in this wagon waits my granddaughter, Magenta, herself well over one hundred. Soon she will dance for you, but first let me tell you of the miracle.

"Long ago, when Magenta was but a child, the Sainted Virgin appeared to her in a dream. In that dream the holy visage beamed down on her beatifically from heaven and spoke in a voice soft as moonlight.

"'Magenta,' she said. 'Your purity of heart is so great that it gives you the power to purify others; but only in moonlight will this power be made manifest, for virginity in women is the seal of God's favor, and the moon my own loving and vigilant eye.'"

As Cesar spoke, members of the crowd crossed themselves, chewing prayers past rubbery lips. Several old women swathed in black who wore about their thick necks yellowed rosaries that hung submerged within their bosoms like spiritual anchors retrieved the beads and worried them from finger to finger.

"Friends!" thundered Cesar. "That same night the Holy Mother placed in my granddaughter's mind the steps to a holy dance, a dance to music our earthbound ears are incapable of hearing, the same music that pushes the planets through their orbits, the music of the angels. And simultaneously in my mind the secret of alchemy was revealed: the sweat of a young virgin blessed by God and kissed by moonlight, mixed with certain chemicals properly sanctified, yields a formula that will cure any ailment, grant absolution for any sin, and force all devils from the body!

Since that glorious day, no one in our family has aged so much as one minute!"

He pulled a thin vial from his billowing cape. "Behold! These few drops are all that remain, so tonight, beneath the full moon, Magenta must dance again! But first—" He uncorked the vial and drank, then smashed it on the stage and cut a caper around the fragments. "Good-bye, old age! Adios, arthritis! Thanks be to God!"

"Thanks be to God!" echoed the crowd as though responding to one of Padre Mendez's Sunday morning exhortations.

Cesar collected his ten knives, depositing them within the folds of his cape, then withdrew a large sombrero from the wagon, which he lay upside down at the fore of the stage. He swept the crowd with his unflinching eyes once more, face by face. "Now, my friends, my granddaughter would like to dance."

He walked to each corner of the stage and extinguished the torches; in the moonlight, the shards from the smashed vial glimmered like stars reflected in the depths of a well.

Then Magenta stepped onto the stage. She was a tiny girl, her limbs frail as matchsticks, with long hair the color of coal and round, hungry eyes as deep and mysterious as the jungle looking out of a face as pale and placid as stone. I felt as though her eyes would devour me if I stared too long, but I couldn't look away, curious to plumb their depths. Her dress hung loose, dwarfing her body in white folds that seemed to radiate a faint light of their own, like woven moonbeams.

Suddenly the tinny dash of cymbals and the rattle of tambourines rose from the wagon behind her. The strings of a guitar were struck, the chord crashing in the air then bending around Magenta as if warped by the heat. She launched into her dance, moving slowly at first, then with greater speed and complexity, until it made me dizzy to watch. As she spun, hair flying, her dress whipping high above her knees, all the light seemed to spiral inward to her eyes, kindling them with a flickering, ghostly fire, though her pale features remained expressionless as ever.

People in the crowd began to hurl coins into the sombrero, but these were snatched by a sudden whirlwind and flung through the air in a crazy dance of their own, some even shooting back at us as if thrown by an invisible hand. In the confusion, as people yelled and ducked for cover, I saw Magenta tread upon the shards of glass from the vial Cesar had smashed. Through her feet were bare, they were not bloodied; it almost appeared that she was floating ever so slightly above the stage, raised by the wind she had spun into being.

Then all at once there came a blinding flash of light accompanied by a sulfurous smell that made me cough and my eyes water. When my vision finally cleared, Magenta was gone. The torches were lit again, and Cesar was calmly picking up the sombrero, jingling the coins inside. I looked around; everyone else appeared as dazed as I, blinking in confusion as if unable to decide whether they were just emerging from a dream or sinking into one. I wasn't sure myself.

"My friends," Cesar said, that same gracious smile frozen on his face, "thank you for your generosity. But I'm afraid you must excuse me now. I go to prepare the elixir according to the instructions of the Sainted Virgin. Tomorrow morning, for a modest fee, I will have the honor of offering you health and immortality! Until then, I bid you goodnight."

He turned to go, but before he could enter the wagon, Captain Ramiro Benítez appeared out of nowhere, clambering weakly onto the stage and calling for him to halt in the name of the law; Cesar, with the ironic deference all gypsies seem to instinctively show men in uniform, stepped back and offered a low bow.

The captain seemed nervous, shivering with a malarial chill in the dense nighttime heat. "I'm told you are the leader here," he said.

Cesar shrugged, smiling agreeably.

"Why wasn't I informed of your arrival? It's your duty to register with me, my friend." He presented his hand crisply. "Your papers."

"Of course, Captain. A simple oversight." Cesar drew a thick bundle of papers from a pocket in his cape and placed them in the captain's outstretched palm.

Captain Benítez examined the papers. The shivers wracking his body worsened as he read, whether from rage or the malaria no one could tell. Meanwhile, the crowd milled noisily, shouting for him to step down. Suddenly the captain tensed, his finger pouncing like a jaguar. "What is this authorizing signature?"

Cesar bent over the page. "That is the signature of the Minister of Internal Affairs."

"What do you take me for? The Minister is Porfiro Velazquez, not this man. You're under arrest."

"Excuse me, Captain," said Cesar. "But Porfiro Velazquez was assassinated three years ago."

The captain sagged visibly at this information, then squared his shoulders. "You're lying, gypsy."

"I assure you, I'm not. Why don't you radio your superiors?"

The fact was, as everyone knew, the garrison's radio had long ago rusted away to nothing.

"Don't tell me who to radio!" the captain thundered. "I'm going to close you down!"

"Come on, Captain," someone shouted. "Forget about your uniform for once!"

"Who cares about some damn signature?" demanded someone else.

Captain Ramiro Benítez was even more outraged by these outbursts. He scanned the crowd for his men, who were with their wives and children in the back, trying to avoid his gaze. "Jose, Alvaro, Eusebio, Quito," he ticked off mercilessly. "Juan, Lupe, Ixca, Carlos, Artemio, Gervasio!"

Grumbling to each other and scowling, the men shuffled forward.

"Men!" Captain Benítez shouted. "Disperse these people!"

The men hesitated as though they had been ordered to betray themselves. In a paroxysm of rage, Captain Benítez drew his revolver.

"Don't shoot us, Captain," cried a drunken voice. "We'll go peacefully!"

Everyone broke up. We sympathized with the ten men; after all, they had long ago ceased to be soldiers. They were our neighbors now, our relatives. No one wanted to give them a hard time, regardless of how we felt about the captain.

I ran straight home. Grandfather was sitting up in his dark room, waiting. I lit a candle and sat beside him: "Grandfather, I wish you could have seen it!"

I told him about Cesar, how he had juggled knives as though they were lighter than air and how in a fit of anger Captain Ramiro Benítez had shut the gypsies down. I was saving the best for last, but before I could mention Magenta's dance, Grandfather laughed and mussed my hair.

"Good job, Pablito," he said. "You are a good son."

The excitement of seeing the gypsies had all but pushed the demands of vengeance from my mind. Only now did I remember why Grandfather had wanted me to keep my eyes open. Ashamed, I listened to him describe the murder of Captain Ramiro Benítez.

Over the years, Grandfather had studied the captain's movements until he knew exactly where he would be at each moment. His nights began in the bountiful arms of one or more of the local whores, but by two or three in the morning he invariably staggered into the street, held upright by some homing instinct triggered by the prodigious amounts of rum he'd consumed, and set off for his bed as though wading through molasses, collapsing there until at least noon.

Grandfather spoke softly, in a rush. "In an hour or two, when everyone is asleep, I want you to take a knife from the kitchen, a long and sharp knife, and sneak into the captain's house. When he comes back and passes out, cut his throat just like a pig's. Then clean the knife on the sheets and bring it back here. Don't let anyone see you. Understand?"

"No . . ." Part of me was still thinking like a child, and murder was men's business.

"Don't worry, you'll be safe. Everyone will assume the gypsy did it. They all saw his skill with knives, his argument with the captain."

At last I understood. The silver earring in my pocket grew heavy as blood money. "Please, Grandfather. There has to be another way. I'll kill the captain, just leave Cesar alone."

Grandfather was furious. "Coward, is this how you honor your father, by throwing your own life away?" His palm stung my ear, and I swallowed a sob. "The life of one gypsy is a small price to pay for vengeance!"

"But the gypsies saved your life!"

"That was long ago, and the debt I owe my son cancels all others—just like the debt you owe your father. No one said it was easy being a man, Grandson. We do what we have to, not what we want."

I took the knife from the kitchen and hung it beneath my shirt on a string. Now that the moment I'd spent my whole life preparing for had arrived, things didn't seem so simple anymore. I asked Cesar to forgive me.

But as I lay in bed, waiting for time to pass, I realized that I couldn't let Cesar take the blame for my actions no matter what Grandfather said. If I warned him of what I was going to do, he would be able to get away in time. Maybe that would make things more dangerous for me; I didn't care. I was proud of the murder I was about to commit. Captain Ramiro Benítez deserved to die; Grandfather was right about that, I knew.

I slipped out my window and made my way to the plaza, sticking to the shadows. The streets were empty, the gypsies' wagons shut up tight. The only sound was the whickering of the horses in the corral. It was hard to believe that just hours ago the whole town had been hopping; that was another one I owed the captain.

I crept up to Cesar's wagon. In the moonlight it loomed vast and ill-defined, its edges sinking into shadow, its bright paint peeling, the colors washed out. I was not afraid; I was filled with a consciousness of the nobility of my mission, already imagining Cesar's effusive gratitude, which I would accept with a heroic dignity worthy of my father.

I raised my fist to knock, but before I could complete the action the door swung open and a huge hand shot out to grasp my own. Before I knew it, I was being pulled inside, too startled to fight or scream. The door slammed shut behind me.

"What do we have here, I wonder? A thief or a spy?"

It was Cesar, his face like cracked, yellowed parchment in the unsteady light of the candles that swung in a brass lamp from the ceiling behind him in the center of the wagon. His eyes were red as the cape he had worn. His fist still engulfed my own, squeezing with a pressure that forced me to my knees. I shook my head no, unable to find my voice.

"Better state your business fast, son," he said, keeping the pressure mounting until I thought my hand would break.

I stuttered, my heart hammering in my chest so loudly that I couldn't get my thoughts straight. I looked past Cesar, glimpsing glass vials filled with a colorful array of liquids and powders below a hopeless tangle of coiled rubber tubing all set on a table in the center of the wagon. A vaguely metallic taste scraped the back of my tongue. Of course—he thought I had come to steal the elixir! And then, in one corner, I caught sight of the pale curve of Magenta's profile.

"Oh, so that's it," Cesar said, following my eyes. 'Don't you think you're a little young for my granddaughter, son?"

Now Magenta spoke from the shadows, unmoving. "Let the boy go, Cesar."

Her voice seemed only inches from my ear. I jumped at the impossible nearness of it. It was a beautiful voice, yet there was no warmth in it; her tone was smooth and cold as ice, delicately sculptured but strong as steel. Cesar released me at once, as if accustomed to obeying that voice without a thought. I got to my feet, flexing my sore hand. Cesar's red eyes were on me, glittering with a malice that chilled my heart. Then I remembered the silver earring he had given me. I pulled it out of my pocket and held it up where he could see it. "Look, you can trust me," I began shakily. "I've come to warn you . . . " And then I told him everything, holding nothing back, not even Grandfather's plan to frame him for the murder of Captain Benítez. But when I had finished, he seemed unmoved; I wondered if he had heard a single word.

"I know who you are and why you've come," he said, his voice as full of hate as his eyes. I had the impression that his yellow skin was hardening before my eyes, that pieces of flesh would soon crack off and drop away, exposing the skull beneath. I looked on in horror.

"You've come to take my place, to take care of her!" he continued like a madman. He took a step toward me, hands outstretched.

"Cesar!"

Again Magenta's voice rang out. Cesar froze, trembling. I looked past him. Magenta was half out of the shadows, gazing at me with eyes that still retained a glimmer of the moonlight they had swallowed in the dance. I gave a strangled cry and backed away. She was not a young girl. She was an ancient, withered girl, her youth mummified and shrunken, the skin of her face so pale and shining in the soft glow of her eyes that her features seemed carved from polished bone. The face we had seen on stage must have been a mask, heavily made up. I turned and wrenched the door open, then ran as if my life depended on it, Cesar's mocking laughter licking my heels like fire.

I wanted to run all the way home, dive into bed and huddle under the covers, wake up in the morning and tell myself that it had all been a bad dream. Instead, I forced myself to stop. I waited to catch my breath, then made my way to the house of Captain Ramiro Benítez. If Cesar was arrested for my crime now, I told myself, so much the better. I tried to forget what I had seen and heard, concentrating on the job ahead.

I slipped into the captain's house through an open window. It was dark, difficult to see. I moved slowly, my hands before me. Then I heard a rattling snore. I followed it to the bedroom. Enough moonlight fell through the window to give me a dim view.

Captain Ramiro Benítez lay on his back on the bed, still wearing his uniform. It was filthy now, stained and missing some buttons. The room reeked of rum. Plainly, he'd been celebrating.

His scrawny neck was a sickly yellow color, stretched across the pillow like a chicken's on the block. There was no anger in me, no thirst for retribution, just the blunt prodding of what had to be done. I drew the knife from beneath my shirt and laid its edge against the captain's throat. He snored on, unaware of how impatiently death crouched above him, how beautifully it shone in the moonlight where I grasped it in my hand.

What was he dreaming of, I found myself wondering, in these, the final seconds of his life? A childhood somewhere, loving parents, loyal friends? All the women he had known and perhaps loved, perhaps hated, all the men he had killed? Was he dreaming of my father, reliving the arrest, the trip back over the mountains, the execution in the capital, wondering why he had ended up here after all those years, what the hell had gone wrong with his career, with his whole damned life? I looked at him, the skin of his face pinched by the malaria into that of a man three times his age, a living corpse, and suddenly knew that for all my hate I couldn't kill him, not even if I had been as blind as Grandfather.

It wasn't that I feared the feel of flesh parting like butter beneath the blade, the thin mouth I carved first vomiting then drooling blood; I'd seen all that before, had myself cut the throats of pigs and cattle. It wasn't that he was a human being or didn't deserve to die; if Grandfather had materialized beside me I would have given him the knife, even guided his hand. Maybe it was a weakness in me, maybe I was a bad son. But after all those years spent rehearsing for this moment, I simply couldn't do it. I wished I could. *We do what we have to, not what we want.* Those words of Grandfather's came back to me, but just the same I knew he wouldn't understand. I didn't really understand, myself. What could I say to him now? In his anger, he might easily kill me, or himself.

It's always hard, the first time.

I recognized Magenta's voice. Her words rang not in my ears but within my head, as though I had thought them. They were accompanied by a cold so intense and permeating that my heartbeat slowed and my emotions deadened, though my senses seemed to crystallize, even sharpen. I felt the chill of her presence all around me, yet when I turned, searching the dark corners of the room, my knife held ready, I saw that I was alone. Her laughter pricked me, sharp and brittle as needles of ice.

"Where are you?" I called out. "What do you want?"

Shh. We don't want to wake the captain, do we? Your thoughts are loud enough for me to hear.

What do you want? I repeated silently, my eyes on the captain, who was still snoring; it would take more than a few words from me to wake him.

That's better. I want to help you, Pablito.

How do you know my name? How are we doing this? The Virgin Mary . . .

I shivered at her laughter.

My secrets come from across the ocean, across the centuries. All that talk about the Sainted Virgin and moonlight and sweat is just to fool people.

Then what are you?

Instead of answering, she asked a question of her own. *You hate that man with all your heart, yet you spare his life. What will your grandfather say?*

I looked down at the knife in my hand, unable to reply.

I'll tell you, Pablito. He will call you a coward. His proud heart will not be able to bear the shame. By letting this worthless man live, you will be killing your grandfather. I can understand your reluctance to kill a man in order to avenge a man you never knew—your father—but it's your grandfather's life I'm talking about now. Can you condemn him through inaction?

I had never considered that. She was right. And yet I couldn't kill the captain as he lay there in his drunken stupor, defenseless, already more dead than alive, not even if it meant Grandfather's death. I guess that made me a coward. Revulsion and shame crawled through me as if called forth by Magenta's voice. I wanted to stab myself with the knife, but I was too much of a coward even for that.

Let me kill him then.

Her words gave me fresh hope, though I could scarcely bring myself to believe them. *Why should you help me?*

Maybe because I met your father years ago over the mountains and believe in what he died for. Or maybe because I can't keep Cesar alive much longer to watch over me while I sleep, and I need someone to take his place.

"You knew my father? What was he like?" In my excitement, I spoke aloud.

Shh. He was a brave man who murdered something precious in himself with each man he killed, even the ones that deserved to die. He was dead inside long before they killed him, but they killed him anyway. I'm sure he appreciated the joke.

I don't understand . . .

You're too young, Pablito.

That's what Grandfather always used to say . . .

I helped your grandfather ninety-five years ago, your father a few years after that. Now I'm offering you my help. Will you come away with me tonight if I kill this man? Will you take Cesar's place, wear the silver earring I made him give you? We'll go into the jungle, find the guerrillas. And when we come out again, in five years or five hundred, we'll be leading an army.

As I listened to her words, I had the feeling that Magenta already knew what my answer would be, that she had always known. But I was just discovering it for myself. For the first time in my life, I had a sense of why my father had crossed the mountains in search of his fate instead of waiting sensibly for it come to him like everybody else. Though I would be going in the opposite direction, I believe he would have understood. *Yes,* I thought. *Yes.*

And there she was suddenly, stepping out of the moonlight as if she'd been hiding there all along, transparent as glass. Her appearance no longer terrified me; instead, I felt almost transfixed by her strange beauty, the face and body of a child aged beyond the grasp of time into something pure and eternal. I offered her the knife, but she shook her head with a smile as she stood on tiptoe and bent over the sleeping form of Captain Ramiro Benítez like a little girl kissing her father goodnight.

THE SILVER GHOST

IT WAS PAST TWO-THIRTY WHEN MIRIAM SPOTTED THE silver mailbox with the neat row of faded black letters spelling out the name HOFFMAN. Gravel crunched as she turned up the driveway. The house, a red-brick rambler, was nestled well back from the road amid trees burgeoning with spring growth. So many shades of green. Miriam felt as though she'd crossed the line separating seasons in leaving the city—the big acacias along her Brooklyn street were still bare, buds clenched tight like tiny pink fists.

Miriam parked beside a black Lincoln whose tinted windows were as impenetrable as the curtained windows of the house. She hurried up cracked concrete steps to the front porch and rang the bell. Her stomach was churning; she was nearly twenty minutes late. She heard heavy footsteps drawing near. The door swung open.

"Mrs. Bowles?" The man seemed a size too large for his dark blue pinstripe suit. He was bald, his tanned face smooth and hairless save for eyebrows so blond and thin as to be almost invisible. A silk tie provided the only splash of color: a floral print like a Renoir left out in the rain.

Miriam nodded. She guessed he was in his early sixties. He smelled faintly of bourbon.

"I'm Henry Hoffman." His lips stretched in a tight smile as he looked her over with eyes like chips of lapis lazuli. "You're late, Mrs. Bowles."

Miriam smiled apologetically. "I took a wrong turn."

Mr. Hoffman engulfed her small hand in his large one. "No harm done. You're here now." He drew her inside.

The air was stuffy and stale, as if the windows were never opened.

Miriam smelled the odor of an invalid; one part sickness, three parts hope-lessness.

"Would you care for some coffee or tea?"

"Tea would be nice, thank you."

"Tea it is, Mrs. Bowles. If you wouldn't mind waiting in the living room, I'll bring you a cup directly. We can have a little chat before you meet the patient."

Miriam would have guessed him to be a lawyer even if he hadn't told her so over the phone when she'd responded to the advertisement for a home-care nurse in Sunday's *Times*.

The living room had seen better days. There was a lumpy couch of faded leather and a dusty wooden end table in need of a good polishing. A coffee table stood before the couch, its glass surface cluttered with old magazines. The fireplace had not been cleaned in ages.

Lined up across the mantelpiece were five large silver trophies also in need of polishing. Miriam read the inscriptions: Eifelrennen, Nurbur-gring—1980; Agadir, Morocco—1982; Reno, Nevada—1983; Long Beach, California—1984; Pebble Beach, California—1984.

A photograph of a silver roadster was mounted on the brick wall of the chimney above the trophies. The car was hunched low, with a sleek, flowing line that made it appear to have been carved and polished by the precise application of hurricane-force winds. Even at rest it exuded speed. A small bronze plate at the base of the frame read: THE SILVER GHOST.

A young man and a stylishly dressed older woman posed arm in arm beside the car. Both had fine blond hair and wore aviator glasses. There was enough resemblance in the handsome, tanned features for Miriam to conclude that the man and woman were related, though in what way—mother and son or brother and older sister—she couldn't guess. Hearing Mr. Hoffman's heavy tread, she turned as he entered the room.

"Your tea, Mrs. Bowles."

Miriam took the steaming cup and saucer. "I was admiring the trophies."

"Ah, yes. Harold's trophies. That's a picture of him there, along with my late wife, May. You'll be meeting him in a moment."

"Your son?"

"Stepson. May and I had no children of our own. We tried, but, sadly, it was not to be. Are you and your husband blessed with children, Mrs. Bowles?"

"I'm divorced, Mr. Hoffman. No children." The tea burned her tongue.

"I'm sorry," Mr. Hoffman said with more delicacy than she'd given him credit for. He gestured towards the sofa. "Won't you sit down?"

"Thank you." Miriam settled onto the sofa and cleared her throat. "As I told you over the phone, Mr. Hoffman, I was laid off two months ago from Columbia-Presbyterian because of budget cuts, and—"

Mr. Hoffman waved his hand dismissively, as if Miriam were a paralegal trying to present him with irrelevant papers in the heat of a deposition. "Please, Mrs. Bowles. Miriam, if I may. There's no need to go over all that again. I'm quite satisfied with what you told me. If you like Harold—and he likes you, of course—the position is yours."

Miriam smiled, flattered and shy. "Tell me about him."

"Harold raced cars." Mr. Hoffman strolled to the mantelpiece. "These are all his. You can imagine how he worried us, May and me. We begged him to stop, but he never listened. No one could tell him what to do. In many ways, he was a spoiled child who never grew up.

"Eight years ago, on his mother's forty-sixth birthday, Harold made a promise he had made and broken many times before. As a present to her, he swore to give up racing from that day forward. May and I pretended to believe him, but, knowing his history, how could we? Even when he showed us his racer—the Silver Ghost—transformed into an ordinary sports car, we doubted. Anyone who knew him would have doubted! And he saw our doubt; we couldn't hide it from him.

"That night there was a party for May here at the house. Harold was moody and reserved, drinking more than he should have. He began to berate us in front of the guests. Professional acquaintances, Miriam, important people. He accused us of treating him like a child, of wanting to keep him a child forever to replace the children we could never have. He said terrible things, Miriam. Awful things. Poor May was in tears.

"When he saw the effect of his words, Harold ran from the room. I tried to comfort May, but she pushed me away and followed him. I went after her, but at a distance; after all, he was her son, not mine.

"When I caught up with them, they were arguing out front. I couldn't make out the words. Harold made to leave several times, but May restrained him. Finally they climbed into the Silver Ghost and sped off. May was driving. She hadn't had as much to drink as Harold, but she wasn't exactly sober either. I called to them to stop, but they didn't hear or pretended not to. They did that sometimes . . . ignored me. Retreated to their own little world, just the two of them."

Mr. Hoffman's shoulders sagged. "They didn't get more than ten miles before May lost control of the car. The local roads are dangerous under the best of conditions. May was killed instantly. And Harold . . . "

Mr. Hoffman fell silent.

Miriam had heard many such stories over the years. Worse even. After a while, they all sounded the same. "What about Harold?"

His laugh sounded bitter. "Harold's injuries left him with the mental capacity of a small child. One year old, perhaps two. But otherwise he's perfect. Handsome as a wax dummy! May was wearing her seatbelt. She was trapped inside the wreck. Harold, who scorned such devices, was thrown free. Is that fair, Miriam? Is it?"

For the first time, Mr. Hoffman's voice cracked. His blue eyes bored into Miriam's in search of an answer. It was a look she knew well. Like Mr. Hoffman, like all her patients and their families, Miriam would have liked to believe there was an essential fairness to life and death, that things happened for a reason and people got, in the end, what they deserved. But she'd decided long ago it was useless to demand answers, far better to quietly mourn the dead while easing the burden shared so inequitably among the living. "I'd like to see Harold now."

"Of course." Mr. Hoffman was his lawyerly self again. "He's in the bedroom down the hall. The nurse is with him—Mrs. Graves. A retired RN from New Ridge. She'll answer all your questions. Now you'll have to excuse me. The house has too many painful memories. I'll be waiting outside for your answer."

There were two open doors in the hallway—a bedroom and a bathroom—and a closed door. Harold's room. Miriam knocked lightly.

A tremulous voice called for her to come in.

Miriam turned the knob and pushed the door open. The contrast with the rest of the house was striking: the bedroom was airy and sun-drenched, the far wall lined with windows that looked out over a long and sloping back lawn. At the bottom of the lawn a thick copse screened the house from the neighboring fields. After half a mile or so the fields gave way to dense woods over which the blue-green shapes of the Adirondacks bulked like clouds above the sea.

A man sat hunched in a chair before the center window. He gave no sign of having heard Miriam enter. His head, with a thick mane of golden hair, bobbed like a sunflower in a faint breeze.

"That's Harold. I'm Edna Graves. You must be the new nurse."

The old woman who spoke so matter-of-factly was perched at the edge of a tidy bed. She looked as sturdy as a house of cards. Her frail white arms, paler than her nurse's uniform, were crossed at the wrists; her hands lay palm up in her lap. Patches of scalp glowed through the chalky mist of her hair.

"Miriam Bowles. Actually, I haven't decided about the job."

Mrs. Graves responded with a canny nod, as if Miriam could say what she pleased, but *she*, Mrs. Graves, knew better. With great difficulty, like a marionette raised by a palsied hand, she rose to her feet.

"Don't make a fuss, dear." She shooed Miriam away. "I'm perfectly capable. Haven't I been looking after *him* for all these weeks?" She shuffled across the room to shut the door. "You're from the city, aren't you?"

Miriam sat at the edge of the bed. Mrs. Graves' body had not left the slightest crease or indentation in the taut bedspread. "Brooklyn. Born and bred."

"What's a pretty young thing like you doing so far from home? Not married, are you, dear?"

"Divorced."

That knowing nod again. "Well, you're not going to find a husband here."

"I'm not looking for one."

Mrs. Graves' giggle seemed less expressive of mirth than peevish malice. "Me neither! I only wish Mr. Graves could get that through his skull! Seventy-eight this July and after me even more than when we were first married. What's a woman got to do for a little rest, eh, dear? Men retire, but a woman's work is never done. I took this job for a rest. Anything to get a moment's peace!"

Miriam had no wish to pursue the subject. "What happened to the nurse who was here before?"

"That would be Louise. Louise Vintner. She didn't last long. Not with him after her every second."

Miriam couldn't conceal her surprise. "You mean Harold?"

Mrs. Graves giggled again. "No, the old man. Mr. Hoffman. Always hanging about, drunk more often than not. Leering at her, finding ways to touch her. She told me everything. *Everything.* The poor girl had no one else to turn to. She was from the city just like you. Running from something. Whatever it was, she's gone back to it now."

"Mr. Hoffman seems harmless enough. Kind of sad."

"Just wait till he's got you alone. He's even had a go at *me* once or twice!" Mrs. Graves smoothed her white uniform with an air of affronted dignity.

"I can take care of myself."

"I'm sure you can, dear. He's more of an annoyance than anything else. Probably turn out to be like Abel—that's Mr. Graves—which is to say *un*able. Harold here is a perfect angel. No more trouble than an infant. And I'll say this for Mr. Henry Hoffman: he pays well. Has to, to keep people out here. It can get pretty dull, especially for a young woman used to what the city has to offer."

"I've had my fill of the city." Miriam felt the prickly sensation of being watched; turning, she found herself the object of Harold's disconcerting stare.

His features, as Mr. Hoffman had said, were blandly handsome, like a mannequin's. He didn't look a day over thirty, as if he hadn't aged since the accident. Every so often a recognizable emotion rippled across his face, a shadow of fear or sorrow or laughter, but there was no sense of an accompanying awareness. His skin was smooth and evenly tanned, his hair as pale as corn-silk. He exuded all the health and well-being of a well-watered plant in a sunny corner.

"What . . . what's the matter with him?" Miriam felt a kind of awe, as if she were in the presence of a creature both more and less than human.

Mrs. Graves pulled back Harold's golden hair to reveal the shape of the skull beneath. The left side of his head was cratered, as though it had not merely collapsed but, like rotten fruit, decayed from within. "There's a metal plate in there. It's a miracle he's able to function at all. Look at him . . . his head always swaying. You know what I think? He's picking up a radio station, listening to music only he can hear!" She giggled at the notion.

Just then, Harold began to stroke Miriam's arm. It felt like tiny cracks were spreading through her bones.

"Pretty," Harold said, his voice gruff and unused.

"He does that sometimes," Mrs. Graves said. "Talks, I mean. I don't think he even knows what he's saying. It's just an old reflex."

Miriam thought she might faint.

"He's not bothering you, is he, dear?"

She shook her head, unable to speak. Gently, she lifted Harold's hand from her arm. He turned back to the window. Miriam took a deep breath and followed his gaze, saw flashes of white and gray in the overgrown copse at the base of the lawn. "What's he staring at?"

Mrs. Graves peered over Harold's shoulder. "In the woods there? Why, that's the cemetery. Gravestones there go back two hundred years and more. This land as far as the eye can see used to belong to the Allistons—Mrs. Hoffman's family. It came to her as a wedding gift. Mr. Hoffman holds it in trust for Harold, but when he dies it goes back to the family—my cousin Vera works at the County Courthouse, so I know. The cemetery's still in use, though badly neglected. Harold's mother—God rest her soul—is buried there. It was one of her favorite spots. Harold's too. I think on some level he remembers that."

They stood in silence, gazing into the woods. Then Mrs. Graves cleared her throat. "I guess you'll be taking the job."

Miriam's skin still tingled from Harold's touch. Though she hadn't forgotten what was left to her, still, for now, she felt strangely at peace. What was past was past, and in the future there was only this house and the man who lived in it, more like a child than any real child could be. "Yes," she said. "I guess I will."

"Come on, Harold," Miriam coaxed. "Time for our walk."

Harold flashed her a look of baffled distress before coming away from his trophies, which she'd polished to a mirror shine. It broke her heart the way he stared at them sometimes, as if seeking in his distorted reflection traces of the man he used to be.

Miriam had asked Mr. Hoffman to give her a week alone with Harold. Now that week was up, and she was sorry to see it end. She'd never known a gentler, more helpless creature. He was almost like a newborn baby. She bathed him, dressed him, saw to all his needs. Nights she sang him to sleep with a lullaby her mother had crooned to her, the words drifting back across the years like a message from an earlier, forgotten self. She liked to watch him sleep, when emotions played across his face like the shadows of dreams. Sometimes he cried, and then she stroked his hair and made soothing sounds, feeling like she mattered.

After leading him outside, Miriam paused to lock the door, a habit retained from a lifetime of city living. It was a gorgeous afternoon, with a breeze blowing from somewhere in the direction of June. The sky was robin's egg blue. Harold was shambling down the lawn with a peculiarly bearish gait, heading for the cemetery—the first stop on their already customary afternoon walks.

Upon reaching the cemetery, Harold squeezed past the bars of the old wrought-iron fence, overgrown with ivy and brambles, and began to wander among the tombstones as he always did. The first time Miriam had seen him there, she'd thought he was looking for his mother's grave and had searched it out to show him.

It had not been easy. The cemetery was in a state of neglect bordering on ruin. Many of the markers were toppled or buried under vegetation. Piles of beer cans and bottles and the occasional discarded prophylactic testified to other visitors. But at last she found the grave tucked in one corner, a small headstone of pink marble lost in a thicket of wild roses that Miriam had since cut back.

Taking Harold's hand as though he were blind, Miriam had guided his fingers over the stone, tracing out his mother's name letter by letter: MAY ALLISTON HOFFMAN. She'd expected nothing but just the same was disappointed when Harold gave no sign of recognizing even a single letter. Not then, not on any of the days since.

Miriam lifted the chain and entered the cemetery through the creaky gate. Harold's head came up like a startled squirrel's; unexpected sounds frightened him.

"Shh," she said. "Everything's all right."

It was amazing, after so brief a time, how he responded to her voice as though he'd been hearing it all his life. Taking him by the hand, she led him to his mother's grave and began once more to slowly trace the letters of her name. She felt a little foolish—who did she think she was anyway, Anne Sullivan?—and glad no one could see her. But she went on anyway.

"It's your mother, Harold. Your mother."

"M—M . . . " Harold mumbled as if straining after the lost word. His head slowly grew still; it was the first time Miriam had seen his head stop moving save for when he was asleep. She held her breath, aware of a sudden hush. Harold seemed to be listening to something faint and far away. Then all at once his bland expression crumpled to one of uncomprehending sorrow, as if the pain of his loss had returned shorn of its memory like a kind of emotional stealth bomber. Tears rolled down his cheeks. He swiped at them with the backs of his hands, shifting from foot to foot and whimpering like a frightened child.

"My God. Harold . . . " Miriam couldn't go on. She was afraid of what she'd set in motion. But it was too late now. She pulled him close and began to cry. Her insides were being wrung out like a sponge; it felt like all the old grief was being reborn inside her. She didn't think she could bear the pain.

Finally Harold gave a perplexed sniffle and pulled away. His features had returned to normal, like the placid surface of a pond after a cloudburst. He looked at her and smiled, and that smile was so open and full of trust that Miriam found herself smiling, a little shyly, in return.

"M-mother," he said.

"Yes," she whispered, the tears coming again. She felt like a miracle had taken place. "Mother."

Mr. Hoffman's Lincoln was parked in the driveway when they returned from their walk. The sight of it brought Miriam abruptly back to earth, dispelling the aura of timelessness that had taken root in the last week. But the annoyance she felt was superseded by the desire to share with Mr. Hoffman the news of what had happened in the cemetery.

She led Harold up the hill and into the house. "Mr. Hoffman?"

He answered from the kitchen: "In here, Miriam!"

"You won't believe what just happened—" Miriam broke off as they entered the kitchen. Mr. Hoffman was just turning from the counter with a glass of bourbon. His smile froze at the sight of them. He staggered as if pushed from behind, spilling his drink on the parquet floor. His mouth worked silently, but no words came.

"Are you all right?" She thought he was having a seizure.

"Get . . . get him out of here!"

Dazed, Miriam ushered Harold out of the kitchen and into his bedroom. He went at once to the window, his thin frame wracked by shudders. She stroked his hair and whispered that everything was going to be all right. She was furious at Mr. Hoffman for having frightened him; for frightening her, too. She marched back into the kitchen.

Mr. Hoffman was on his knees, wiping up the spill.

"Are you trying to scare him to death?"

"I'm sorry." He heaved to his feet, brushing the knees of his dark blue pinstripe suit. "Seeing him like that was . . . unexpected." He finished what little bourbon remained in his glass and poured another.

Miriam felt for him, but Harold was her responsibility now. "Surely you must have been expecting to see him! How could it surprise you?"

"It was the suddenness of it, a trick of the light. He looks so much like his mother. So very much." Mr. Hoffman was pale as a ghost and trembling; he brought the bottle to the kitchen table, pulled out a chair and sat down. "It gave me quite a shock. I didn't mean to upset the boy."

"He'll be all right. But I think it would be best if you didn't see him again today."

Mr. Hoffman nodded, obviously relieved.

"And in the future, perhaps you could call first? That way we can avoid any further surprises."

"Of course. I tried to call on my way over, but there was no answer."

"Yes, we'd gone out. An afternoon walk; Harold loves to be outdoors. The exercise does him good."

"Exercise?" Mr. Hoffman raised his glass in a mocking salute. "He's healthy as a horse! *I* should be so healthy!"

Miriam realized belatedly that Mr. Hoffman was drunk. She remembered Mrs. Graves' warning. "I should probably check on him."

"Have a drink with me first."

"No thank you."

"Admirable," he said, refreshing his glass. "You're an admirable woman, Miriam. That husband of yours was a fool to let you get away!" He shook his head as though deeply puzzled by the quirks of human behavior. "Still, it's a blessing there were no children, I suppose. The children never do well. Harold was raised by a single parent, and he was no prince, believe me . . . or, rather, too much of one."

He spoke as if he knew her history. As a lawyer, perhaps he had access to the records of her divorce. And other records. Suddenly Miriam felt very vulnerable. "I'd rather not talk about my personal life, if you don't mind."

"I just want us to be friends, Miriam."

"You hired a nurse."

Mr. Hoffman looked startled, then laughed. "Very good. I don't blame you for being upset. I have a distressing habit of upsetting people, perhaps because I make my living that way. Rattling people on the stand. Harold used to call me Dr. Jekyll and Mr. Lawyer." He laughed again. "He had a sharp tongue. His mother too. I respected them for it. Just as I respect you."

"I really should look in on him."

"Trying to get rid of me, Miriam? But I'd much rather stay and talk to you. For instance, I believe you were telling me that something rather remarkable had taken place today."

She felt like whatever she said could and would be used against her in his private court of law. "A week ago, I showed Harold his mother's grave in the cemetery. I held his hand and traced out her name with his fingers. There was no reaction. But I didn't give up. I thought that sooner or later, by sheer repetition, something might click. And today it finally did. He recognized her name. It was . . . beautiful." She couldn't keep a catch from her voice.

"An emotional moment, evidently. What was it that alerted you to this epiphany?"

"He cried."

"I thought as much. You're deluding yourself, Miriam. Harold cries at the drop of a hat. It's one of his favorite pastimes. He can barely recognize his *own* name, let alone anyone else's."

His patronizing attitude angered her. "You've had too much to drink, Mr. Hoffman."

He lurched to his feet. "It's my house, my liquor. You don't know what it costs me to come here. You can't know."

Though frightened, she forced herself not to back down. "Then why come? Not for Harold's sake!"

"No, not for Harold's sake. Believe me, I'd stay away if I could."

"Why can't you?"

He looked away as if ashamed. "She won't let me. May. I dream of her, you know. Yes, it's true. She haunts my sleep if I stay away too long. Only by coming back here can I make the nightmares stop . . . for a while! And when I'm here, every moment is a concentrated nightmare. Even alcohol barely dilutes the horror. She blames me, Miriam! She does! She torments me! When I saw Harold, I thought . . . " He began to weep.

"Mr. Hoffman, please . . . " She crossed the kitchen to him, no longer afraid or angry, and tried to take his hand.

"For eight years it's been this way. I don't know what to do anymore. I think I must be sick. Yes, I'm sick. Forgive me!" He brushed past her, out of the house. She followed, but he was already getting into his car.

"Forgive me!" he called again, and she knew that he was addressing the spirit of his dead wife as much as, even more than, her. The door slammed and the Lincoln backed out of the driveway in a spray of gravel.

That night Miriam dreamed she was running through a thick fog. Behind her, a pair of headlights drew closer and closer. An engine growled at her back. Waking with a start, she clutched the blanket and gazed fearfully into the darkness as if the engines she was hearing had pursued her out of sleep.

Then she heard shouts and laughter in addition to the engines. The noises were coming from behind the house. Miriam got out of bed and went to the window.

The fields were dotted with the headlights of dirtbikes. They bounced and swerved like frantic will-o'-the-wisps. Heavy metal music was a faint but constant presence, filling the gaps. Miriam was more annoyed than afraid; a call to the police in New Ridge would put a quick stop to the party. But first she checked on Harold.

The door to his room was open, his bed empty. Through his window, she saw flashlights in the cemetery.

"Harold!" she called, afraid now. "Harold!"

No answer.

Miriam ran to the back door. As she'd feared, it was open too. She fetched her robe and hurried outside, calling his name as she stumbled down the lawn.

A group of shaggy-haired teenagers in jeans, leather jackets and torn black t-shirts were clustered among the gravestones. Flashlights cast a gloomy light on the androgynous faces that looked up with indifference as she reached the cemetery fence. She smelled marijuana; the dull orange tips of cigarettes or joints floated in the air.

"Have you seen a tall, blond-haired man?" The faces regarded her without answering. They made her feel self-conscious, as if she were the one trespassing; she wished she'd thought to bring a flashlight. "Please, it's important! I'm his nurse!"

One of the faces smirked and whispered something before replying. "Harold? Sure, we seen him."

"Where is he? Is he all right?"

"Sure, he's cool," came the same laconic voice. "He's hanging with Joey."

The sound of the dirtbikes suddenly registered. "You don't mean he's riding one of those things? Are you crazy? Do you want to kill him?"

"Chill out, nurse lady. I said he's cool."

"He's *not* cool," she shouted. "Get him now or I'll call the police!"

More whispers. One of the group ran off.

"He's coming, lady. You got a serious attitude problem!"

"If you've hurt him . . . "

"Nobody's hurt nobody. He's with Joey, okay?"

"Who's Joey?"

"I am."

A tall young man strode out of the woods. He was almost as thin as Harold. He wore a leather jacket and had a motorcycle helmet tucked under his arm. His face was in shadow, but Miriam felt his eyes on her. She pulled her robe tight and tried to keep her voice from shaking. "Where's Harold?"

"I heard about you," Joey said. "Grandma says you're on the up and up, not like the others."

"You're Mrs. Graves' grandson?"

He nodded. "Harold and me is friends, okay? He heard the music and came down; he digs heavy metal. I was just giving him a ride on the back of my bike. Real slow, so don't freak. I was gonna bring him back. I always do."

Miriam was almost speechless. "You've done this before?"

"Lots of times. It's no big deal. Harold digs it. Reminds him of the good old days, I guess."

"Let me see him."

"No problem. Yo, Harold!"

Harold shambled out of the woods. He looked ridiculous in his blue pajamas and a red motorcycle helmet but didn't seem hurt in any way. He was grinning from ear to ear.

"Dude!" Joey stopped Harold and removed the helmet. "We didn't get him high or nothing, if you're worried about that."

"I'm worried about you giving him rides while *you're* high, Joey. Does your grandmother know you're out here at this time of night?"

"I don't do nothing when I'm on the bike, okay?" He gave Harold a gentle push in her direction.

"Are you all right, Harold?" Only the presence of Joey and his friends kept her from giving Harold an unprofessional hug. "You had me worried half to death, running off like that!"

Harold gurgled happily, his head bobbing.

Joey spoke up. "You ain't gonna say nothing to Grandma, are you?"

"Well . . . " She just wanted to get Harold back to the house. "Not this time. But no more bike rides. And you kids have to stop coming around here like this. A cemetery is no place to party—have some respect!"

A chorus of groans from the gravestones.

"Shut up, you guys," said Joey. "Here, I'll help you with Harold."

"I can manage."

But Joey was not to be denied. As they walked up the lawn, Harold between them, he said: "Look, is it okay if I stop by during the day sometime to see Harold and stuff?"

Miriam was surprised. "You really do like him, don't you, Joey?"

Joey shrugged. "I knew him before. Maybe I can give him rides in the driveway with you watching. It's the closest he gets to racing anymore. Man, that was his *life*. He was the baddest thing on four wheels. Drove a souped-up Porsche called the Silver Ghost. That car was cherry. Now what's he got to look forward to?"

Miriam was touched. "Come by whenever you like. On second thought, call first. I don't think Mr. Hoffman would understand."

They walked on in silence. Then Joey said: "That was the car his mom was driving when . . . well, you know."

"The Silver Ghost?"

Joey nodded. "After the wreck, they couldn't get her out. That's how bad it was. I mean, they would have had to cut her up into like ten thousand pieces. So Hoffman had them haul the car away. You know those junkyard compactors? That's what he used on her. Crushed the car around her for a coffin, then buried her." Joey gave a half-admiring laugh. "Ain't that some wild shit?"

Miriam stopped. "You tell me."

"It's on the level. I swear."

"But that's terrible. Poor Mr. Hoffman!" She felt she had a better understanding now of the guilt and fear that haunted him.

"Poor *Mrs.* Hoffman, more like."

"Harold visits her grave every day."

"No shit? I didn't know he was that together."

"He's more together than a lot of people give him credit for."

"I hear that. Sometimes when we're riding, I feel him hooked into the bike like he could drive it by himself if he had to. Almost like he *is* driving it, only *through* me. You know how they say when you lose one sense the others grow stronger to make up for it? Harold's like that. Maybe he ain't smart no more, but everything else is working overtime."

"I hear *that*," Miriam said with a smile.

The next day was Friday. Miriam and Harold went shopping in New Ridge with Mrs. Graves. The old woman called early in the morning and arrived to pick them up in an ancient brown and tan station wagon at ten o' clock precisely.

The winding, hilly road cut through thick woods to emerge amid fields that fell off sharply on either side. Miriam tried to imagine Harold and May careening around these curves on that fatal night. But in daylight it looked peaceful. There were cows and sheep and an occasional slow-moving tractor. White farmhouses varied with suburban brick homes and shabby aluminum trailers whose muddy yards featured rusting cars raised on cinderblocks and emaciated mongrels chained to satellite dishes.

"I met your grandson last night," Miriam said as, beside her, Harold gazed out the open window like a dog.

Mrs. Graves' bright eyes darted from their contemplation of the road. "Joey? Runs with a bad crowd, but he's a good boy. How'd you meet him?"

Miriam recalled her promise. "He came by to say hello to Harold."

"Harold was a real hero of Joey's back in his racing days. Gave him a ride once in the Silver Ghost. Joey's never forgotten that. He likes to return the favor."

"He told me about the Silver Ghost. Is it really true?"

"That Mrs. Hoffman's buried inside it, you mean? Sure, it's true. Mr. Hoffman swore everyone involved to secrecy, but my cousin Earl's boy, Earl, Jr., works down at the junkyard, and he saw everything. My heart goes out to that woman. What she had to put up with!"

"What do you mean?"

"Has he had a go at you yet, dear? You can tell me!"

Miriam shook her head. "He came by for a visit yesterday. He was very distraught, almost irrational." She related what had happened but left out Mr. Hoffman's conviction of being haunted, feeling that she would be betraying a confidence. "It's easy to see that he still suffers from what happened."

"He's got you feeling sorry for him; that's half the battle." Mrs. Graves reached across Harold to pat Miriam's knee with a bony hand. "I didn't want to mention this before, but you're the first real nurse he's hired for Harold in years."

Miriam looked at her blankly. "*Real* nurse?"

"Your predecessors were paid for other services than nursing Harold, if you get my drift."

"Joey said something last night, but I—"

"The way I heard, Mrs. Hoffman had had it about up to here with his constant philandering. Vera—that's my cousin works down at the courthouse—says there was even talk of a divorce. That was before the accident, of course."

"What are you saying? That he murdered her?"

"Quick, hold Harold's hands down! Do it!"

Confused, Miriam obeyed. As the car came around a bend, Harold reached for the wheel. He was not strong. Miriam easily stopped him. Then they were past, and Harold's struggles ceased as abruptly as they'd started.

"What was that all about?"

"Back there's where the car went off the road that night. It always affects him . . . like he's back in the Silver Ghost, grabbing for the wheel. Don't ask me how he knows."

"I'm beginning to think Harold knows a lot."

"He knows the answer to your question."

"My question?"

"You asked me if Mr. Hoffman murdered his wife. Aside from Mr. Hoffman—and Mrs. Hoffman, of course—Harold is the only one who knows. The only problem is, he doesn't *know* he knows." Mrs. Graves had a good laugh at that.

"Sit still now," Miriam admonished. It was later in the evening of the same day. Bath time. Harold was more trouble than a big puppy. She was soaked to the skin. "I'll take my bath later, Harold, thank you very much."

Naked, Harold was an odd sight, a study in contrasts. His thin body was finely tanned wherever the sun reached and pale as plaster where it did not, heavily scarred in some places and unmarked in others, covered with a fuzz so light as to be almost invisible. His golden hair darkened to brass when wet, clinging to the sunken planes of his skull where the metal plate was. The effect was to throw both the shape of his head and the harmony of his features weirdly out of balance, like a Picasso come to life.

"Out we go."

Soapy water cascaded into the tub as Harold stood. Miriam guided him onto the bathmat and patted him dry with a fluffy white towel. Harold giggled, entranced by his reflection in the full-length mirror behind the door.

Suddenly Miriam gasped and drew back, clutching the towel as if she, and not Harold, were the naked one. In all the times she'd bathed him, dressed him in the morning and undressed him at night, never had he reminded her in this way that he was a man and not a child. She'd assumed his injuries had rendered him incapable; surely Mrs. Graves would have said something to prepare her, however obliquely. Harold, meanwhile, was happily if clumsily stroking his erection.

Dizzy, Miriam dropped the towel and leaned back against the door. She knew she was on the edge of something, a line that, once crossed, could never be crossed over again. She'd crossed a line like this once before, though not by her own choice. She remembered that night, how she'd lain in a pool of blood at the foot of the stairs, half-unconscious. Her then-husband, Michael, swayed drunkenly above her, his raging eyes wide with the horror of what he'd done. Much later, in the hospital, the doctor had told her about the miscarriage. He'd told her there would be no more children. She'd been hemorrhaging inside. They'd had to remove her uterus.

She wasn't whole anymore. Wasn't a woman.

She divorced Michael and threw herself into her work, seeking substitutes for what she'd lost. But they said she was unstable and fired her from job after job, Columbia-Presbyterian only the latest. Not until Harold had she found what she was looking for: a perfect child whom she could care for without interference.

Except he wasn't just a child. He was both man *and* child. And men were a problem. Miriam couldn't feel attracted to a man without feeling a deep sense of guilt, as if she were forgiving Michael for what he'd done to her and to the life within her. She hadn't been with a man since that night. But

Harold had awakened more in her than she'd realized. She felt that everything had been building toward this moment, this chance to feel whole again . . . or, if not whole, then at least to know her wounds were matched by the wounds of another.

She led Harold to her bedroom and sat him on the edge of the bed. She undressed quickly, trembling with a desire that had gone unsatisfied for too long, a desire she'd thought dead inside her along with everything else. Then she went to him. She knelt between his legs and pressed him back onto the mattress. The air between them seemed to carry an electric charge, a passion all its own.

Sensing Harold's impatience, Miriam guided him between her legs and rocked back with a groan. Harold squirmed beneath her. Miriam steadied his head between her hands. She brought her face close to his and saw her reflection in his blue eyes, tiny and distinct as an image in still water.

"Pretty," Harold gasped.

"Yes," she said, feeling him swell then come inside her with a heat that left her quaking. He was asleep before he slid from her.

Miriam began to cry. Gentle tears. There was no going back. Not that she wanted to, but she knew, though she hadn't had much of it in her life, that this happiness wasn't the kind that came cheaply or lasted very long. She turned out the light and hugged Harold close under the blanket, smelling the clean fragrance of his hair. When she fell asleep, all boundaries dissolved between them.

She was driving. Harold sat beside her. It was night, and they were going very fast, scarcely watching the twisting road as they shouted back and forth, arguing about something. Suddenly, out of nowhere, a deer leaped into the road, its eyes shining like the headlights of an oncoming vehicle. Miriam screamed and stamped the brake. There was no response. Again and again she pushed it to the floor. A sick look of understanding spread across Harold's face. He grabbed for the wheel as Miriam sent the car swerving to one side. They shot off the road. For a second, they were flying.

Miriam woke covered in sweat. Her heart was pounding. Harold snored softly. The luminous dial of the clock beside the bed read 4:27.

Miriam rose and went to the window. The sky was paling. Gray clouds moved in packs that drifted slowly apart, revealing in their ragged gaps the cold and distant glimmer of a star. She thought of Harold's mother wrapped in the wreckage of the Silver Ghost at the base of the hill, where a line of darkness dissolved bit by bit in the face of the oncoming day, and shivered. What dreams troubled *her* sleep?

Harold woke as he did each day, to a world freshly made, without precedent or puzzle. A world in which there was no past or future, no regrets or hopes, only the eternal instant. Looking into his eyes, empty of memory and desire, Miriam saw something almost holy, something she could learn from. Nothing else made sense to her now.

The next week passed smoothly, in a kind of Indian Summer glow. Joey came by once to give Harold a ride on his bike under Miriam's watchful eye, down to the end of the driveway and back. Mrs. Graves called to chat and grouse about her husband's sex drive. Miriam didn't hear from Mr. Hoffman at all.

It seemed to her that she slept through the days and came awake only in the nights. Then, trembling with excitement, she brought Harold to her bed and made love to him, crying out without fear or shame. Afterwards, as he slept, she stroked the dented crucible of his head as if it had the power to grant her wishes like some magic lamp in a fairy tale. Each night she dreamed of the car crash, the episode growing more vivid, the emotions more intense. One night she was awakened by the growl of an engine, but when she went to the window the moonlit fields were empty.

Finally Mr. Hoffman called to say he would be stopping by that evening. His voice carried a chill to Miriam's heart, a killing frost. Even Harold seemed aware of a change; on their usual afternoon walk, he found his mother's grave and traced the letters of her name all by himself, something he'd never done before. Back at the house, Miriam kept hearing a car turn into the driveway, tires crunching on gravel. She ran to the window, but there was never anyone there.

After five or six false alarms she stopped looking. She nearly jumped out of her skin when the doorbell finally rang. Harold, who was in the living room, looked up sharply from his trophies and headed for the sanctuary of his bedroom, as if he knew very well who had come to call.

Miriam opened the door. Mr. Hoffman stood there, sweat dripping from his bald head though the evening was cool. He wore what she had come to think of as his standard uniform: a dark blue pinstripe suit.

"Good to see you, Miriam. How's the patient?"

She smelled bourbon. "In his room."

"Good." He brushed past her into the house. "We wouldn't want any more surprises, would we?"

Something in his tone put her on guard. She trailed him to the kitchen, where he immediately poured a shot of bourbon, gulped it down, then poured a larger glass.

"I don't suppose you'd consider joining me?"

"I'll have a scotch and water." She needed something to steady her nerves.

Mr. Hoffman's eyes grew wide. "This *is* an occasion!" He fixed the drink and handed it to her, then raised his glass: "To friendship."

Miriam drank, wondering what he was up to. The drink was strong. "You look tired, Mr. Hoffman."

"Yes, well, I haven't had much sleep, you see." He laughed. "I'm afraid that May is up to her old tricks. The nightmares. So I've come back. But not just because of May. No, I've come to see you, Miriam. There's something we need to discuss."

"About Harold?"

"About all of us. But not here. Why don't you wait in the living room?"

As she left the kitchen, Miriam heard the cough of an engine and the crunch of gravel. She hurried to the living room window and pulled aside the curtain. It was too dark to see clearly; a light glimmered at the foot of the driveway, then vanished. Maybe Joey had come for a visit, she thought, only to leave after seeing Mr. Hoffman's car.

"Expecting someone?"

Miriam turned. "I thought I heard something."

Mr. Hoffman held a tray on which he'd set the bottles of scotch and bourbon along with a pitcher of water. He placed the tray on the coffee table then lowered himself onto the couch as if doubtful of its ability to support his weight. "Perhaps it's May."

"May?" Miriam was confused.

"A joke." There was a brittle edge to his laugh that made her shiver. "Do I frighten you, Miriam?"

"Of course not," she lied.

"You think I'm crazy."

She weighed her words, afraid of setting him off. "I'm not a psychiatric nurse, Mr. Hoffman. But I can see that you're very tired. Under a lot of stress. I could recommend a psychiatrist, someone to talk to. It helps."

"You're an expert on that."

"I told you, I'm not . . . "

"I meant as a patient."

Miriam thought she might faint. She sat down on the nearest chair and gulped the rest of her drink.

"I've done some checking into your references, Miriam. I'm on the boards of quite a few hospitals and charitable institutions. I know about your dismissal from Columbia-Presbyterian. It wasn't a matter of budget cuts at all, was it? It was razor cuts."

Miriam was trembling.

"According to the records, you have a tendency to become, shall we say, a little too involved with your patients. Especially those least able to care for themselves. The very young, the very old, and the ones who, like Harold, fall somewhere in between. Unprofessional to say the least, but understandable in light of your history. I mean, what your husband did to you. You should have prosecuted, you know."

"You had no right . . . "

"On the contrary. But let's not argue about rights. I know what I know. And I'm prepared to use it."

"You mean fire me?"

"I would hate to have to do that, Miriam. I honestly would. It's not easy out there right now. And I'd feel it my duty to pass on what I know. God knows you're no murderer or child molester, but, still, the whiff of scandal clings to every page of your files. A hint—more than a hint—of the improper. Your influence on certain patients has been far from beneficial, Miriam. The psychiatrists, for once, agree. That kind of dependency is not healthy. It has a tendency to get very messy. Need I remind you of Alyson?

Of course, it wasn't really your fault, despite the poor girl's note. Just the same, I don't think you'd have much luck finding another nursing job. Do you?"

Miriam shook her head, remembering Alyson. A recovering anorexic. Her face an angel's. It had all been an accident. A horrible misunderstanding. Kindness mistaken for something more. They'd found her in the bathroom, her wrists cut. She'd lived, thank God. But they hadn't let Miriam see her again. They'd fired her.

"How are you and Harold getting along?"

Miriam felt herself blushing. Did he know? She averted her eyes but was unable to keep her voice free of feeling. "Please, Mr. Hoffman, I couldn't bear . . . "

"I told you, I have no wish to fire you, Miriam. It's entirely up to you whether you go or stay. As far as I'm concerned, what you do with Harold is your own affair. Mother him to your heart's content. *Smother* him. But I have needs too. The needs of a man, not a child. It can be very pleasant here for all three of us, Miriam."

"Mrs. Graves was right." Miriam stood on shaky legs. "You disgust me!"

"So you've been listening to that old busybody. What else has she told you?"

"That you murdered your wife!" The words slipped out before she knew it.

Mr. Hoffman's face turned bright red. He pushed to his feet. "It was an accident!"

Suddenly Miriam understood. Her voice was a whisper. "It was *Harold* you meant to kill, wasn't it?"

Mr. Hoffman controlled himself with an effort. He poured another glass of bourbon. "That's ridiculous, Miriam. Stop trying to change the subject."

"You did something to the car. Fixed it so the brakes would fail. Only you never figured your wife would be driving that night, did you? You thought it would be Harold! What went through your mind as you watched the two of them drive off in the Silver Ghost?"

"You don't know what you're talking about!"

"I've dreamed it. Every night for the past week I've dreamed it! You're not the only one with nightmares, Mr. Hoffman. Why did you do it? Because she was going to divorce you? Did you think that, with Harold gone, she'd be bound to you more tightly?"

Mr. Hoffman set his empty glass carefully on the coffee table. His hand was shaking, but his voice was calm. "My dear Mrs. Bowles. You're making me very angry. You don't want to make me angry, I assure you. You can't know what it was like living with those two. They were closer than a mother and son should be. Do you understand what I'm saying?"

"I don't believe you."

"What matters is that no one will believe *you*. You can't prove a single word of it. Dreams are not yet admissible in a court of law. I, however, possess ample proof of your repeated unprofessional conduct. I advise you very strongly to forget this nonsense and cooperate with me if you want to continue caring for Harold. You *do* want that, don't you?"

She began to cry. "Yes. Yes, I want it, you bastard!"

"We all want something, Miriam. That's the way the world works. You give something, I give something back. Shall we go to your room?"

"After all this, you still want . . . "

"I'm a passionate man, Miriam. As you'll soon discover."

"I need another drink."

"By all means."

In the bedroom, Mr. Hoffman sat on the bed and ordered Miriam to undress. She tried not to think as she removed her clothes. Her head swam from the scotch and water. Mr. Hoffman's stare was itself an assault. He massaged himself through the blue pinstripe suit, his face reddened and running with sweat. He sat upon the bed like a fat toad oozing poison. The bed where she and Harold . . . Miriam couldn't stand it. She started to cry again.

"No crying!" Mr. Hoffman snapped. "Come here!"

Miriam tried to make her mind go blank. She told herself over and over that she was doing this for Harold. So they could be together. She repeated it like a mantra.

At first, Mr. Hoffman barely touched her. There was almost no contact between them. He told her what to do. She had never felt so degraded, like she wasn't a person anymore, but only a hollow object. Yet that feeling made it somehow easier to bear, as if the real Miriam were somewhere else, far away from what was going on, safe in the changeless world that Harold inhabited.

Time passed; how much or how little, Miriam couldn't say. All she knew was that there came a time when Mr. Hoffman was no longer content to watch, when he could no longer give coherent commands but only grunt his dead wife's name as though undergoing a violent exorcism. He rolled on top of her. Miriam closed her eyes and was back at the foot of the stairs, lying in a pool of blood, her baby already dead inside her.

Then suddenly the pressure was gone. She opened her eyes. Mr. Hoffman was on his knees on the floor, his pants around his ankles. He was babbling to a figure in the doorway. The figure of a middle-aged woman with long blond hair. His wife. May Alliston Hoffman.

Miriam felt herself move. She was not aware of willing her movements. It was like a dream . . . and not even her own dream, but someone else's. Her hands found the lamp on the bedside table and ripped its cord from the socket. She got to her knees, raised the heavy base over her head and brought it down hard on Mr. Hoffman's skull. There was a dull, sloppy thud, as if she'd hit him with a sack of wet cement. She struck him again. Mr. Hoffman fell over. His head resembled what Harold's must have looked like after the wreck of the Silver Ghost.

Miriam scrambled to her feet. The figure in the doorway began to moan. It was not May Hoffman at all, but Harold.

Miriam ran to him and hugged him hard. She was shivering; she didn't think she would ever be warm again.

"Mother," Harold said.

Mr. Hoffman lay where he had fallen. Miriam had seen enough death to recognize it now. Its smell was on her: bourbon and sweat and sex. She ran to the bathroom and threw up. Then she took a shower as hot as she could stand it. She threw up again in the shower.

Miriam dressed quickly, avoiding the sight of the body as best she could. She got Harold from his bedroom and took him out to her car. She buckled him in, then backed out of the driveway in a squeal of tires. She didn't know where they were going, only that it lay far away from where they were now, across lines she couldn't imagine.

Back there on the other side were all the things she knew, things left behind like so much excess baggage when she'd crossed over. Her profession, her ideas of right and wrong, her sense of who she was. All gone, along with her patients, her ex-husband, her dead child, all the children that should have been. The only thing left was Harold. The two of them against the world, just like in the song. There was a place for them out there. There had to be.

Miriam drove fast. After a while, she noticed the appearance of bright headlights behind her. Harold began to whimper, not in fear, but with excitement, like he did when they made love.

"Shh," she said, stepping on the gas.

The headlights grew brighter as the car overtook them. No question; it was following them. Who could it be but Mr. Hoffman? She should have checked to make sure he was dead! Now he was coming after them.

The car was right on their tail. It swerved into the oncoming lane and pulled alongside, then swerved again, right into them. Miriam braced for the impact, but there was nothing. Only a strange flutter of coldness, as if two liquids of differing densities had passed through her and each other, mingling.

The other car was gone. Miriam looked in the rearview mirror, thinking it had dropped behind. But beneath her features, as though her skin had grown translucent, she saw the face of an attractive, middle-aged woman with blue eyes and long blond hair.

Miriam screamed and hit the brakes. At the same instant, Harold grabbed for the wheel. Only then did Miriam recognize the stretch of road.

The car swerved and accelerated sharply, as if racing toward a finish line. There was a flutter of foliage before the windshield like a checkered flag coming down, and then they were across.

WHERE BALLOONS GO

O N HIS THIRD NIGHT IN THE NEW APARTMENT, JUST WHEN HE'D
begun to feel at home, Felix Cody was jolted out of a sound sleep by a
noise he had not heard before. His heart rose in his throat like a balloon
that had snapped its string. Then he realized that it was only the buzzer. He
lay back on his new mattress, no longer frightened but uncomfortably
aware of how alone and vulnerable he was, knowing none of the neighbors,
the phone not yet installed and the windows barless until tomorrow
evening, when the locksmith was coming by.

Felix groped behind him for his watch and pressed the button that illuminated its face. It read 3:37. Who could be buzzing him at this hour on a
Monday morning? No one came to mind. He lay tensely in the loft he'd
inherited from the previous tenant, waiting for the drunk or street person
to get tired of the game and move on. What had he done to deserve this?
Every day he deposited a quarter into the first outstretched palm he saw.
The idiot was going to wake the whole building!

There were four apartments on each floor, one in each corner. The brick
walls functioned like taut strings linking tin cans. Every day hollow waves
of conversation, the words indistinct but the tones tantalizing, suggestive of
murmured endearments and muffled cries of passion or rage, wafted into
Felix's apartment along with the drone of televisions and radios and the bass
thump of speakers. As if that wasn't bad enough, his bedroom abutted the
bathroom of the apartment opposite his. Each morning he'd been awakened by the horrible intimacy of what was presumably a toilet seat being
flung down, followed by an assortment of grunts so graphic that the wall
might as well have been made of glass. The name on the mailbox down-

199

stairs was B. Waite; Felix had decided the "B" stood for Bruno. He'd seen Bruno through his peephole a few times: big, fat, mean-looking, with a forehead that suggested a throwback to Neanderthal times. The thought of Bruno rudely awakened for a change made Felix smile.

But in the next instant he expelled a breath of infinite suffering as the finger ceased jabbing the buzzer and pressed it down in a sustained assault. That was too much to bear. Felix swung his legs over the side of the bed, questing for the smooth wood of the ladder with his toes, and climbed down. He felt his way through the maze of still-unpacked boxes to the apartment's other, scarcely larger, room, where he flicked on the light and lunged for the buzzer beside the door. He pressed the "talk" button. "Who is it?"

There was no reply. In his anger, he'd neglected to press the "listen". He did so now and heard an unintelligible voice sink into static.

"What?"

This time the voice, though tinny, was identifiably male and clear enough to understand: "Stop fooling around, Frieda! Buzz me up!"

Felix heaved an exasperated sigh. "You've got the wrong apartment!"

"Doesn't Frieda Gombrowicz live here anymore?"

As if the last name would make a difference: Oh, *that* Frieda! "No, she doesn't! Goodnight!"

Felix wished he'd said something more insulting, but he hadn't wanted to antagonize the guy, wind up being held hostage by the buzzer for the rest of the night. But he hadn't even turned off the light before it buzzed again.

"Now what?"

"Where is she? Where's Frieda?"

"How should I know? Look, it's almost 4 a.m.! I'm going to call the cops if you don't leave me alone!"

Felix prayed the bluff would work; the only way he could call anybody was to open the window and shout. But the buzzer was quiet. After a while he cautiously pressed the "listen" button. There was only white noise, the forlorn sound of an empty city street.

Felix rose to the chirping of his watch alarm. Groggy and irritable, he navigated the obstacle course of unpacked boxes as he showered, dressed and fixed breakfast. God, the place was a mess. He must have been crazy to think that he could fit all his stuff into a place this size, but he'd been desperate to get away from Washington Heights, where salsa blared at all hours of the day and night, punctuated by sirens and gunfire. On the plus side, at least there was no bathroom reveille from Bruno; aside from the burble of water through the pipes and the frantic buzz of radio d.j.'s, the building was quiet.

Felix hurried out of his apartment and down the stairs, hoping to avoid his neighbors. They probably thought that it had been a friend of his, that he was the kind of guy who had friends who routinely pressed his buzzer at 3:37 on a Monday morning. Not that he cared what they thought.

Except for Marjorie Jett. Felix didn't actually know her; in fact, he'd seen her only once, on Friday, when he was moving in. Their apartments were side by side, not end to end like his and Bruno's. She was standing outside her door as he staggered up the stairs under a load of boxes. The first thing he saw was her legs, slender and fit in jogging shoes and silky red shorts. She was fishing in her waist pouch, presumably for her keys. She glanced up and gave him a harried but not unsympathetic smile that made something swell in his chest. Without staring, she seemed to see right through him. He stumbled and nearly dropped the boxes.

The funny thing was, he couldn't say for sure what color her eyes were, or even what she looked like. He thought there had been a flash of green and gold, and he remembered pale skin and long dark hair, but it all happened so quickly that she was inside before he could think of anything to say. Downstairs he'd found her name on the mailbox between his and Bruno's. Marjorie Jett. Since then he'd often pressed his ear to the wall they shared, but heard only muffled footsteps and classical music.

Outside, the sun was bright, the October air crisp, the sky a gorgeous, clear blue against which the Chrysler Building shone like tinsel. Felix started up the sidewalk at a brisk pace; one of the best things about the new apartment was that he could walk to work in fifteen minutes. From the Heights it had taken up to an hour by subway.

"Mister . . ."

A collection of rags stirred on the steps that led to the basement of the building next door. There was a methadone clinic around the corner on Second Avenue whose sad habitués haunted the neighborhood like corpses evicted from a graveyard. Felix held his breath and produced his daily quarter.

"Put your money away." The threadbare voice had a strange dignity.

"Suit yourself." Felix pocketed the quarter without breaking stride.

"Wait."

Felix hurried away. He heard footsteps . . . the man was following him.

"You live in number 17, don't you? Frieda's apartment."

Felix groaned. Out of the corner of his eye, he saw a man old enough to be his father, rake-thin, with clothes like Robinson Crusoe's and a huge floppy hat whose brim came down over his eyes. People stared, enjoying the show, glad it wasn't them.

"Don't you?" The man grabbed Felix's elbow.

Felix tried to pull away, but the old man's grip was surprisingly strong.

"The name's Gregson. Frieda had something of mine. We were supposed to meet last night, but she never showed. Now you tell me she's moved away. Where?"

Felix gazed into the old man's face. His mouth was like a pit of tar; his left eye was covered with a black patch, and his right eye sparkled with a hard, predatory glint, like a raven's. Gray hairs sprouted from his nose and ears. "I don't know."

"She had something of mine," Gregson insisted. "Didn't she leave anything with you?"

Felix looked desperately for a policeman. The smell was awful. Why did these things happen to him? It would be just his luck if Marjorie Jett walked by and witnessed his humiliation. "I didn't even know her! There was nothing in the apartment when I moved in."

"She might have left it behind. An aggie. Very rare. Worth a fortune."

"A what?"

"Aggie. A marble made of agate. You know, a shooter."

"You're looking for a *marble*?"

"An *aggie*," Gregson repeated with particular stress. "A *starburst* aggie. Have you seen it?"

Felix decided to play along. "I've got it right here. If you just let me go . . . " Gregson looked so happy that Felix almost felt guilty. But the instant the old man relaxed his grip, Felix ran like he'd never run before.

"Damn your eyes!" Gregson thundered behind him.

Felix cringed but didn't look back. He hailed a cab and jumped in. "Go! Go!"

As the cab sped off, Felix hammered down the locks and sank low into the seat. Gregson chased the cab, shaking one fist while holding down his floppy hat. Soon he was lost to sight.

"What'd that son of a bitch want?" the cabbie asked.

Felix shook his head. "A marble." He couldn't help laughing, but it was brittle laughter.

"I'm telling ya, the bums are dragging this city into the sewer. Just yesterday I was . . . "

Felix tuned the driver out, watching the flow of traffic and pedestrians as he rubbed his arm where Gregson had grabbed him. The homeless were everywhere. They stared after the cab with knowing eyes.

Felix worked in the proofreading department of Gentry & York, a law firm located on four floors in the Chrysler Building. He loved passing through the huge, high portals framed in black marble, loved the delicate inlaid wood paneling and bristling silver fixtures of the murky interior, which reminded him of Captain Nemo's submarine, the *Nautilus*. He especially loved the elevators, like kitschy time machines, up for future, down for past.

His job he wasn't too fond of. He'd started as a temp at Gentry & York when he moved to the city last year, then signed on full-time two months ago when a 9-5 spot had opened unexpectedly; the extra salary had been just enough to finance his move downtown.

The five other proofreaders had known each other for ages and still treated him like an outsider. The worst was Ms. Thiem, the supervisor, a middle-aged woman with rusty hair, flushed, sagging cheeks and wet blue eyes ballooned to such a degree by her thick glasses that Felix half-expected them to drift free of her face and float about the office, peering over everyone's shoulder. Each day the floating eyes would sag a little lower, until they swayed listlessly upon the carpet like undersea plants. Then one morning someone would notice quite suddenly that they were gone, vanished to wherever it is that balloons go.

Such fantasies brought a secret smile to Felix's heart as he sat poring over some interminable brief or other, the lawyerly language more deadly than any over-the-counter soporific. But in reality, Ms. Thiem's eyes never drifted anywhere, least of all away from the pile of work ever-growing upon her desk.

"Cody," she would snap. "Full-read!"

Or: "Cody! Redline!"

She saved the worst jobs for him. Jobs like black and white whirlpools into which he sank with pen and ruler and didn't surface for hours, his hands filthy with ink, his eyes seeing spots everywhere. He wondered if he was ruining his eyes.

He'd thought of looking for another job, but jobs were scarce and he'd put himself in debt by moving. He'd rather die than wind up back in Ohio with his mother, who'd warned him against moving to New York in the first place, predicting his return with her customary assurance even as she'd presented a powdered cheek for him to kiss goodbye.

Ms. Thiem glanced meaningfully at the clock as Felix passed her cubicle, a tiny space with windows but no door that she persisted in calling an office. He gave her an apologetic smile at which she appeared to scribble herself a note. Her desk was feathered with notes written on post-its. Passing the cubicles of his fellow proofreaders, he nodded his good-mornings. The usual pile of work was waiting on his desk. He plunged in, hoping it would take his mind off Gregson.

But Felix grew more apprehensive as the day wore on. What if the old man were waiting for him after work? The more he thought about it, the more likely the possibility seemed. Gregson, though obviously insane, did not seem like a man who gave up easily. Felix's arm still ached from the old man's grasp. There would probably be a bruise.

It was just after lunch when Felix was summoned by Ms. Thiem: "Cody! Into my office!"

The other proofreaders smirked as Felix put aside his work and walked up to Ms. Thiem's cubicle.

Ms. Thiem gazed at him for a long moment. Her eyes had never seemed so blue or so terrible. "Well, Cody. You've been here, what, two months now?"

Felix nodded, mouth gone dry.

"As you know, the first two months of employment are a probationary period. We get to know you; you get to know us. I think we know each other pretty well by now. Don't you?"

"Yes, ma'am."

Ms. Thiem began to tap her pen against the edge of the desk. His mother had the same habit, only with her foot. Tap, tap, tap as she ticked off his flaws, inherited from his father, one by one.

"I'll be frank," Ms. Thiem was saying. "There have been complaints about your work, Cody. From lawyers. Partners in this firm. We're going to let you go. You can finish out the week or not; it's up to you."

"I'll finish," he heard himself say.

"Nothing personal, Cody. I have to think of what's best for Gentry & York."

"I understand."

"Good." Her eyes released him.

Felix passed the rest of the day in a daze. Gregson's shadow seemed to have fallen over his life, blighting all that it touched. He felt that if he started to think about getting fired, about all the money he owed, a black pit would open into which he would fall and fall without ever touching bottom. He remembered when his father had lost his job. That had been the beginning of the end. Everyone said so, not just his mother.

That evening, Felix approached his street from an angle that gave him an unobstructed view of the places where someone might be lurking. There was no sign of Gregson. After waiting a good five minutes, during which time it grew noticeably darker, Felix decided to take a chance. He ran. He fumbled breathlessly with his keys, then was safely inside the building, the door slammed shut behind him. Only then did it occur to him that Gregson could have gotten inside during the day.

Felix crept up the stairs past the closed doors of his neighbors' apartments, each the same dull gray. He listened for the slightest suspicious sound and sniffed for the old man's stink. He was ready to run, his stomach churning. But each landing was empty, and there were no sounds other than the creaking of the stairs and his own scraping footsteps. When he reached the fifth floor landing, he saw with relief that it, too, was empty. There was, however, a small sheet of paper taped to his door.

It was a note from the police. A man had been arrested trying to break into his apartment from the fire escape. There was a number for him to call.

Felix laughed. So much for Gregson. He felt like his luck was changing at last. The apartment was just as he'd left it, boxes stacked in their already familiar disorder. His relief at finding everything safe made the place seem like home for the first time. A home he could no longer afford, but he wasn't going to worry about that. He had a credit card, and a whole month before the next rent check was due. He changed out of his work clothes and decided to call the police before he got bogged down in unpacking. Then it occurred to him that he could ask to use Marjorie Jett's phone.

Felix brushed his teeth and combed his hair. He gazed through his peep-hole—the idea that he might encounter Bruno in the stairwell was repugnant. The coast was clear.

Faint strains of music wafted through Marjorie's door. Felix hesitated, afraid of interrupting a private moment. He wondered if she was alone or with someone. Finally, after smoothing back his hair, he delivered a timid knock.

Footsteps drew near. A woman's voice asked: "Who is it?"

"Your new neighbor." He positioned himself so that she could see him through the peephole. "I wonder, can I use your phone? Mine's not in yet, and I need to make a call."

Felix heard the click of turning locks. The door opened a crack, still secured by a chain. There were no lights on in the apartment although it was by now quite dark outside. He saw a hint of pale skin, dark hair, dark glasses. The sounds of classical piano—perhaps Chopin, but he was no expert—cascaded out of the darkness like snowflakes. He had a crazy idea of catching them on his tongue. "Hi. I'm Felix Cody."

The woman nodded but said nothing. Her head was cocked at an odd angle, as if she were straining after the echoes of his words.

"We saw each other on Friday, when I was moving in. I've been meaning to introduce myself, but, well, you know how it is." He smiled uneasily. "If I've come at a bad time . . . "

"Not at all." As the edges of her mouth rose in a smile, Felix felt a tug on his heart. "You saw my sister, Marjorie. I'm Margaret. Margaret Jett."

Felix shook his head. "You look just like her."

"We're twins. But not just like, Felix. I'm blind."

He fumbled for something to say; he'd never known a blind person before. "I'm sorry."

"Don't be. We're not to be pitied; at least, I'm not."

He was glad she couldn't see him blush. "Now I'm really sorry."

She lifted her chin and laughed. "Come in and call the police, Felix." She unfastened the chain and opened the door.

"How did you know . . . ?" He stepped past her into the dark apartment.

"I've got sharp ears. I heard someone on the fire escape and called 911. I spoke with the officer who left the note on your door."

She shut the door. In the darkness, Felix could see only the silhouettes of furniture against the barred windows opposite, thick, mysterious shapes that seemed not quite solid, capable at any moment of flowing into new forms or dissolving altogether.

"The phone's right over here . . . "

"The lights are off," he said. "I can't see."

He heard her laughter again, counterpointing the piano. The lights came on with a snap. "I'm sorry; I forget sometimes."

He doubted that. She seemed to be gazing at him, as if she could see perfectly well. She wore faded blue jeans and a green blouse dotted with small red and blue flowers. The sight of her rekindled his memory of Marjorie. The sisters had the same dark hair, though Margaret's was straighter and shorter than Marjorie's, curling past her ears; the same pale skin, somewhat pinched nose and thin lips. He wondered what her eyes looked like behind those glasses.

"Help yourself." She indicated the phone.

"Thanks." He made the call. Sure enough, it had been Gregson. The old man was charged with attempted burglary, but was currently under psychiatric observation. According to the officer on the phone, Gregson claimed that he had been trying to retrieve property originally stolen from him, a valuable antique marble now in Felix's possession. Felix related what had happened that morning.

As he told the story, he watched Margaret move about the apartment, which was as cramped as his own although much less cluttered. The small room in which they stood had a beige sofa, a glass coffee table, a television and a stereo. There were neatly filled bookcases—mostly paperbacks—and framed prints from shows at the Met—two by Van Gogh and one by an Impressionist whom he recognized but whose name he could never remember. There was a coat rack by the door, beside which leaned a slender white, red-tipped cane. He imagined Margaret making her way down the bustling city streets, the cane tapping the ground like an insect's busy antennae. Such a fragile substitute for sight. He'd seen blind people on the streets before, but most of them had dogs, though even that seemed unbelievably courageous. A stove, sink, midget refrigerator and cabinets in another corner served as kitchen, where Margaret now busied herself fixing tea or perhaps coffee with a competence he found fascinating. The fact of her blindness made him feel invisible, adding a voyeuristic acuity to his vision.

"Sounds like your friend's lost more than one marble," Margaret said when he hung up.

"He's no friend of mine," Felix laughed. "The guy's a lunatic. You must have heard him buzzing me last night."

"So that's what it was." She took some teabags from a jar in the shape of a black and white cat. "Will you stay for tea, Felix?"

"I'd like that. Can I give you a hand?"

"Thank you, but I can manage perfectly well. Why don't you sit down?"

"I'm here at the end of the couch," he said, wanting to make it easy for her.

Margaret approached the coffee table with precise steps, carrying steaming cups on a tray. She stopped inches away and lowered the tray expertly to the table.

"It's hard to tell you're blind, you move so confidently."

She straightened up with a laugh, hands quickly tucking her hair back behind her ears. "You don't see the bruises that went into that confidence."

She came around the table and sat at the other end of the sofa. When she reached for her cup, it was as though her fingers had eyes. "Be careful. It's hot."

He watched as she blew on the tea, dark glasses fogged with steam. "Did you know the woman who lived next door? Frieda something? That's who Gregson was looking for."

Margaret ducked her head. "Frieda Gombrowicz. She was nice, but weird. Into some kind of occult stuff. You know, that New Age witchery. Used to burn incense constantly and play this strange noodling synthesizer music. Marjorie knew her better than I did."

Felix gave a nervous laugh. "You're saying she was a *witch?*"

"Not black cats and broomsticks. Earth magic. Gaia; you know, the Goddess. You've heard of politically correct? Frieda was what you'd call magically correct. She tried to get Marjorie interested, but we're kind of traditional when it comes to religion. I'm not even sure what happened to her. Marjorie might know."

"She sounds as loony as Gregson. I wonder—" Felix was interrupted by the sound of his own buzzer, muted by the wall but still loud enough to wake a sleeper. He winced, then remembered the locksmith. He put down his tea. "I've got to go, Margaret. I'm getting bars put in the windows."

"That'll keep the crazies out." She nodded approvingly. "Do you mind if I don't . . . " She gestured toward the door.

"Of course not. Thanks for everything."

"Stop by any time."

Back in his apartment, Felix pressed the "talk" button, suddenly afraid that Gregson had somehow gotten out of jail and returned to torment him. "Who is it?"

A voice growled: "Locksmith."

Felix buzzed him up.

The locksmith was a large, burly man in a Mets cap, a red and white checkered flannel shirt and faded blue overalls. He set right to work installing the iron grills that Felix had ordered, which he dragged up in two trips. As he drilled into the window frames, he kept up a steady stream of chatter about the ingenuity of the local burglars. Felix ignored him as best he could by unpacking boxes in his bedroom.

He'd scarcely begun when the abrupt clatter of the toilet seat being flung down on the other side of the wall made him flinch as though struck. This was followed almost immediately by grunts of such surpassing eloquence that Felix felt physically ill. He closed his eyes and leaned against the wooden frame of his loft bed, seething with embarrassment and rage.

"Jeez Louise." The locksmith poked his head into the room with an awestruck whistle. "What you got next door, a gorilla?"

"Sometimes I think so."

"I never heard nothing like that. It ain't natural."

"You don't have to tell me."

A moment later, the noises stopped. As usual, there was no sound of a flushing toilet.

"Mind lending a hand?" the locksmith asked. "My partner, he usually helps, he's sick today. Just hold the grill steady while I drill it in."

"Sure."

The grills were heavy, but the locksmith lifted them into place with seeming ease. Felix held tightly to the bars as the locksmith, balanced on a chair, drilled in the long screws that would hold the grills in place. The vibrations shook the windows, making his reflection in the dark glass tremble. Something hit the wooden floor with a small, hard crack. He looked down, expecting a screw. Instead, a black and white marble lay glittering beside his sneaker.

The locksmith saw it too. He stopped drilling. "Jeez, will you look at that! What a beauty! I ain't seen an aggie like that since I was a kid."

Felix groped under the windowsill; he felt a hollow space. Something else was in there. "An aggie?"

"Sure! Didn't you play marbles when you was a kid? Aggies make the best shooters." He smiled and shook his head as though reliving a fond memory. "I can still hear them clicking together. That could be the sweetest or the saddest sound you ever heard, depending on whose aggie was knocked out of the circle, yours or the other guy's. There was friendships stood every test but that one! You lost your best aggie, you lost a part of yourself with it."

Felix remembered what Gregson had said about the aggie being a valuable antique. It seemed impossible, as crazy as everything else about the old man. But still . . . he could use some extra money right now. "Is it worth anything?"

The locksmith laughed. "To me, yes. To you, no. See, it ain't a question of money. It's rich in memories. Good times. Like if you was to find a part of your childhood again, a part you'd given up for lost so long ago that you forgot it had ever existed."

Felix nodded, thinking of his father despite himself. He tried to remember him as he'd been long ago, when they'd thrown the football back and forth on blustery fall afternoons, or when they'd laughed together over Marx Brothers videos, he watching them for the first time, his father for the millionth but laughing every bit as hard. He wondered where he was now . . . the frail, foul-tempered drunk he'd turned into. More than once since he'd come to New York, Felix thought he'd seen his father on the street among the legions of homeless, but it had always been a false alarm. Some lost things you never got back.

Felix picked up the aggie. It was smooth as glass and cold, heavier than he'd expected, a deep, glossy black webbed with white pinpricks. What had Gregson called it? A starburst aggie.

"Say, why don't you let me have that old aggie?" the locksmith asked.

"I think I'll hold onto it." Felix slipped the aggie into his pocket.

"I swear it ain't worth a cent."

"I believe you."

"It don't mean nothing to you."

"You don't know that."

The locksmith breathed heavily. For a moment, his position above Felix, and the drill in his hand, made him appear threatening. Felix drew back. Then the locksmith sighed again, seeming to deflate. "Look. You go on out and see how much it's worth. Go ahead. Just don't sell it without calling me first, okay? That's all I ask."

"Okay," Felix promised.

After the locksmith had gone, Felix returned to the space below the windowsill and, kneeling, pulled from its tight and dusty confines what turned out to be a pocket address book. The book was filled with a dark and sinuous writing that flowed unbroken from line to line and page to page, the characters intertwined like branchings of a single black vine. The lush script resembled nothing he'd ever seen or imagined.

Suddenly dizzy, he shut the book; the dizziness disappeared as though caught between the covers. Margaret had called Frieda Gombrowicz a witch, and Felix was no longer so inclined to laugh at that characterization. He slipped the book into his shirt pocket.

Standing, Felix felt a coldness against his thigh, as if the aggie in his pocket had grown rimed with frost. He fished it out and held it in numbed fingers. The white pinpricks sparkled in the agate like stars on a crisp winter's night, when the air itself seems frozen, brittle as the thinnest ice over the deepest, darkest pond, yet so clear it makes the eyes ache.

Fascinated, shivering, he raised the aggie to his eye. Perhaps it was the reflection of his eye, but he thought he saw something coalescing in the depths, a milky emulsion that suddenly, like a bubble of gas, shot toward the surface. Before he could react, the aggie was gone, fumbled through his fingers and fallen, with a soft squishy plop, into his eye.

An icy needle pierced his brain. The floor fell open at his feet. He hung there, in space, as stars blew by in a fierce cold wind like streamers of snow. Far below he saw a pale string rising up out of the nothingness in a slender curve like a swan's neck, and he knew that he was attached to it somehow, floating.

Then Felix was back in his apartment. He noticed that his hand had gone gray and filmy, translucent. There seemed to be other hands there, like the blurred afterimages of a vibrating guitar string. He stumbled to the bathroom and gazed at himself in the mirror above the sink. The aggie glittered coldly where his right eye had been. Everything else trembled.

Behind, or, rather, beneath his features a gallery of ghostly, overlapping faces gazed back at him with expressions of stony indifference. He recognized his father's face, so close to the surface that it pressed against his skin as if determined to hatch out. There was no awareness in the ghastly features, no hint of regret or recrimination, no recognition, no memory, only a dull insistent half-life. It was the face he dreaded seeing every day on the street over the top of a coffee cup rattling with coins as he added his quarter.

Felix clapped his hand over his eye. The apparition vanished; he saw only his own ashen face glistening with sweat and tears. The pain in his head intensified, but he didn't dare take his hand away. Whimpering, he staggered to the bedroom with a dim intention of finding something to wrap around his head and cover his eye. Then he would go to the hospital. That was as far ahead as he could think; if the pain grew much worse, he was afraid he'd claw his eye out like some maddened animal.

But it was impossible among all the unpacked boxes to know where to look, or for what. Meanwhile he thought his head would burst. With a groan of terror and pain, he dropped his hand. There was an answering groan from the other side of the wall. Felix looked; he couldn't help it.

The wall had turned transparent. Seated upon a mound of bones, a shaggy, apelike creature gnawed at what appeared to be the forearm of a human being. Drooling gore, the creature tore away mouthfuls of flesh while grunting as if in sexual ecstasy; a huge erection rose from between its legs. Its great head lifted slowly, throat convulsing, as though aware of Felix's gaze but untroubled by it, like a feeding lion at the approach of some lesser beast. A single placid eye regarded him serenely for a moment before the head bent to resume its grisly supper.

Felix vomited. The contents of his stomach splashed against the wall. There, in his own sickness, writhed shapes he couldn't bear to see: half-digested fears and longings, rancid guilts and ulcerous hates, spoiled regrets, curdled pride, forgiveness gone sour.

He staggered from the bedroom, wiping his lips and chin. In so doing, his vision pierced the wall dividing his apartment from that of Marjorie and Margaret Jett.

Margaret stood before a dresser. Her back was to him, but he could see her reflection in the mirror there. Her dark glasses were off. The sockets were gaping wounds that lay open to the bone, burrows in which delicate veins and nerves wriggled like a nest of baby vipers.

As he watched, Margaret took from a jar upon the dresser what appeared to be a large olive or cocktail onion. Calmly, as though inserting a contact lens, she tilted her head back and dropped the thing into one socket. She repeated the process with the other eye, then contemplated her reflection in the mirror.

The eyes were green and piercing, flecked with gold. Eyelids fluttered like the damp wings of a moth freshly crawled from its chrysalis. Tilting her head from side to side, Margaret began to make faces like an actress rehearsing a demanding role.

It was Marjorie.

Felix ran from his apartment and down the stairs. Behind him, a door slammed. He heard Marjorie call his name. He kept running, his hand back over his eye despite the pain, terrified of seeing past the closed gray doors of his neighbors and into the secret horrors of their lives.

He burst onto the dark, deserted street. Dirty light pooled beneath the streetlamps, illuminating fallen leaves and loose garbage. There was something menacing about the cars parked along both sides of the street, as if they were watching his every move, radios tuned to the same station. Traffic streamed brightly by to the east and west, flowing uptown and down.

Felix ran west, toward Third Avenue, where the lights of the Chrysler Building shone a cold and steady white, like lightning bolts hammered free of all imperfections and harnessed in place by a magic more potent than technology. He hadn't gotten far when a hand reached out of the darkness of a stairwell and pulled him down. Another hand clapped over his mouth. His attacker was behind him, unseen, but Felix struggled less against whoever held him than against what he could see now that his eye was uncovered. He heard the slap of running feet on the sidewalk.

"Shh!" a voice hissed low in his ear.

Bruno shambled by, in his hand a gleaming bone, his nose raised as though sniffing the air for a familiar scent. After him came a woman who moved without a sound. A sickly phosphorescence moldered in her eyes like a guttering flame on the candle of sight. Felix shut his eyes tight.

After a while the voice hissed in his ear again: "Quiet now, on your life, for I'll kill you myself if they don't."

Felix nodded as best he could.

The hands relaxed a bit, but not enough for Felix to break free. Then he felt himself being lifted off the ground and turned around as though he were a child.

"Open your eyes."

He was looking at Gregson. The old man looked just as he had that morning, with his eyepatch and floppy hat, his fanatic eye, the tufts of gray hair sprouting from his ears and nose. Felix stared at the black patch.

"Yes," Gregson whispered. "You've got something of mine."

"You can have it," he gasped.

The old man squeezed him silent. "You're a fool. It's too late for that now."

Felix shook his head. "Please, no . . . "

Gregson smiled grimly. "Even with one eye I can see right through you. Hasn't it occurred to you yet to wonder why, of all the people you've seen with your new eye, yourself included, I alone am unchanged from what I was?"

It was true. The old man was solid, complete, as if, despite his missing eye, nothing could be added to him or taken away. "How . . . who are you? Who are those people? Please, what's happened to me?"

"Here, you'd better take this." Keeping hold of Felix with one hand, Gregson removed his eyepatch with the other. His socket was a cigarette burn in the fabric of the night.

Felix felt an icy wind blow into his soul. The edges of the socket glowed orange-red, fanned to life. The pressure in his head vanished as Gregson slipped the patch over his eye. He heaved a sob of relief and gasped out his thanks.

Gregson chuckled. The wind flowing from his socket reversed direction, sucking inward now. The edges glowed ever brighter, chewing up the old man as if he were made of ancient parchment. The socket spread wider and wider until there was nothing left of Gregson but a ring of raggedly pulsing fire.

Felix fell to his knees in the stairwell and began to weep. The awful pressure had returned to his head with Gregson's disappearance, as if his weirdly altered vision, blocked by the eyepatch, had turned against him, pressing a buzzer within his skull.

"Felix . . . ? Are you okay?"

Marjorie stood at the top of the stairwell, gazing down at him with concern. Bruno was beside her, holding a flashlight. They looked completely normal, backlit by a streetlamp, but Felix couldn't forget how they had appeared moments before. He backed against the damp brick wall.

"What is it, Felix?" Marjorie asked.

"What are you on, man?" Bruno demanded gruffly.

"What's happened to your eye?" Marjorie stepped down into the stair-well.

"Stay back, I'm warning you . . ." he croaked.

"We want to help, Felix." She took another step.

By some reflex, he lifted the eyepatch. He saw them again in their hideous forms. Marjorie drew back. The creature that had been Bruno snarled and raised its flashlight, which was once more a massive thighbone.

"Give us the eye, Felix," she said. Her foot tapped the ground nervously. "You don't know how to use it. It means nothing to you but madness. Pluck it out!"

He shook his head. A strange wisdom had come over him. "Those are Frieda's eyes, aren't they?"

"She had no more use for them. She'd found the eye and was going to restore it to its rightful owner. Why? So he could cast it down a well! What a colossal waste of power! But it's just as wasted in your head, you fool!" She lunged for him, her fingers sharp as knives.

He blinked; but it was the world that blinked instead, flickering on and off like a lightbulb in an electrical storm. When the world came back, Marjorie and Bruno were gone from it.

Felix felt a curious elation. His pain was gone, and he felt stronger, as if he'd absorbed their essences into his own. He noticed that he could see perfectly well in the darkness. His hand was more solid, with only a trace of the ghostly afterimages he'd seen before; they seemed to be fusing together, matching their vibrations to his own frequency. Then he remembered the address book in his pocket.

The exotic script made sense to him now. The words whispered their meanings in his mind, unraveling the tangle of things past and yet to come. He read about a well and a tree, a serpent and a wolf. There would be a battle, and he would have his place in it, a place of honor long foretold, whose bitterness he already tasted. But that was far ahead, farther than he could express in time, and now he had other tasks to perform, equally important.

For the rest of the night Felix roamed the city, visiting the haunts of the homeless. Those who asked for change he gifted with the oblivion of his sight. Others, too, he took; men and women whose shapes hid fouler things, though he spared some of these as well, for, like him, their purpose was not yet done.

Somewhere, his father was waiting. He would find him. If not this night, then another. And in Ohio his mother was expecting his return. He would not disappoint her. But there was no hurry. He had all the time in the world.

Morning saw Felix at the Chrysler Building, eyepatch in place, watching as the rising sun kindled the silver spire. Soon people began to arrive for work. They came in a trickle, then a great flood, moving along in their thousands as though blown by a relentless wind. They jostled against each other as their feet scraped over the ground.

Ms. Thiem floated by, her eyes fixed on the neck of the man preceding her. His fellow proofreaders passed, looking right through him. Lawyers in expensive suits and messengers in jeans and t-shirts swept by in bunches. He watched them drift through the great black portals of the Chrysler Building, whose shape, he noticed for the first time, was exactly that of coffins stood on end.

LEFT OF THE DIAL

THE SUMMER MY MOTHER DIED, I SPENT MORE TIME IN RESTON, the Northern Virginia community where I grew up, than I had since college. My mother still lived there, in the townhouse she'd bought after her divorce from my father. Although I was thirty-eight, with college and graduate school long behind me, it felt like summer vacation, a break between semesters. A period of waiting—in which days and weeks blurred together, giving the illusion of timelessness so familiar from childhood—for an interrupted life to resume. Not only mine, but my mother's, for she was determined to beat her disease, acute myelogenous leukemia, or AML, and I had enough experience of her will power to fully believe she would do it.

The sense of in-betweenness was enhanced by the fact that I'd recently lost my job as a content provider for one of the internet start-ups ubiquitous at the time. Fortunately, unlike many who wound up with nothing when the bottom fell out of the boom, I received a modest severance package—enough to finance a few months of back-and-forthing from my apartment in New York to my mother's place. I would stay for a week or ten days, visiting her in the hospital or caring for her at home after the completion of what became a series of failed chemo treatments, then jump on the train back to Manhattan. After a while, it came to seem that I was living in a house whose rooms were not physically contiguous: one in New York, two in Virginia (the hospital and the townhouse), and one on board whatever train I traveled by. I began to feel like I was leaving bits and pieces of myself behind in those rooms, ghostly remnants that languished, half-forgotten, until I reclaimed them like checked baggage. My sister, Ellen, who lives in Richmond with her family, was usually able to drive up to

Reston when I couldn't be there. Despite the divorce, my dad chipped in, too. But he was remarried, with a new family, and had responsibilities of his own. Besides, my mother didn't like feeling beholden to him. So it was mostly down to me; in the circumstances, losing my job turned out to be a blessing.

My days in Reston followed a comforting routine. I got up early, worked for a few hours on a novel I was trying to write (a satirical dot-com exposé, since abandoned), then went for a run along the bikepaths before the heat and humidity grew too punishing. The bikepaths of Reston are famous in the D.C. area: more than fifty-five miles of paved and unpaved trails snaking through thick woods and along rushing creeks while skirting baseball and soccer fields, playgrounds, highways, parking lots, and people's backyards. In the summer, when the foliage is at its fullest, it can seem like you are miles from human habitation . . . except for the stream of joggers, bikers, dog-walkers, and roller-bladers. I varied my route each day, always aiming for about five miles. I had picked up a map of the paths, without which I would have become hopelessly lost; the network had branched and tangled considerably since I'd moved to New York. Even with the map, there were times I lost my way in its mazy meanderings.

Reston is one of those planned communities, like Colombia, Maryland, that were supposed to be the wave of the future back in the Sixties. Experiments in enlightened social engineering meant to provide civilized, even artistic, alternatives to the bland conformity of suburban sprawl. Advertisements for a better, saner, more fulfilling way of life, places where you could feel that, every time you stepped onto a tennis court or dove into a pool, you were making a moral statement, setting an example, helping to bring the American dream, or one of them, closer to reality for everyone. Once upon a time, people really did think that way.

Built around a man-made lake, there was little about Reston that was not artificial . . . including, or so it seemed to me after we moved there in 1976, when I was eleven, the people. Especially the adults. There was a kind of Stepford utopianism about them; they saw themselves as pioneers in the brave new world of daily commuting beyond the D.C. beltway. Like my parents, they were liberal, highly educated, ambitious, and so determined to enjoy the cornucopic amenities of Reston—swimming pools, tennis courts, golf courses, shopping centers, affairs—that they did not merely pursue happiness: they stalked it. My father wore the same grim grin whether pushing a lawnmower or pulling a golf-cart. It didn't occur to me then, nor would it for many years, that it wasn't happiness he was seeking, but escape, not pursuing but fleeing what pursued him: what, in one form or another, pursues us all.

As my friends and I entered the wilds of adolescence, we viewed our parents with cynicism, seeing them as ridiculous, deluded, hypocritical. Reston held no wonders for us. We hadn't asked to be brought here. To be brought up here. Trapped between playground sandboxes and senior citizen centers, there was nothing for us to do, nowhere to go. We were bored.

Some of us turned to drugs and sex . . . more like our parents than we knew. There was always a house with absent or uncaring adults; if not, once the sun went down, the bike paths opened to us like ley-lines leading to another country, a shadowy, lamp-lit land of adventure and refuge. Or were themselves that land. I smoked my first cigarette there, squatting troll-like under a wooden bridge as a creek burbled by the toes of my Converse All-Stars. I gulped down my first cans of Stroh's like some bitter magic brew, toked on my first joint, wriggled my hand for the first time down the front of a squirming girl's tight bluejeans (her name is long gone, but the perfume of her sex clings to my memory, and always will).

Being back in Reston, running each morning along some of the same paths, brought these and other memories to the surface, sprinkled with the pixie-dust of nostalgia. It seemed to me that I'd been happier in those days than I'd ever realized, happier, in some ways, than in all the years since . . . though I wouldn't have lived through them again for anything. My parents were still together then, my mother was healthy, and I didn't have to worry about finding a job. Life was simpler, events less consequential. Of course, my experience was altogether different at the time, with the import of every thought and action magnified and distorted out of all proportion through the paranoiac lens of teenage hormones.

After my morning run, I would shower, pick up the *New York Times* and the *Washington Post* from the nearby Harris Teeter, and either drive to the hospital to visit my mother, or, if she was home, return there to fix her breakfast. Getting her to eat was a struggle; from the first, the chemo afflicted her with almost constant nausea, and frequently the best she could manage was a few spoonfuls of oatmeal or jello or sherbet. She was weak, emaciated, with the gaunt and haunted look of an anorexic. She joked that this was the best diet she'd ever been on, but her failure to gain back any of the weight she had lost was an ominous sign, as she fully recognized.

After breakfast, my mother would lay back in her hospital bed, or I would help her to the living room couch, her bones birdlike, her blood count so decimated that her white skin bloomed with bruises, a neutropenic garden. Settled in, she closed her eyes, and I read to her from the papers until she fell asleep. When she woke, we would go for a walk around the neighborhood or up and down the halls of the hospital ward; her doctors had impressed the value of daily exercise upon her. She remained an early riser; often, I would arrive at the hospital in the morning to find her already up and about, trudging stolidly down a corridor in her ill-fitting green gown, hospital-issue slippers, and the dark blue headkerchief she wore to cover what she called her "fifty-thousand dollar haircut," pushing Sisyphus-like the wheeled tree of her intravenous medications. I was in awe of these exertions, my heart torn with pride and anguish at the sight of that failing body driven by a will as fierce and indomitable as ever.

Our lunchtime routine was similar, except I read to her then from her favorite magazines, *New Scientist* and *The New Yorker*, or from a collection of essays by Stephen J. Gould; she was fascinated by the biology of her disease, the Darwinian battleground her body had become. The leukemia had started with an error in just a single cell—one her immune system, for reasons the doctors couldn't explain, had been unable to weed out. Free to reproduce, the cell had spread its genetic flaw with astonishing speed, a blitzkrieg in the blood. But for all her interest in the microscopic war being waged within her, my mother was not detached from the world. She followed current events with her customary keen interest and sharp-humored cynicism, engaged her doctors and nurses in political as well as biological discussions. She remained involved in the lives of her children and grandchildren. If there was a tennis match on TV, she watched it, cheering on her favorite players and cursing their villainous opponents.

She was used to being independent, and it was painful to see how humiliating it was for her to have to place herself in the hands of strangers. With family it was even worse; to be cared for by her children seemed to go against the natural order of things . . . though she knew, of course, that the very opposite was true. Still, at seventy-two, she didn't feel ready to accept that role-reversal. Until the sudden onset of the AML, she'd been in perfect health. She bowed to the reality of her situation but was determined not to let its indignities—and they were many, both small and large, physical and otherwise—diminish her own dignity.

Even so, she apologized to me more than once for, as she saw it, thrusting me prematurely into the role of caretaker, forcing me to put my life on hold just when, jobless, I could least afford it. I didn't see it that way; it wasn't her fault she'd gotten sick. Nor, I told her, did I feel put upon. Thanks to my severance pay and unemployment insurance, I had enough money to tide me over until she was back on her feet, and with the Internet, I could look for a new job just as easily from Reston as from New York. All true. All utterly beside the point.

"You're a good son," she said, patting my hand, "but I know this is tedious for you. You need to get out a little, have some fun. Look up your old friends. I'm sure Eric would be glad to hear from you. And Lisa."

I said I would, but in fact, I had no intention of doing so. It had been years since I'd seen or spoken to Eric or Lisa, though I wondered what had become of them, whether they'd escaped from Reston like me or were still there. I could have easily found out, of course. Looked up their names in the phone book or searched on the Internet, but I'd burned those bridges, and there was no sense in looking back.

Eric, Craig, and I had met in junior high, bonding over Avalon Hill military strategy games, science fiction and fantasy stories, and comic books. By our sophomore year of high school, our interests had expanded to include Dungeons & Dragons, rock and roll, drugs, and girls . . . though we were beginning to suspect that our obsession with the first term of that series precluded significant experience of the last. Most girls shunned D&D like they did the 3 Stooges, and those that didn't were about as attractive to us as Moe, Larry, and Curly. They were the kind of girls who made *you* cry if you kissed them, as Eric once put it. Of course, we'd closed our eyes and kissed them anyway whenever we could, and sometimes done more than that; Eric even boasted of having gone all the way, though his refusal to identify the girl convinced Craig and me that he was lying. Either that, or she was truly hideous. But we wanted more than furtive gropings in dark places that stank of spilled beer and bongwater with girls who did not meet the high aesthetic standards inculcated in us by the voluptuous paintings of Frank Frazetta and Boris Vallejo. We wanted girls with whom we could walk hand in hand through the halls of our high school. Girls we could kiss while lounging against our lockers or lying on the front lawn of the school during lunch period. Girls who shared our obsessions, who were just like us . . . only less so. We wanted girlfriends. We wanted love.

We got Lisa.

She appeared suddenly one day a week after the start of sophomore year. Her parents had moved to Reston from South Korea, where her father, who worked for the State Department ("You mean CIA," said Eric smugly when she disclosed this factoid; "Whatever," she replied, rolling her eyes), had been posted to the embassy. Not only did Lisa play D&D—which is how we met; she noticed the *Dungeon Master's Guide* I carried around with me everywhere and introduced herself—her comic collection put ours to shame, and she opened our eyes to the strangely retro yet undeniably cool and sexy world of Japanese anime: *Speed Racer* on, well, speed.

Plus, she was *hot*. Willowy and tall, with creamy skin, ice-blue eyes, and short, spiky black hair streaked (at first) with pink, blue, and pale, metallic green. Her fingernails, and very often her lips, were painted black. She favored short skirts and fishnet stockings and Doc Martens, wore a battered old leather jacket even in September, rolled her own cigarettes, and carried a perpetually disintegrating backpack covered with patches and buttons of bands, a surprising number of which we'd never heard, or even heard of, before: Spaceman 3, The Residents, Hawkwind. Surprising because, thanks to WHFS, a local left-of-the-dial radio station, we prided ourselves on being ahead of the curve when it came to cutting-edge or just plain weird music. Needless to say, the three of us fell in love with her immediately.

Friendships have foundered in less stormy seas. And for the next few months, as we strove against each other for the prize of Lisa's affections, it seemed like that would be the fate of ours. Real malice crept into the casually obscene insults we'd always traded as surrogate terms of affection, and we found ourselves remembering a host of old injuries and resentments that had somehow kept their sting, or even sharpened it, across months and years. We were sullen, tense, edgy. We never spoke openly of the true cause of our contention; instead, every day became a minefield it was impossible to cross, however carefully we stepped, without triggering an explosion. We exchanged shouts, shoves, and even, on a few memorable occasions, punches. None of us wanted any of this, but (as we later discovered, comparing notes) we felt helpless to break free of the destructive pattern, swept toward disaster by a force outside ourselves. Was Lisa the cause of our misery or its cure? We scarcely knew or cared; we were too far gone for that. Only in her defense would we band together willingly, the three of us staunchly denying the malicious rumors that sprang up around her, as they did around any new kid in school: how Lisa had put out for the football team, how she was really a lez, that sort of thing.

It all came to a head one Saturday afternoon in December. We were playing D&D in the moldy-smelling basement of Craig's house (our usual spot, thanks to his parents' benign neglect), when an argument erupted between Eric and me over a roll of the dice. This was, of course, merely the pretext for another display of testosterone-fueled chest-thumping. We stood up, shouting across the table. Craig was quick to join the fray. It was nothing Lisa hadn't witnessed a hundred times before, rolling her eyes and waiting for the storm to pass. But now, suddenly, she'd had enough.

She slammed her palm down hard on the table, sending dice flying and knocking over the screen of books from behind which, like a priest in a confessional, I carried out my dungeonmasterly duties. "I am so sick of this shit!"

"Jeez, Lis," said Eric. "Take a chill pill, why don't you!"

"This isn't fun anymore," she persisted. "You guys are always fighting. You don't even know why, do you?"

"Sure I do." Eric blinked. "Dweeber rolled a six-sided die when it says right there in the fucking *DMG* to roll an eight-sided!"

"I can roll whatever the fuck I want, whenever the fuck I want," I responded. "I'm the fucking dungeon master!"

"Jesus Christ," Lisa said, shaking her head and leaning back in her chair. "It isn't about dice, okay? You idiots are fighting over me."

Nervous laughter was the best we could manage.

"I thought maybe boys would be different back in the States. But you're just the same. Your heads are so filled up with romantic bullshit that you let your dicks do your thinking for you."

"What is with you today?" Eric demanded. "That time of the month or something?"

"Fuck you, Eric," she said coolly.

"So, what are you saying?" I asked. "Are you dropping out of the game?"

"You know, that's all sex is, really," she said. "A game. It's not some big, serious deal all full of love and tragedy and suffering. It's not about happy ever after or till death do us part or any of that crap. At least, it doesn't have to be."

I sat down. I felt like she'd punched me in the gut. "What they're saying about you at school," I said. "It's true, isn't it?"

She shrugged. "Maybe. Some of it. I don't pay attention to what people say."

Eric sat down with a groan. "Fuck me!"

"What?" Craig's wide-eyed gaze bounced between the three of us. "You mean . . . ? Are you saying . . . ?"

"I've been with some boys, if that's what you're asking," Lisa said without a trace of shame. "They wanted it, and so did I. It's no big deal. Like I said, a game."

Eric began to chuckle softly, while Craig actually burst into tears.

"Oh, for Christ's sake, grow up," I said, biting back my own tears.

Lisa shot me a glare and moved to his side, putting her arm around his heaving shoulders. "I'm sorry it hurts, Craigy," she said.

"Why?" he asked, turning up his lumpish, tear-streaked face. "Why them and not us?"

"It's easier that way," Lisa said. "I don't give a shit about them, and they don't give a shit about me. No misunderstandings. I care about you guys. I didn't want to come between you. I didn't want to hurt you."

"But you *are* between us," Eric pointed out, dark eyes glittering. "You *have* hurt us."

She had no answer for that.

"Look," I said, "let's just forget it and get back to D&D, okay? It's none of our business anyway."

"I don't feel like playing anymore today," sniffled Craig, and since it was his house, that was that. We went our separate ways without bothering to schedule our next gaming session. I think we were all wondering if there was even going to *be* a next gaming session.

But there was, of course, and many more after that. Things had changed, though. Eric, Craig, and I were no longer at each other's throats. We looked at Lisa differently now. It was as though a glamour had been dispelled, revealing her to be more like us than our clouded senses had been able to perceive, subject to the same desires . . . if less inhibited in satisfying them. For Eric and me, the liberating effects of this disenchantment extended beyond Lisa to girls who had always seemed out of our league. I realized suddenly, with the force of a revelation, that whatever barriers existed between me and these girls were largely in my own mind, of my own making, as if I had needed to put them safely out of reach. Now I began to find girlfriends, as did Eric; not right away, but gradually, over the following months. Some of them even joined us in D&D sessions, but they never cracked the core of our clique; they were like comets whose orbits carried them close for a time, only to escape our gravity in the end. Nor did we try to hold them. We had adopted Lisa's philosophy of sex divorced from love, sex as game, and it had set us free. Not that every girl I went out with slept with me, or even most of them (this was, after all, still high school!), but the possibility was always there, or so it seemed, just as every hitter who steps up to the plate envisions a home run no matter how many times he's struck out. And a surprising number of the girls I went out with—surprising to me, anyway—turned out to be as relieved as I was to dispense with all that love business. We enjoyed each other without jealousy, without expectations. We were using each other, of course. But at least we weren't lying to each other about it. It didn't occur to me until much later, after college, that this was itself a kind of lie.

Perhaps the strangest, or at any rate most unexpected, result of that December afternoon was that Lisa and Craig became an item, joined (as the high-school saying went) at the hip. His tears had melted something in her heart, and she had abandoned her hedonistic philosophy even as Eric and I became its adherents. As for Craig, he had achieved his heart's desire and couldn't have been happier. There were times, even in the midst of my own happiness, that I found myself envying him. What he had with her. But I felt sorry for him, too, as though in advance, wondering how long Lisa would be satisfied, and what would happen on the day she was not.

Eric, Craig, and Lisa went to the University of Virginia, while I attended the College of William & Mary. I'd been accepted at UVA, too, but decided in the end not to go. The others thought I was nuts. Or pissed at them for some reason. But I wasn't. I couldn't really explain it to them, or even to myself, not at the time. I just knew that if I joined them at UVA, I would wind up drifting through my college years the same as I had through the last two years of high school, drinking, partying, playing D&D, never really emerging from our snug cocoon. I wasn't sure why this prospect suddenly struck me as something to be avoided when up until then it had satisfied me completely. And it still did satisfy me. But when I looked ahead, trying to imagine my future, it was as though I could see a variety of paths leading to different destinations, and the path that went through UVA disappeared into a thick, dark, tangled woods, and I couldn't see it come out again. So I didn't go that way. It was the first, but not the last, time I would experience this kind of vaguely premonitory impulse, not so much toward one thing as away from another. Or perhaps it was only a fear of becoming stuck, trapped, nothing more than a flaring up of the instinct to escape that impels every hunted creature, for I've felt that, too, more often, and more strongly, as I get older.

There with my mom in her hospital room, waiting at her bedside as death drew near, confident and unhurried in his approach, a huntsman whose prey had run itself out, I felt that fear crawling over me so intensely—though I knew he hadn't come for me, not yet—that it was all I could do not to bolt, leaving her to face him alone. Of course, in a sense she *was* alone; we all are. But it was precisely because of that fundamental, irreducible aloneness, hers and mine, that I was determined not to desert her. To bring what comfort I could by my presence, the sound of my voice, the touch of my hand. Even if there was no way to tell for sure that she knew I was there. I believed that she knew. It was a kind of faith, the most I was capable of. And talking to her, reading her favorite poems aloud, stroking her warm, waxy skin, dribbling water into her mouth with a straw or moistening her lips with a sponge, studying her face (her features sometimes as innocently expressive as a sleeping infant's, other times so ancient and wizened that it seemed I was not looking at my mother any longer, but at some eternal archetype of motherhood shining through translucent skin and bone), brought me comfort and gave me strength enough to face her death, which was also a foretaste of my own.

In the end, it was a case of the cure being as deadly as the disease. My mother's battered system began to break down under the onslaught of chemo. There was damage to her heart and lungs. Her kidneys were failing. And the AML, following the last, ineffective treatment, had come roaring back stronger than ever. Literally overnight, her options narrowed from more chemo and various phase-2 clinical trials to a choice of where she preferred to die: at home or in the hospital. She chose the latter—more, she admitted, for our sakes, my sister's and mine, than her own, wanting to shield us from any small household disasters, such as a broken bone in a fall, that might add immeasurably to whatever burden of grief and guilt we would carry through the rest of our lives. Her mother, recovering at home from surgery, had died following a fall, so she was especially sensitive to this possibility. Ellen and I knew our limits, and we did not argue . . . which only added to the burden my mother wished to spare us. But not even a mother's love can spare her children every burden. Isn't love itself a burden, however willingly we bear it?

As we drove up to the hospital for the last time, my mother—hunched in the front seat, where Ellen and I had, with difficulty, maneuvered her and strapped her in—said in a voice as reduced as the rest of her, "Back to where my journey started." I thought at first that she was referring to the

AML, for it was to this hospital that she'd driven herself months before when she thought she'd contracted pneumonia, only to learn from emergency room physicians that her disease was far more dire, that by rights she should have been incapable of driving herself anywhere in her condition, and that if she'd delayed coming in by even an hour, it would have been too late. Later I wondered if she hadn't meant the whole course of her life, birth to death, a transit from one hospital room to another.

That was the longest sentence she spoke until she died. The doctors said it could happen at any time, but she continued to surprise them, holding on for another ten days. But the power of speech ebbed rapidly from this articulate, well-read woman, a former English teacher and professional editor who delighted in the play of language. By the second day, she could reply only in monosyllables to our questions. Are you comfortable? Would you like some water? Do you need to use the commode? Are you in pain? Her replies slipped over the threshold of coherent speech, into grunts and moans and sighs that for a while still communicated intent and desire. Then that threshold, too, was crossed and left behind, and she entered a country of silence.

My mother's accelerating deterioration was painful to watch, all the more so because she was conscious of it. At least it seemed that way to me. The knowledge was there in her eyes, which at various times glittered with a cold, hard, gemlike fear, or melted with compassion and love, or flashed with anger at her inability to make herself understood . . . or at our inability to understand her.

It was there, too, in the language of her body. In the naked expressions that flitted across her features. And in her restless, repetitive, and sometimes violently agitated movements. There most of all, and most heartbreakingly of all. She would kick her way free of her sheets, pluck at her hospital gown as though trying to remove it, slip her wasted arms out of the sleeves or pull with fierce determination but scant strength at her collar. She would raise her hands to touch the slim, transparent tubes carrying oxygen to her nostrils, seeming to remember, forget, and remember again what they were and why they were there all in the space of moments. She explored her features with her fingertips like a blind woman puzzling out the mystery of a strangely familiar face. And over and over, for hours, days, at a stretch, like a zoo animal caught in some behavioral cul-de-sac of instinct, she would hoist herself into a half-sitting position, grasping one-handed and with all her strength the raised side-bar of the bed, and hold herself there until her arm, her whole body, shook with the effort of continuing the motion, swinging her legs around, pushing herself to her feet, standing, walking out of the room, out of the hospital, leaving her sickness behind and returning to the life she knew, picking up right where she'd left off on that spring morning, months ago, when she'd driven herself to the emergency room. But however far she progressed down this path in her mind, her body would at last sink slowly back onto the mattress and pillows, where, exhausted but undefeated, she would rest for a time, gathering herself for the next attempt.

Were these efforts indicative of pain and suffering? The nurses and doctors couldn't say, but advised morphine anyway, just to be on the safe side, and to smooth away her evident distress. But Ellen and I were wary of acting to ease *our* distress, not hers. It was torture to watch my mother's futile struggles, knowing they were foredoomed. But who could say what purpose they served for her? Perhaps what seemed futile to us, young and healthy as we were, was crucial to her, an experience we had no right to rob her of. Besides, she had made it crystal clear over the years that she didn't want to spend her last days in a drugged fog, bound body and mind in a pharmaceutical straightjacket. As long as there was no obvious pain, we would not permit morphine. This proved an unpopular, indeed incomprehensible, decision to the hospital staff, and I think they saw us as deluded or even cruel. But at this point in the long march of my mother's illness, the path that Ellen and I were on diverged from that of the doctors and nurses. Once we had been united in our desire for a cure. Now their goal had shifted to a peaceful death, in comfort and dignity . . . as they defined those terms. But as guardians of my mother's ever-dwindling autonomy, we had to take her wishes into account, as best we understood them, and balance those wishes against the medical advice we were getting. If they didn't like our decisions . . . too bad. As for my mother, her path had taken her ahead of us all. Soon she would cross the final threshold and pass beyond the reach of any decisions we had the power to make.

For days her eyelids sank lower and lower as though heavy with drowsiness, until at last they closed for good, leaking gummy tears as if her body were sealing itself shut, becoming a cocoon. But behind those fleshy screens, thin as rice paper, her eyes rolled and darted, responding to our voices, the sounds we made, or to memories, dreams, visions. Again, the doctors couldn't say how conscious she was. All they could tell us was that hearing was the last sense to go. And so, as her struggles weakened and finally stopped, her body lying still at last (and how precious those struggles seemed to us then, how we mourned their passing, for every new stage in my mother's journey, because it brought her that much closer to its end, and took her that much farther away from us, filled us with a kind of nostalgia for what had gone before, no matter how awful it had been, and they were all uniquely awful), I began to talk to her as I hadn't before.

As soon as she'd gone back into the hospital, Ellen and I, along with her husband, Greg, had divvied up each 24-hour period into four-hour shifts, so that one of us was always with her. As the days wore on, and this grueling schedule began to wear us down, our father took a shift as well. We rotated the schedule so that no one had the same shifts twice in a row. We slept when we could, sometimes at my mother's house, sometimes in the hospital. We left the orderly rhythms of daily life behind, the regimented structure of seconds, minutes, and hours that we humans have laid over the wilderness of time to make ourselves feel at home there, safe and civilized, the future predictable, the past conveniently labeled, the present visible on our wrists, captured in the circular sweeping of a second hand, the morphing of one gray number into the next. All of that is a kind of grid, a prison so comfortable and internalized that, most of the time, like the beating of our heart, we never even know it's there. But it's possible to slip through the grid, exist for a while outside it. Drugs can do it, and illness, and sex. Religion. Art. Any number of things. And that's just what happened to us. At least, it felt that way to me, as if I were standing on the fringes of an ancient, untamed forest, into which my mother had wandered, and where I longed to follow but dared not for fear of becoming lost myself, unable to find my way back to the warm and well-lit village still close behind me.

So I talked to her from the fringes. Told her I loved her. Reminisced about vacations we'd taken, experiences we'd shared, people we'd known:

friends, relatives. All the sad and funny landmarks of our lives. And spoke of the future, too, my dreams of making it as a writer, of finding a woman to cherish and share the rest of my life with, of bringing children into the world, grandkids she would never know but who, I promised, would know and love her through all that I would tell them. Most of all, I read to her. Shakespeare's sonnets and soliloquies from his plays. The poems of Dylan Thomas, Gerard Manley Hopkins, Yeats, Auden, Eliot. Stories by Lawrence, Fitzgerald, Joyce. I felt that these old, well-loved friends might bring more comfort to her now than anything else I could tell her, that the combination of their words and my voice could still reach her, give her something useful to cling to, like a flashlight she could hold as she followed her lonely path.

The intravenous tubes were removed from her arms. The clip feeding oxygen to her nostrils was replaced by a clear plastic mask covering her nose and mouth. Her breathing grew labored, arrhythmic, interspersed with microseconds in which it ceased altogether, or seemed to, a pause that lasted just a fraction of a beat longer than normal between breaths, as though some mechanism was resetting itself. Her motions stilled. Her pulse fluttered visibly beneath the lily-white stem of her throat, mesmerizing in its fragility, a butterfly's shadow. I dropped my voice to a whisper, afraid of startling it away, though I knew there was nothing I could do to hold it there.

And then it was as if the butterfly shifted position, partially obstructing her windpipe in its efforts to lap up every last drop of nectar. I listened for a while before it occurred to me that I was hearing her death rattle, that old literary cliché proved true, like so many of them. I called in the nurse, who verified my fears; when she had gone, I phoned the others. Minutes later, Ellen and Greg arrived from my mother's house. My father showed up shortly thereafter. Then my mother left us. It appeared as simple as deciding not to breathe. A burden laid down after seventy-two years. Was this a power everyone possessed, a choice we could make at any time, if we only knew it? Later, Ellen told me she had felt my mother's spirit depart in a great *whoosh*, like a vacuum imploding, but I felt nothing like that, only a gentle absence, as if the butterfly had taken wing while I blinked, leaving behind an empty husk that bore a striking resemblance to my mother, but was not her, was not anyone anymore. A doctor came to verify time of death; nurses descended; this was their place now, their time. We left them to their ancient ablutions.

I saw the body once more, two days later at the funeral home. This was a legal requirement, to ensure that no mix-up had taken place at the hospital morgue and we did not bury a stranger. And yet, I thought, as I looked at the painted, doll-like features, the arms stiffly arranged over the drab brown dress that Ellen had picked out, the hands cupped one atop the other, positioned as I had never seen them in life, the hands of a modest churchgoer posing for a formal portrait, that was exactly what we were doing.

I was reentering the world of normal time. It was to be a gradual process, a slow and painful awakening . . . or a slipping back into sleep, depending on your point of view. Perhaps it has not yet fully stopped; perhaps it never will. It had commenced when I glanced at the clock in the hospital room at the moment of her death and saw the second hand jerking steadily forward; until then, my mother had been drawing away from us with a similar fitful motion; now it was we who were being carried farther and farther away . . . though again, depending on your point of view, drawing nearer to her, too. I felt both at once, a dizzying sense of in-betweenness that lingered through the sweltering, mid-August funeral two days later and the open-house we held at the Reston townhouse immediately afterward.

Later that evening, when everyone had gone, Ellen and Greg returning to Richmond, my dad to his family, I wandered through the townhouse. The task of sorting through my mother's possessions lay ahead, determining what to keep, what to sell, what to throw away. But that grim festival was for the coming weeks and months; in the meantime, I had to catch up with my life. By this time tomorrow, I planned to be back in New York. Now, though, the emotional toll of the previous days and months hit me in waves of desolation and loss and grieving.

Everything was as she'd left it, the furniture, paintings, photographs, books all in their accustomed places . . . Yet they were different, existentially askew, like Christmas ornaments displayed out of season. Some were drained of significance, emptied by my mother's death and become mere objects, while others were like emotional mirrors, reflecting back everything I felt in distorted ways, so that they seemed to be aware of her absence, and to share my mourning, or to blame me.

Finally, I had to get out. I got in her car, a Toyota Corolla, and drove, the windows down, the muggy night air buffeting my skin, drying my cheeks. I had no destination in mind; I didn't want to be around other people; even the sight of other cars, the flash of their headlights on the winding, darkened streets, was intrusive. I found myself in our old Hunters Woods neighborhood, near the house where I'd grown up, which my parents had sold after the divorce. I drove past; the lights were blazing; other lives filled it now. Just so would my mother's possessions find new owners, new uses; we treasure our things, but they are not faithful to us.

I turned in the cul-de-sac at the end of Fowlers Lane, made my way back up Whip Road, and hung a right on Steeplechase Drive. I continued past the elementary school, where I had attended sixth grade, across Colts Neck Road, and past Paddock Lane, where Craig's parents' house had been. I wondered if they were still there, but I didn't make the turn; instead, I stayed on Steeplechase for a quarter-mile or so, until it ended in a tree-fringed cul-de-sac. There were no houses here, no cars, just empty parking spaces beneath overhanging boughs. I stopped the car, turned off the engine and the headlights, took a deep breath.

Tall trees shook their shaggy limbs in a breeze that carried the tang of chlorine. The asphalt sparkled in the false moonlight of surrounding street lamps. I felt like climbing the chain-link fence, stripping off my clothes, and jumping naked into the swimming pool beyond. I thought of all the times that Craig and Eric and Lisa and I had done exactly that, drunk and stoned after a late-night game at Craig's house, daring the cops to catch us, which they never did. But that fence looked higher now; I doubted I could scale it with the ease I remembered. And even if I did, even if I went up and over as easily as a squirrel, what would have changed when I came down on the other side? Who was I trying to kid? Suddenly I felt old, thirty-eight going on sixty, and sad past all weeping.

I started the car, switched on the headlights, made the slow turn past the padlocked tennis courts and the entrance to the pool. Then, impulsively, in a kind of fuck you to my own timidity, as if the ghost of my younger self, disgusted, had risen up to grab the wheel, I swerved right, inching the car around the yellow concrete posts that stood sentinel to this section of the bike paths just as they had twenty years ago. It was a near thing; branches scraped one side of the car, while, on the other, the rear view mirror slid perilously by one post. Then I was through.

I laughed, pumped my fist in the air. I tapped the gas pedal and crawled the car forward into the compact green and brown tunnel carved out of the woods and the night by the beams of my headlights. The silence was tangible, profound, spooky. The air had acquired a mythic density, as though I'd crossed into a fairyland of dreams and nostalgia. I breathed it in like a drug. Driving the bike paths by night had always been an eerie experience, like exploring the bottom of an uncanny ocean, the trees moving their limbs languidly, seaweed drifting in lazy temporal tides, quantum currents, elves and orcs and aliens and other creatures from D&D and movies and all the fantasy and science fiction I'd read seeming to spill from my perfervid imagination into the world, every ordinary object, natural or manmade—a tree, a wooden foot bridge, a lamp post—drenched in a rime of enchantment, a precipitate that only appeared in conditions such as these. Now all of that was present again, as if it had been waiting patiently all these years for me to submerge myself once more, but the familiar atmosphere of heightened perception was further glossed with memories of nights like this from twenty summers ago, memories which had themselves acquired a mythic patina with time.

Impossible now to say who started it, which of us first came up with the idea of driving down those winding paths by night. A lot of the time we were bored out of our minds, or stoned out of them, or both at once, sitting around Craig's basement playing Nintendo or watching TV with the sound off and his stereo or HFS blasting soundtracks of bizarre serendipity. Reruns of *Star Trek* choreographed to Johnny Lydon's bitter PIL or Julian Cope's suave, psychedelic growl. Baseball and soccer games whose events seemed not so much accompanied as orchestrated by the music of Pink Floyd, like the fabled pairing of *The Wizard of Oz* and *Dark Side of the Moon*. We were starved for novelty and diversion. Taking our cars (or, in my case, my parents' car) onto the paths had in addition the lure of the forbidden, the element of risk that woke us like nothing else from our suburban stupor and allowed us, for a time, to feel free, superior to our surroundings, as if we had escaped them, not by leaving Reston for some outward destination, as I was to do later in moving to New York, but *inwardly*, by crossing a secret, interior border that most people couldn't cross, or even recognize, like Alice stepping through the looking glass. There was something strongly if obscurely transgressive about it, empowering; we felt that we were flouting more than just the law, chancing more than arrest or tragedy, a midnight encounter with someone's dog or kid, an insomniac jogger, or even another carload of idiots like us, mirror images colliding, canceling each other out.

I do know that it was sometime during the summer after our graduation from high school that the practice began. We were eager to escape the nominal control of our parents but also loath to leave this part of our lives behind, conflicting aims that made the summer seem endless at one moment, evanescent the next. We were anxious, impatient, a little bit afraid. We longed for the experiences of college but wondered if those experiences would lead us away from each other, though we never talked about that possibility, or anyway Eric and I never did. Craig and Lisa may have discussed it among themselves; in fact, I'm sure they did, but they kept their discussions private.

The bike paths proved the perfect remedy for what ailed us. We couldn't wait for the sun to set. We would stoke up on pot and beer, cram into someone's car, and head off to explore this fanciful new realm we had so unexpectedly, fortuitously, discovered. I think we must have driven every mile of the paths, mapping them as we went, cranking tapes or HFS on the stereo, as if we were still playing Dungeons & Dragons. We saw animals that were rarely glimpsed by day, our headlights drawing them like moths: possum, raccoons, deer, foxes, once even a coyote, or what looked like one. The usual rules of engagement did not apply; the animals did not flee from our approach; instead, they seemed as fascinated by us as we were by them, regarding us with eyes that glowed like moonstones.

We became experts in navigating our vehicles through tight squeezes and sharp turns, experts, too, in dodging the cops who soon began to stalk us. Their cruisers were too wide to fit onto most of the paths, but they knew every exit and entrance, often lying in wait for us, their lights off, and we had our share of narrow escapes. By the end of the summer, we were stopping well back from any potential exit and reconnoitering on foot, creeping along like commandos, though I doubt commandos ever had to worry about giving themselves away by giggling. I guess we should have taken them more seriously, but to us, the whole thing was a cartoon cat-and-mouse game, part of the fantasy world of the bike paths, and not the most important part, either. Anyway, they never caught us.

The exhilaration of those nights came back to me now. I turned on the radio, stumbled across a station at the extreme left of the dial playing what a New York friend of mine called "the New Oldies" (that is, tunes from the 80s; as for HFS, it had long since been assimilated into the Borglike empire of conservative talk radio), and began to drive slowly, staying under five miles an hour. If I'd had a joint, I would have smoked it. Not that I needed one: I already felt high. My body recalled the route better than my mind did; I found myself making turns without hesitation, by instinct instead of memory, even after I'd passed beyond any landmark of bridge, playground, or lamp post that looked remotely familiar in the headlights and I knew I'd entered a new section of the paths. New to me, anyway; the network had expanded considerably since I'd last driven it. Occasionally I saw the lights of houses winking through the trees, but I had no idea where I was. Nor did I care. Being lost suited my mood perfectly.

At one point, a fat possum wandered onto the path ahead of me. It trundled along, in no hurry, showing no inclination to skedaddle. Every so often it turned its ratty face back at me as if in annoyance, its eyes splashes of emerald fire. *What?* it seemed to be asking. *Are you still here?* It looked so self-important that I had to laugh. I followed it until, with one final backward glance, it veered off into the woods and was gone. I continued on, knowing that sooner or later I was bound to emerge onto a street that would take me home, but in no hurry to get there. I would have been happy to keep driving forever, spiraling deeper and deeper into the interstitial spaces of Reston and never coming out again.

The radio station was really amazing, playing all kinds of obscure and semi-obscure bands without commercial interruption, just like HFS in its glory days. Martha and the Muffins. Romeo Void. The Minutemen. Lene Lovich. Holly Beth Vincent. Joy Division. I heard them all that night, as well as stuff by the usual suspects: The Replacements; Siouxsie and the Banshees; Gang of Four; Talking Heads; Billy Idol; Bowie; U2. I began to spin out a fantasy that I'd traveled through time, the twists and turns of the paths driving me backward to the 80s. I kept waiting for the DJ to come on, half-expecting that I'd hear Weasel or Damien or one of the other old HFS hands, but no one ever did. I figured I must have caught the beginning of an hour's block of music. Unfortunately, the reception was spotty, and the station kept fading out, until at last it slipped off the edge of the dial into a sea of static and did not return. But the static seemed to hold a buried music of its own, spacy and alluring, if only I could surrender to it, as if there were a whole other spectrum of stations there to the left, beyond the reach of conventional radios.

It was right about then that I saw an approaching headlight. My first thought was that it was the cops, that they'd finally taken to patrolling the paths by bike or motorcycle like they should have been doing twenty years ago. Backing up was out of the question; where was I going to back up *to*? Nor was there any convenient side path down which I could duck. Besides, my lights were on, as visible to him as his were to me. I was as good as busted. I pulled as far over to the side as I could, letting the branches scrape the sides and windows of the car, and waited.

As it turned out, it was neither bike nor motorcycle, but a car with a broken headlight. Not a cop, then, just somebody out for a late-night drive, same as me. Still, the appearance of another vehicle had shattered the spell of the paths, and I felt foolish to have come here, a middle-aged guy trying to recapture his youth, trying to escape the reality of his mother's death. The oncoming glare was blinding, and I waited nervously for the car to reach me, wondering whether it would stop or pass by. I didn't want trouble; I just wanted to go home. The swirl of static from the radio was suddenly annoying, and I stabbed it off as the car slowed and pulled to a stop beside me, an old Dodge Dart. The driver's side window was down, and even before it drew even I heard the hiss of static from inside like a shivery wind blowing through the trees. Then I was staring at a face I hadn't expected to ever see again.

"Jesus," I said. "Lisa, is that you?"

She took the cigarette from her lips and exhaled, cool as ever, acting unsurprised, as if she'd been expecting me. "Hi, Johnny. Been a long time." Blue-gray smoke drifted between us like static made visible.

I laughed, all at once aware how much I'd missed her, how glad I was to see her after all this time; it wasn't that I'd forgotten the reasons why I'd avoided her, but suddenly they didn't matter so much anymore. "Jesus, Lis, you haven't changed a bit! What are you doing here?"

"That's a trick question, right?" She raised a ring-pierced eyebrow, took another drag on her cig. "Look, I'll go down a ways and turn around, then you can follow me home, okay? We'll talk there. Catch up and shit."

"That'd be great."

She pulled away without another word. In less than five minutes, she was back, motioning with one hand for me to follow as she glided by. I pulled in behind her and let her lead me out of the maze.

All the way back to her place, I was thinking about the last time I'd seen her. It was right before I'd split for New York, the summer after we graduated from college.

The summer Craig died.

As usual, we'd come home that summer and slipped back into our high-school way of life. Drinking, drugs, D&D. I'd been seeing someone at William & Mary, but we'd broken up before graduation, her choice, and I was glad of any excuse to numb the pain I was feeling and to avoid thinking about my responsibility for what had happened . . . which, put briefly, was that my philosophy of high-school hedonism hadn't gone over too well in college, at least not after the first few semesters, and it was only now, a little too late, that I was being forced to admit it. Or *was* it too late? My ex-girlfriend, Donna, had gone to New York, and the notion of following her was percolating in the back of my mind, not yet something I considered seriously, more of a romantic fantasy. Plus, that was the summer my folks finally split up, and while I welcomed the step (long overdue, as far as Ellen and I were concerned), it only made my life more unsettled just when I needed all the stability I could get.

Hung up on my problems, I didn't pay much attention to the others. Because I didn't want to admit that I had changed, neither did I care to admit the possibility that my friends, too, might be different. But of course they were. How could they not be? After four years of college, we had all changed. We didn't fit comfortably into our old friendship anymore. The roles that had once come naturally were forced, artificial. Maybe they always had been. It wouldn't have taken much to shatter the complacent illusion of timelessness with which we were deceiving ourselves. Anything at all might have done it.

If I'd been less self-absorbed, perhaps I would have seen it coming. Done or said something in time to make a difference. I've wondered about that a lot. But I didn't notice a goddamn thing. One morning I got a call from Eric; Craig was in the hospital. Apparently, he'd tried to hang himself in the woods the previous night. The limb of the tree he'd chosen had snapped, and he'd somehow managed to crawl out of the woods to the side of Glade Drive, dragging the fucking branch behind him the whole way. There he'd lain, unconscious, until he was found by passing motorists. By the time I got to the hospital, he was dead.

It was big news for a while. Everybody blamed drugs and rock and roll: the autopsy found pot in his system, and he'd actually been wearing a Walkman when he'd hung himself. Even D&D got dragged in, as though he'd been possessed by demons summoned up at a roll of the dice. His parents were devastated and angry; they believed we'd corrupted Craig, Lisa especially, whom they'd never liked, and they made it clear we would not be welcome at his funeral. We stayed away out of respect for their grieving (he was their only child), but that same night we visited the gravesite for a service of our own, sneaking on to the moonlit cemetery grounds . . . the same cemetery where, years later, I would see my mother buried. We sat beside the freshly turned earth and sickly sweet, already-wilting flowers and passed around a joint and, after pouring out a libation, a bottle of Virginia Gentleman bourbon. No one said a word. Lisa wept quietly, steadily, and Eric scowled into the night, his body hunched as if in expectation of another blow. By then they'd told me the real story.

It seemed they'd been fucking behind Craig's back for pretty much the whole last year of school. It had, Eric told me, just happened. They'd never meant for it to continue so long, and they'd never meant to hurt Craig. But things got out of hand. They got careless and slipped up, and about a week ago he'd apparently seen enough to make him realize what was going on, and how long it had been going on. At least, that's what he'd written in a note to Lisa (the existence of which she kept from the cops and his parents; she didn't even offer to show it to me, nor did I ask to see it). Lisa said that he'd believed she didn't love him any more, that she wanted to be with Eric now. And so, like a gentleman, he'd stepped aside. That was, she said, her voice half-angry, half-incredulous, really how he saw it. Or how he'd written it, anyway.

"Like offing himself was some big act of chivalry," snarled Eric from the driver's seat. We were in his car, heading to the cemetery. For once, no music was playing. He thumped the wheel with the palm of his hand. "Asshole! He didn't even talk to us! Didn't give us a chance to explain . . . "

"What if he had?" I asked after a moment from the back. "Did you still love him, Lis? Did you want to be with him?"

"I don't know what I wanted," she said, half-turned to me, features sunk in shadow. "Not this. Never this."

I could feel Eric's gaze in the rear-view mirror, his eyes boring into me as if I'd accused her of murder, accused them both. But I felt too guilty myself just then to cast any stones. "Poor Craig. When I think of him all alone, crawling through the woods . . . "

"Fuck!" Eric exclaimed. "Will you shut the fuck up?" And he jammed a tape into the stereo and cranked the volume.

A week and a half later, I was on my way to New York and Donna. We never did get back together; she accepted a job in Boston that fall and left the city, while I stayed. I kept in touch with Lisa and Eric at first, but we knew that our friendship had died with Craig. Or, more accurately, it had been dead for a long time already, and what had happened with Craig just made the fact of it undeniable, like a marriage that unravels at the death of a child. Thanksgivings and Christmases, when I went back to Reston, I avoided looking them up, avoided driving past the cemetery where Craig was buried (and where, before leaving that summer night, we had planted a handful of pot seeds). And they avoided me in turn. My mother would ask about them from time to time, tell me what a shame it was that we'd let Craig's tragedy come between us, encourage me to look them up again. I always had the feeling that she knew the truth about what had happened, although I never confided in her. Anyway, it seemed to be important to her that I make an effort at reconciliation. Even at the end, from her hospital bed, she was urging me to get in touch.

And now, here I was, following Lisa home. I'm not ordinarily superstitious, but I felt that something beyond mere chance was at work, that my mom had taken a hand in our meeting, bringing us together like she'd always wanted . . . though for what purpose, I didn't know. Corny as it sounds, I sensed her gazing down on me. I felt surrounded and protected by her love, felt it shining all around me like the headlights of another car, and for the first time in days, I found myself thinking of her without pain. *Why, I haven't lost anything,* I remember thinking in surprise. *She's still right here.*

Lisa led me to an apartment complex off South Lakes Drive. She parked her car; I pulled in beside her. When I got out, she put her arms around me and hugged me hard, and I hugged her back; she was as slim and strong as ever. She smelled of lavender and cigarettes.

"Jeez, it's good to see you, Lis." I studied her in the light of the streetlamps. She wore cut-off jeans and a black Hello Kitty t-shirt that left her midriff bare. A tattoo of a blue and silver lightning bolt or thorn circlet ran around her left arm. Her hair was long now, pure, glistening black, and there were new piercings (nose; eyebrow; belly-button) and a hint of crow's feet at the corners of her eyes, but otherwise she looked no more than five or six years older than the last time I'd seen her. If I hadn't known better, I would have guessed her to be in her mid-twenties, tops, instead of more than ten years older: my age. "You look fucking great."

She gave me a crooked, incongruously shy, smile, one I'd seen a million times before but until that instant had forgotten about completely. It floored me, that smile. "It's good to see you, too," she said.

I knew that I looked every bit of my age, and then some. I had lost some hair and put on some weight. And I'd stopped wearing an earring years ago. Silence descended as we sized each other up. I had so many questions, I didn't know where to begin.

"Come on." She took me by the hand and led me into the apartment building, to the elevator, which opened its doors as soon as she pressed the call button. We stepped on. "We live on the third floor," she told me.

"We?"

"Eric and me." She flashed that shy, crooked smile again. How could I have forgotten that smile?

"So you guys stayed together," I said. "I always wondered. Married?"

She laughed. "Not hardly."

"How is he?"

"He was diagnosed with MS a few years back."

"Shit. That really sucks."

The elevator stopped. The doors slid open.

She lowered her voice. "He doesn't like people to make a big deal out of it. He's in remission now. Uses a cane, has a bit of a tremor, but that's about it. I mean, he's not crippled or anything."

"That's good to hear. I don't know much about MS. How did . . . ?"

"Nobody knows how you get it," she said. "One more thing. Seeing you is going to be a surprise, and he doesn't like surprises much anymore. He likes things predictable, safe. So at first he might come across a little harsh."

"Maybe I should wait out here while you talk to him."

"Do you mind?"

"Of course not."

"I'll just be a minute. Believe me, he'll be glad to see you."

By then we had reached the door. From behind it I heard the thump of heavy bass. She opened the door with her key and slid inside. "I'm home," she called above the music, which I recognized as the first song off the Talking Heads' *Fear of Music* LP, whose name I could never remember. "I, Zebra," or something like that. Over her shoulder, I glimpsed a paperback-filled bookcase and, hanging at an angle from one corner of the ceiling, the black rectangle of a stereo speaker; then the door closed, though not before I smelled the unmistakable odor of pot.

I leaned back against the wall with a sigh, suddenly aware how worn out

I was. It had been a long day, and now it was late, after midnight. And I had a reservation on the ten o'clock train to New York the next morning.

The volume of the music swelled as the door swung inward. I straightened as a face I recognized with difficulty as Eric's poked into the hall. "Fuck, look who's back! Get the fuck in here, Dweeber!"

I laughed; it had been a long time since I'd been called that . . . although, when your last name is Weber, you get used to it pretty quick, and deep down inside you never really stop expecting to hear it. "Hey, Eric." I put out my hand; he clasped it with his own, pulling me through the door and into the apartment before releasing me. "Sorry to come by so late."

"Fuck, you call this late?" He stumped past me, leaning heavily on a cane of polished blond wood. "Come on in and have a beer."

I followed him into the living room. I didn't know if the MS was to blame, but he looked to be around two hundred pounds, which, for a guy who stood about five-seven, with a bad leg, was serious baggage. His face and cheeks were puffy behind a scraggly brown beard, and when we'd shaken, I'd noticed that his hand was swollen, though his grip was firm enough. He wore jeans and a gray sweatshirt with the sleeves cut off. He smelled of sweat.

"Make yourself at home," he said, and let himself fall with a satisfied grunt into a well-used leather recliner.

I surveyed my options. The room was a cluttered mess. A leather couch strewn with paperbacks, magazines, and comic books, a couple of wooden chairs with clothes draped over their backs, a glass coffee table covered with CDs, albums, more books, comics, and magazines, beer and soda bottles and cans, two overflowing ashtrays, computer and video game boxes, and a cherry-red plastic bong. Along one wall was a desk with a PC on it; the monitor was on, a screensaver endlessly generating the fractal patterns of a Mandelbrot set. Set against the opposite wall, as though in obedience to a law of techno-feng shui, was a TV; Letterman was on, sans sound. There were three bookcases, all stuffed full, one holding the stereo and hundreds of CDs. A few framed photographs hung on the walls, along with a reproduction of *Starry Night* and a large map prickling with colored pins. Curtains were pulled shut over the windows. As for the floor, it was basically a legless table with a carpet on top.

"Go on," Eric urged, tilting back in the recliner; swollen, filthy feet levered up into view, and I looked away. A side table at his elbow held a second bong, this one blue, and a remote. He picked up the latter, thumbed it repeatedly, and the volume of the music dwindled slightly. "Sit your ass down."

I cleared a space on the couch and sat. Lisa, meanwhile, entered the room, carrying three bottles of Rolling Rock beer. She handed one to Eric and one to me. I thanked her, and she sat beside me on the couch, raising her bottle in a toast.

"To old times."

"Old times," Eric and I chorused, and drank.

"Lis says she ran into you on the paths," Eric said.

"Yeah," I said. "Old times, right?"

"Are not fucking forgotten," he said. "Not around here, that's for fucking sure."

I didn't know what to make of that, so I had another swallow of beer.

"Back for a visit, Dweeber?"

"Not exactly." I told them about my mother.

"Shit," said Eric. "Leukemia, huh? That sucks, man. How the hell'd she get that?"

"No one knows."

He grunted. "Fucking doctors don't know shit, man."

Lisa slipped her arm around my shoulders and squeezed. "I'm sorry, Johnny. She was a good lady. I liked her."

"Thanks," I said. "She was."

"I used to see her every once in a while," Lisa went on. "Not to talk or anything. Just in passing. You know, in the Giant or whatnot. We'd wave, say hi. I always thought about asking how you were."

"She asked about you guys a lot," I said. "She wanted me to look you up."

"Well, now you have," said Eric.

I couldn't tell if that was sarcasm or not, so I simply nodded, drank more beer. No one had mentioned Craig yet, but he was right there with us, his absence filling the room. I thought I would finish the bottle and split.

"So, how long are you staying?" Lisa asked, offering me a cigarette from her pack.

I shook my head no. "I'm heading back to New York tomorrow."

Eric's laugh was a sharp, ugly bark. "Figures."

"Eric, please," Lisa began, lighting a cig.

"No," said Eric. "I mean, listen to this fucking guy. Dude disappears for what, seventeen years, then when he finally does show his face again, and not because he decides to look up his old buds after all this time, but because he gets his ass busted on the bike paths and has no choice, he can't wait to get out of town! What's the problem, Dweeber? Don't like hanging out with murderers?"

I could only stare. Had Eric been storing up all this vitriol for seventeen years? It was like a switch had been thrown, transforming him into a red-faced, spittle-spraying lunatic.

"Eric—"

"Shut up, Lis! Well, Dweeber? I'm waiting for your answer."

I set the bottle down on the glass coffee table. My heart was pounding. "It's not like that, Eric. It never has been, and you should know it."

"Yeah? How should I fucking know it? Not from you. You made your feelings fucking plain as day, taking off like you did, leaving us behind to, to . . . " He spluttered, gesturing with his beer, as if whatever he was trying to say was summed up perfectly by the cluttered room around us, the over-flowing ashtrays, the mindlessly cycling loop of the screensaver on the computer monitor, the tightly drawn curtains, the piles of books and maga-zines on the carpet, David Byrne's yelping, growling voice on the stereo, the smell of stale beer and bongwater.

"I'm sorry you feel that way." I got to my feet. "I guess I'd better be going."

"Going?" Eric blinked in surprise.

"You obviously don't want me here." I turned to Lisa. "It was good to see you again, Lis."

"I'm sorry, Johnny," she said. She looked angry and mortified at once.

"Shit, man," said Eric. "Don't get your fucking panties in a wad! Nobody said anything about not wanting you here. Fuck! You always were too sensi-tive for your own good, Dweeber!"

"Yeah, well, fuck you, Eric," I said, and started for the door.

"Don't let him go, Lis," Eric directed. "Go after him, for Christ's sake. He's not gonna fucking walk out on us again, goddamn it. Do you hear me?"

That stopped me. I was at the door, but I turned around. "Is that really how you see it, Eric? I walked out on you?"

"Well, you did, didn't you? A week after they put Craig in the ground, you were gone. I mean, you didn't even wait long enough for those pot seeds we planted to sprout!"

"Did they?" I asked.

"You bet your ass they did!" he affirmed with pride, and his face glowed as he thumped one armrest of the recliner with an open palm and let loose with a string of wheezy chuckles.

Lisa, still sitting on the couch, the cigarette held between the fingers of her drooping hand, its tip pointing toward the ceiling, smiled. "His parents were *not* pleased."

Eric nodded. "Man, that's the understatement of the century! They had cops crawling everywhere. You would have thought we'd desecrated the tomb of a saint instead of a guy who was like the biggest head in Reston at the time. Of course, they never knew it was us."

"Oh, they knew," said Lisa. "They just couldn't prove it."

"Same difference," said Eric. "Shit." He was breathing heavily, almost gasping. It was alarming to witness; there was a stroke somewhere in his not-too-distant future.

"Are you okay?" I asked.

He waved away my concern. "Nothing a bong hit won't cure."

I glanced at Lisa, but she only shrugged. I figured she saw this sort of thing a lot.

"Come on, Dweeber," he wheezed, prepping the blue bong for action. "Stay. At least finish your fucking beer."

I sighed. "All right." And returned to the couch. "You know, you guys could have left the same as I did."

Eric shook his head vigorously as he sucked in a lungful of pot smoke. "Why not?"

He gestured to Lis, who sighed. "It's hard to explain," she said.

"Fuck if it is!" said Eric, smoke exploding from his lips.

"Let me do this my way," said Lisa.

"Whatever."

I looked from one to the other. "Jesus, you sure you two aren't married?"

"Funny, Dweeber." He had packed another hit into the bong, and he now extended it to me. "You still toke, don't you?"

I hesitated; for the first time, I noticed the tremor that Lisa had mentioned.

"You're not gonna catch MS, if that's what you're thinking."

I took the bong. "Jesus, Eric! I know that." I picked up Lisa's lighter from the coffee table and lit the bowl, drawing the hot, harsh smoke deep into my lungs. I rarely smoked pot any more, an occasional drag from a joint at parties, and it had been a long time since I'd last used a bong. Something akin to what occurred in the seconds following the Big Bang began to take place in my chest. I started hacking like a neophyte.

Eric giggled delightedly.

But if my lungs had forgotten how to expand with the intake of pot, my brain still remembered. "Wow," I said, when I could talk again. "Good shit."

"Eric grows it himself," Lisa said, taking the bong from me and passing it back to him. "This strain goes back to those seeds we planted at the grave."

"Wow," was all I could say.

"Yeah, we managed to save some of the plants," Eric said. "Transplanted 'em."

Tina Weymouth's bass line was wrapping itself around the drift of smoke from Lisa's cigarette. Or maybe it was the other way around. I closed my eyes for a second, or what seemed like a second, and it was as if seventeen years had fallen away, and I was sitting in the gloomy basement of Craig's parents' house waiting to start a game of D&D.

"So, tell him, Lis," came Eric's voice.

I opened my eyes. There was a beer in my hand, so I took a drink.

"Why were you on the bike paths tonight?" she asked.

I shrugged. "It wasn't anything I planned. I was just driving around." I found myself speaking slowly; the words had an unfamiliar feel in my mouth, like they'd changed shape slightly and no longer fit as they once had. "I ended up down by the Hunters Woods swimming pool. We used to sneak in, remember? Anyway, that's where I got on the paths. Got lost after about five minutes! But I didn't care, you know? I mean, shit, I buried my mom today." I realized that I was about to start blubbering, and suddenly Lisa was handing me a bunch of Kleenex.

"*Had to*," Eric drawled in imitation of the voice of W.C. Fields, and I knew exactly what he was going to say, the line from *My Little Chickadee*, a movie we'd watched a million times on video, along with everything from the Marx Brothers, Laurel and Hardy, and the 3 Stooges, and while on the one hand it was wildly inappropriate and insensitive, on the other it was perfect, and so I joined him in completing the quote: "*She died.*"

Then we were cackling like idiots. Lisa shook her head and smiled her lopsided smile.

I wiped my eyes with the Kleenex. "Man, I found this kickass station on the radio when I was driving the paths! Way down to the left of the dial. Played all these cool tunes from back in the day. I kept waiting for a DJ to come on, but it faded out before anyone did. You guys know that station?"

They were looking at me like they couldn't believe their ears.

"What?" I said.

"You heard it?" Lisa asked.

"Yeah, I heard it. What's the big deal?"

"You remember what you heard?" Eric asked in turn. He was rummaging around through a stack of papers on the floor beside the recliner.

"Just that it was a lot of great shit I hadn't heard in years."

He pulled out a crumpled and stained sheet of paper and passed it over to me. "Any of this ring a bell?"

It was a handwritten list of songs. I was pretty sure that I'd heard most of them on the radio. And even in the same order. "What's this?" I asked, looking up. "The playlist? Are you guys running some kind of pirate radio station or something?"

"Yeah, it's the playlist, all right," Eric said. "Craig's playlist. This was the shit he was listening to on his Walkman when he fucking did the deed."

"No way." I looked from one to the other; their faces were dead serious.

"You can listen to the goddamn tape yourself if you want," said Eric. "I managed to grab it that night at the hospital, when things were so confused. Before his folks went psycho on us."

"A few months after that, Eric and me started hearing the station," Lisa said. "It was freaky. I mean, it only happened on the bike paths, and only when we were there at night, and only if it was one or both of us. If there was anybody else in the car, we could never pick it up."

"Why didn't you tell me?" I asked.

"Shit, you'd split by then," Eric said. "Anyway, we never figured you'd hear it, too. Nobody else could. Just Lis and me. We figured he was, you know, haunting us."

Lisa picked up the story. "We tried all sorts of shit to get in touch with his ghost or spirit or whatever you want to call it. Trying to find out what he wanted. Trying to make him go away. Seances, Santería, exorcism. Nothing worked."

"That's when I thought, what if we found the source? I mean, we were picking it up on the radio, right? So it had to be broadcasting from somewhere." Eric heaved ponderously to his feet, the recliner squealing in protest, and lumbered across the room to the map I'd seen earlier, hanging on the wall, covered with different-colored pins. "C'mere, Dweeber. Take a look at this."

I joined him. I wasn't sure how to take all this. If Craig could reach out from beyond the grave, what was to stop my mom from doing it? The idea creeped me out, but at the same time, there was nothing I wanted more than some concrete, unmistakable sign that she still existed, that she was watching over me, that she forgave me for all the times I'd caused her pain or disappointment, that, in those last horrible days, when she'd been buried alive within the coffin of her body, unable to communicate, she hadn't been suffering, or, if she had, that she didn't blame me for it, for withholding the morphine the doctors had wanted to give. Earlier, it's true, as I'd followed Lisa out of the paths, it had seemed to me that I'd felt her presence, but now that seemed no more than the product of wishful thinking and a grieving, guilty heart.

"Like you noticed yourself," Eric said, "the station fades in and out. It's a weak signal. So Lisa and me started tracking it."

"That's what you were doing tonight," I said to Lisa as she walked over to stand beside Eric and slipped an arm around his ample waist.

"We were both out there chasing it," she said. "Eric just got home first."

"We bought ourselves a couple of walkie-talkies and started driving around the paths at night, noting down where it got stronger, where it got weaker, where it faded out altogether."

"And the times, too," Lisa added. "I mean, it only happened at night, and only between certain hours."

"Which turned out to be no earlier than around ten-twenty, and no later than a little before midnight. In case you were wondering, that's when they figure he strung himself up and when he was found by the side of the road."

The map was thumbtacked to the wall. It was fairly large, a square about three feet to a side. It showed all the roads, parks, lakes, developments, and bike paths of Reston. It was bounded by Leesburg Pike to the north, the Fairfax County Parkway to the west, Lawyers Road to the south, and Hunter Mill Road to the east. Within those borders were clustered hundreds of push pins with different-colored heads. From a distance, the thing had resembled a pointillist abstraction. Up close, no pattern of colors leaped out at me, but it was clear that most of the pins were in and around the same area I'd driven earlier, which made sense, as much as any of this did, because it was close to Craig's parents' house, near the woods where he'd hung himself, though no one knew the exact spot, since he'd managed to crawl out to Glade Drive.

"And this is why you've stayed in Reston all these years?" I asked. "Chasing a fucking ghost?"

"I think he needs us," Lisa said. "I think Craigy is stuck or something. He needs our help to move on. To find peace. And we owe him that, Johnny. You know we do."

"The problem is," said Eric, "two people isn't enough. Lis and me have never been able to get a fix on the source. We've come close, I think, following the signal when it's at its clearest and strongest, but it always fades out before we can home in. With three people, though, I bet we can do it. We can triangulate on the motherfucker!"

"And then what?" I asked. "What do you expect to find out there, Eric?"

"An answer, that's what." He gave me a cold-eyed, challenging look. "So, what do you say, Dweeber? Are you in? I've got an extra walkie-talkie you can use."

"I told you," I said. "I've got to be back in New York tomorrow. I've got my ticket and everything."

"Don't be a pussy," Eric said. "Your mom just died, okay? You can take an extra day off work or whatever. Nobody's going to deny you that."

"Please, Johnny," said Lisa.

"Don't beg for his help," Eric snapped.

The truth was, my own words had shamed me more than Eric ever could. "I think the two of you are out of your fucking minds," I said. "But I'll do it."

"Good man, Dweeber," said Eric, and gave my shoulder a hearty thump as Lisa leaned over and kissed me on the cheek. "Come by around ten; that'll give us enough time to get high first."

"Does that help?" I asked, genuinely curious.

Eric winked. "It don't hurt."

On the drive home, I tried to find the station again, but there was only static. And not like before, when it had seemed to me that I could discern faint patternings of sound beneath the hiss, otherworldly melodies that might spill over into this world at any moment, or might lure a listener from this world across the dividing line there at the left of the dial. No, what I heard now was empty, dead, a noise as blank as entropy, without order or design, a hissing that filled my head like a sandstorm. I thought of my mother in her coffin beneath the ground, of the profound silence that must reign in that dark space, broken only by the sounds of decomposition, or perhaps the echoes of footfalls from above, faint, murmurous voices carrying on one-sided conversations as the flesh melted from her bones and her bones crumbled to dust, until all that was left of her was held in the air like a last breath never to be released, a final secret forever unwhispered to any living soul. Was that what Craig was trying to tell us? A secret that hadn't died with him? Or, as Lisa had suggested, one that had somehow prevented him from dying, from moving on to whatever country the dead call home? For a moment I felt the car take on the shape of a coffin around me, as if I, too, were dead and buried, my shabby secrets interred with me. I knew these morbid thoughts and fantasies had their origins not only in the circumstances of the day, dreary and eerie by turns, but in the pot I'd smoked. I'd only had the one hit, but it had been kick-ass shit, and now the high had burned away, leaving ashes that I could taste on my tongue. Tomorrow night, I told myself, when Eric handed me the bong, I would Just Say No.

Back at my mom's, I dragged my ass to bed and fell asleep at once, waking late the next morning with a dry mouth and a pervasive lethargy that kept me in bed for another hour. By then, it was too late to make my train, even if I'd wanted to. I got up, drank a cup of coffee, ate some cereal, did my stretches, and went for my usual run along the bike paths.

As I jogged, sweating out the poisons of the night, I began to regret my decision to help Lisa and Eric. The firmness of the path beneath my feet was a rebuke to everything they'd told me, everything I'd experienced, or thought I'd experienced. In the brilliant light of day, so much of it seemed improbable, foolish. I had no doubt that something deeply weird was going on, but their explanation for it, to say nothing of their proposed remedy, struck me as equally weird, if not more so. I told myself that I could still leave, catch a later train. But by the time I'd finished my run and showered, I knew that I wasn't going anywhere. I wanted to find that station again. Prove to myself that it really existed. Or that it didn't. But one way or the other, I had to know.

At ten o'clock, I knocked at Eric and Lisa's door.

"C'mon in, Dweeber." Eric's voice issued from inside. "It's open!"

I found the two of them exactly where I'd left them, Eric sprawled in the recliner, Lisa seated on the couch. With the drapes drawn, a miasma of pot and tobacco smoke drifting through the air, and *Fear of Music* playing on the stereo, I could almost believe that I'd circled back in time, entering the apartment just seconds after I'd closed the door behind me the night before. Only the fact that they were dressed differently dispelled the illusion.

"Jesus," I said. "This place reeks of dope. Aren't you worried about the neighbors?"

"Hell, they're my best customers," said Eric. "The whole fucking floor is nothing but heads. Relax, Dweeber." He held up the blue bong. "Have a toke."

"Thanks, but I'll pass. Whatever happens tonight, I want a clear head."

"Shit, my head's so clear, it's fucking transparent," laughed Eric, and Lisa laughed along with him, then asked me if I wanted a beer.

"Thanks, Lis. Don't get up; I'll get it myself. Where's the kitchen?"

"Straight on back."

"Bring me one, too," said Eric.

"How about you, Lis?"

"I'm fine."

To my surprise, the kitchen was immaculate. There were two refrigerators, one normal-sized, the other a mini, like the fridge I'd had in my college dorm room. Instinct steered me there, and sure enough, it was filled with bottles of Rolling Rock. I pulled out two, twisted off the caps, and returned to the living room, where I handed one of the bottles to Eric.

"My man!"

"You're in a good mood," I commented after a swallow of ice-cold beer.

"Fuckin-A," he agreed. "Tonight's the night. I feel it."

"Don't get your hopes up too high, Eric," Lisa cautioned.

"Are you kidding? With Johnny here, we can't miss."

I didn't share his confidence. I wasn't even sure what I wanted to happen. "Shouldn't we get going?"

"That's the spirit," said Eric with a grin. "Lis, give the man his walkie-talkie."

Lisa rose from the couch and handed me a black device slightly larger than a cell-phone. She demonstrated its use, then led me over to the map. "We'll each enter the paths from a different point," she said, indicating them to me with the antenna of her own walkie-talkie, like a commando explaining a mission. "You'll use the same entrance you did last night, by the pool. I'll get on near where they found him, on Glade. Eric's going to come in from the east, from over by Steeplechase. Tune in to the station and follow it as best you can; if it starts to fade out, backtrack and go in a different direction until it comes in stronger."

"We'll use the walkie-talkies to stay in touch," Eric said. "Now, here's the thing, Dweeber. The bike paths don't go everywhere, right?"

I nodded. I'd been wondering about this.

"But check it out: the walkie-talkies can pick up the FM band. So once we've driven as far as we can, we ditch our cars and start walking into the woods, converging on ground fucking zero." His eyes glittered with enthusiasm. "Just keep the station strong and steady, and it'll guide us right where we want to go."

"Aren't you guys afraid of what we might find there?" I asked.

"Fuck, no," said Eric. "I *know* what I'm gonna find."

"What's that?"

"Redemption, Dweeber," he said in a voice that sent a chill down my spine, as if he were defining that word in a very different way from any dictionary I knew. "Sweet, fucking redemption."

I kept the car radio on as I drove to the swimming pool, the tuner all the way over to the left. There was no sign of the station, or, for that matter, of any station at all, but the hiss of static no longer seemed empty. Perhaps it was just my own anticipation, but once again, as had happened last night after I'd lost the station for the final time, I thought I detected a hint—or something even less substantial than that, call it a premonition—of musical structure buried deep in the swirling wash of white noise. I began to think of that noise as a kind of spooky camouflage, a surface deception not unlike the protective coloring of an insect, beneath or behind which a presence lurked. I couldn't help but reflect that such strategies of disguise, in nature, frequently concealed a predatory intent. I decided it was a good thing I'd turned down that bong hit. I was paranoid enough already.

As before, the cul-de-sac fronting the swimming pool and tennis courts was deserted. I pulled the car to a stop under a street lamp and contacted Lisa and Eric on the walkie-talkie. "I'm in position," I said, feeling ridiculous, like a kid playing at *Mission: Impossible.*

"You're supposed to say 'over' when you're finished talking, Dweeber," Eric's voice crackled condescendingly.

"Fuck you, Eric," I said. "Over."

Lisa entered the conversation. "I'm ready, over."

"All right," said Eric. "Let's do it, over."

I coaxed the car past the guard post and onto the bike path. The hairs at the back of my neck stood to attention as the music I'd heard the previous night came ghosting out of the static. It was like the car had passed through an invisible veil. A shiver ran through me, vaguely electrical, a tingling that reminded me of Halloween haunted houses I'd navigated as a boy, in which threads dangling from the ceiling had trailed across my face and arms like the strands of spider's webs. The sensation was so strong that I actually raised a hand to brush them from my face. Of course, there was nothing there.

"Shit," I said, and took a deep breath. Had I felt this same creepy caress last night? I couldn't remember for sure, but I didn't think so. I squeezed the steering wheel tightly and let the music draw me on.

For the next hour or so, I chased the signal along the bike paths. I drove at a crawl, stopping frequently to back up, retrace my route, take a bypassed turning. All the while, the music flitted in and out of existence, coming through loud and clear one minute, disintegrating into static the next, then, when I thought I'd lost it altogether, reappearing suddenly, until it seemed to me that there was a playful intelligence at work. *Billy Idol. The Au Pairs. Devo. Gary Numan.* I didn't sense any maliciousness to it, any intent to cause harm, but it was frightening nonetheless, a game of hide-and-seek or Blind Man's Bluff that was leading inexorably, although not directly, to a place where neither I nor any living being belonged. At least, that's how it felt to me as I drove, ears alert to the slightest change in reception, skin crawling with the imminence of the uncanny. The meandering nature of the pursuit seemed an indication of the difficulty of the journey, as if we were threading a labyrinth that extended through more than the four dimensions of space and time. The bike path was nothing more than an analogy of this N-dimensional maze, a flat and simple shadow. *Blondie. Television. The Ramones. X.* Even the songs seemed encoded with a significance beyond themselves, beyond their nostalgic potency, which was itself a kind of magic. But this was a more powerful magic, darkly brooding, primal. Not for one second did I forget that I was listening to the soundtrack of a suicide. My imagination persisted in picturing the acts which corresponded to the music, the ungainly dance of death whose steps Craig had executed in the dark of the night, alone, so many years ago. I saw him picking his way through the woods by flashlight in search of a suitable tree, a length of rope coiled in his backpack. I saw him stop, shine the light upward, then, satisfied, shrug out of the pack. I saw him open it, remove the rope, the noose already knotted, and clamber with it up into the branches of the tree, where he made it fast. I saw him sit then and smoke a final joint, his head bobbing to the music coming through his headphones, the same music I was now hearing, but though I tried to glimpse the expression on his face, I couldn't do it. His features were lost in the darkness.

The voices of Eric and Lisa grounded me, and we kept up an almost-constant chatter over the walkie-talkies, each of us, I think, dependent on that contact. I certainly was. I would have broken without it, turned tail and fled. I came near to doing just that a dozen times. And I sensed the same was true of them. If one of us had bolted, the others would have followed, our resolve crumbling like sand. Strangely enough, it was my awareness of the precariousness of our efforts, how quickly and easily we could fall away from the task we'd set ourselves, that enabled me to go on. It wasn't any strength I possessed, but an acute apprehension of my weakness.

At last, we reached the point that Eric had predicted, where we had to abandon our cars and enter the woods on foot, tracking the station by walkie-talkie. Lisa had given me a flashlight, and now, even more than before, I found myself picturing Craig's last moments. I saw them so clearly that it was as if I were reliving them, retracing his steps exactly. I saw him stub out the joint, slip the noose around his neck, careful not to disturb his headphones, and cinch it tight as a tie. I saw him climb shakily to his feet, one hand on the trunk of the tree to steady himself as he prepared to step off the branch. A cold sweat poured off my skin as the beam of my flashlight probed and darted, populating the woods with shadowy witnesses to my stumbling progress, dark shapes that clustered at the edges of my vision, slinking from tree to tree.

The crack of a gunshot split the night. I stopped dead still, my lungs, my heart, paralyzed with terror, as the echoes faded. Only then did I notice that I'd lost the station. Static was pouring from the walkie-talkie. I fumblingly switched from FM to broadcast. "Did you guys hear that?"

"Fuck yes," came Eric's voice.

"I've lost the station," came Lisa's panicky voice a second later.

Then I heard a sound that froze the blood in my veins. It was a low, protracted, inhuman moaning, as of some helpless animal suffering the ravages of fear as much as pain, alone and baffled somewhere in the dark nearby. I think I must have known right away, deep down, what I was hearing, but it wasn't until Eric's shout reached me in disjointed stereo, over the walkie-talkie and through the air, that I consciously realized the import of the ghastly sound.

"Shit! It's Craig! Get the fuck over here!"

Haltingly, as though emerging from shock, I began to crash through the woods toward Eric's voice.

"Oh, my god! Oh, my god!" Lisa's cries mingled with Eric's shouts and the steady moaning that I knew was coming, impossibly, from Craig. Not a ghost returned to haunt us, but the flesh-and-blood original.

"Oh fuck!"

"Oh god!"

"Can you hear me, Craig? Can you hear me, buddy?"

"Oh god, Craigy!"

I saw the frenzied strobing of their flashlights up ahead. I picked out the shapes of my friends in the criss-crossing beams and, huddled on the ground between them, a dark shape reminiscent of a huge tortoise.

"Cut the rope, Eric! Cut it!"

"I'm fucking trying! Shit! Dweeber, get your ass over here!"

Instead, I came to a stop, struck by a sudden thought. Or not even that, more like an intuition. I switched the walkie-talkie back to FM and sent the glowing display of pale blue numbers climbing.

"Dweeber!"

There it was, as I'd somehow known it would be. 98.1. WHFS. The whiny voice of Weasel rambling on about nothing, or everything, in one of his drugged-out, late-night monologues.

"Get his feet, Eric! We've got to carry him out of here!"

"Careful, Lis! Dweeber, we need you!"

But I was already moving away from them, heading for my car. I didn't understand how or why we had traveled seventeen years back in time, to the moment of Craig's suicide, but I didn't doubt that, whether by magic or mechanism or miracle, we had done exactly that. Nor could I guess how long we might remain here, what rules governed our presence, and whether, through ignorance, I might hasten—or prevent—our return to the present. Perhaps by separating myself from the others, I was running the risk of stranding myself, or them. Perhaps we would remain trapped here, or wander the bike paths forever, seeking a way back that no longer existed. But I didn't care about any of that.

"Dweeber!" Eric shouted hoarsely. "Where the fuck are you going?"

"My mom," I yelled back, crashing headlong through the woods.

"Get back here, you asshole! Don't you run out on us again!"

I ignored him. Here in this place, this time, my mother was still alive, and the thought that I could see her again drove out every other consideration.

Back in my car, I turned the radio to HFS and drove down the paths like a maniac, scraping against branches and swerving against the trunks of trees until I forced myself to slow down, afraid I would crash. I pulled out on Steeplechase. I kept to the speed limit only by an exercise of superhuman will, knowing I couldn't afford to be stopped by the cops, driving a car from seventeen years in their future. I'd gone almost five miles before it occurred to me that I was driving in the wrong direction, toward a house that hadn't been built yet. Cursing, I made a U-turn and headed for our old place on Fowlers Lane.

The walkie-talkie lay on the seat beside me. I picked it up as I drove and tried to raise Eric and Lisa. But whether I was out of range, or they were too busy with Craig, or angry with me, to answer, my attempts were unsuccessful. I felt guilty for leaving them, but I still didn't see what choice I'd had. I told myself that, if it had been Eric's mom, or Lisa's, they would have done the same thing. But at the same time, I wondered what it was that I hoped to accomplish. What could I say to my mother now that would have any meaning to her? She wouldn't even recognize me, this stranger claiming to be her son . . . or, if she did recognize me, how could it not freak her out?

By then, I was turning onto Fowlers Lane. The HFS signal was holding strong and steady. There was our old car in the driveway: the ugly and ungainly red Oldsmobile Omega that I'd taken out on the paths dozens of times, the car I'd learned to drive with. I pulled past the driveway and stopped. I killed the lights and turned off the engine, though I left the radio on, the volume low.

Just as before, the lights of the house were blazing. But I knew that everything else had changed since my visit hours earlier . . . or, rather, years later. Inside that house were not strangers, but family. My mother, miraculously alive again. And my father—or, no, I remembered; they had just separated, and he had moved out, into an apartment in D.C. But Ellen was there. And me.

What would happen if I confronted myself? I knew all the sci-fi paradoxes, the weird temporal loops and knots that writers had devised over the years. But this was real. This was my life, my past. And, I was beginning to suspect, my future.

I got out of the car and crept close to the house, coming up through the narrow strip of woods that stood between the back of the house and our neighbor's yard. From the shelter of the trees, I could see through the sliding glass door that opened onto the back porch from the empty kitchen. I could also see one of the windows of my bedroom on the second floor, the light on behind a creamy white curtain. Against that backlit scrim a dark silhouette suddenly appeared, drifting like a filmy ghost, and I felt a rush of sheer, atavistic horror that would have sent me scrambling back the way I'd come if my legs hadn't simultaneously turned into limp noodles. I clung to a tree trunk, heart hammering, my jaw clenched against the unreasoning scream that was trying to claw its way out of my throat, as I watched my younger self, or his shadow, move back and forth behind the window. There was nothing extraordinary in those movements, nothing unusual at all, yet to me they seemed invested with superluminal significance, and I felt an unmistakable sense of trespass, as if I, a mere mortal, had stumbled into a god's private bower.

And yet it was not my past self that was the god here. How could it be?
No, if my presence was offensive to some immortal power, what could that
power be but time? I felt that I'd made a grave mistake in coming here, in
deserting Eric and Lisa, leaving them to assist Craig by themselves while I
chased after what was, it suddenly seemed, nothing more than a
memory . . . or something even less than that: a delusion borne of pain and
denial. Oh, how I wished then that I'd stayed with them, helped them to
get Craig to the hospital! I moaned in misery, for I realized then, without
understanding why or how, that a rare choice had been offered to me there
in the woods, and I believed that I had chosen foolishly, selfishly, taken the
wrong path, and it was too late now, too late forever, to undo the result of
that choice, whatever it might be, or come to be. The humid air around me,
the scents and sounds of the Virginia night, seemed to recognize the wrong-
ness of my presence and to recoil from it.

I'd told myself that I'd come running here to see my mother, but there
was more to it than that. I'd also been running from what lay on the
ground, under the trees, that horrible tortoise shape. I hadn't wanted to face
it, to face Craig, for to do so would mean acknowledging my part in his
death. To see that knowledge reflected in Craig's eyes had been more than I
could take.

Craig had never seen them together. He hadn't had to. I'd told him about
Eric and Lisa. And I hadn't even known it was true. It was a spiteful aside,
a taunt I flung at him because I was jealous, miserable over my smash-up
with Donna. She'd caught me cheating once too often, and now I threw my
own failing in Craig's too-trusting face, wanting to hurt him for no better
reason than that he was happy and content, while I was not. And it was
even worse than that, because what really rankled me, and had for years,
deep down, was that Lisa had chosen him over me. So I stabbed at him
with my crude lie, never dreaming that it would open his eyes to the truth.

Or was that, too, a lie? Had I known somehow, on some instinctive,
unconscious level, that Eric and Lisa were involved? I'd always wondered if
Craig had told Lisa what I'd said, written it in his last note to her. She never
gave me any cause to believe that he had, but I couldn't be sure. And even
if he hadn't, even if she didn't know, *I* knew, and that had been enough to
make her presence, and Eric's, unendurable.

I'd never told anyone what I'd done. Not even my mother, at the very end, when I'd wanted more than anything to confess my secret to her—not to receive her forgiveness, but just to share the burden with another soul. But I'd been too ashamed. Too afraid. I'd picked up a book of poems or stories instead, and read to her, telling myself what a good son I was being. That I was keeping quiet for her sake, so as not to add to her distress. The cowardice and hypocrisy of these rationalizations appalled me now, and I grew convinced that my silence had in fact deprived her of something precious, something that, far from adding to the pain and confusion of her last days, would have eased them, or at least made them easier to bear. And what's more, would have done the same for me. But it was too late now. For both of us.

A phone rang inside the house. The ringing went on, urgent, strident, and I think I must have known right away what it portended. I watched with mounting dread, sinking little by little to the brittle leaves and twigs covering the ground, as an attractive middle-aged woman in a ridiculous green pantsuit stepped into the kitchen, framed by the sliding door, and picked up the receiver.

It was, of course, my mother.

This was the choice I'd made. It was for this moment that I'd come. But I hadn't guessed that it would prove so awful a sight, so cruel in its immediacy and its distance, for now that I saw her, a healthy woman still in her prime, with no suspicion of the betrayal that lay quiescent in her cells, I didn't feel in any way that I'd recaptured her. Not for a moment did I feel reunited with her, as if I'd stolen her back from the dead or come to visit her among the shades. No, this woman was not the mother I'd lost. She was a stranger to me. And I was a stranger to her. There was nothing I could do or say that would help her avoid what waited patiently in her future. No confession I could make to her, no forgiveness I could ask or offer. Nothing. I felt like a ghost. Like I was the one who had died.

My mother put one hand over the mouthpiece of the receiver and shouted my name in a voice that carried through the glass door, shrill with emotion. Even from a distance I could see how the blood had drained from her face.

The shadow behind the curtain of my bedroom window vanished.

I wanted to look away then. I tried to turn my head, avert my gaze, but I didn't have the strength. Or perhaps, deep down, I needed to see myself as I had been on that long-ago night, the night when my casual betrayal reached its terrible fruition . . . although, had I been able to think clearly, I would have realized that things had already departed from how they'd been, for if this was the call from the hospital—and given my mother's reaction, I had no doubt that it was—then it was coming far earlier than had originally been the case. But I wasn't thinking clearly. Wasn't thinking at all.

What entered the kitchen to take the phone from my mother wasn't me. That is, it didn't look anything like my younger self, or like anyone at all. It was less solid and substantial even than the shadow I'd watched moving back and forth behind the curtain. It was an amorphous grey blur with a vaguely human shape, as if it were composed of many separate, overlapping selves, none of which truly or fully existed, a kind of coalescent cloud of potential mes. Yet as it held the phone to its "ear," it began to grow sharper in outline and detail, and I knew that with every passing second it was turning into a single self, the many fusing into one. Or perhaps not fusing but falling away, alternate versions of myself, possible futures, competing in some Darwinian struggle for survival, from which only one could emerge supreme. And would that newly constituted self lead, in turn, to me? Once it had, but was that still true? Or was I superfluous now, superseded, extinct?

It was the terror of ceasing to exist, of seeing my skin degrade into smoke or mist and blow away in the night breezes that finally gave me the strength to tear my gaze away. Breathing raggedly, I examined myself by what little light there was. I seemed solid enough. I lay there gasping, drained of energy and intelligence, for what seemed an endless time before I heard the front door of the house slam and, seconds later, the Oldsmobile's engine roar to life. I glanced back into the kitchen.

My mother stood at the sliding glass door, tears running down her cheeks. This was the first change I consciously recognized; in the past that I remembered, she had driven me to the hospital. But now I became aware of other departures from what had been, changes radiating outward from the first and biggest change of all: that we had found Craig in the woods, long before he'd crawled out to Glade Drive. I realized then that he was going to live. Knew it absolutely, without question, as if that future had already taken precedence over the one I hailed from. But where did that leave me? My mother seemed to be gazing right at me, though I was sure I couldn't be seen. And yet she did see me. She must have. For she drew back sharply, as if she'd seen a ghost. But then immediately pressed her face closer to the glass, hands cupped around her eyes. Her mouth shaped my name, and though her voice did not penetrate the glass as it had when she'd called my younger self a moment before, I heard it as clearly as I've heard anything in my life. And then, seconds later, her voice cut through the night, sharp and querulous: "Johnny? Is that you?"

But I was already running for the car.

I got out fast, propelled by grief and terror. I didn't understand what had happened, what it meant that my mother had seen me. Was this a memory she'd carried through the rest of her life, a secret she'd kept even on her deathbed? Was this why she'd wanted me to get back in touch with Eric and Lisa? Had she known somehow of the part I'd played in his death? Or had she learned of it after her death, in a place where all secrets are exposed? Had she orchestrated these events from that place, or at least my part in them, to give me a chance to make up for what I'd done, for what I hadn't done? What were the limits of a mother's love?

HFS was still playing loud and clear as I drove toward the hospital. But by the time I got there, I knew that I couldn't go inside. Craig's parents would be there by now, in addition to my earlier self, whom I still dreaded encountering face to face, as if, in close proximity, with no glass door between us, his reality would prove superior to my own, and I would wink out of existence. Besides, there was nothing I could say to them, nothing I could do that would be of any help. Even if I avoided the fate I feared, I would come across as a lunatic, and perhaps a dangerous one. His parents might think me involved in what had happened to Craig, as indeed I was . . . but not in the way they would imagine: easier to suspect a stranger of attempted murder than to encompass the fact of a son's suicide. It was funny; all the time-travel stories I'd read, all the movies I'd seen, presented the time traveler as someone possessing immense power, a godlike figure able to change the future, the fulcrum of a cosmic balance to be shifted for good or ill. But here in the past, I had no power. Yet was that powerlessness really so different from how I had lived my life in the present, back—or, rather, ahead—in my own time? Drifting from job to job, relationship to relationship, I saw now that nothing had really changed for me since those days in Reston, that my participation in Craig's suicide, and my need to keep it a secret, had curtailed what was possible for me, caused me to reject, again and again, opportunities to grow, to change. I was already trapped in the past long before I came here. I just hadn't realized it.

I pulled into the hospital parking lot, mostly deserted at this hour, and prowled it slowly. I saw the red Oldsmobile at once, and then other cars I recognized: Craig's parents' car, and Eric's car, and Lisa's . . . not the cars they drove now, but their old cars: their younger selves were also present, holding vigil. But there was no sign of the Eric and Lisa from my time. Neither of their cars was parked here. They had brought Craig to the emergency room and then split. But where had they gone? Back to the future, deserting me as I had deserted them? Or were they still here, waiting for me?

The walkie-talkie lay on the seat beside me, turned off, forgotten. Perhaps they'd been trying to reach me all this time. I grabbed it, switched it on. "Eric, Lis, can you hear me? Over."

There was no reply, only static.

"Come on, guys. I know you can hear me. I'm sorry, okay? Just answer, will you, for god's sake!"

Nothing.

"Fuck!" I threw down the device, feeling a pit of frustration and despair yawn open in my stomach. They had left me. I was alone.

But was I trapped? Could I get back to my proper time in the same way I'd come here, by driving the bike paths? It seemed the only chance, other than parking somewhere and waiting for whatever might happen next. If my mother was behind all this, pulling the strings from somewhere beyond time and space, then surely she wouldn't abandon me. But what if it wasn't her? What if it wasn't my mother's compassionate ghost, but Craig's vindictive one? I shivered. Even more reason not to give up. There was nothing for me here, just a past that no longer belonged to me, people I no longer knew, though my feelings for them were as strong as ever, these familiar strangers who had once been my family, my friends, my self. It tore at me to leave the hospital. I knew I would never see any of them again.

I drove back to the swimming pool and got on the paths there; it seemed important to follow my earlier steps as precisely as possible. Until that moment, the HFS signal had been unwavering. But as I slid past the guard post, the voice of Weasel faltered, static slipping in between his words like grains of sand through the cracks in a seemingly solid wall, and I felt a flicker of hope. Seventeen years from now, there would be no HFS. The station would have vanished into the ether, replaced by talk radio. Perhaps I could use HFS to steer by, letting the weakness, rather than the strength, of its signal dictate my route along the paths, until, in losing it completely, I might find my way home.

"Buddy. Hey, buddy. Wake up!"

I started awake to find myself staring into the beam of a flashlight. "Wh-what?"

"Police," growled a gruff male voice, and the light swung away.

"Shit." I rubbed my eyes.

"Sleeping it off?"

I shook my head, groggy. An unctuous voice was oozing softly from the radio. I remembered driving the snaking paths for what had seemed like hours, following a route more convoluted than that which had led me into the past. I remembered seeing the lights of other cars winking through the trees, shining around turns, appearing and disappearing in my rear-view mirror like will-o-the-wisps. I had been convinced that they were all me, or versions of me, all seeking a way back. But I never caught up to any of them, and they never passed me.

And then what? Where was I? *When* was I?

"Come on, buddy," said the cop, rapping his knuckles sharply on the roof of the car as he trained the flashlight on my features again. "Wakey, wakey."

"All right," I said, annoyed. "I'm awake!"

"Good. Now, turn off the engine."

I did so.

"Step out of the car. Slowly."

I unfastened the seatbelt, opened the door, and got out. I saw now that I was back at the swimming pool, in the parking lot. Overhead, the sky was just beginning to lighten. "Sorry, officer," I said, trying to appear non-threatening, grinning at him all bleary-eyed and apologetic. "I had a rough night."

His laugh was unpleasant. He was young, pink-faced in the flashing red and blue lights that crowned his cruiser. A thin blond mustache gave him the look of a high-school kid trying to pass for a grown-up. I was acutely aware of his gun, and the proximity of his hand thereto. "I can see that," he said.

"My mom passed away . . . I was having trouble sleeping. I came out for a drive."

He shifted his stance, fitting my words into his threat assessment. "Sorry for your loss, but you can't be sleeping here. Let's see some ID. Slowly."

I pulled my wallet from my back pocket, withdrew my driver's license and handed it to him. He examined it, his eyes flicking from my picture to me and back again. "You live in New York, Mr. Weber," he said, as if it were a foreign country suspected of terrorist ties.

"That's right," I said. "My mom lives . . . lived here. I grew up over on Fowlers Lane."

"Is that where you're staying now?"

"No. My mom has a townhouse in Lake Anne."

He nodded. "Let's see the registration on the car, Mr. Weber."

I ducked back into the car, opened the glove compartment, pulled out the registration, and passed it over to him.

"I'm going to call this in," he said. "You sit tight, Mr. Weber."

"Sure."

I watched him walk to his cruiser. Then I turned the radio back on. The carnival-barker's voice of a certain conservative commentator emerged, and I actually laughed, glad for the first time in my life to hear that hypocritical asshole. I'd done it. I was home.

I itched with impatience to be off, but forced myself to wait until the baby-faced cop returned with my license and registration. He handed them through the window. "Everything checks out, Mr. Weber. You can go. Just do me a favor and check into a motel or something next time, okay?"

"There won't be a next time," I told him fervently.

"And I'm sorry again for your loss."

"Thanks, officer." I drove off slowly, into the dawning of the new day. The night was like a vivid dream. Had it really happened? I headed for Lisa and Eric's place.

It wasn't there.

The apartment complex was missing. Where it had stood was a shopping mall.

I sat there for a while in shock. Clearly, the future I'd returned to was not the same one I'd left behind. I drove over to a pay phone and called information. There was no listing under Eric's name. Or Lisa's. With my scalp prickling, I asked for Craig's number. And got it.

It took me some time to summon up the nerve to call.

"Hello?"

I nearly hung up right then. "Lis, is that you?"

"Who is this?"

"It's me, Johnny."

"Johnny?"

"Weber. Johnny Weber."

"Christ, from high school! Shit, man, how are you doing?"

Her words erased a whole history. I didn't know what to say.

"Honey, it's Johnny Weber," she said meanwhile.

I heard Craig's muffled voice, sleepy and annoyed. "At five a.m.?" Then he came on the line. "Hey, Johnny. Long time."

"Hey, Craig. Look, I'm sorry to bother you guys so early . . . " I groped for an excuse, an explanation. The whole thing was both horribly real and unreal.

"Yeah? What is it, Johnny? Are you okay? You sound like shit."

"Forget it," I said. "I never should have called. I'm sorry."

"Wait," he said. "Don't hang up! Shit, we haven't seen you since . . . well, you know."

But I didn't. And yet, somehow, I did. Not in my mind, as a memory, but as an ache in my soul. "Since Eric died, you mean."

"Yeah," he said, and sighed.

"Fuck," I said, and before I knew it, I was crying.

"Johnny . . . ?"

"I gotta go," I said. And hung up.

So this was the redemption Eric had spoken of with such fevered intensity. He had blamed himself for Craig's death. And sacrificed his own life somehow to bring him back. A life for a life, so that the books stayed balanced. Or that's how I thought of it, weeping there in the phone booth as the sun came up around me, grieving not just for his death, but for the death of everything and everyone I knew, the time I could never go back to now, that had never even existed. I felt the pain of all this so deeply that I knew it was true, but I didn't understand how it could be true, or why I had been spared.

If indeed I had been spared.

At last I got back in the car and drove off. I was heading home, but the cemetery was on the way, so I pulled off to visit my mom's grave.

I wasn't really surprised to find it gone. I think I was expecting it on some level. Even so, it was a while before the static ebbed from my senses and I could think more or less clearly again.

But it was instinct more than thought that sent me to the hospital. I parked the car and hurried through the emergency room entrance; the main doors weren't open at this early hour, as I knew from previous visits. I pushed the button for the elevator; then, when it didn't come right away, I took the stairs, dashing up them two at a time. But when I reached the landing for the third floor, the cancer ward, I stopped. I didn't want to just come bursting out. I felt foolish, afraid of what I might find. Afraid of what I might not find.

I took a deep breath and opened the door.

A frail and solitary figure was shuffling down the white hallway before me. Even from behind, I recognized my mother. She was holding on to her IV-tree like a wheeled cane as she walked with her typical steadfast bravery and determination. I didn't think then about guilt or forgiveness. Didn't think about prices paid, debts owed, second chances. All my questions fell away, and with them, the need for answers. Nothing mattered but the woman before me.

I came up beside her and took her gently by the arm. She smiled at me and said my name as if she'd known I was there the whole time. As if she'd been expecting me. And perhaps she had. I didn't know anything anymore. As we advanced step by slow step down the aisle, our paths paralleling for at least a little while longer, I couldn't even tell which of us was supporting the other.

"Mayaland" first appeared in *Night Cry*, Spring 1986; "Red Shift" first appeared in *Asimov's*, January 1984; "Lighthouse Summer" first appeared in *Asimov's*, April 1991; "Changeling" first appeared in *Fiction Inferno*, 2003; "The Cats of Thermidor" first appeared in *Night Cry*, Summer 1987; "Moonlight Becomes Magenta" first appeared in *Twilight Zone*, February 1988; "Left of the Dial" first appeared on *SciFiction*, September 2004; "Twilight of the Dogs", "After Ivy", "The Silver Ghost", "Where Balloons Go", and "Everland" are original to this collection.